Pride Publishing books by
Catherine Curzon and Eleanor Harkstead

Single Books
An Actor's Guide to Romance
The Captain's Cornish Christmas
A Late Summer Night's Dream

Captivating Captains
Captivating Captains: The Captain and The Cavalry Trooper
Captivating Captains: The Captain and The Cricketer

Also by Catherine Curzon

Anthologies
I Need a Hero: The Angel on the Northern Line

D1744796

The de Chastelaine Chronicles

THE GHOST GARDEN

CATHERINE CURZON
&
ELEANOR HARKSTEAD

The Ghost Garden
ISBN # 978-1-78686-398-0
©Copyright Catherine Curzon & Eleanor Harkstead 2019
Cover Art by Erin Dameron-Hill ©Copyright April 2019
Interior text design by Claire Siemaszkiewicz
Totally Bound Publishing

THE GHOST GARDEN

Dedication

CC — To all the ghosts I've known, especially the dapper ones!

EH — For Maria.

Chapter One

1925

The gap between each floorboard seemed to call to Cecily. *Drop the ring.* But she gripped it even tighter.

She'd cleaned off the dirt after finding the ring in the rose garden. No one ever went behind the ancient brick walls, and Cecily had only braved its thorns and twisted branches to rescue a cricket ball. The pupil who had accidentally knocked it in there had cried, frightened of a telling-off, and Cecily hadn't had to go far into the overgrown garden to retrieve the ball.

And there had been the ring, half-hidden in the ground as if it had risen up through the drought-parched earth just for her.

Cecily glanced over her shoulder, along the length of the corridor, but Hugh, her husband, was nowhere to be seen. *Busy in his study,* Cecily supposed as she knocked on the Culpecks' door.

The late summer sun was dying, throwing a blood-red tide over the floorboards of the masters' quarters and she knocked again, keen to be in the cozy confines of the Culpecks' rooms. Somewhere, someone was tuning a piano and she could hear the occasional sound of leather on willow from the playing fields outside, where school life went on as it ever did, as it ever had since she could remember. She was part of the fabric here, as constant as the buildings themselves.

"Close the curtains," Harriet instructed from inside the rooms. "Our circle is now complete." The bolt slid back with a metallic thud and the door opened to reveal Harriet Culpeck, her yellow summer dress a flame in the gloom. She smiled and said, "I was worried you'd thought better of it!"

"No, not at all!" Cecily stepped inside. Harriet's curious glance fell on Cecily's knitting bag. "Just in case the spirits are quiet, I have a pullover I'm knitting for Hugh, you see."

"Graham has a meeting with the headmaster," Harriet explained as her husband appeared on the threshold of the sitting room, struggling to find the sleeve of his dark gray suit. He greeted Cecily with a warm smile, as different from Hugh as any man could be. "It'll just be you and I."

The headmaster. Never 'Hugh', never 'Mr. James', always that stern-faced, rheumatoid-eyed headmaster, even to the people who have known him all these years.

"Good evening." Cecily nodded. "I hope your meeting goes well."

His look was one of sympathy, the same look the world had given Cecily all her thirty years, when the world looked at her at all. Then Graham fastened his jacket over his rounded belly and said, "And your circle of two."

"We shall see — perhaps it will be more by the end of the evening. There might be quite the party going on by the time you get back!" But Cecily still clung to her knitting bag. Until the bolt was drawn on the door, she couldn't trust Hugh not to arrive unannounced. He would be extremely displeased to know that Harriet was holding a séance in the masters' quarters. And even more so if he knew that Cecily was taking part.

"We shall be one hour," Graham told them, holding up his index finger. Cecily nodded an acknowledgment as the clocktower chimed its mournful six bells. When the clock chimed again, *the headmaster* would stalk along the narrow, dark corridor that led to his study, his black cape billowing at his back. He would descend the wide staircase into the oak-paneled hall and make his way over the courtyard, through the archway and around the path — never over the grass — toward the rooms she shared with him.

And she *must* be at home to meet him.

Harriet presented her cheek for a kiss, then Graham was gone. She slid the bolt back into place and asked Cecily, "You have the ring?"

Cecily put her knitting bag down behind the sofa, then held out her palm to Harriet. The gold ring, with its inlaid pattern of white and dark red stones, shone in the dim light.

"I managed to get the dirt out of the inscription this afternoon — it says '*My love, my secret*'. And then a letter C. I suppose an antiques dealer would know how old it was, but they couldn't tell us who this C is, could they?"

Cecily glanced expectantly toward the séance table. Or dining table. She had never been to a *circle* before but whatever Cecily had been expecting, it hadn't been a cheery crochet square in the colors of the rainbow, nor a bowl of russet apples beneath the pink lampshade, its tassels blowing a little in the breeze that fluttered the closed curtains. Two stubby candles already burned, settled into green saucers, and a steaming teapot sat next to the bowl, alongside two cups and a milk bottle.

A milk bottle on the table. She couldn't even imagine what Hugh would have to say to *that.*

"Would you like a tea before we start?" Harriet held out her hand. "Can I see the inscription? How romantic, a ring in a rose garden!"

Cecily nudged the ring into Harriet's palm. "Yes, it is romantic, isn't it?"

Romance was lacking so entirely from Cecily's life that she wondered if it was just something made up for songs, books and films, a lie to cling to. Harriet squinted at the inscription and gave a sigh of appreciation before she handed it back.

"I'll pour and we can start!"

Cecily held the ring tight once more. It had become her little piece of treasure, something she wrapped in a handkerchief and kept under her pillow. Hugh knew nothing of it. If he did, he would send it to the auctioneers in Tiverton. But it was hers — the one little piece of romance that had fallen to her.

She pulled out a chair at the dining table and sat down, her chin in her hand. "I wonder if the *C* stands for Caroline?"

"Once we've reached your brother, God rest him, we can ask!" Harriet took her seat and poured out two cups of tea. Then she clasped her hands in front of her breasts and told Cecily, "We'll start with a prayer."

Cecily placed the ring down in the center of the table and pressed her hands together. Sitting around the table, she and Harriet looked as if they were about to say grace before dinner, rather than contact the dead. Together they recited the Lord's Prayer as the candle flames fluttered and the curtains moved gently. Then

Harriet reached her hands across the table and offered them to Cecily.

"We mustn't break the circle until we've said goodbye," Harriet told her. "Ready?"

Cecily took her hands. She would grip on for dear life, because what would she do if Sandy got trapped in limbo, or wherever it was spirits went if the circle broke too soon? "I'm ready."

Harriet tossed her head to throw her graying copper curls from her eyes, then closed her eyelids. She took a deep breath, then another, and asked in a clear voice, like the dorm matrons ordering the boys into line, "We wish to speak with Lieutenant Pincombe. Sandy. Are you there, or is anybody with us who can call Sandy forward?"

Cecily stifled a sob. She'd promised herself not to cry, but the thought of her poor brother lying cold in the cemetery outside Ypres for a decade was too much to bear. Though she hadn't cried when news had reached them that Sandy had been killed. Her father hadn't allowed it.

"Sandy, it's me, it's Cecily. Please talk to us."

The mantelpiece clock ticked on, counting out the empty seconds. The sound of the piano had stopped and, into the silence, Harriet called, "Can anybody come forward? Sandy or perhaps the lady who lost her ring in the rose garden? We'd love to know who gave you such a pretty trinket. Who was C? Were you one of the Whitmores of Whitmore Hall?"

One of the candles guttered, the flame sputtering and dying as though someone had passed a breath across it. Then it flared again, the wick spitting back into life.

"Is there a Whitmore with us?"

Thump.

11

Cecily jolted and almost let go of Harriet's hands. Cautious, she asked, "Is that a footstep, Hattie? What is it?"

Harriet's fingers tightened and she gripped onto Cecily as her eyes sprang wide open and her mouth grew slack. As Cecily watched, her friend began to work her jaw as though chewing tough leather, then she asked, "What ring?"

Yet it wasn't Harriet's voice at all, but a rasping, low, male voice. A voice that sounded as though it hadn't been used in a very long time. It sounded like alcohol and tobacco and a stern loathing that Cecily had heard from her father, just as she heard it from her husband and now from this unnamed, uninvited visitor.

"Answer me, my girl." Harriet stared at her, unblinking. "Whose whore are you?"

"I'm not anybody's..." Cecily swallowed, her throat dry with alarm. Her voice had become tiny again. "Not anybody's whore. I'm not."

"Don't take it!" Harriet's voice was a scream of terror, a woman's scream, high and shrill. Her hands were so tight on Cecily's now that her knuckles were white as bleached bone. "No!"

"Take what? The ring?" Cecily implored Harriet, or whoever was speaking through her. This wasn't what Cecily had hoped for when she'd agreed to sit in Harriet's circle.

"Keep it safe," the woman's voice implored. "Keep it from him."

"I will, I promise." Though Cecily had no idea who *him* was supposed to be. "Is it yours? Are you C?"

"Shh." Harriet looked over her shoulder, as though listening for someone. Cecily found herself listening too, her heart pounding at the approach of whoever the woman was so afraid of. The clock ticked again and

Harriet leaned forward across the table to whisper. "Isabella."

Cecily recognized the name. She closed her eyes, trying to recall where she had heard it in relation to Whitmore Hall. Of course, the memorial inscription on the floor of the chapel.

Isabella Whitmore, whose earthly remains lye interr'd elsewhere, under her husband's connstant gaze untill the Daye of Judgement.

Isabella, the woman whose own husband had tried her and found her guilty of murder.

A chill rushed through Cecily. Whyever had she agreed to this? Her brother had not spoken, and instead Harriet had managed to dredge up a dark, dark episode from the old days of Whitmore Hall. Long before her grandfather had bought it and turned it into a school.

"Find me," Isabella's voice implored. "And let us rest as one."

The candle flames flared again then went out, plunging the room not into the gloomy sunlight that the curtains should allow, but an inky blackness, darker than any night she had ever seen. Cecily willed herself not to move, not to cry out as the hoarse rasp of the man's voice sounded again and told her, "I am *always* watching."

Cecily shivered. It sounded just like Hugh. Could it really be that Harriet had made contact with the dead, or had she managed to read what lay hidden in the depths of Cecily's mind?

"You leave her be, you bully!" Cecily said under her breath. Yet she could be entirely alone in the room if not for Harriet's grip on her hands. The clock was silent, the birdsong too, and here they sat in this sudden, unexpected tomb, watched by whoever possessed that ancient, cobwebbed voice.

"Sorry to interrupt, but the door was open," a new voice said in an accent that she didn't recognize. For a second Cecily readied herself for a new horror but instead a match sparked into life and the candles were illuminated. As though someone had flicked a switch, the clock resumed, the piano sounded and outside the window with the billowing curtains, a bird was singing.

Cecily blinked against the light and saw a man in the doorway. She had no recollection of ever having seen him before. He was rather short, an imp of a man, with an uncombed thatch of tousled dark hair and bright blue eyes. He was grinning — beaming in fact.

And he was handsome.

Still holding on to Harriet's hands, Cecily gave him a polite nod to mask her mounting surprise. "Good evening. And you must be...?"

"Rafael de Chastelaine. *Raf.* They tell me you're having a problem keeping your Latin masters?" As he replied, Harriet sucked in a gasp of air as though she had just been revived after drowning. She released Cecily's hands, just as she had told Cecily *not* to do. As she did, Raf took a step into the room and pressed his hand to his crumpled shirt, holding it over his heart as he told the unseen visitors, "Thank you, spirits, for joining us, go safely on your way. Lord grant peace to us and those who speak here."

He recited it as though it had been learned by rote, his accent lending the words a strange flamboyance, a world away from the hideous rasp of the spirit. Then he dropped his hand and Cecily realized that the new arrival wore no tie.

Hugh won't like that at all.

"I am so, so sorry!" Harriet settled her wide gaze on Cecily. "Did we get anyone, Cecily? Did your brother come through?"

Cecily stared at her open-mouthed. "Did you not... You couldn't hear what you were channeling?" Maybe it was better to pretend. She could tell her that Sandy had said hello, and that he was playing cricket in Paradise with the shade of W.G. Grace. But no, she couldn't lie to Harriet—she had few enough friends as it was. "A gentleman and a lady came through. He sounded angry. And she said her name is Isabella."

Cecily took the ring from the table and held it safely in the hollow of her palm once more. She offered the new arrival a smile. "Sorry."

"Did your bro—" Only then did Harriet seem to notice the crumpled Latin teacher in the doorway. She rose rather shakily to her feet and said, "Did my husband let you in?"

"The door was wide open!" Raf repeated, still beaming. He gave a very polite nod of greeting. "I'm a day early but there wasn't a reply from Dr. James' rooms so I thought I'd give his deputy a try instead!"

The bolt was fastened, Cecily remembered, a chill running through her again.

"Graham— Mr. Culpeck, the deputy headmaster, is with Dr. James." Harriet rose to her feet and quickly swept the curtains open, flooding the sitting room with welcome light. There was a giggle in her voice, an obvious note of excitement at this new arrival who seemed so untypical of the men of Whitmore Hall. "This is Mrs. James. Cecily—Mrs. Headmaster!"

Cecily rose from the table and, with a confidence she didn't feel, approached the new arrival. "How do you do, Mr. de Chastelaine? Have you traveled far? We are rather tucked away in our corner of Exmoor—I trust you did not have too many difficulties finding your way here."

"All the way from the Yorkshire coast," he admitted, though he didn't sound like any Yorkshireman Cecily had heard before. "By way of Romania, in case you were wondering if this is a typical Yorkshire accent!"

"Romania?" *No White Russian emigré, then.* "My goodness, I don't believe I've had the pleasure of meeting someone from your country before. You are very welcome here in Devon, Mr. de Chastelaine."

"I've been wandering around the grounds," he admitted in a conspiratorial whisper, as though it was quite the shocking confession. "It's a beautiful place."

"Mrs. James was born here." Harriet beamed. "Tea, Mr. de Chastelaine?"

He took a battered silver pocket watch from the pocket of the rather rumpled tweed jacket he wore and opened the case with a flick of his thumbnail. "I wouldn't want to hold you ladies up."

Cecily glanced at her watch. "We have twenty minutes."

"Mrs. James is a marvel in the gardens." Harriet smiled and Cecily couldn't help but return it, because she knew her friend well enough to recognize the embarrassment in her bluster. She had been caught in her séance by this newcomer, and she felt rather silly about it. "Cecily, dearest, why don't you show Mr. de Chastelaine the grounds before he meets the headmaster?"

Cecily's heart blanched at the very thought of it, the idea that she would stroll alone at dusk with a man, any man. She had been punished for far less over the years.

"I can show you from the window, if you'd like. There's something rather special for you to see, actually."

Maybe Mr. de Chastelaine would be interested in what Cecily had spotted, even if her husband had not been. Yet Harriet wasn't about to let the matter drop so easily and suggested, "Oh, you can't see anything at twilight! Take Mr. de Chastelaine to see the gardens, Cecily." Then she patted Cecily's arm. "They never end their meetings early. Nobody need know."

Something in Harriet's voice implied, *I won't tell.* But someone else might if they saw Cecily and the substitute teacher through the school's many windows.

"If you should like to see the grounds quickly, then I have no objection in showing you, sir."

"Really, call me Raf," he told her. "And I'd love to see the grounds with you. Don't tell, ladies, but gardening's what I do these days. Gardening and enough Latin to help a mate in need!"

Nerves. That's what Hugh had said was wrong with Mr. Brennan when he went off in his father's car, whiter than anyone Cecily had ever seen in her life. *It's always nerves.* Mr. Brennan had nerves, she had nerves. Nerves were for weak people, Hugh always said.

Where on earth did the bookish Latin teacher meet this man, though? They hardly seemed to be from the same planet, let alone be mates.

"This way please, Mr. de...Raf." Cecily gestured toward the door. Over her shoulder, she said, "Thank you, Harriet. That was certainly...interesting. Oh, I nearly forgot my knitting bag!"

Cecily's emergency excuse sat behind the sofa, and she hurried to pick it up, the ring still clutched in her other hand.

"Never break the circle," Raf told Harriet with a very mischievous wink indeed. Not the sort of wink that one saw in a school intended to turn out middling cabinet ministers and respectable bastions of the civil service.

In reply, Harriet giggled and held her hand to her lips like the girl she had once been. Her giggles grew a little sillier when Raf added, "You never know who might be knocking about."

Chapter Two

The clocktower chimed the three-quarter hour as Cecily led Raf through the grounds. They cast stick-figure shadows stretching over the lawn before them in the evening light.

"I didn't learn Latin," Cecily admitted.

"It's the only thing I was good at in school," Raf confessed. Raf, who knew how to close a séance. "I was that lad the teachers always said should work with his hands, because they didn't reckon my brain was up to much!"

As Cecily nodded, a strand of her hair fell loose and she tucked it back behind her ear. Hugh had insisted she have it cut short, but not bobbed, because that would be fashionable. Her light brown hair, which had always been straight, had developed untamable kinks once it had been cut. She was convinced it looked scruffy, and couldn't imagine what impression it would give someone new to the school. Someone like Raf.

"And now you're teaching Latin at Whitmore Hall! Poor Mr. Brennan. You said he was your friend?"

"He's a good bloke." It sounded odd in that accent, so unlike any she was used to hearing in this quiet corner of Devon. "Can I carry that bag for you? My mum wouldn't think much of me not offering!"

"Oh—thanks ever so!" Cecily handed it to him. Her fingers accidentally brushed against his and a blush rushed to Cecily's cheeks. He grinned, then paused to look back at the school, a glowering monolith against the setting sun.

"You were really born here?"

Cecily nodded. "Oh, yes. My father was the headmaster. I've never lived anywhere else. Me and my brother, Sandy. Father schooled me here himself, but Sandy was a pupil."

"And now you're married to the headmaster." He raised his eyebrows. "He must be young to be in charge!"

"Erm...actually, he's..." *He'll realize soon enough.* As soon as Cecily introduced Raf to her husband, he'd see that she had married a man who was old enough to be her father. Because what else could she have done when her father died and Sandy hadn't been there to take over the school? "Anyway, this is what I wanted to show you. Look!"

Cecily pointed to the lawn. It had dried out from lack of rain, but hadn't all gone the same color, so a pattern of lighter grass was visible below their feet. He wouldn't care, of course, because only *she* cared about such things. Hugh made sure Cecily knew that.

"It's a ghost garden!" Raf's tone was alive with excitement, his delight even reaching through Cecily's own melancholy, through the memory of that rasping voice and the woman's whispered plea.

'*Find me.*'

'*Let us rest as one.*'

"I've seen them before but nothing on this scale — it must've been magnificent!" And it must have, the yellowing ghost of the garden that had once been there stretching across the lawn, its paths and borders forever lost until the hottest summers parched the grass. "It's huge!"

"Isn't it!" Buoyed up by Raf's enthusiasm for the garden, Cecily went on. "And do you see what's at its center? It's terribly overgrown now, of course, but see the walls in the middle? That's the old rose garden. It always seemed so odd stood there in the middle of the lawn, but now we can see that it was once the centerpiece of a formal garden. It must've looked fantastic in its heyday, mustn't it?"

"I'll bet it was!" He began to walk backward across the lawn, chatting to her as he went. "So this place was a house once, yes? Your family's house?"

"No. The Whitmores built the house, and now it's a school."

"Someone knew their gardens — there're some exotic specimens scattered about!"

"That was Captain Whitmore — Matthew, I believe he was called. He was an explorer and used to bring plants home from his travels. The poor fellow was shipwrecked in the end." Cecily shivered. There was a chill in the air and she pulled her home-knitted cardigan more tightly around her. "It's in a remote spot, really, and the house sat empty for a long time before my grandfather bought it for a song. Borrowed some money and turned it into the school you see now."

"Right on the edge of Exmoor." Raf ruffled his hand back through his tousled hair, messing it even more. "I love the wildness of it. I was born in the mountains and now I live on the cliffs. Nature is magic, no need for a classroom!"

"I believe my husband might disagree with you on that score!" Cecily tried to make a joke of it, but the last thing she wanted was for this unusual character to leave the school in under a week. She hoped he'd at least make it until the Christmas vac.

"I've been warned he's one for tradition." Raf reached into his pocket and brought out a deep blue silk tie, which was as rumpled as the rest of his clothes. "Don't worry, I can put on the act when I need to. Good references too, because I thought I might need them."

It felt like a secret, as though he were confiding something in her with what was nothing but a joke.

A secret, she thought, feeling the ring warm against her palm.

Cecily laughed politely. "Yes, I'm afraid he will want impeccable references, or to have drunk brandies with your father. Perhaps we should make our way back to the house?"

"Believe me, he *definitely* won't know my dad." The way he laughed suggested another story, one that would remain untold for now. "Can we see the rose garden before we run?"

"Yes, we could have a peep, but the gate's locked so we shan't be able to go inside. I do apologize." Cecily glanced away from Raf's sparkling blue eyes and up at the clocktower. She could almost swear she heard its tick, advancing each second toward the time when she must go indoors.

"Locked?" He sounded halfway between surprised and horrified, then amusement crept into his tone again. "Were the boys sneaking in for a cheeky woodbine?"

She couldn't even smile, for the boys at Whitmore Hall knew better than to do such a thing *anywhere*. The cane and slipper had never been spared under her father and now, with her husband's regime in place, that hadn't changed. In fact, for the thirty years that Cecily had been on this earth, *nothing* had changed beyond her transition from the late headmaster's daughter to his thin-lipped successor's wife.

"It's—it's dangerous. I went in there the other day, and I scratched my hand on the thorns." Cecily offered the back of her hand to him, scored by a red line which she had told Hugh had been caused by clumsiness in the kitchen. "It's so terribly overgrown. And the walls...they're ever so old. Unstable. There's danger of subsidence, you see."

"I have something for that." Raf reached into his pocket and brought out a tiny bottle of brown glass. "From my own garden. Dab this on there three times a day and it'll soon be gone. It's good for bruises too, if you ever have any."

Cecily froze, her hand halfway toward the bottle. Did he know? Could he see it in her? A weak, nervy woman who received a slap now and again from her husband to keep her on an even keel? "Thank you, you're very kind. Are you sure you won't need it yourself, though?"

"I have more," he told her as though confiding a great secret. "When you spend as long as I do digging gardens and snagging every bit of yourself on thorns, you pick up plenty of bruises!"

Cecily took the bottle from Raf and put it in the pocket of her gingham dress. "Will you miss your garden at home while you're here? I would say you're welcome to work on this garden, but you ought to speak to my husband first."

"It's always better to ask for forgiveness than permission." And he winked. He must be mocking her, Cecily knew. He didn't seem to be, but he must be. Then Raf turned to the walled garden and closed his fingers around the rusted gate.

The garden within the walls was pitch-black despite the red flood of the setting sun, a twisted labyrinth of vines and boughs, with thorns threatening to snare any who dared go near. Cecily wondered now how she had ever slipped into the garden at all, let alone found the ring. It seemed to have become impenetrable in the short time that had passed. Whatever ghosts the boys in the dorms teased walked within the walls must walk alone for now — the rampant growth of the roses had ensured them their privacy.

The judge is going to get you.

"Is Sleeping Beauty in the middle of it?" Raf put his face to the gate and squinted into the darkness beyond, though Cecily doubted he could see anything more than she in the thicket that lay behind the walls. She shuddered, realizing that the birdsong that had accompanied their tour was silent now. "There's history in there, who knows what's hidden under all those thorns!"

Cecily wondered if she should show Raf the ring. But Isabella had begged her to *'keep it from him'*. And who was *him*? Raf seemed to be the sort of chap a lady could trust, but they had only just met. Even so...

"Yes, there is history in there." She recalled how her heart had leaped on spotting the half-buried ring. *My secret.* "I suppose the ladies of the house used to wander there in days gone by. They might have left all sorts of things behind them."

"It's a place for secrets." As Raf spoke she met his gaze again, that sparkling, bright blue. "I'll miss my garden, but I'll enjoy this one instead."

"I do hope so." Cecily's attention returned to the clocktower. Five minutes to seven. "We really should go back to the house now. Mustn't keep the headmaster waiting!"

"Lead me to him!" Raf laughed. "And let's see if my references pass muster!"

Cecily went at quite a clip over the lawn toward the school building, one eye on the clocktower as she went. Her heart hammered and her palms grew clammy — turning up late and accompanied by a strange man would never do. It had been bad enough when her husband had seen her talking to the homewares salesman who'd turned up at the school. Even by showing Hugh the brochure of saucepans and vacuum cleaners that the cheery salesman had left behind, it had been difficult to convince him that she wasn't a hussy. *'Were you flirting? Were you? Did you smile at him?'*

Cecily opened the side door from the courtyard. Raf was close behind and she quickly moved her hand away from the door handle in case it should accidentally brush against his. The interior of the school was gloomy, lit sparsely by electric bulbs that fizzled out whenever the weather was stormy. The boys would be in their studies now, dutifully writing letters home or reading of adventures or probably getting up to all sorts of mischief, but there was no sign of them here. The wide, empty hallways echoed with their footsteps, the sound dulled only when Cecily led her charge through a narrow door to what was once a servants' staircase, glad for this far quicker route up to their quarters as she heard the first chime ringing in the clocktower.

Hugh would end his meeting now, she knew, and escort Graham from the study, past the portraits of founders and peers and the illustrious men who had made their names here. They would part company at the end of the hallway and Graham would make his way through the school, looking in on his charges as he left, but Hugh would stride downstairs and out into the courtyard. She could almost see him now as he swept across the flags, the gown a bat's wings that engulfed him. Through the archway he would walk and into the main doors, simply so he could use the grand staircase that she knew made him feel like a man of means. The very act of ascending that ancient flight made him *somebody*.

We have three minutes left.

Cecily scuffed her way up the stairs in her cheap lace-up shoes, hurrying to offset the rage that would be unleashed if she was late, but not rushing too much in case Raf thought her rude. Her father had always told her, *'A woman must please others, not herself.'*

Breathless, she quipped, "So many stairs in this place, it keeps one fit!"

"I'll never find my way around." He laughed. "Ten years from now you'll stumble on a man wandering the corridors, gabbling in Romanian, his beard to his knees, and you'll say…*is that Raf, we wondered what had become of him!*"

Cecily giggled. Then hid her mouth behind her hand, silencing herself. It wouldn't do for Hugh to hear her laughing with a man. "You'll soon know this warren like the back of your hand!"

She pushed wide the door at the top of the stairs, which led onto the masters' corridor. Doors opened off from it, but at the end was the headmaster's residence, where Cecily had lived her whole life. "Your room is underneath the clocktower, by the way—but you'll soon get used to the chimes. You'll find it strange if it falls silent."

"It'll make a change from seagulls." Raf paused and looked along the corridor, his eyes narrowing. "Wait now, this is familiar. This is where I started, frightening you two ladies, isn't it? I came up the main stairs—this *is* a labyrinth!"

Cecily flinched when he mentioned the main stairs. Her husband would be heading up them as they spoke. "Erm…yes, it is a labyrinth!" *With its very own monster crouched at its center.*

She took her small bunch of keys from her belt and went to unlock the door, but as she leaned against it, it swung open. Cecily's heart shot into her mouth. "I believe my husband has already arrived…"

She could hear the sound of hammering, three sharp knocks of a nail then Hugh's voice summoning her with one word.

"Study!"

Forgetting Raf was following her, Cecily darted for the study. Whenever her husband demanded she enter, she was taken back to her childhood, already preparing herself for a reprimand.

"Sorry, I'm so sorry, I do apologize, I'm not so terribly late, I do hope your meeting went well with Mr. Culpeck, can I bring you a cup of tea? I made flapjacks earlier if you should like one and…and…"

She had never liked the study, with its dark, heavy furniture, in her father's time or now. Hugh was turned away from her, swathed in his black teaching gown. The back of his shiny pink scalp showed through his thinning scraps of hair. He was so tall that he had no need of a stepladder as he hung a painting on the wall.

Cecily had never seen it before, a portrait of a man with graying hair that fell from under his black cap to his shoulders. His mouth was set in an unsmiling line, and his heavy-lidded eyes seemed to bore into her from the depths of his thin, fleshy face. He was dressed in a vast black cloak decked with an elaborate collar and gold braid, with a scroll in one hand and a skull under the other. The painting was too old to be anyone connected with the school — it had to show one of the Whitmores.

"Good evening, husband." Cecily folded her hands in front of her and inclined her head.

"Witness the return to Whitmore Hall of its founder, Judge Edward Whitmore!" Hugh didn't turn to look at her but instead gestured toward the vast portrait. "Vilified in his day, let him be properly honored in ours!"

Cecily raised her head and the man in the portrait fixed his scrutiny on her once more. Judge Whitmore, the man who had tried his own wife for murder, and sent her to her doom.

"It looks well on your wall, husband," Cecily lied.

Isabella's voice came back to her. *'Keep it from him.'* Cecily clutched the ring firmly.

"Would it've killed him to smile?" At Raf's words, time seemed to stop. Cecily's heart plummeted into her stomach as the man beside her, his hands in his pockets and his tie there too, smiled that carefree smile that barely seemed to leave his face. Hugh turned in one movement, the cape flowing around him as he did. As his pale gaze settled on Rafael de Chastelaine, Cecily saw only one thing there, utter disdain. Then he slid his gaze across to her and that disdain grew deeper even as he twisted his thin lips into a grimace of welcome.

"And you are?" Hugh asked in his quiet, considered voice.

"Rafael de Chastelaine, I'm your emergency Latin teacher!" Raf held out his hand. "Raf."

"Tea," Hugh told Cecily as he took Raf's hand and shook it. "Chop chop, Mrs. James, Mr. de Chastelaine shall need a libation once he has fastened his tie and combed his hair."

Cecily bustled from the room. Must her husband talk to a grown adult like Raf as though he were a pupil? Not that she could risk Hugh's rage and protest on Raf's behalf.

She went through the ritual of making the tea, willing the water to boil faster, but it seemed to take forever. Once she had loaded the tea tray, she returned to the study and knocked at the door, waiting for Hugh to admit her. He wouldn't like it if she burst in.

"Enter!" Hugh announced, but before Cecily had a chance to move, to struggle with the stiff door handle and the tray, the door was opened by Raf. His tie was fastened, though not with the precision needed for Whitmore Hall, and if his hair had seen a comb, it wasn't today. With his back to Hugh he gave a small smile for Cecily and nodded toward the tray, mouthing, *Need help?*

Cecily shook her head. She wouldn't have minded Raf's help at all, but there was always the danger that Hugh would read something into it that wasn't there.

Cecily laid the tray down on the table and, without waiting to be asked, poured Hugh his tea, exactly as he liked to take it. She placed it down beside the blotter in front of him, then offered Raf a little grin. "Milk and sugar, Mr. de Chastelaine?"

"I have so much sugar I daren't say," Raf told her as he settled back into the hard wooden seat opposite

Hugh, who was as resplendent as ever on the enormous padded chair that had once belonged to her father. "You don't have to wait on me."

"Mrs. James likes to be useful," Hugh told him with an attempt at a smile of his own. "It helps to keep her nerves at bay. Nerves, it seems, have afflicted more than our ailing friend Mr. Brennan."

"Yeah, he's doing a lot better now he's had some time to rest." Raf nodded, heaping spoonfuls of sugar into his cup. That was good news at least, Mr. Brennan had always seemed such a gentle soul on the few occasions Cecily had met him. "He reckoned you'd lost a few teachers and that even some of the boys have been a bit anxious. Queer business."

"Adolescence on one hand, middle age on the other," was Hugh's smooth reply. "And in the case of the ladies, mere femininity. Nerves might be taken as a warning of a weak character, I think. When that warning manifests in the boys at Whitmore Hall, it is my duty to cut it off at the root. We are in the business of forging *men*."

Cecily shouldn't be listening to their conversation, but she hadn't heard anything about the boys being anxious. Other than the usual issue of nightmares, which were common in children sent to live in a large old house like Whitmore Hall. But as she laid the plate of flapjacks on the desk between the two men, something occurred to her. The boy whose cricket ball had gone into the rose garden had been terrified. Was he anxious too?

"Will that be all for now?"

"Of course." Hugh waved his hand toward her. "You may go."

As Cecily left, she felt Raf's smile rather than saw it, and it warmed her. Though her life hadn't been filled with kindness, it wasn't entirely unknown to her, but she only ever saw it in slivers, like sunlight falling through railings.

Chapter Three

Cecily went to the bedroom and hid the ring under her pillow again, wrapped unobtrusively in a handkerchief. She returned to the kitchen and occupied herself in tidying up, until no reasonable person could object to its neatness. But there was always something she forgot, and her husband always spotted it.

She had been late returning to their rooms, and her husband wouldn't hold back his displeasure. And if the sight of Raf had annoyed him too — and Cecily was sure that it must have — then Hugh would be more of a grump than usual. She took the bottle Raf had given her from her pocket and dabbed some of the substance on the cut she had received from the thorns. Cecily recoiled, preparing for it to sting, but it didn't hurt at all.

Maybe Hugh would only shout at her. It wouldn't be so bad. She *had* been tardy, even though she had tried her best to be quick. She shouldn't have lingered so long in the garden with Raf, but it had been so nice — *he* was so nice. And she was wrong to notice it in a man who wasn't her husband. Hugh *was* kind to her—after all, he sometimes gave her a lift into the village if it was raining and she had shopping to do and he wasn't too busy. It was very wrong of her to show her ingratitude by not being ready for him when he needed her to be. She was his wife, his helpmeet. She had sworn to love, honor and obey, and she was very bad at all three. He would shout, and she would say sorry, and there would the end of it.

For today, at least.

She heard the study door open and two pairs of feet walking along the hallway, away from the kitchen as Hugh showed Raf from their rooms. At the last, however, one of those pairs of feet stopped then she heard them approaching her at a rapid speed.

"I just wanted to say goodbye." Raf appeared in the doorway. "And to thank you and Mrs. Culpeck again for showing me the garden. I'm going to drop by and say thank you to her on my way to settle in."

He lied. Why would he lie? Why would he tell Hugh that we hadn't been alone in the gardens? It wasn't as though he owed Cecily anything, after all.

"Goodbye, Mr. de Chastelaine. And I'm glad you enjoyed the gardens." *As much as I enjoyed showing them to you.*

"Come along, sir." Hugh appeared in the doorway behind him, filling the narrow space. "You have missed supper with the boys, but I shall send word to the kitchen and have them provide a light meal. Good evening."

"Good evening, Mrs. James." Unseen by her husband, Raf beamed, then composed himself and turned back to Hugh. "Good evening, Dr. James."

There it was again—the sensation that his smile had touched her. Like a kind brush of his hand against her arm. An unfamiliar warmth spread within her, and Cecily realized she was blushing. "It's terribly warm. I must open a window."

"Clear the study," Hugh said in a clipped tone before he escorted Raf away, along the corridor and out of sight.

Cecily ducked out of the kitchen, a tray under her arm, and began to collect up the tea things in the study. A syrup of half-dissolved sugar sat at the bottom of Raf's cup.

A very sweet man!

Cecily smiled at her own terrible joke, and was still smiling as she left the study, heading straight into her husband's path.

"Hurry along," he instructed, his gaze fixed over her head as he approached the study at a pace. "When the crockery is washed, dried and put away, I shall see you in my study, Mrs. James."

Only then did she see her knitting bag on the hallway side table, where Raf must've placed it when Hugh had called them to his study. Thank goodness he had thought so quickly — the very idea of Hugh seeing him carrying her bag sent a fresh chill through Cecily.

She washed and dried as fast as she could without breaking anything. Still wiping her hands on her pinny, Cecily went into the study. Hugh's displeasure radiated from him.

"Yes, husband?"

"Dr. James," he corrected, not turning from the portrait to look at her.

"Sorry, Dr. James."

"How have you passed the day?" He finally turned to face her, knitting his hands behind his back. "Were the hours well spent?"

Cecily tried to ignore the disapproval on his lined, gray face. "Yes, of course. I tidied and cleaned, I read a recipe book, and Mrs. Culpeck and I did some knitting."

"And showed Mr. de Chastelaine the garden."

Cecily nodded. "Yes, and showed Mr. de Chastelaine the garden."

"Indeed." Hugh nodded and drew in a breath. "And at no point as you *showed him the garden* did it occur to either of you tell him to put on a tie?"

Cecily had learned over the years to keep her answers short, volunteering only the most pertinent information. Which worked, as long as she didn't get flustered and erupt into waffle. "There wasn't really time."

"What will people think, seeing his sort — *a foreigner* — with my wife? You've much to be thankful to the Culpeck woman for." Hugh jabbed his finger toward her. "If you and he had been alone, my girl, there would be hell to pay!"

Cecily flinched away from his finger. God willing, no one had seen them together. "You were busy, and as your wife, I felt I should be hospitable to Mr. de Chastelaine…as a help to you. My mother was often hostess when my father was headmaster."

He nodded slowly and peered at her, as though he could see her soul. Then he said, "I recall. Another one for her nerves, I seem to remember the late Dr. Pincombe would lament. A charming hostess, though. *Accomplished.* Would that you had inherited her skill."

Cecily pursed her lips. If only her mother hadn't passed away. Or Sandy. But there was no point in wishing to mend the past when it couldn't be done.

"I try my best," Cecily replied in a small voice.

"You are my burden to bear, such is the lot of the husband." He sighed. "You may go about your business. And brush your hair, you look like a daily woman."

Better, perhaps, than last week when he'd said she looked *'like a scarecrow'*. "At once, Dr. James."

Cecily went to their bedroom and sat down in front of the dressing table, her wan face and gray eyes reflected back in the mirror. The dressing table was bare apart from a silver-backed brush lying on its surface, with no clutter of powder-pots or compacts. The last time Cecily had worn makeup had been on their wedding day, and Hugh had banned it ever after.

She began to brush her hair. If only Hugh would let her grow it again, or allow the hairdresser in the village to shape it at least, it wouldn't look such a mess.

At least he didn't hit me.

Cecily went on brushing. One hundred strokes, they said, to make hair shiny and beautiful. She lost count somewhere around forty-three.

Maybe in his room along the corridor, Mr. de Chastelaine was at this very moment brushing his hair too. If he even owned a brush. He was so very kind. So very nice. If only her husband were more like him, then perhaps she would not be so afflicted with nerves.

As her husband didn't like to be disturbed in the evenings while he was reading, Cecily knitted for a while on the window seat in the bedroom, glancing out at the garden every so often. There was no one there — no Mr. de Chastelaine, no boys creeping about where they shouldn't. Only the brick walls of the rose garden in the center of lawn held her attention.

How had Isabella lost her ring there?

Once it was time for bed, Cecily changed into her plain cotton nightdress and climbed under the bedsheets. She reached under the pillow and held the ring, safe in its wrapping, and began to fall asleep.

* * * *

She wasn't sure how late it was when the sound of Hugh coming into the bedroom woke her and she kept her eyes tight shut, listening as he went about his routine. Cecily could picture his every movement as he hung up his suit in the wardrobe, placed his shoes neatly beside each other and changed into his navy blue pajamas. She felt the mattress sink as he climbed into bed beside her and waited to discover whether he would expect her to perform what Hugh called *'a wife's duty'*, praying that he wouldn't. After a few minutes had passed, Hugh's breath evened out into sleep and Cecily allowed herself to breathe, lying stock-still beside him.

It had been such a warm day that Cecily had left the window slightly ajar. Now she wished she had not as a distinct chill came into the air. She pulled the bedclothes more tightly around her, but she was still cold, right into her bones. If she started to shiver, it would only annoy Hugh, and she tried her best not to move. The only comfort she allowed herself was the secret of the ring, and she let it slide its way onto her finger, the band warm around her skin.

Then she heard it. Someone was crying.

Cecily opened her eyes. It was probably one of the boys in the dorm below, another nightmare for Matron to deal with, but the crying didn't seem so far away. Cecily blinked.

It was from somewhere in the bedroom.

And Hugh slept on.

Thank God.

The curtains shut out most of the light, the darkness only alleviated by the luminous dial of the alarm clock. The weeping went on, gaining in volume, and in a blink a figure appeared at Cecily's bedside, emitting its own pale glow as if reflecting moonlight. Cecily shrank back against the bedsheets as the room grew colder still.

There, standing right in front of her, was a woman. She looked as if she had stepped down from a painting, and was dressed in Puritan garb, her gown as black as the night beyond, her white lace collar immaculate. Her face was lowered, bordered with ringlets, and Cecily couldn't see her features, but there was no mistaking her visitor's despair and desolation.

"Isabella?" Cecily whispered.

The crying stopped. The woman began to raise her head and Cecily felt her gaze on her though she could not see her eyes in her shadowed face.

Then she was gone.

Cecily rubbed her eyes. She had obviously been dreaming. Nerves.

That séance was a terrible idea. Dreams of crying ghosts, whatever next!

But Cecily knew, deep down in her marrow, that she had just been visited by a ghost.

Chapter Four

Cecily always rose before her husband did, so that his breakfast would be ready when he woke up. She laid out his boiled egg and toast and his pot of tea, and brought him his newspaper. He would only speak if there was a problem—a creased page in his paper, or a smear on his cutlery invisible to everyone but him.

After he'd gone into the school for the day, Cecily tidied up, but this morning she couldn't get the memory of the ghost out of her mind. As she made the bed, the memory became more intense, and she felt the woman's woe all over again.

I'll go half-mad thinking about it.

So Cecily headed off to see Harriet Culpeck, hoping she'd be in and not at her dance class in the village. As she went along the corridor, Cecily glanced outside at the garden. She stopped and clutched the windowsill, amazed at the sight before her.

Rafael de Chastelaine, Whitmore Hall's temporary Latin master, was standing in the center of a semicircle of pupils who were sitting on the parched grass beside the ghost garden. She recognized them as the youngest boys in the school, those who had come up from prep and were just a couple of weeks into their first term. These were the boys who could look so small and lost, so very afraid.

But not this morning.

This morning they were rapt, some neatly cross-legged and a few even kneeling, the braver of them sprawled back, blazers set aside and ties loosened in the morning sun. Their teacher was no better, his jacket flung over the box hedge behind him and his own tie nowhere near straight.

Raf was speaking with such animation, such excitement, that it radiated from him even though Cecily couldn't hear his words. He gestured to the flowers that bloomed beneath the hedge with an enthusiasm that was mirrored on the faces of his young charges, all of whom seemed to be enjoying this unorthodox Latin lesson.

What Cecily wouldn't have done to be one of the pupils.

She continued on her way to Harriet's rooms, her heart buoyed up now with unexpected joy.

Cecily knocked at the door, not as furtive as she had been the evening before. "Hattie — are you about?"

"Come in," Harriet called. "Floury hands!"

The door was unlocked so Cecily let herself in. "Oh, Hattie, you'll never guess what's happened! I don't know where to begin!"

She followed the sounds to the small kitchen where Harriet was kneading out bread on the narrow worktop. It was a perk of being the deputy headmaster, of course. Rooms plural, not as spacious as those of Cecily and Hugh, but better than the single studies awarded to the masters who occupied the remainder of the corridor.

"You'll never guess what Mr. de Chastelaine's doing, Hattie—he's got the first form out on the lawn!"

"I know!" Harriet pulled a face of pantomimed scandal. "I admit, as soon as Graham left for school I enjoyed a welcome cup of tea watching our new arrival begin his first class with us. I don't think we've had such a rakish teacher before! I could watch him all day."

Cecily giggled. "If we could borrow some blazers, maybe we could disguise ourselves as pupils? No one would ever notice!"

"He came by last night on his way to his study." Harriet picked up the dough and threw it down against the worktop, sending a cloud of flour into the air. "And thanked me for accompanying you and he on a wander in the gardens! I asked no questions, Cec, but as I said to him, it was a pleasure."

"Thank you." Cecily's joy began to deflate as she recalled her husband's interrogation. "And if anyone else says anything, please do say that you were in the garden with me. It's for the best—you know how protective my husband is. It was nothing, really, I showed Ra—Mr. de Chastelaine the gardens and he was the perfect gent."

"I know your husband," Harriet told her darkly. "There's tea in the pot—help yourself if you like. What've you done to your hand?"

"I scratched it on the roses when I found the ring." Cecily held out her hand. The scratch had lost its angry red tinge and was well on the way to healing. "Mr. de Chastelaine gave me something to dab on it—I do believe it's working."

"Well, if he has something for a lady going through that time of her life, he's welcome to stop by and see me." Harriet laughed. "If you're pouring, I'll have a cup too. Graham says he's wonderfully exotic, filled with stories and fun. A breath of roguish fresh air — I said that, not Graham!"

"Roguish — that's certainly right." Cecily turned her back to Harriet as she poured the tea. The blush had crept back into her face and she didn't want Harriet to see. "Sorry...all this excitement... I almost forgot what I actually came here for. But you might want to take a seat before I tell you."

"Can't leave the bread at a crucial moment — I'm a doughty girl, tell me your news!" Harriet took a breath then asked, "Did Sandy come through after all?"

"No, he hasn't. Instead..." The chill Cecily had experienced last night returned to her and her heart beat as heavily as if it had been made of lead. "There's no simple way for me to say this, and you'll doubtless think I was dreaming, but last night, while I was lying in bed...I was visited by a ghost."

Harriet stopped kneading. "What?"

Cecily's teacup rattled in its saucer. "A ghost. Hattie, I think...I think it was Isabella. It was a lady, a Puritan lady going on how she was dressed, and she was so sad. Her crying woke me. And when I said her name, she almost looked at me, then she vanished."

"What exactly happened last night in our circle?" Harriet plunged her fingers into the dough again but remained unmoving. "There was an angry man?"

"Yes. He was saying someone was a...a whore." Cecily repeated the hateful word under her breath. "He was so nasty, Hattie. He said, '*I'm always watching.*' Then a woman came through, and said she was

Isabella. Wasn't she Judge Whitmore's wife? There's that memorial inscription in the chapel."

Just before the altar rail, where Cecily and Hugh had stood as they were married.

"It seems as if it's her ring," Cecily continued, "and she said something about wanting to *'rest as one'*. Who with?"

"Oh, how horrible!" Harriet shuddered. "She isn't buried with him—perhaps she wants to be? I don't think *I'd* want to be!"

"No, I certainly wouldn't want to be either!" Cecily grimaced. "Anyway, she was hanged, wasn't she? So I suppose she would've been buried within the prison walls. We'd never have a chance of finding her, and can you imagine even asking for the exhumation?"

And it was the judge who had sent Isabella to a mass grave. The judge in that horrible painting. "Anyway, when I got home, guess what Dr. James was up to?"

"I bet it wasn't a séance!"

Cecily had to chuckle at that. "No! He was—the Lord alone knows where he found it—he was hanging up a portrait of Judge Whitmore in his study."

"Why on earth would anybody do that? The parents wouldn't like it if they knew!" That was an understatement. The school had done all it could to quell the legend of its very own bloody judge from before Cecily was even born. The hall might still bear his family name, but other than that simple stone in the chapel, Edward Whitmore was nothing but a bogeyman. "Oh, Cecily, you don't think Mr. de Chastelaine would tell the headmaster about our circle? I mean, Graham doesn't mind but Hugh— Do you think it was the judge I channeled? I've never managed to reach anyone before, so two in one night!"

Cecily froze, her teacup halfway to her lips. "You'd never...really? Well, that *is* impressive. Maybe my husband digging out that portrait has stirred things up? But we do need to make sure Mr. de Chastelaine won't say anything. Would Graham be able to have a word with the new master? I really can't knock on his door myself — Hugh wouldn't be pleased."

"I'll ask Graham." She nodded. "But if you do happen to spot our rogue first... Wherever did he find that painting anyway? He must've been digging around in the most cobwebbed corners!"

"I honestly don't know where he found it. I'd never seen the ugly thing before. It's horrible — it's as though he's staring right at you." Cecily shivered. "But yes, if I bump into Mr. de Chastelaine, I'll have a word. I'm sure, if he's perceptive enough, he'll realize Hugh's not the sort to be pleased about spiritualism under his roof."

It sounded so normal spoken like this in broad daylight, as though the weeping woman was nothing to be afraid of at all. Yet she was. The sound of her sobs and the memory of her form beside the bed were something that Cecily already knew she would never be able to forget. Whatever would she do if the specter returned tonight?

"Ghosts can't hurt you, though, can they?" Cecily asked. "I mean, it's not like the lady will try to wring my neck while I'm sleeping?"

"When Mr. Brennan and I used to do our circles, we never conjured up anyone." *Mr. Brennan? Raf's quiet, timid predecessor shared Harriet's love of the spiritual world?* Cecily would never have expected that. "But he knew more than anyone I've ever met about the other realm. A lifelong passion, you see. He assured me that no harm could come to the living from the dead. Of course, he did have his nerves..."

"So if she comes back, I oughtn't fear her?" Cecily felt strengthened at that thought. "I mustn't be nervous, must I?"

Harriet shook her head. "She was an innocent, wronged by that devil of a husband. She's to be pitied, not feared. Poor thing, to suffer in life and find no peace in death."

"I can't imagine how awful it must've been. He watched her hang, so they say, and he knew all along she was innocent, because *he* was the one who'd committed the murder." Cecily put aside her cup. "Oh, I could slash that portrait with Hugh's very own paper knife! Honoring a murderer, indeed."

"Far be it from me to speak ill of another's husband but your Hugh has always been a queer fellow." She kneaded her knuckles hard into the dough. "I wonder if Mr. de Chastelaine likes bread?"

"Hugh...he's under a lot of pressure running the school." Cecily didn't want to say any more. No one knew anything about Hugh's behavior toward her, although she had often wondered if the masters who lived nearby had ever heard Hugh's voice raised against her. Cecily dabbed her fingertip in the spilt flour. "I'm sure Mr. de Chastelaine must like bread — a fresh, homemade loaf would be a lovely gift for the new teacher."

Harriet beamed and Cecily followed her gaze to the open window and, far below them, the impromptu Latin class that was taking place. The laughter of the boys drifted up and she heard Raf's voice proclaiming in a language that she had never learned. Cecily might not know what he was saying, but from the raucous howls of mirth that accompanied his teaching, she guessed it wasn't the days of the week.

"I hope he stays. For a while. Until Mr. Brennan's better. I'd hate for him to find it too isolated and stuffy here and vanish before the week is out." Cecily went to the window and looked down at the class, who appeared to be even more rapt, and even more relaxed, than they had been before. "The boys think he's marvelous!"

"He's already a breath of fresh air blowing through this dusty old place." Harriet smiled, just a little sly. "The headmaster must *hate* him."

"Not so much that he sacks Mr. de Chastelaine before the day is out, I hope!" Cecily had read about the *feminine wiles* of women who convinced men to bend to their will. But she didn't seem to have that power herself over Hugh. If only she had, then she could convince him to allow Raf to stay.

Raf. Such a lovely name. It suited him. Not that she should think it.

"You didn't hear it from me, but Graham says he doesn't think our gypsy rogue has ever set foot in a school. You have a sixth sense for it when you've been in the game as long as Gray." Harriet picked up her cup and took a sip, still watching Raf and the boys. "But his references are *impeccable.* Some very important people, as the saying goes!"

"*Really?*" Cecily gasped. "I suppose he might have been a personal tutor, and in that sort of job no one would blink if he took his charge outside for a lesson. Oh, I do so hope Hugh's busy and doesn't see him."

'A breath of fresh air.' Harriet was certainly right about that. She was probably right about Hugh hating him too, since Hugh had very definite ideas for the school

he was in charge of. Cecily had seen enough teachers come and go to know that Raf didn't fit the mold at all, but for a man with the ambitions of her husband, a man who aimed to see his school mentioned alongside the likes of Eton and Marlborough, she could only hope that those apparently marvelous references would be enough.

Cecily finished her cup of tea and bade Harriet goodbye. There were dumplings to be prepared for supper, vegetables to chop, the table to lay for lunch and the bathroom floor to scrub.

But despite her list of tasks, on the way back to her rooms Cecily paused by the window to peer once more at Raf's open-air lesson.

Oh, to be one of his pupils, how lucky they –

In alarm, Cecily stared down at the garden. Hugh was striding across the grass toward Raf and his group and she could see fear writ across the faces of every boy, all of whom were now sitting bolt upright, their smiles gone. Raf looked a little less concerned as he approached Hugh, his jacket still abandoned and his sleeves rolled to the elbow. Very carefully, she lifted the sash window just in time to hear Hugh thunder, "You boys, indoors now! Mr. de Chastelaine, at bell I expect to see you in my office. Properly dressed!"

"Dr. James—" When Raf spoke, Cecily flinched, though she knew her husband wouldn't show a teacher the same punishment she would have received for daring to answer back. Instead Hugh drew himself up to his full height, thin as a stick insect, pale as a ghost. She couldn't see his face but she could picture it, could see the barely contained fury there all too clearly.

"This is a British school," he bellowed. "And in this school we behave as civilized men. My office at bell. Now inside!"

Chapter Five

All day, Cecily fretted over what had happened to Raf, a sense of dread afflicting her as she wondered what her husband had said to him in the privacy of his office. The thought of him leaving, of one of the few sparks of life at the school guttering out, left her desolate. More than it should — she had only met him the day before — but there was something about him that Cecily liked. His unorthodox teaching methods charmed her, and he *saw* her. Not *the headmaster's wife,* but *Cecily.*

After putting the stew to bubble on the hob, Cecily decided to clear her head, if only for a short while. She made her way down to the garden, retracing the steps she had walked yesterday with Raf. Cecily lingered on the darkened stairs for longer than she should, running her fingertips over the polished banisters.

I wish he was in the garden with me again.

The thought brought a smile to her face, and she decided that Raf would've survived her husband's wrath with aplomb. And as she walked the paths, she started a conversation with Raf in her head. What a brave, unruffled chap he was as he faced down the headmaster.

Cecily glanced up at the house, and found the window of Raf's room, but she couldn't see him inside. She wouldn't have been at all surprised if Harriet had invited him to play a game of cards.

Her attention moved to the clocktower above. Something wasn't quite right—there, below the clock face, was a crack.

It looked almost like a thunderbolt, an angry zigzag in the brick and stone. Cecily had lived here all her life and never seen the masonry in less than perfect repair. She'd have to tell Hugh.

And he wasn't going to be pleased.

The clock chimed the hour, and Cecily knew that once again she had displeased her husband. She hadn't meant to be late, and now she ran as fast as she could over the lawn. If anyone saw her ungainly sprint, she didn't care. Back into the building, then up the stairs, expecting at any moment to hear a master bellow, *No running in the school! Save it for the rugby pitch, you louts!*

Maybe he'd be late. A last-minute letter for him to dictate, an important phone call from a parent, or an offer of sponsorship from a Devonshire worthy. If Cecily wished it enough, might it not come true?

No.

The door to their rooms was open. Hugh was already home.

Cecily combed her hair with her clammy fingers before announcing, "Dr. James? Supper's on the hob— I'll dish up in a minute."

"There is an imbecile in my school!" Cecily heard him bellow. "A foreign incomer, a bit of rubbish washed up on a beach somewhere who has infiltrated Whitmore Hall and brought his heathen ideas with him. Study, Mrs. James, now!"

Cecily smoothed down her rumpled skirt and headed into the room. She flinched as soon as she saw Hugh. "I'm terribly sorry you're upset. Can I get you anything?"

He stood before the portrait of the judge, his hands behind his back, his pale gaze filled with fury. On the desk in front of him was a pile of letters, strewn across the blotter in a manner that she would never have expected from her exacting husband.

"References from leaders of men!" Hugh roared, spittle flecking his lips. He swept one spindly arm across the surface of the desk, sending the letters fluttering onto the floor. "From the Home Secretary himself! Yet this creature has the temerity to tell me he has never taught in his life! They have sent me a damned gardener!"

"Oh—oh, dear. How terribly unfortunate." Cecily grabbed the back of the chair that Raf had sat in only the evening before and tried to steady herself. "The boys seemed to enjoy the lesson, though."

"And who is to be found in that class of boys?" He waited for a moment, no doubt to ensure the full impact might land. "That same Home Secretary's damned grandchild! I would send the imbecile back to the sorry land that spawned him tomorrow if not for that. Instead I am stuck with the creature. Mark my words, Mrs. James, he'll put more than a foot wrong and when he does…"

Hugh drew one long, thin finger across his throat then told her, "Clear up this mess!"

"Yes, of course, at once." Cecily fluttered about the desk, trying to impose order on the scattered letters. She stood with a bundle of them in her hand, anxious now in case she put them in the wrong place. Lucky guesses were required. "Oh, and by the way, there's something I need to tell you."

"What could you have to say that I might need, let alone wish, to hear?" He turned and straightened the immense portrait. "Speak, woman."

"The—the clocktower. There's a huge crack in it. I thought I ought to mention it. It wasn't there yesterday. What if it should fall?"

"I have seen the crack," he said quietly, his back still turned to her. "It wasn't there when the clock struck five. By the striking of six, it had appeared." Hugh turned, slow as a spider moving in its web. "More to the point, Mrs. James, what were you doing outside at such an hour, when you might have been better employed preparing supper?"

Cecily clutched the letters before her. "I—I *had* prepared it. I only wished to take the air. It was rather stuffy in the kitchen and it brought on a pain in my head. I wasn't gone for long, I promise."

"It doesn't do for the boys to see you wandering." Hugh pointed to the desk to indicate that she should put the letters down. "Supper, I think. The day has been most trying."

Cecily disguised her sigh of relief as she laid the letters on his blotter. A slap had seemed to be in the offing, and by the grace of God or someone else, he hadn't been in the mood.

"The table's laid, if you'd like to go through. I'll bring you your plate in a jiffy."

Hugh walked around the desk and Cecily followed him toward the door. At the threshold however, he turned, locking his fingers around her upper arms. For a long moment he studied her face and she dropped her gaze, deferential as ever. Finally he said, "Take care around our new Latin master — one never knows with these foreign folk. They've a fire in their blood."

Cecily dished up their dinner, ensuring she gave herself a modest portion — Hugh had views about matronly women and expected her to avoid their fate. She carried his plate through first, then brought her own, and sat bolt upright in the chair with her napkin on her lap. Cecily clasped her hands, her head inclined but her gaze fixed on Hugh, waiting for him to say grace. He knitted his thin fingers and bowed his head but remained silent, his eyes open. How old he looked, how tired, not at all the fearsome figure she knew him as. Looking at Hugh James like this, he didn't look remarkable at all.

"How dare he come into my home and impose himself," he murmured. Cecily felt her breath catch and clutched her hands tighter than ever. "A man's home is his castle, and this house has been allowed to run out of control. What say you, woman?"

"Our rooms are very neat, Dr. James. I see to that. I know how particular you are, and I would hate for you to be put out." Her throat dry, Cecily eyed her glass of water, but she knew she couldn't take a sip yet. "And as for Mr. de Chastelaine, he'll grow accustomed to our ways soon, I'm certain of it."

"He shall have to." Hugh picked up his cutlery, the prayers forgotten. "I thought his sort might have enough to worry about in their own land without invading ours."

Romania, Cecily reasoned. *Not Yorkshire. Although with Hugh, anything is possible.*

A dull thud from above reminded her again of the crack in the tower. Cecily glanced toward Hugh but he didn't seem concerned. Instead he was shoveling stew into his mouth as though he hadn't eaten in days. She had to remind herself not to stare, but in their ten years of marriage, she'd never seen anything like it.

Under her breath, Cecily recited, "For what we are about to receive, may the Lord make us truly thankful. Amen."

"Beer!" He clicked his fingers, ladling more stew into his mouth. *Beer?* It wasn't something they kept in the kitchen, because it wasn't something the refined Dr. James would want. "Now!"

"We haven't any." Cecily began to shiver. "I'd have to go to the pub in the village for a bottle. Or ask one of the masters, though I doubt they'll have any as the school's regulations won't allow it on the premises." *As the headmaster, of all people, should jolly well know.*

"Ale, woman!" Hugh slammed his fist into the pristine tablecloth. "Or by God I'll give you something to be sorry for!"

Cecily was out of her seat like a shot. The stew she'd spent all afternoon preparing would have to go cold. "I'll try, but I can't promise."

She hurried out of the dining room and blinked back tears. If she did find any beer, and it wouldn't surprise her if Harriet had some stashed under the bed, then would she not get the Culpecks in trouble too? But — *oh, damn* — it was whist night in the village, and the Culpecks wouldn't be in.

The first master's room Cecily came to was Raf's, and she was hesitant to knock but what else could she do? Hugh would bellow at her for not bringing him beer, and bellow if she had to speak to another master to get it. She let her hand fall against Raf's door, as if it could be mistaken for an accident.

"Mr. de Chastelaine? Are you in?"

"I am to you," Raf announced as he pulled the door open. Cecily knew immediately that the very sight of Raf, barefoot, tie gone, collar opened and sleeves rolled up, would have driven her husband into a fresh rage. "What's the drama, Mrs. J?"

How on earth did he come by those references?

Cecily didn't like to have to lie to Raf, but she was certain she couldn't tell him the truth. "My husband has fallen under the weather. I don't suppose you could help? He...when he feels peaky, only ale will do. But we haven't any, and I wondered...might you have some?"

"I've never met anyone that talks like you." He stepped back into the room but Cecily didn't move, the thought of going into a master's study one that she couldn't countenance. "You're what my mum would say is *proper*, like a queen. How many beers does he need?"

"Well, I don't really sound like I'm from Devon, do I!" Cecily stifled a nervous laugh. She shouldn't be making chit-chat, she should be finding beer. "Look...how many beers do you have? He's...well, I'm not sure that only one bottle will satisfy him at the moment."

"I've got a few." He grinned, then seemed to recognize the urgency in her and said, "Will two do?

Enough to make him sleepy, not so much that he'll get into a temper."

"Yes—yes, that's it, two." Cecily caught Raf's eye. He knew, didn't he? He could see just what a bully she had married. Wagging her finger at him playfully, she told him, "Although you do know you shouldn't have beer in school."

"I know! If he asks, tell them I found them under a very generous hedge." Raf disappeared into the room and called back, "How's that hand of yours? Did my potion do the job?"

"Yes, it did, thank you!" Cecily leaned against the doorframe. "What's it made from—magic?"

"Witch hazel from my garden," he replied over the sound of clinking glass. Then he appeared in the doorway again, holding out two bottles of ale. "I chucked some lavender in to make it smell a little sweeter. Keep it, you might need it again."

He was standing very near her. He smelled of the gardens, of earth and moss, of rain on long-parched soil. She swallowed, taking the bottles from him, trying to understand what the tightening in her stomach meant.

"Thank you. For everything. I mean it." Cecily began to turn away, then stopped. "And if it means anything—anything at all—I saw you teaching the boys outside today, and it was marvelous. I wished I could be among them."

"It means a lot to know that," he told her softly. "We all need a taste of freedom now and again, Sissy."

Sissy.

Cecily turned away and hurried back to her husband.

"Dr. James—Dr. James, I've found you some beer!" Cecily called as soon as she was through their front door. She found him still at the table, running a chunk of bread around his plate, greedily mopping up the gravy. He gestured to the table, ravenously chewing as he did.

Proudly, she set the two bottles down on the table, and ducked to reach inside the drinks cabinet where Hugh kept his ancient bottles of brandy and whiskey. There was a bottle opener in there somewhere, she was sure. As she searched, she thought about Raf and she heard him says *Sissy* again in that accent of his. She had never had a nickname before, she had always been a Miss or a Mrs., rarely a *Cecily* even, let alone anything else. One headmaster's daughter, another's wife.

"Here, Dr. James." Cecily offered him the bottle opener, but suspected that, as ever, he would demand she do it. "Shall I open them?"

He reached out and took the bottle opener from her roughly. "More stew, woman, and more bread!"

Cecily scraped her dinner from her plate onto his. There was some spare stew in the pot, and that at least would still be warm. "There—and I'll fetch your bread."

She closed the kitchen door behind her and ate the leftover stew directly from the pot with the serving spoon. Certainly unrefined, but Cecily didn't care. It was either this or go hungry. She ate as fast as she could, then sawed four slices of bread off the loaf for her husband. A quick swipe of butter across each was all she seemed to have time for, and she headed back to the dining room.

"Bread, husband." She placed it on the table beside him. He snatched it up and plunged it into the gravy again, pausing only to take a swig of beer. *It must be the stress of today*, Cecily decided, because she'd certainly never seen such a display from Hugh before. He was exacting, fastidious even, sipping claret from crystal and eating in measured, bird-like mouthfuls, yet here he was eating like a man enjoying his last meal.

Did Raf de Chastelaine really annoy him so much that he'd forget himself like this?

Surely not.

"Steamed pudding and jam for afters," Cecily reminded him. Their menu hadn't wavered since the first week of their marriage. Hugh nodded keenly as, above, a dull thud sounded, not enough to be of concern if not for the cracks in the stone. The clocktower had looked over Whitmore Hall for centuries—it was inconceivable that it might be vulnerable.

"Dr. James, that thudding noise—do you not hear it?" Cecily looked up to the ceiling, wondering if a crack would appear across it too. Hugh wouldn't be happy about an unknown racket above his rooms, but he seemed not to notice. "Dr. James?"

He paid her no attention, going on with his food as another thud sounded, then another. If Cecily were being fanciful she might even imagine them as footsteps, but nobody climbed the clocktower without Hugh's permission and nobody *could*, for only the headmaster held the key.

Unless… Could it be Raf? It wouldn't surprise her at all if the unorthodox teacher had fancied a ramble and gone wherever he chose to. Cecily rather liked the idea of that, though how he'd get the door unlocked, she couldn't guess. But it had to be said that Raf did look like the kind of man who could get himself out of a fix.

Then again…oh, why hadn't she warned him not to say anything to anyone about the séance while she'd had the chance?

He wouldn't. He'd already lied for her, not to mention discreetly deposited her knitting bag, so surely he wouldn't be so silly as to mention the séance.

But what if he does?

Hugh would be furious — she couldn't even imagine what he'd do if he knew. The thought of it was almost as chilling as the memory of that weeping woman in the darkness.

Cecily returned to her chair and waited for Hugh to finish. He was eating at such speed that it didn't take long. She gathered up the plates and returned with the pudding. Although she usually left something for the next day, she heaped up Hugh's bowl. He devoured it just as he had the stew, then snatched up the second beer bottle and took it with him to his favorite armchair, where he slumped beside the window as Cecily cleared the table.

Usually, on any other weeknight, there would be half an hour of reading the newspaper, then an hour of work in the study, but when Cecily returned to the sitting room once the pots were washed and put away, she found Hugh still in the chair where she had left him. He was asleep, his mouth gaping, drool glistening on his lip and the empty beer bottle still in his hand. Standing there in the doorway with her husband sleeping in the gloomy dusk, Cecily wondered, for just a second, what she would have done if he hadn't been sleeping, but dead.

What then?

What freedom.

Above her, she heard another thud. Would the whole place fall down around them? A second thud sounded then a third and she realized, there in the gathering shadows, that the thuds were settling into a rhythm. Above them, in a locked tower where nobody ever trod, somebody was pacing. Something unseen was walking back and forth and Cecily remembered looking up at the crack in the wall with a shiver that ran through her very bones. Had something been looking back at her?

Chapter Six

Hugh's odd mood persisted, and Cecily made sure to stock their cupboards with a larger order from the grocer and a supply of beer from the pub. Steak and sausages, pie and potatoes might satisfy him — she hoped. Although she had never told Hugh where she had found the beer to start with, for he had never asked, it was as if Raf had been given a reprieve. Maybe it was the recommendation from the Home Secretary.

She no longer kept the ring under her pillow, but had hidden it under a loose floorboard in what had been her childhood bedroom and was now a storeroom for Hugh's books and files. Raf's bottle of witch hazel joined it. They would be safe there, with her mother's locket.

Cecily saw Raf from the windows as she went about her daily round of housework, with pupils or sometimes on his own. As the days passed the crack didn't grow and the boys who hurried beneath the clocktower soon found other things to look at once the novelty of the fissure began to fade. Yet Cecily never found her fascination with Raf fading and she was warmed by the way he didn't simply seem to tolerate the pupils, but to actually pause and give them his time. It was against the rules, of course — boys were supposed to seek out a master in his study or schoolroom, not in the busy courtyard — but Raf didn't seem to follow those rules.

From her lonely window Cecily saw him bowl a cricket ball or fold a paper plane, even kneel on the parched grass of the ghost garden and pour over an exercise book with a boy whose face had been a frown of confusion at whatever the prep was that day. She watched Raf tend the garden when he thought he was unobserved, deadheading roses and tying back trailing plants and even, on one occasion after twilight, kneeling at the cluster of flowers at the base of the old sundial on the lawn. Only the next day, as she walked into the village for Hugh's newspaper, did Cecily steal an opportunity to investigate the sundial. There she discovered a small piece of rosemary, seemingly already rooted where Raf had planted it.

He was becoming the highlight of her day, those snatched glimpses like a ray of sunlight through a cloud, and it just made her lonelier than ever.

At night Cecily lay beside Hugh with her eyes tight shut, not daring to open them for fear of who might be standing beside her bed. She told herself that the sounds that echoed from the clocktower were nothing but bats or mice, that the soft sobs she heard after dark were bad dreams, though she knew all too well that they weren't. Instead she thought about Raf's smile and his crumpled clothes, the tousle of his hair and his blue eyes.

And the way he said *'Sissy'*.
It had sounded like a secret.
One more secret, to go with the ring and the witch hazel.

When Hugh announced that he was off to a meeting in Plymouth—with whom, he didn't say, because it was not the business of the headmaster's wife to know—Cecily hid her relief. For a whole day there would be no bellowed demands for beer, no enormous meal to cook, no fear of a lashing out.

She went into the storeroom and levered up the loose floorboard with a spatula. Opening her mother's locket, she saw once more the face of Sandy as a little boy, and herself as a small girl with a serious face. Cecily carefully took out the ring, still wrapped in the handkerchief. As soon as she opened it, the sun caught the gold and made it shine. Without Hugh around to question her about it, Cecily put it on and admired it. *What a perfect fit.* She dabbed more of Raf's witch hazel lotion onto the back of her hand and the scratch seemed to fade further before her eyes.

She slipped a note under the Culpecks' door inviting Harriet for a sherry that evening and settled on the sofa with a book. She'd found it on the shelves by Hugh's armchair, a ponderous tome called *Puritan Devonshire Gentry*. The Whitmores had to be mentioned somewhere, Cecily was sure, but the book didn't have an index. She had to skim through lengthy passages on the theology of antinomianism and Arminianism, all of which made Cecily's head spin.

Fortunately, someone knocked at the front door. It was a jaunty knock, a quick tattoo that she didn't recognize, and Cecily thrust her hand into the pocket of her cardigan as she approached, the little secret of the ring one that only she would know.

She patted her hair in a pointless gesture before she opened the door, her heart already pounding at the ridiculous notion that the caller might be Hugh himself, testing her.

Nobody visits, after all. It's not so absurd.

"Morning!" Raf was standing in the hallway, beaming as bright as the sun that streamed through the windows.

Cecily took a step backward in surprise. She hadn't expected Raf of all people to turn up at the door. "Oh, I'm sorry, Mr. de Chastelaine, Dr. James is away. He won't be back until tomorrow now. Can I help?"

"He's away?" *Don't go,* she thought suddenly, *but you must.* Raf reached into the pocket of his dark blue jacket and produced a small, folded parcel of dark purple paper. Then he quirked his eyebrow and asked, "Shall we be naughty then and have some chocolate?"

Cecily glanced over Raf's shoulder at the empty corridor beyond. No one was there to see. She nodded eagerly. "Come in. Do. I'll make us a pot of tea — if you have time."

"I've got loads of it!" Raf was already tugging at his tie as he stepped over the threshold. "And this thing can be the first to go since the foreman's not around."

Cecily giggled. She took her hand out of her pocket as she closed the door behind him, the gold of the ring flashing. "No classes this morning, Mr. de — Raf?"

"Done!" He shoved his tie into his trouser pocket and took off his jacket, which he threw across the chair outside Hugh's study. "And my next lot are so petrified of an algebra test they have after lunch that I've told them to skip the Latin and spend the time trying to make sense of the numbers instead. If anyone asks though, we were Latin-ing like mad all morning."

"The mathematics master *does* like to drill his pupils." Cecily had heard him in Hugh's study, the two men loudly agreeing that cracking a ruler over a boy's knuckles while he recited the seven-times table was the only way to make the numbers stick. "Do take a seat in the lounge, and I'll bring the tea through."

"I can keep you company if you like," Raf suggested, following her into the small kitchen. "Your hand's totally healed?"

Company? Hugh rarely set foot in the kitchen. It was far too beneath him.

"Almost!" She held it out toward him, and the ring glittered. He caught her fingers, lifting her hand closer to his eyes, and Cecily found herself caught on his gaze as if it were a hook, watching him as he studied the skin where the angry scratch had been. Finally Raf released her fingers and smiled.

"A perfect job!"

"Thank you." Cecily turned away from those dangerous blue eyes and set about making a racket with the kettle and the teapot. Anything to distract herself from the tightening inside her, as if a thread were tugging at her from somewhere.

From Raf.

She opened the window. "Gets a bit steamy in here when the kettle's boiling."

"It's been a steamy year," Raf replied but Cecily wasn't listening. Instead she was looking out over the courtyard to the lawns, and there on the grass, standing in broad daylight with her face turned toward the impenetrable walls of the forgotten rose garden, was the weeping woman.

Cecily froze on the spot, staring at the phantom, and as she did, a crocodile of older boys emerged from the shadows of the building. At their head was one of the tallest in the school, a rugby ball tucked beneath his arm. She saw him glance back to make sure nobody was watching, then, rather than trail his team around the paths to the playing field, he cut across the garden, taking the boys on a collision course with the woman. They didn't see her, of course, and as the chattering pupils drew nearer, she flickered out of existence like a mirage.

"Raf...when you saw Mrs. Culpeck and me the other evening — when you first arrived, and we were holding a circle...you've not mentioned it to anyone else, have you? I'm sure you haven't, and I feel as though I can trust you, but you do understand, don't you?" Because Cecily knew it wasn't just herself at stake. Not only Mrs. Culpeck, but the ghost of Isabella Whitmore.

She heard the rustle of a wrapper and the smart *snap* as he broke the chocolate in half, her nerves tense with every moment that passed until Raf said, "It's nobody's business but yours what you do with your mates. I'm not going to run to the headmaster."

Mates. Not a word that she heard often in Whitmore Hall, where diction and the King's English were everything. *A boy could be thrashed for less.*

"Besides," Raf went on, "if I did, you might tell him that I've not been inside a classroom since I was twelve years old. A secret for a secret, it seems like a fair swap."

"I've never been in one at all!" Cecily was relieved to admit that, amongst all the scholarly types who taught here, and all the talk of lessons and matriculation, boys being sent up to university, tests and rote learning. "My parents taught me when they had time, until my father decided that I would only be any use as a wife. I sneaked books in and taught myself."

"So, in the spirit of confession, not only have I never passed an exam, I have *word blindness.*" That *was* a surprise — how on earth could he teach Latin in that case? "When the third school told my parents I was a hopeless idiot, they said *enough is enough, let's teach him ourselves.* And in between building bat boxes and working in the garden, they managed to trick me into actual lessons! How do you think I got those amazing references?"

How indeed? The sparkle in your eyes suggests it wasn't in the schoolroom.

The kettle interrupted with a whistle, and Cecily poured the boiling water into the teapot. She swilled the water around then, satisfied the pot was warmed, tipped it out and added the tea leaves. Barely any thought was required — she had done it every day since she was six years old. "And you only took this job to help out your friend... How *did* you get those references? Dr. James mentioned you even have one from the Home Secretary."

"Who do you think landscaped his country estate?" He winked again as she looked at him, another secret shared. "Brennan needed a mate, I wanted to have a look at Whitmore Hall, so..." Raf shrugged. "So I asked Lord Whatsit for a favor. He knew what it was for, I didn't tell him I wanted to come here and dig out the flowerbeds!"

"So even the Home Secretary knows you're not a teacher?" Cecily set out the teapot and cups on the tray, the bone china ringing as she laid teaspoons on the saucers. "And yet he wrote your reference! Goodness me, his country estate must look beautiful!"

"It looks good, but not as good as my garden." He put the broken squares of chocolate on the tray too. "And I got rid of his banshee too, so he owed me one. Should I lug the tray? My lugging's on a par with my Latin!"

"Yes, if you wouldn't — " Finally, her brain caught up with what Raf had just said, and she stared at him. "Sorry, you did just say *banshee*, didn't you?"

"Did I?" Raf blinked as though she had caught him scrumping apples and quickly took up the tray. "I probably shouldn't have if I did. If I said *banshee* I probably meant greenfly. English is my second language, you know."

"Oh...oh, I see." For a moment, Cecily had wondered if she could have told him about the ghost. But if he meant greenfly, then — "Lounge is just through here. Although the armchair is the more comfortable of the chairs, it's probably best you don't sit in it. I am sorry, I don't sound very hospitable, do I, but it's Dr. James' and he's...he's very particular."

He didn't mean greenfly. Word blindness or not, Cecily knew that.

"That makes me want to sit in it all the more." Yet Cecily willed him not to settle in the armchair, because Hugh would just *know*. She didn't know how, but she knew that he would. "But I don't want to make trouble, so let's share the sofa, you and me?"

Raf stooped to put the tray down on the coffee table then unfastened his collar and settled down on the sofa. He was rumpled already, hair tousled, jaw stubbled, and as he leaned forward to pick up the teapot, Cecily caught a glimpse of what looked like a tangle of leather necklaces beneath his creased shirt.

Perhaps it's something Romanian.

Cecily sat down on the sofa, deliberately wedging herself into the corner. That pull was even more intense and when she glanced at Raf, she knew at once what that sensation was.

I want to kiss him.

She glanced away from him and, in a fluster, put the tea strainer over a cup. "I'll pour. Sugar, yes? Oh, and milk first. Gosh, I'm doing this all wrong." She knocked the strainer onto the tray with a clang. Raf gallantly rescued it, then reached out and closed his hand over Cecily's.

I've never felt anything so gentle.

"Sit back, eat chocolate, let me pour the tea?"

"I wouldn't mind. Sorry. I'm a bag of nerves, as Hugh always says." Cecily had an odd sensation then, as if there was someone else in the room watching them. Though when she looked up, all she saw was the wedding photograph on the mantelpiece. Hugh in his best suit, *almost* happy. Cecily beside him, unsmiling and resigned, in her best dress and a wide-brimmed straw hat, because Hugh had thought wedding dresses, veils and bouquets mere frivolities.

"If you've been awake half the night listening to the building fall down like I have, I'm not surprised." But that meant she *wasn't* alone, someone else *could* hear the bumps from above. "Have you really been here all your life?"

"I have, yes. Always lived in this very apartment, in fact!" It hadn't changed a great deal, either. Hugh wasn't one for unnecessary expense when it came to living quarters. His car, however, was quite another thing, for what headmaster of an up-and-coming public school wouldn't drive about in a Daimler? "Raf...what you said about *'the building falling down'* — I've heard it too. Thumping. It sounds like footsteps. I did wonder the other evening if you'd managed to get up into the attics for a nose about, but...I don't think you did."

"Honestly? I did try but the door to the staircase is locked," he admitted with a mischievous smile as he poured out two cups of tea. "And now there's that crack too. I've had a few lads wanting to know if the building's going to drop on their heads and I tell them I hope not, or it'll hit me first!"

"Dr. James is aware of the structural...issues. If he knew the boys were talking about it, he'd have to arrange some builders to come out because if they tell their parents—no, that wouldn't be at all good for the school." Cecily had reverted to *the headmaster's wife* again. It wasn't a costume she liked to wear very often, so she shrugged it off. "Anyway...so you did try to go up? Dr. James has the key—and I haven't a clue where he keeps it."

"Can I tell you something odd that happened?" Then he frowned and shook his head. "I probably shouldn't, but— I don't want to scare you, but I never know when to keep my trap shut!"

Cecily closed her hand over his. "*Please* tell me. I won't be scared."

Raf put the teapot down and turned just slightly, studying her gaze. "So I don't usually let a lock stop me if I need to be somewhere. I'm not a thief, but sometimes in my business, locks are old and locks get stuck." Cecily nodded, waiting for him to continue. "And I was going to open the lock on the stair door so I knelt down and I had a peep through, just to check there was nothing stuck in there and —"

Raf fell silent and looked around as though someone might be concealed in the room to hear their conversation. He lifted his gaze to the ceiling for a split second then dropped his voice to a whisper.

"There was an eye looking back at me."

Cecily nearly dropped her tea. "An...an eye? Oh, my word, Raf...a *human* eye? Is there a person up there? Have the boys got in somehow and made a den? Or was it perhaps a pigeon?" Though she knew what the answer would be.

"A human eye and I wondered—" He closed his fingers around their joined hands. "You're under the tower too and I haven't had any impression from the other teachers that they've heard anything but I thought you might have. Sissy—Mrs. James, sorry—does anyone at the school have... What's the word?"

She saw the frustration in his face and he narrowed his eyes, seeking for the right word. "Cloudy on the eye? Cataract! Does anyone here have a cataracted eye?"

"I don't believe so. Dr. James is very strict about who he hires, and the boys who are taken on as pupils. Must be in fine fettle, he says, so he certainly wouldn't take on a master who has a cataract. Nor a pupil." Cecily thought some more. "There's Matron, and the kitchen staff, and of course, Mrs. Culpeck... I have very little to do with the running of the school, but as far as I know — I can't think of anyone."

"I don't know that I'm in fine fettle but your husband told me that I wasn't allowed any *followers* while I was here." Raf laughed. "So Mrs. Culpeck and you are rare creatures indeed as wives!"

But he *was* in fine fettle, she could see it despite the creased shirt and the suit that looked as though it had seen better days. And he was happy, which far too few people at Whitmore Hall were these days.

"*Do* you have a follower, Raf?" Cecily asked in a saucy tone. One she only used when Mrs. Culpeck was showing her movie magazines with photographs of Rudolph Valentino in them. "Surely you must. Although not a wife, not in *that* creased shirt!"

"Looking like this?" He squeezed her hand. "No followers for me. Not in Romania, not in Devon, not at home in Yorkshire."

Cecily was mesmerized by the twinkle in his eyes. Why was he telling her? She should not even have asked. "That's a shame. You'll have to find one when you've finished here — I'm sure there's just the right lady out there for you somewhere."

"She'd have to like gardens and the seaside." Raf smiled. "And chips out of newspaper."

And a rogue with eyes as blue as the ocean.

Cecily put her teacup on the table. She couldn't behave like this. It was surely bordering on flirtatious. And there was something she needed to tell him.

"Erm...Raf. About the banshee — I know you meant to say it, it wasn't greenfly. They're women, aren't they, who go about crying, inconsolable?"

"Believe me, if you heard one, you'd know." He shook his head and winced as though the memory were a trying one. "The noise wakes the dead — it's like something you'd hear in a nightmare. Where I come from, we know the veil can be thin. Here in England, though, it takes a banshee screaming your child's name at midnight to convince you."

"Oh, how horrible!" Cecily clutched the collar of her blouse. "So if a ghost weeps instead, that's not a banshee?"

"A crying woman? She could be all sorts of things but if she's not wailing and carrying on like her finger's in the mangle, she's probably not a banshee." He began adding sugar to his cup as though this was a perfectly normal conversation. "So you're like Godfrey too? Our Mr. Brennan had an interest in everything spooky."

"I didn't realize he had until the other day!" Cecily shuffled a little nearer to Raf along the sofa. "Listen...there's a woman in this house, she's so desolate and sad. She goes about weeping. She comes to me at night and I even saw her by the bed. I hear her crying and I keep my eyes tight shut, but just now, when we were in the kitchen, she was outside! In the ghost garden."

"I know." It felt as though someone had taken a weight from her shoulders. Not only did he believe her, he *knew*. Or was he humoring her? *No.* That much was clear from his expression alone. "That's how I got to know Godfrey — we both love a ghost story."

"He saw her too? And...and have you?"

Raf shook his head. "No, but he heard noises above his room — *my* room now. Feet scraping, somebody pacing, muttering, scratching, all the classic haunting whatnots. By the time he wrote to me, he was scrying every night, using a spirit board, staring into a black mirror, all the things you don't do unless you know who you're talking to."

As Raf spoke he glanced up toward the mirror above the mantelpiece and Cecily followed his gaze. It needed resilvering, she realized, for the reflection had become a touch hazy.

Hugh won't like that. A waste of good money.

"Do you think Mr. Brennan could've stirred it up, whatever it is?" Cecily thought back to the séance. "And Harriet and I — we only wanted to reach my brother, and find out who owned the ring I'd found. And instead..."

Oh, what have we done?

"If he stirred it up, it was pretty stirred already when he first wrote to me," Raf assured her. "And in my experience, if you're a toe rag in death, you were a toe rag in life. If you didn't like clumping about frightening people when you were on this side of the grave, you don't suddenly turn into a bastard on that side." He put his hand to his mouth for a second and laughed. "Pretend I said greenfly again, sorry!"

Cecily laughed too. *"What a bloody greenfly!"* She looked down at the ring. "I think she came through at the séance, the lady who once wore this. And I think she's the ghost I've seen."

"Your brother —" His voice grew softer. "Was it the war?"

"Yes." Cecily nodded. "I've never not missed him for a second since he died. It sounds silly, but I knew when he died. I was in the kitchen one afternoon, peeling the potatoes, and I felt as if I'd been punched. Here, in the chest. I had to sit down, I couldn't breathe. And I felt such awful sadness. I thought, *Sandy's gone.* Then the telegram came. And he'd died just when I'd felt it — I did, Raf."

"I'm so sorry," he whispered, and in those simple words she heard more emotion, more compassion, than she had ever heard from Hugh. It wasn't the words or the tone but something in the air, a gentleness from this earthy, unusual man who had come into her life. "Those years were hell, but those we love don't leave us. You might not see him, but he's walking there beside you. My mother walks with me, Sandy walks with you."

She remembered the rosemary he had planted beneath the sundial.

For remembrance.

Cecily blinked back her tears. "I wish he... When we were children, and Father was displeased, Sandy took my punishment as well as his own. He was the kindest of boys, Raf. The kindest of men. So selfless. I hope he *is* here."

"Was there a lot of punishment to take?" He handed her one of the pieces of chocolate, the gesture as kind as it was simple.

"Sometimes. My father was very strict." Cecily grimaced comically, trying to make light of it. "Well, he was the headmaster!"

Raf nodded and she looked down at the chocolate he had given her. He was too kind though, seeing everything and saying nothing. How had he known them for a week, barely even that, and still know what others didn't. Or what they simply chose to ignore.

She popped the chocolate into her mouth. Its flavor was dark and rich, utterly forbidden. Cecily savored it, then washed it down with tea. She couldn't grow accustomed to such a thing. "Gosh, this chocolate's awfully nice."

"I've got piles of it. Chocolate and beer, what more do I need?" He dropped his voice again to tell her, "I sneak out after dark to tend the gardens, armed with chocolate and beer. You've done a wonderful job on them, but there's a lot for one lady to deal with!"

"Thank you, I do my best! I don't have the time I'd like, to be honest." Cecily grinned. "If only I could come out after dark with you — I'd love to work on the gardens at night."

"I'd love that too, and if you can get away this weekend, I'll be in the garden in the daylight!" Raf promised. "I came here to ask your husband how I'd get started on taking the young lads up to the moors for a bit of an outing. Graham thinks it'll be a no, but I didn't think it'd do harm to ask. Do you think he'll just say no?"

From cataracts and weeping women to school outings, it seemed as though Cecily's day wasn't going as she might have expected. And what a refreshing change that made.

Cecily folded her hands on her lap. "He might. He doesn't like the amount of school they lose if they're off for a day out. He says it excites them too much, and he complains about the cost of hiring a charabanc." She could already picture the castle at Dunster, and the fast-flowing water at Simonsbath, the ferns in the Valley of Rocks and a pheasant flying low over the scrub. "But I think it's a wonderful idea! Where were you going to take them? I haven't been up on Exmoor for so long."

"I was going to ask them what they'd like to see," he admitted. "But if we make them toil through Latin, let's at least show them where the Romans trod too? If your husband is away all night, will you come to our cricket later? It's masters against pupils and I expect to be shown right up. I'm half English, but my cricket skills are *all* Romanian. Come and cheer for me!"

A thud sounded overhead and he tutted, handing her another piece of chocolate.

"Whoever that is, he's *not* invited."

"I'd love to come. I shouldn't really, but...oh, I will!" Cecily wondered where her nerves had got to. She knew Hugh wouldn't be happy if he found out, but Cecily wanted to be happy herself. And that meant going to the match. "I tell you what, I baked some biscuits yesterday—I'll bring them along."

"Promise not to laugh at me?" Raf grinned, tutting away another heavy footstep from above. "Does this happen all day while you sit here? I've never had such a noisy neighbor!"

"It happens on and off, but it's worse when Dr. James is here in the evening. He can't hear it though!" Cecily fidgeted with her cup. "Oh, Raf, is there nothing we can do to get rid of it? And poor Isabella, weeping… I wish I knew what to do to help her."

"You know who she is?" His gaze dropped to the ring again and the levity vanished from his tone. "Have you actually spoken to her?"

"Isabella Whitmore. I'm certain of it. I found the ring the other week in the rose garden. One of the boys had lost a cricket ball in there, and I managed to get in and…and there it was! I cleaned it up and I showed it to Harriet, and that's when she said we should do a séance." Cecily worked the ring off her finger and held it out to Raf. "And Isabella begged me to *keep it from him*. And a man's voice—oh, it was so horrible!—it said, *'What ring'?* And shouted about someone being a—a woman of light virtue. And she told me—the woman actually said her name is Isabella. There's a letter C inside the ring and I thought it could be Caroline. Or perhaps even Cecily! Not Isabella."

"This is the wife of the man who built this house, yes?" He glanced up to the ceiling, where the pacing had resumed. "His wife hanged for the murder of a stranger?"

"Yes. And my husband has dug out his portrait and hung it on the wall." Cecily put the ring back on her finger. "A stranger came to this house and was murdered, and Judge Whitmore presided over the trial of his wife, who was accused of the crime. She was hanged. And afterwards, Judge Whitmore went mad, and finally confessed to having killed the stranger — raving, he was — that she had come to him every night, had followed him about during the day, lamenting and sorrowing for what he had done. So he was imprisoned, but before the trial could start, he'd died."

"So he's the miserable-looking bugger in the headmaster's study!" In response to Raf's unflattering but truthful comment, there were three sharp stamps from above and Cecily glanced up before returning her gaze to Raf, who seemed untroubled by the noise. "So he did for the stranger, right?"

"Yes! And accused his wife. Can you imagine someone being so cruel? There's a pamphlet somewhere that my father had — a local historian wrote it. Said the judge did it all for money — for Isabella's inheritance. The boys have all heard about Judge Whitmore. They won't go into the rose garden because they all say, '*The judge is going to get you.*' Why there, exactly, I don't know, but it *is* creepy."

"Money?" Raf asked. "More likely sex."

Cecily choked. "Erm…ah…erm…" *Sex.* No one discussed such a thing. Not even her husband. And despite Harriet's movie magazines — no, the word was never spoken. "Who was having…*relations* with whom? The judge, to marry someone else, do you mean?"

"So, let me get the family straight. Three brothers, one shipwrecked, right? Is it too obvious to say that *he* was the mysterious lover?" Raf quirked his eyebrow. "The eternal triangle!"

"But surely the chap's name would begin with C? The shipwrecked brother was called Matthew."

"Stop ruining a perfectly good theory with your facts! Why can't Matthew begin with a C and make all our lives easier? Matthew, Judge Edward and...Benjamin?" He drew the word out as a question, earning a nod of confirmation from Cecily. "And Matthew's shipwreck makes Judge Edward heir to a fortune, yes? Or not a fortune, but a house. Did he have to marry Isabella to get the fortune?"

"Benjamin inherited the Hall once the judge was dead. And Isabella — she came from a wealthy family — the only other gentry in the area, so the marriage was inevitable, I suppose. He was a man of influence, she was a woman of wealth. A perfect match in those days."

"I feel sorry for her." His gaze was fixed on her now. "Shackled to a man like that. Trapped for the sake of money and mortar. You know if the world was right it'd be your name engraved on that list of head teachers in the hall, not your husband."

"Oh, I wouldn't know the first thing about running a school!" Cecily replied. She didn't want him to say she could, because she knew she'd have no idea how to be a headmistress. She had once allowed herself to daydream that she could have run the place, if only she'd been schooled. But that chance had been denied her and it made her heartsore to think of it.

"After a lifetime watching men *try* to do it?" He laughed. "You'd shame the lot of them! If I'd had a few less Dr. Jameses and a few more Miss Sissys, I might even have passed an exam or two!"

"You're flattering me, you're very naughty!" Cecily hadn't lived at the school all her life without forming her own ideas on how things could be run. Not that her father or her husband had ever cared to hear, but she thought Raf might. "However…if this was my school, I'd let the masters teach the boys outside whenever they liked. And take them out on a trip once a week. And we'd put on plays. And concerts. We'd have a dance once a term with the girls' school over by Dulverton. And we'd bring back the vegetable patch that we had in the war. And we'd be more involved in the village, too — oh, dear, you've started me off now!"

"It's not a veg, but I snuck a bit of rosemary into your garden," Raf admitted brightly. "You know what I'd *definitely* do? I'd let women teach here too — boys can't be with men *all* the time! Women shouldn't only be serving their food and cleaning up their messes. My mum would have had plenty to say about *that*!"

"Rosemary smells so lovely, doesn't it?" Cecily grinned. "I think we should put more herbs in the garden, in secret. Mint here, parsley there! And as for women teaching here, I think that's a splendid idea. Mrs. Culpeck was a teacher before she got married, and when we've had masters on sick leave, her husband has put her forward to cover. But my husband won't hear of it."

"Let's fill the garden with sweet-smelling herbs!" Raf seized her hands in his, fired by enthusiasm. "A little victory, but ours."

Cecily giggled at the thought of such subtle rebellion. She had another ally now in Raf. "And we can say they seeded themselves."

"I could be wrong but he doesn't strike me as the sort who stops to smell a flower," Raf decided. "So we won't have to say anything at all." He glanced over his shoulder then said, "Mrs. C's on her way, she's doused in rose water!"

All Cecily could smell was furniture polish and gravy. "Are you sure? You're pulling my leg, Raf!"

As the words left her mouth there was a knock at the door. Raf inclined his head politely and said, "See you and Mrs. C down on the field at four? Bring biscuits and sympathy. And you just ask her if it's rose water."

"Will do!" Cecily rose from the sofa. "This unexpected chat has been lovely, Raf! And I'll definitely be down at four with Mrs. Culpeck for the cricket."

Cecily hoped to goodness that it really was Harriet at the door — there was always a risk that someone in the school might want to create some entertainment. Reporting back to Hugh that the new teacher had been in his rooms, alone with Cecily, might be too much to resist. But as she heard the knock again, she knew that Raf was right. Maybe it was all that gardening that had given him such a good sense of smell, but that was definitely Harriet's knock.

"I'm sorry not to have found Dr. James at home," Raf told Cecily with theatrical volume as they approached the door. He picked up his discarded jacket and took another block of chocolate from the pocket, this one unopened. "For you. For friendship."

"Thank you, you're so kind." Cecily wedged it into her cardigan pocket as she answered the door to Harriet. "Ah, Mrs. Culpeck!"

"Mrs. James!" At the sight of Raf the older woman's cheeks flushed a little and she smiled like an auntie welcoming her favorite nephew. "And, Mr. de Chastelaine, what have *you* been plotting?"

"Just a game of cricket, I'll leave Mrs. James to issue a proper invite." He kept a comically scraping bow and slipped past her, pausing only to say, "I like your rose water."

Chapter Seven

Cecily brought the biscuit tin, and Harriet the picnic blanket and a flask filled with tea. The boys and the masters were already out on the pitch, and Cecily sensed Harriet's happiness at the forthcoming match. If only Hugh would let Cecily join in, and not insist that she keep herself hidden away. It was a rare thing indeed for Cecily to see the boys play.

As they got nearer, she could identify the staff and some of the older boys and, at last, Raf. She waved hello and he raised his hand in reply.

He was standing beside the wicket, rubbing lotion from a small glass jar over his exposed forearms, and Cecily couldn't help but be glad at how different he was to the other masters, every one of them the product of a school just like this one. From the youngest to the oldest they had that British bearing, at ease with their place in the world and their pristine, pressed whites. Raf was easily the shortest of the impromptu team and his whites were easily the most creased, but he was the one her eyes went to.

Down the gentle hill toward the pitch came the boys, the team in their whites, the spectators in their uniforms. There was an excited buzz in the air that Hugh wouldn't have stood for. If he were here, they would have proceeded in silent, single file, greeting each master with a polite nod. Instead Graham rested one hand on his rounded belly and called, "Get ready to lose, boys, the moment of reckoning is nigh!"

How unlike the headmaster was his deputy.

It was lovely to be out there, the sun warm on Cecily's skin and such a happy atmosphere in the air. She realized she was attracting a few politely curious glances, but it didn't surprise her, and as long as she stayed with Harriet, there could be nothing for Hugh to complain of.

Cecily took the lid off the tin and the scent of fresh baking and lavender wafted out. "Biscuit, Hattie?"

"Ooh, lovely. I'll pour," her friend decided, taking a biscuit.

"Lavender?" Raf called. "Can we come and eat biscuits and you ladies come up and wield the bat?"

That incredible sense of smell! Cecily cupped her hands around her mouth. "There's plenty for everyone!"

"Afternoon, miss," the boys greeted her as they trotted past, each a credit to their school.

Graham, ever ready to make sure the waters of the school were smooth, told them, "Mrs. James has generously agreed to come along and represent our headmaster. She is, let's not forget, the granddaughter of our founder." And Cecily knew some of them *would* have forgotten, because she was so rarely allowed to see the pupils. "So, let's have a fair game and, as ever, keep your language sporting."

From the gaggle of boys, a voice shouted, "Tell Mr. de Chastelaine that, sir!"

"Bloody hell!" came another cheeky cry, in a terrible approximation of Raf's accent and the boys all laughed. Raf laughed too but Graham and the masters, to their credit, did their best to look disapproving.

"You've all just failed!" Raf told the pupils as he put the lid back on his jar and approached Cecily. "Would you mind looking after this? It's just for the sun."

"Of course, Mr. de Chastelaine." Cecily held out her hand. He looked so handsome in his whites and that tightening inside her visited again. He placed the jar in her palm, brushing his fingertips against her skin as he murmured his thanks.

Cecily closed her hand around the jar as firmly as she could. "I'll save you the biggest biscuit," she told him.

Raf smiled, his eyes shining as he whispered, "I can't wait." Then he turned and strolled back to the pitch, leaving the women to their picnic. Harriet filled two cups of tea and put them on the blanket between her and Cecily.

"Look at Gray," she said affectionately. "I should stop baking those pies and buns for him, but we do love them so. I hope he scores a run or two at least!"

"I'm sure he will — no boy would dare get the deputy headmaster out! This is so much fun. I haven't done this in years, not since —" *Sandy was alive.* Cecily sipped her tea. "Anyway, who do you think will win?"

Cecily and Harriet cast their gazes over the motley collection of old boys and their *slightly* younger fellows, each more at home in the stands at Lord's than standing at the crease. Raf was by far the youngest, and if his self-professed ineptitude at the wicket wasn't an exaggeration, then there could only be one answer.

"Cecily, my love, the boys are going to mop the floor with them!"

"Good-oh!" It appealed to Cecily's growing sense of quiet rebellion. "Raf says he's a terrible cricketer. I wonder how long he'll be able to stay in bat?"

"Men always say that when they're secretly W.G. Grace." Harriet watched the teams meet in the middle of the pitch as the boys settled down onto the grass. Yet Cecily had a feeling that Raf wasn't one of those sorts of men and that he might well be as bad as he claimed. The fact that he was currently being shown by a child of about ten how to hold the bat was hardly a good start.

"Double-bluff?" Cecily got up from the blanket so she could get a better look. Not at Raf's bottom as he leaned forward in those white trousers, of course.

Perish the thought.

Where had these unfamiliar feelings come from? She had never found Hugh attractive, never wanted him to kiss her or to feel his touch. She accepted it as his wife, but she was in treacherous waters indeed, wanting the kiss of another man.

I don't care.

She'd never had a choice, and if she had failed to love, honor and obey her husband, then he had most definitely failed in his promise to cherish her. He barely even seemed to like her.

And there was nothing wrong with looking. Besides, she had precious little to offer Raf other than biscuits.

He glanced over his shoulder and offered her a thumbs-up even as Harriet said, "Oh, he doesn't look at all at home with his stance. Maybe bats aren't him."

Harriet's observation made something Raf had said stir to the surface. "He told me he makes bat boxes! You know, for the flying sort of bat."

"Oh, that's very fitting!"

"Really? Why's that?"

Harriet nudged her and laughed, "Transylvanian bat boxes!"

"Oh, I see!" Cecily had once read Bram Stoker's novel, after Sandy had found a copy abandoned in a classroom, but it hadn't occurred to her that Raf was from the very country where most of that novel was set.

And besides, Raf wasn't exactly *Gothic*. Cecily could hardly see him climbing down the sheer castle walls to terrorize the locals. No, Raf wasn't that sort of Romanian at all. He was very real indeed.

And about to play cricket.

"Simmer down," Graham told the boys as the excited chatter fell to a buzz. "Boys on bat, masters out to field. May the best team win."

"Don't knock it into the rose garden!" one of the older boys called, to murmurs of ominous agreement. "Don't want to wake the old judge up!"

"Settle now," Graham warned again, amid calls of *the judge is going to get you*. "Play on!"

Cecily sat down again beside Harriet and watched as the game began. The boys quickly racked up the runs, the masters fumbling as they tried to catch the ball. At one point the master of geography collided head first with the master of history, and both went tumbling backward. But neither had sustained too serious an injury, and both were back on their feet again after good-natured laughter from all.

Raf was in the outfield, valiantly trying and failing to field. He was so popular with the boys already, that much was obvious from their jolly shouts at his failed efforts. It was all Cecily could do to take her eyes off him, and she found that she didn't want to.

He was the most hapless cricketer she had ever seen, but he was so full of roguish smiles and clowning grins that Cecily decided she could watch him play for hours. He'd brought life to Whitmore Hall.

"We should do this much more, Mr. Culpeck!" Harriet called during a changeover. "Perhaps we could have a little test match season!"

Some of the boys had overheard and clapped loudly at Harriet's suggestion. Some even began to cheer.

"The boys certainly like your idea!" Cecily pointed out.

"Mr. de Chastelaine can captain you," one of the boys called. "Then you definitely won't have a chance!"

She saw Raf laugh at the suggestion, but she knew too that he wouldn't be here. This balmy Indian summer couldn't last.

All too soon, the boys' innings was over. Their score was unlikely to be beaten, and the masters gamely readied themselves for defeat. As they changed sides, Raf wandered close to the women and said, "Prepare to be amazed, ladies."

He already *had* amazed her. Blushing, Cecily glanced at Harriet. "And just how will he do that, I wonder?"

"Knocking the lads for six." Her friend laughed before crunching down on a biscuit. To cheers from the boys and polite applause, Raf took up the bat and squared up before the wicket. The bowler he faced was a boy of sixteen, the son of some viscount who had left Hugh virtually speechless, so busy had he been being deferential.

"I'll try to go easy, sir." The boy touched a salute to his floppy red fringe. "And I'd really like to pass my Latin!"

"Then you'd better pray that this wicket stays standing," Raf told him, tapping the bat on the grass. The boy took a run and let fly, and perhaps to everyone's surprise, Raf's bat connected. Up into the air went the cricket ball and down it came again, heading straight toward Cecily.

Blinking against the sun, she leaned back, hands cupped against her chest, and caught the ball. She still remembered how to catch, even though it had been so long since she'd played out here with Sandy.

Cecily got to her feet, still holding the ball, as applause rang across the field. She awkwardly dropped a curtsey as her gaze settled on Raf.

"Sorry!" she called, and threw the ball to the nearest fielder, then sat down again.

"Howzat, miss!" the peer's son shouted in delight. He turned to the other boys and asked them, "Mrs. James for honorary captain? What do you say, team?"

A roar of approval went up for her, with even the long-jaded masters awarding Cecily a round of applause. Raf, meanwhile, bowed to the field and trotted over to the picnic blanket, where he settled beside her.

That desire to kiss him returned again and Cecily passed him the biscuit tin, as if that would salt her need away. "Your well-earned prize, Mr. de Chastelaine."

"Howzat!" Harriet echoed the bowler, clapping her hands. "We have a secret cricketing fiend in our midst! Honorary Captain Cecily!"

Raf selected two biscuits from the tin. He gave one to Cecily then settled back on the grass, propped on one elbow as he bit into his own biscuit. She wondered what he made of her, sure that the answer was very little indeed, because what was Cecily if not instantly forgettable? Yet there was a sense of such warmth in the air when he was near and she was sure, though she wasn't sure *how*, that her affectionate friendship was returned.

How she would miss him.

The game continued, but Cecily barely noticed. She ate her biscuit, watching Raf, whose lips looked so soft and were now edged in crumbs and sugar. Were those even little moans of delight he was making at her cooking? Maybe he was teasing her. Maybe he was like this with everyone. But it made her happy to be with him, and that was the most important thing of all.

Cecily watched the boys on the field, heard the laughter of those seated on the grass and recalled the steady trickle of news from Europe, the reports of another old Whitmorian dead, some of them so young it was a wonder they were there at all. Looking at the youngsters here today, she wondered how many of them had lost fathers or brothers and prayed that they would never see such days again. No other sisters should lose their brother, their protector, on a blood-soaked foreign field.

Let it all be biscuits and cricket and endless summers like this.

"Can I have another biccie?" Raf asked, leaning a little closer to whisper, "I'm glad I got caught out, especially by you."

Cecily moved closer to Raf and pulled the lid off the tin. A length of her hair escaped from behind her ear and brushed Raf's forehead, and a static charge shot through her. Certainly not something she should feel from a man who wasn't her husband. But she couldn't help it.

"Erm…sorry. A biscuit…" She attempted to balance the tin on her lap while rearranging her hair clip to rein in her hair. "Sorry, hang on…"

"Let me." Raf sat up and carefully unclipped her hair. To anyone watching it would look like nothing, a clumsy woman and a gallant man, but nobody else would see the way he looked at her, the affection in those blue eyes. He murmured, "Your hair's all wild."

"I wish it wasn't—I'd kill for Marcel waves!" Cecily looked away from him, pretending to be interested in the English master's plodding run between the stumps. She felt Raf clip her hair back, his hands surprisingly soft as he took the tin from her and retrieved another biscuit. Then he settled back on the grass again, apparently without a care in the world.

Cecily dared herself to think about the night to come. She thought about the weeping woman and the eye behind the keyhole and Raf in the garden by moonlight. Whoever Hugh had gone to meet, he had told her that he wouldn't be home until tomorrow, that his business with the man from the ministry would keep him in the city overnight.

Raf gardening in the darkness, his skin silvered by the moon.

Would she dare to join him?

The ring she had found in the rose garden seemed to warm on her finger, and Cecily allowed herself a glimpse of Raf, tousled and happy beside her.

My love, my secret.

Cecily's breath caught in her throat. Was that why the weeping woman cried? Had she desired someone she couldn't have?

'*Sex*', Raf had said, the word so forbidden and so thrilling on his lips. He shifted slightly on the grass beside her and when she dared glance his way again, she found him chancing a look at her in return. They shared a smile, another little secret that she would remember when the world reclaimed Rafael de Chastelaine.

There was clapping from somewhere but Cecily was barely aware of it. All she could do was glance at Raf. And offer him another biscuit.

Hugh would say no, would lecture her on profligacy and greed and tell her she'd eaten too many biscuits already. Raf, however, said, "I will if you will."

And he makes it sound so decadent.

Cecily took a biscuit then held the tin out to him. "They're full of butter and sugar. All the naughty things. Though I stopped short of coating them in chocolate — do you think I should try?"

"Everything's better covered in chocolate," Raf replied. He took one of the biscuits from the tin. "Thank you, Captain Sissy."

"My pleasure, Mr. de Chastelaine." As Cecily was about to return the lid to the tin, she spotted a ladybird crawling around its edge. She carefully picked it up and it sauntered over the back of her hand, which showed no sign of the scratch. There it remained, settled happily on her hand as the game went on, the afternoon stretching toward the early evening and the ever-encroaching dinner bell. Soon the clock would chime in the tower and boys and masters alike would file off to the dining hall, leaving Cecily and Harriet to finally enjoy that sherry they had planned.

And no Hugh until tomorrow.

Cecily watched the ladybird lift into the sky and fly away and allowed herself to imagine a world in which Hugh didn't come back at all. She didn't imagine him dead or injured or anything other than just not there, no longer at her back, watching her every move.

What a wonder it would be.

"The boys and their honorary captain, our excellent Mrs. James, claim the victory!" Graham exclaimed as a cheer rose up from the pupils on the field and in the audience. Some of the older masters who had managed more runs than Raf had managed seconds on the field, gave cheery heckles yet they were smiling too, despite the groans of aching bones and sore muscles as they levered themselves up from the grass. All of it was in good part though, because who could be anything but happy on an afternoon like this?

Tonight, Cecily decided, she would walk in the gardens beneath the moon.

Chapter Eight

As Cecily headed back into the cool of the house, her skin retained the sun's warmth. She balanced the empty biscuit tin on her hip as she dug for her door key in her pocket. But even before she had put the key to the lock, she was aware of discord in the air. Maybe she'd left a window open and a bird had got in?

The door was already unlocked.

Cecily pushed open the door. "Hello?" she called into the empty hallway. Behind her, Harriet waited on the threshold, her face no longer ruddy from the climb upstairs but washed pale by this unexpected hitch in their plans for a cheery evening.

"Study!" Hugh's voice thundered along the hallway like a storm breaking. "Now!"

"Should I—" Harriet began but the sentence remained unfinished because both women knew that there was nothing to be done. Cecily must answer the summons of the headmaster.

"Hattie, I'm so sorry… Let's have our sherry another day." Cecily hoped she hadn't heard Hugh boom at her. Embarrassment took hold of Cecily, but it wasn't the first time Harriet had heard Hugh order Cecily about as if she were a difficult pet.

Harriet's answer was to hug Cecily as though she were going to face the executioner. She pressed a kiss to Cecily's cheek and whispered, "Honorary captain, don't forget." Then, with a gentle smile, she retreated onto the landing and closed the door.

With trembling hands, Cecily put the tin down on the chair then took off Isabella's ring and pushed it into the farthest corner of her pocket. She tried to smooth down her hair and her clothes, and rubbed at her face to brush away all trace of biscuits.

Or any trace of the afternoon's happiness.

The door of the study was already open but Cecily paused in the doorway and knocked anyway. He would only accuse her of *barging in* if she didn't. "Dr. James?"

"In!" he roared and Cecily scurried to obey, quailing at the sight of Hugh in his black suit and robe, standing before the portrait of the judge. He was white with rage, his lips a thin, tight line and on his desk was the brandy decanter that she topped up dutifully. It was half empty now and the air was filled with anger, the scent of alcohol enveloping her. "Upon arriving in Plymouth today, I found that circumstances had conspired to postpone my meeting. Did I remain anyway, drinking and wassailing away the night in a hotel that my school was paying for? No, madam, I did not. I climbed back into my car and endured the drive home, home to my loving, waiting wife. Except I found no wife waiting, because my wife was flaunting herself to the boys, coquetting herself to young men who will be the future of this nation. What is in your head, girl? Will you ride roughshod over their unblemished characters with your whorish ways?"

Cecily folded her hands neatly in front of her. "Harriet and I were enjoying the cricket, and I was representing you." Rather than rattle off an excuse, a new voice came from Cecily. "I...I must say, Dr. James, it upsets me when you accuse me of being *whorish*. It's very hurtful. I've never been unfaithful to you."

And yet you're stupid, she realized, surprised at the very idea of thinking such a thing. *The boys? When Raf's sitting there beside me, you look to the boys?*

"Because you wouldn't have the opportunity, Mrs. James!" He threw his head back and laughed, a hollow, mirthless sound. "Look at you, what man but I would take pity on a creature like you? Those young men will become husbands one day to the finest stock in the land. If they see you at all, it's to laugh at you. To pity you your utter insignificance!"

Cecily lowered her head. Not because she felt subservient, but because she couldn't trust herself not to sneer back at his vileness. And she couldn't bear to see Judge Whitmore glowering behind him, as if there were not one but two enemies in the room. "I heard laughter, but they were enjoying the game, Dr. James."

Without you there, you joyless tyrant.

"Masters lolling about on the lawn, men of my age lumbering over the grass, turning themselves into figures of fun. And with you and the Culpeck creature there at the heart of it, brazen as a couple of common tarts!" He took a deep breath and asked, "Why must you drive me to this?"

Cecily flinched. His words were like a jab in the ribs. She clasped her hands tighter, her short fingernails digging into her palms. *I'm the honorary captain.* Cecily could have apologized, but what would be the point? She had done so hundreds of times before, for every tiny infraction he had claimed to see, and it had never softened his cruelty. The insults and the blows would still fall.

She raised her head and settled her gaze on him. Not imperious, not unblinking, merely an honest gaze. He was going to hit her whether she apologized or not, she could sense it in the atmosphere. She could fall to her knees, weeping and begging for his kindness until her face was blotchy with tears. Nothing would stay his hand.

I am the honorary captain.

Keeping her voice as level as she could, Cecily said, "I thought husbands were supposed to love their wives."

"Only if the wives are worth loving." He walked around the desk to stand before her. "Who on earth would love *you*?"

Cecily didn't look away from Hugh's rheumy eyes, despite the loathing and the threat of violence that burned there. He smelled of booze and something else — something spicy, like a heavily scented flower at dusk.

Perfume.

She took a step away from him. Maybe she was imagining it — but no, it was definitely there. He'd been with another woman. *Bloody hypocrite.*

The knowledge of it felt like a punch. Even though she had no love for him, how dare he, how dare he, *how dare he!* Calling her a whore, a tart, when he was carrying on with someone else.

"*I* love me." Cecily's voice quavered with hurt as tears sprang into her eyes. "*I* do."

Hugh matched her step away with one of his own, seizing her by her upper arms with a fierce grip. Then he shook her as though she were a rag doll, bellowing as he did. Above, the footsteps sprang to life in what seemed to be celebration, the ceaseless pacing replaced by a sprightly tread directly above their heads.

"You will *not* fraternize with the boys, you filthy creature!" His spittle landed on her face, hot and stinking of alcohol. "By God, my girl, you won't ensnare them as you ensnared me!"

And Cecily knew the slap was coming before it landed, his palm hitting her face with enough force to twist her head. Then he threw her down onto the floor and landed a kick in her belly, the polished toe of his shoe — the shoe *she* had polished — knocking the breath from her lungs.

"Refill the decanter," Hugh snarled, stepping over her. "Then go to your room."

Cecily couldn't speak and lay there gasping like a fish dragged out of a river. But she knew she'd have to get up or he'd kick her again. She wiped her tears away on her sleeve and as she pulled herself back to her feet, grasping the desk, she shot him a glare. *You bloody hypocrite.*

I am the captain, she told herself, tasting a tang of blood in her mouth. Let the feet stamp and dance above, let her husband crow. *The filthy bloody hypocrite.*

The phone jangled into life on the desk and Hugh called as though nothing untoward had happened at all, "Answer it then, woman!"

Cecily spat blood into her handkerchief before lifting the receiver. In a bland chirrup, she rattled off, "Good afternoon, Whitmore Hall School, the headmaster's residence. To whom am I speaking?"

The line was silent and she listened to the echo of emptiness down the miles. Then a man's voice could be heard, clearing his throat. He took a deep breath and told her in a Devon accent so thick that even she, a native of the county, had to concentrate, "Tell that bastard headmaster that if he comes near my wife again, I'll wring his scrawny neck."

And the line went dead.

Cecily stared at the receiver. A shock of cold went through her, then she held the bloodstained handkerchief over her mouth to stifle the giggle rising up her throat. But she couldn't fall foul of hysterics.

Cecily composed herself quickly, and told the *hypocritical, philandering bastard*, "A wrong number, Dr. James."

"Then go to bed," was his flat response.

Without offering him supper, without wishing him good evening, Cecily went to the bedroom. The giggle threatened her again, and she held it back. As she sat in front of the dressing table to comb her hair, she realized that out there was a woman who had been caught out. Had she been slapped by her husband too? But why on earth would she willingly liaise with Hugh? Maybe he spent money on her, took her out in his Daimler, paid for expensive meals and gave her pretty presents. Flattered her and loved her. Everything that he didn't do for her.

How many others had there been over the years?

Cecily took the chocolate Raf had given her, which she had hidden in the drawer with her stockings, and sat on the wide windowsill to gaze outside at the garden.

And I wished my husband dead.

Cecily snapped off a piece of chocolate and put in on her tongue, letting it melt there as she watched the gathering evening. Away across the courtyard, a breeze disturbed the trees that surrounded the lawn, the ghost garden burnished brown in the setting sun. From the open windows of the dorms drifted the sound of the boys' laughter and chatter and below she saw a figure amble into the courtyard, the tousled black hair giving away its identity before she saw the creased cricket whites and bare feet.

Raf must have sensed her watching because he paused and turned back to the building, then lifted his face to her. He smiled and raised his hand, waving as he mouthed the words *Hello, captain.*

Cecily waved back, mouthing *Hello, Raf,* then held the chocolate up to the glass. She pointed to it then gave a thumbs-up.

He answered with a thumbs-up of his own, his smile even brighter. When Hugh fell asleep, Cecily decided, she would dab witch hazel on these newest bruises. He always slept heavily after brandy.

And she would think about Raf and she would think about Hugh's pathetic attempts to philander.

And how he had failed.

On her way to the bathroom, Cecily hid her treasures under the loose floorboard. The ring and the chocolate and the grass that had fallen from her hair as she had combed it — she would visit them again when Hugh was next away. She washed and slipped into her nightie and sank under the covers. Wrapping her arms around herself as she began to fall asleep, she thought of Raf. *Lovely, lovely Raf.*

* * * *

Cecily didn't know how long had passed when the sound of sobbing woke her. She blinked into the darkness, just able to make out the phantom of Isabella Whitmore, the woman who had died to satisfy the whim of a brute. Isabella was facing toward the door, her back to the bed, her shoulders heaving beneath the weight of what seemed to be eternal misery.

Pulling herself up against the pillows, Cecily asked, "Isabella, who did you love?"

Perhaps it was the darkness playing tricks, but did Isabella's head turn just a little, as though she had heard?

Could they make contact?

Cecily sat up in the bed. "Isabella, don't be afraid. Your secret love — what was his name?"

The door opened and Isabella shimmered away as Hugh stumbled into the bedroom, grunting an oath when he collided with the dresser. Cecily tried to slip down under the covers again, hoping he wouldn't notice she was awake. He staggered this way and that, trying to hang up the suit, set the shoes down neatly, determined to remain the headmaster. Only when Cecily realized that he hadn't completed the ritual and put on his pajamas did she steel herself, her stomach clenching at the sound of his hoarse breathing as he approached the bed.

Cecily closed her eyes. She recalled the flavor of Raf's chocolate, she pictured the picnic blanket and the cricket match and remembered the warmth of the sun.

What a lovely afternoon it had been. And in her mind, it still was.

As Hugh pulled back the sheets and climbed into bed, his body heavy atop hers, she could smell the perfume again, mingling with brandy and sweat and pipe smoke. Instead, Cecily conjured up the scent of the rosemary Raf had planted beneath the sundial and recalled the slight hint of exotic cologne that he wore, a world away from the husband who was possessing her now, with no care for what she might want. And she had never wanted *him*.

She pictured Raf with a woman, in a garden in full bloom. The roses' drooping, silky petals nodded in the breeze and their scent filled the air. Raf and the woman were laughing and he gazed at her in a way that Cecily had never been looked at. She saw him comb his fingers through the woman's hair, so tender and slow, then she saw them kiss. And when they paused, Cecily realized that she knew the woman.

My God, it's me.

"*Damn it*," Hugh grunted, the brandy having robbed him of his ability to do anything other than sweat and pant atop her. The headmaster, it seemed, had no mastery over himself.

Cecily dared to peek open one eye. The room was so dark, dark as a cellar, but above her she saw — no, how could it be? The silvered swirl of a cataract.

Cecily turned her face away and clawed at the bedsheet in terror. The eye at the door. Raf had seen it, and there was no one at the school — not even Hugh — who had a cataract. So who was looking at her? Cecily caught the scream that was building in her throat. It would only end badly for her if she yelled, but she couldn't bear the weight of Hugh on top of her, couldn't understand why his eye had changed.

"I need to sleep, Dr. James. I feel unwell."

"Lost with all hands. All. Hands. Drowned," he snarled against Cecily's ear in a voice thick with drink and vitriol. The words meant nothing to her but the cold mirth that ran through them chilled her blood. Then he rolled his bulk onto the mattress beside her and began to laugh, a sound like glass shattering. "You are bound to me after all, you damned deceitful whore."

Cecily jammed her hands over her ears and curled up in a ball, her back to him. She wanted to scream in his face — *I'm not! I'm not!* — but she knew that would only make him worse.

There was something very wrong with the headmaster.

Chapter Nine

In the days that followed the cricket match, for that was how Cecily preferred to remember it, not the days that followed the beating, nor the vision of the cataract just inches from her face, Cecily knew what it was to be a prisoner. She was watched at every turn when Hugh was at home and even when he was in the school she dared stray no farther than Harriet's rooms for fear of encountering her husband in the hallways. On the kitchen calendar, back in the winter, Hugh had marked two days in red ink, writing in his exacting script *London* across them.

Two days of freedom. Forty-eight hours in which Hugh would be far, far away, sharing his wisdom at a conference, winning the plaudits of other men in academic gowns and chalk-dusted suits. Men who hardly knew who was in their midst.

The Cecily who packed her husband's case was meek and obedient but the Cecily who dabbed witch hazel to her bruises and waved to Raf from the window each night was defiant. She who knew the building better than anyone had always watched the world from a window, this was no different. She saw the butterflies in the sunlight and the bats at dusk, tiny pipistrelles that fluttered past the window and, sometimes as she sat there, one small, black bat paused on the sill to rest, looking back at Cecily as she looked out at him.

The honorary captain.

Even the footsteps seemed to sense a change in her for they grew less frequent and far quieter, and for a few days Isabella confined herself to just one appearance, treading the crisp lines of the ghost garden in the sunlight as Cecily prepared Hugh's breakfast.

"I have asked a tradesman to give us his opinion on the clocktower," Hugh told her as he stood on the threshold at dawn, his case clutched in his thin hand. "He shall visit the school upon my return." Then he stopped and kissed her cheek. "Behave during my absence, Mrs. James, or I shall know if you don't."

"I always behave," Cecily told him. *Unlike you,* a waspish voice added in her mind. "Safe journey. I hope the conference goes well."

And I hope the cuckolded husband wrings your neck.

After breakfast, and once their rooms were tidied, Cecily felt restless. She couldn't wander far, because there was always the risk that Hugh would telephone. But there was nothing wrong with a stroll outside. She retrieved the ring and the chocolate from their hiding place and wandered out into the garden. The boys were all busy at their lessons, the sounds from the classrooms floating out on the still air. The raised voice of a master, a pupil answering a question, the squeak of chalk on a blackboard.

She wandered over the ghost garden, following the paths she had seen Isabella walk. Perhaps she had met her lover here.

"My love, my secret." The forbidden nature of the words sent a thrill through Cecily. Maybe if she went back to the rose garden she could make some sense of what Isabella wanted — and perhaps who Isabella had loved.

Cecily had left the key upstairs, but she could at least peer between the railings, and maybe Isabella would come. Just as she rounded the wall, and was screened from the school building, Cecily's skin prickled. She wasn't alone. She could hear someone.

"Isabella?" she called, as loudly as she dared.

"Not the last time I checked," she heard Raf reply from the other side of the wall. "Guess again, Captain!"

"Oh, Raf, how are you? I've missed you so — my word!"

She stopped, her hand over her eyes. Her pulse had quickened, racing as she tried to rein in her surprise. "You're...erm...you don't appear to be wearing a shirt."

"I'm wearing trousers," he pointed out. "And shoes and gloves. And a welcoming smile!"

Cecily slowly parted her fingers and peered between them at Raf. He really was wearing a welcoming smile. *Too* welcoming. Those beautiful eyes... Her gaze tracked down and there was his chest, proudly bare and muscled. The necklaces she had had a hint of before through his unfastened top button were visible now, a collection of leather and chain with metal, glass and pottery shapes dangling from them that rested against the modest tangle of hair on his chest.

Desire tightened within her — she had never seen a sight like it before.

Finally Cecily dropped her hand and shoved it into her pocket, trying to appear relaxed. "I — I was going for a wander."

"I'm glad you wandered over here." Raf was holding a fearsome-looking ax the head of which rested atop the pile of twisted wood and vines that carpeted the few feet of exposed earth in the choked rose garden. Cecily saw the sunlight glisten on his skin and was reminded again of the jar of sun lotion, the same sun lotion he must have applied to the very naked torso before her. "I have no classes until after lunch, so I thought I'd make a start on our rose garden."

Our rose garden.

"You're doing a splendid job — won't it be wonderful when it's returned to how it must've once looked? All those beautiful roses!" Cecily turned Isabella's ring on her finger, glancing over Raf's shoulder into the garden beyond. She lowered her voice. "By the way, I was thinking about what you said. The motive for the judge to commit murder."

"Sex," he reminded her playfully, drawing the back of his arm over his brow. "I'm just trying to fathom how the murdered pauper got dragged in. What's your thoughts on it all, Sis?"

"I think..." Cecily's gaze had dropped to Raf's chest again, his nipples dark pink against his pale skin. She looked up again to focus on his eyes. "This ring, it was Isabella's, and there's an inscription inside it. It says *My love, my secret.* With a C following. What if the pauper was in fact her..."

Raf's masculine presence was impossible to ignore. That scent he wore, mingled with fresh, honest sweat.

'*Sex*', he said it so easily. Cecily took a deep breath before saying, "...what if the pauper was Isabella's lover?"

Raf turned to prop the ax against a thick tangle of boughs and Cecily heard herself gasp. He was covered in tattoo on top of tattoo, a wild jumble of images and colors that somehow came together to tell a story. What the story was she didn't know, but each piece seemed to fit with the next despite the random manner of it all. Some crept down under the waistband of his trousers, and Cecily forced herself not to picture what that would look like. *Not bad, at any rate...*

"And if she said that in defense," he murmured, turning back to her, "they'd condemn her for adultery instead. Or more likely she never got the chance to defend herself at all."

Cecily took off the ring and held it out to Raf. "But look at what a beautiful ring it is. I can't see how a pauper could have afforded such a thing."

"You know in the colonies the Puritans could hang a lass for adultery." Raf took off his glove and threw it down before accepting the ring. "Maybe that's what old Judge W thought he was doing. Not the most balanced bloke in the land."

"Killed her lover, and had her killed..." Cecily shivered. "Beastly man."

"Is she with us now?" Raf slipped the ring onto his little finger.

"I don't think she is." Cecily shook her head. "But she's always there at night, in the...the bedroom."

Raf nodded and held out the ring to Cecily again. Among the wilderness of the garden, his hair so tousled and his chest bare but for the tangle of charms, he looked like a tempting, mischievous Puck. Cecily took the ring back and put it back on her finger.

"I want to find out, Raf. I want to know what happened. Someone was lying — a pauper, indeed, it wasn't at all!" Cecily turned the ring again. An idea had occurred to her. "I wonder if maybe she was buried in the family chapel after all? I can imagine a jealous man like the judge doing just that. I'm tempted to look — I can get the key to the vault easily enough."

"Do you want some company? I've got plenty of time before I have to be in the classroom."

"If you'd like!" There was no one else Cecily knew who would've volunteered to go with her into a vault. "You'll need a shirt, though — it's chilly down there."

"I can manage a shirt." Raf threw his other glove down then knelt on the floor and sifted through the cuttings. Eventually he dug out a canvas knapsack that he'd managed to bury and from it he pulled a crumpled cotton shirt of pale blue. The knapsack, khaki and old, made Cecily think immediately of the war and she wondered if Raf had served. He must have though — he was certainly no boy.

She would wait for him to tell her, if he ever could. "Do you know the way to the chapel? The key to the vault's in the caretaker's office — I'll fetch it and meet you at the chapel in ten minutes."

"See you there, cap!" Raf executed a lazy salute, his shirt still bunched in his fist. "Without an ax."

* * * *

Cecily knew exactly which key would let her into the vault, although it didn't have a fob. A heavy, ancient thing, hidden behind a forest of other keys, disguised deliberately should the pupils find their way into the caretaker's office. The man himself had his back to her as he poured a cup of tea.

Cecily arrived at the chapel to find Raf already there, kicking up the dust. She turned the heavy handle of the chapel's unlocked door. "Ready?"

"Always."

The ancient wooden door squeaked open and Cecily reached inside for the light switch. "It gets a bit gloomy in here," she explained. "I brought a torch from the caretaker's office too, for when we go downstairs."

The light revealed row upon row of dark wooden pews and gray stone walls. By the door were two wooden panels — one listing the three headmasters with space for many more below, and another beside it naming the pupils and the two masters who hadn't survived the war. Around the walls and set in the floor were memorials to the Whitmores, with a modest plaque beside the pipe organ to remember Cecily's family. She didn't like to look at it — she was the last Pincombe left.

Above the altar light flooded through a stained-glass window from which the crucified Christ looked down on them, his face passive and, Cecily had always thought, rather resigned. Perhaps, like her, he had just had enough of trying to measure up.

She looked to Raf, who was frowning as he took it all in. As the colorful light spilled through the window, Cecily was reminded again of his tattoos as he worked in the garden.

The locked garden.

Cecily leaned against the end of a pew. She arched an eyebrow playfully. "I'm impressed that you managed to find the key to the rose garden."

He shrugged one shoulder and replied, "I might not be a teacher, but I've got one or two other talents."

Cecily's giggle echoed around the chapel as she nudged him with her elbow. "Oh, you didn't—you did, didn't you? You picked the lock!"

"You're asking a man with word blindness who manages to teach Latin if he's got the odd trick up his sleeve!" Raf scrubbed his fingers through his hair. "What do *you* think?"

Cecily grinned. "I think you did!" She held out the vault's key on the flat of her hand. "I *did* get the key to the vault, but if you fancy picking an extremely old lock, now's your chance."

"What will you give me if I can?" he asked, voice filled with mischief. "I like chocolate a lot."

"I made some more lavender biscuits yesterday," Cecily confided, "and they might just have a dab of chocolate on them."

"Let me at that lock." Raf rubbed his hands together, all enthusiasm now. "And if anyone asks, I was never here."

"This way…" Cecily headed up the aisle with Raf at her side. Once they were at the top of the aisle, where Cecily had stood at Hugh's side on that miserable day when she had reluctantly said '*I do*', she pointed down at the floor. "There—it's worn somewhat but that's the stone. See…Isabella first, no mention of any murders, only that she is under his gaze. Horrible. And below, the inscription to him—the *worthye, honourable* Judge Edward Whitmore."

"Under his gaze," Raf said thoughtfully. He dropped to his knees and ran his hands over the stone, tracing the letters one at a time. Then he closed his eyes and reached into the open neck of his shirt. Cecily saw Raf's fingers close around one of the charms and his lips were murmuring something in a language that she didn't understand.

She crouched down beside Raf, watching him, wondering what on earth he was doing. Communing with the long-dead judge, or uttering a prayer of protection?

"Sorry," Raf said finally, releasing the charm. She saw a faint bashful blush on his cheeks as he turned to look at her.

"That's all right—you know more about this sort of thing than I do!" Cecily said. "Was that to protect us?"

"When Mum was here, she was fierce when we needed to be protected," he told her gently. "And she still is. I was just asking her to look out for Isabella. You might be pretty annoyed, but after the match, I asked her to look out for you too. I kept thinking of that bloody eye!"

Cecily shuddered and reached for Raf's arm as the memory of that dreadful night came back to her. "Oh, Raf, it was horrible—I saw it! The eye!"

"You didn't go up to the clocktower, did you?" Raf closed his hand over hers.

"No. I..." Cecily bit her lip, trying to think of a delicate way to put it. "I was in bed. And...Hugh happened to look at me, and there it was. He doesn't have a cataract, but he did then. And he was drunk, and angry, and he—"

Hit me.

"And I found out that he's having an affair. Or at least was." The husband's furious voice returned to her mind. *'I'll ring his scrawny neck.'*

Raf nodded, studying her face. "How did you end up shackled to him?"

"It's what my father wanted." Cecily wiped her hand across her face. She didn't want to cry, but Raf's expression was so sympathetic, so kind, that she was fairly sure her restraint would falter.

"It was a great shock when Sandy was killed, and my father had a heart attack the next day. He was weakened, and took to his bed, and I was there beside him, and Hugh—his deputy and his friend—was there too. And he clasped our hands together, and he asked Hugh to look after me, and he said to me, '*You are a good, obedient girl when you choose to be, and a headmaster needs a wife. And you'll be Dr. James*'. *You'll struggle to find a husband, you're only a slip of a thing.*' I didn't want to marry Dr. James, not really. I wanted to go into nursing and be a VAD, but I was only twenty and neither Father nor Hugh would let me. I couldn't leave the school— there was nowhere else for me to go. All my family had gone, and I'd never had friends, not the kind who would have taken me in. Father appointed Hugh as my guardian and a month after Father died…Hugh married me."

Cecily's view of Raf became distorted by her tears and she rummaged in her pocket for a handkerchief. "Sorry. I shouldn't cry. I should've run off, I daydreamed that once, I even half-packed my bag. When they said I couldn't be a VAD—I was going to run away to Exeter and find work in a munitions factory. Those girls made good money, I heard. But I didn't. I was too scared, and I stayed here."

"*Obedient*," Raf repeated, as though he couldn't think of anything more insulting to call a young woman. He took a clean white handkerchief from his pocket and pressed it into Cecily's hand. As she wiped her eyes, he said, "The world hasn't done right by you, Sissy, and that brute you're married to—" Dabbing at her tears, Cecily heard the loathing in his voice. "Believe me, I've seen his kind before. So-called pillars of the establishment. I lost my mum because of a bloke like him, on his knees every Sunday trying to hide a soul that's blacker than midnight."

Cecily glanced at the pulpit where her husband held forth to the school, expounding his theology of fear and obedience. *The hypocrite,* when all along he had done his best to break Cecily while he cavorted with another man's wife. Her gaze returned to Raf and his gentle blue eyes. "What happened to your mother, Raf?"

"A supposed godly man killed her," he replied, his voice filled with vitriol. "And left five kids without a mum and a man without a wife. He followed us all the way across Europe just to kill my mum. What sort of *piety* is that?"

Cecily rested her head on Raf's shoulder. "You poor things. What an evil man."

"So now *I* travel about too." She felt his cheek against her hair, warm and stubbled. "Tidying up gardens and dealing with the nasty whatsits that go *bump* in the night."

"Is that what your mother did?" Cecily couldn't hide the note of surprise in her voice. "Gardens and beasties?"

"That was Dad. And Dad's dad, and Dad's dad's dad and on and on way back as long as Yorkshire can remember. Handymen and gardeners first, vanquishing beasties second." He shook his head and sighed. "Mum's people aren't gardeners, they're proper nobility. But if I say to you *Transylvanian nobility,* what's the first thing you think of?"

Cecily recalled her conversation with Harriet. *Transylvanian bats*. "I'd think of Dracula! Which patently can't be—" But if a long-dead woman could walk through a ghost garden, if mysterious feet could stamp in the attics, if a cataract could appear then vanish from an eye... "Oh, I see!"

"Yeah, exactly, that's what *everyone* thinks!" He laughed softly, as if to say, *how absurd*. "But Dad had a bit of a name for himself for heroics as well as landscaping so he got invited over to the old country. There'd been a few killings in Mum's neck of the Tihuţa Pass and people were pointing the finger at the glamorous family up in the mountaintop castle. Mum and Dad teamed up, saved the day, and when the time came to say goodbye, they realized that they didn't want to. A few years and four kids later, yours truly came along!"

"So your parents fought vampires? They *really* exist? Raf, that's amazing, I had no idea."

"I never said the word vampire," Raf pointed out breezily. "I just said they saved the day!"

"Sorry. It would be a bit odd if vampires were real. Ghosts are one thing, but vampires? No, how silly." Cecily got back on to her feet. Raf hopped up beside her, smiling that slight smile she had pictured so often.

The clocktower chimed the hour. Cecily looked at her watch. "We ought to go to the vault now—my husband said he would ring from London once he arrived and I can't miss his call."

"Let's hope there aren't any vampires down there." He quirked his eyebrows. "I might've been born in a Transylvanian castle, but I'm not one. Don't ask if Grandpa is, though." Raf laughed, silly and playful as ever.

"And I'm a Cornish piskie!" Cecily led the way to a curtained arch, behind which was the clutter common to most churches—a stack of numbers for the hymn boards, watering cans for the flowers that Harriet sometimes put in the chapel, kneelers embroidered with the school crest and piles of mildewing books.

A doorway with a pointed Gothic arch waited innocuously. It could have led to a vestry, but Cecily knew better. "That's the way into the vault. Your lock-picking exercise begins," she told Raf. He rolled his shoulders and swaggered over to the door.

As Cecily watched, Raf took a battered leather pouch from the back pocket of his trousers, the sort one might use to carry a penknife or even small screwdrivers. He dropped to one knee and was about to open the pouch when he looked over his shoulder and asked, "Can I borrow a hair grip, if you're wearing one?"

"Yes, of course." Cecily went over to stand beside him. As soon as she pulled out the grip, her hair fell into her face and she scraped it back behind her ears. She held the grip out to him on her palm. "Here it is."

"Your hair's like mine." He took the grip. "Untamable. I like it!"

Cecily grinned. She wasn't used to receiving compliments. "You always look so tousled."

"I swear, I brush it every morning!" Raf shrugged. "I'm a handyman, I'm allowed to be a bit of a mess!"

"I like you being a mess." Cecily's gaze dropped away from him. "I like it because no one else here is like you."

"I like you because—" *He won't be able to think of anything*, Cecily knew. *How embarrassing for him.* A moment later, though, Raf decided, "Because you like chocolate and laughing and you're gentle but tough, I reckon, even if you don't know it yet. I think you're a lot like me, Sissy."

Tough? She had never thought of herself as tough, but maybe she was, if Raf thought so. "Maybe we are alike. I'm so glad you came to Whitmore School."

"So am I," he told her. "And I think you need to be very careful around your husband."

Cecily tried to suppress the shudder that went through her at Raf's words. She knew very well that something was out of kilter, that Hugh was even more unpleasant than usual. All that drinking was so out of character for him. "Do you think he could have something wrong with his eye, like a cloudiness that only comes on when he's…well, I won't lie to you, Raf, he was drunk when I saw it. And maybe he went up to the clocktower one day, in his cups, and that's when you saw him?"

"Do you want the honest answer or the comforting one?"

"Be honest with me, please. I know something's badly wrong." Cecily's stomach lurched. She fixed her attention onto the repeating whorls in the wood of the vault's door. *Don't be scared, honorary captain.*

"Come and help me pick the lock?" Raf asked. "You don't want to stand around doing nothing."

"Well, if you like, but I'm not sure I'll be all that useful." Cecily leaned forward anyway, closer to the lock, like a keen pupil awaiting instruction. Raf withdrew the now-bent hair grip from the lock and put it between Cecily's finger and thumb. Then he took her hand in his and guided it toward the lock as he spoke.

"I think there's two ways of looking at what's going on," he said, helping her to slide the grip into the lock. "Either your husband's got some serious problems with his temper and his eye or—what was he like before this year? Has his behavior changed?"

"Only recently…" Cecily's shoulders loosened as the weight left her now that she had someone to confide in. "He demands beer and wants huge amounts of food, and he says things—weird things. He was rambling on about a shipwreck the other night, gloating that all hands were lost. What shipwreck? Is he remembering something from the war? There was someone in his family in the Navy—a great-nephew, I think. Not that his family ever have much to do with him."

"He's got a hell of a temper," Raf commented. "Is that new?"

Cecily shook her head. "No—he's always been a spiky sort of man. I so easily put a foot wrong, and then he's off."

Raf turned her hand a little this way and that and Cecily felt the workings of the lock grind and resist beneath their combined touch. "So, from your opinion, what's changed the most? And when?"

"The drinking," Cecily decided. "It's almost as if he's losing his grip. He was so fastidious, he'd have a drink, but not get drunk. The other evening he couldn't even walk straight. And he's put that horrible portrait up. I answered the phone to a man threatening him if he ever went near his wife again—maybe something's gone on with his fancy woman, and it's sent him to the bottle."

"A few nights back, after the cricket, when the feet were stomping… Was your husband at home?"

Cecily swallowed. "He was, yes. And that's it—the stamping got worse when he was angry with me. It sounded like it was doing a jig! Like it was happy that he…that he…hit me."

"He what?" Raf's hand stopped guiding her and she heard a jolt of anger in his words. "I thought — Does he do that a lot?"

"I shouldn't have told you that." Cecily closed her other hand over Raf's. "Please promise me you won't say anything."

"Of course I won't but — I can't ever understand it. That's not a man to me."

"He's a bully, Raf." Cecily saw kindness in Raf's eyes, nothing patronizing. No *poor little Cecily, what a shrinking weed*. "He's like it with the boys, too. He'd hit the masters as well, but they'd hit him back."

"If he hits me, he's going to know about it," Raf told her casually. "I might be little, but I'm fierce when I need to be. You don't grow up as one of five siblings without knowing how to take care of yourself. You don't become a handyman with a sideline in long-legged beasties without learning a thing or two either. Know this, Captain Sissy, I won't leave this school until I know you're safe."

"Thank you, Raf." But the thought of him leaving one day still saddened her. "Where will you go when you leave?"

"Home to Yorkshire, to my house beside the sea." He gave her hand a gentle squeeze. "Do you like the seaside? I love it."

"Yes! I've been a couple of times. I miss the sea." An idea struck her then. A way out. "Raf...if I could prove that Hugh's been unfaithful, then it's grounds, isn't it? For...you know what."

"Good grounds," he agreed. "But I think there's more to it than just being unfaithful."

Cecily's hands grew clammy. She didn't want to hear it, but she needed to. However bad it was, there was no use living in ignorance. "What do you think?"

"I think you picked your first lock, but I forgot to tell you how!" He laughed as there was a dull, metallic click from within the door. Cecily felt a thrill of forbidden triumph, yet it was tempered by this talk of Hugh and of a world that she'd had no idea existed, a world in which mothers were murdered by godly men and gardeners did battle with dark forces. "We'll have to do another so I can give you a proper class."

"Of course—there's lots of places in the school that Dr. James keeps locked up—not for much longer, anyway, if we're brave enough. Ready?" Cecily turned the door handle, releasing the smell of stale air and dust. Raf rocked back, waving his hand in front of his nose. Then he gave a sound of utter disgust, as though she had smashed a rotten egg atop his breakfast.

She'd forgotten about his keen sense of smell. "Sorry. All those dead people! They're not particularly fragrant, are they? You're all right on the steps, aren't you? They're not too steep, and not even worn as hardly anyone comes down here."

Cecily primed the torch. Its light was weak against the vault's eternal darkness. "Off we go!"

"Two more questions. It was a week ago last Wednesday that I saw the eye, just before midnight." As he was speaking, Raf took a small bottle from his pocket. It looked like smelling salts and he took the cap off, wafting it beneath his nose for a few seconds. "Was your husband definitely at home all night?"

Cecily paused on the top step, thinking. She looked back at Raf, who was outlined in the doorway by the chapel's electric light. "Yes, I'm sure he was."

"And this might sound odd but…have you noticed any smells? Just the odd whiff of something bad?" He wafted the bottle under his nose again then offered it to her, a subtle fragrance of citrus and summer filling the air. "Not like this. This isn't bad, I mixed it."

"That's a lovely smell!" As she thought, Cecily danced the torch beam around the staircase, catching the stone. "I don't know…it's hard to say really, because it might be connected with Hugh's drinking. Stale alcohol, that sort of thing. Something…that's it…something *unwashed*, if you see what I mean. Dirt."

"Yeah, I smell it too around him." Raf followed her down the stone steps, their feet echoing as they descended. "That's why I mixed this, because I have a talented nose. Too talented sometimes!"

Cecily held the rope bannister with one hand, not entirely trusting it as she could never remember it having been replaced. It was probably centuries old. "It must be all that gardening you do! So what can that unpleasant smell around—?" Her torch beam hit the first coffin and she recoiled with a gasp. "Sorry, it always makes me jump! It's not as if I wasn't expecting the coffins, but still, the thought that there's someone in there. At least, what they once were…"

At the bottom of the steps, Raf came to stand beside Cecily, so close that their arms were touching. As he looked around, Cecily swept the torch beam to illuminate the dark corners, the shelves where generations of Whitmores rested.

"What does the ring tell you now?" Raf asked.

The ring had behaved all morning as if it were just a normal ring, but now they were in the vault it felt cold, and a sense of loss swept through Cecily that was so strong it left her breathless. "Grief. That's what I feel.

121

Horrible grief. That shouldn't surprise me, though, not down here."

"Where are you, Isabella?" he asked the emptiness, receiving no answer in reply. Cecily, however, felt that wave of misery again, a lonely desolation that was as real as the slap Hugh had dealt her.

She reached for the first thing to hold herself up, and realized too late that she was holding on to the edge of a coffin. The wood had warped over the years and its metal trim was loose and tarnished. One of the handles had evidently dropped off long ago. Cecily shone the torch on the coffin's lead plaque, illuminating the dusty legend — *Benjamin Whitmore Esq. 1614–1698.*

In a whisper, as if she was frightened of waking up the coffin's occupant, Cecily told Raf, "Look — this is the judge's brother. He was the youngest of the three, but inherited everything when the judge died."

Raf placed the flat of his hand on the coffin and said, "Three brothers. Tell me about this shipwreck that did for the eldest?"

"He went off to France, I believe, and never came back, so we won't find him in here. There was a storm, and everyone on the ship drowned. All hands —" Cecily blinked. "Oh, Raf — that's it, that's what Hugh was wittering on about the other night. A shipwreck, and all hands lost! He sounded so pleased."

That silvered eye too…

"Sometimes, when a person dies, their spirit gets stuck," Raf said carefully, the explanation one that Cecily had the feeling he might have used before. "And some spirits, like some people, aren't the sort you'd want to meet. You know those crabs that can wear another crab's shell? Once in a while, not often, a spirit can do that too."

Cecily turned to face him, the torch beam striking him full in the face. He squinted and she lowered it to the floor at once. "Sorry, I didn't mean to—a possession, you mean? Like when Hattie did her séance. Only the spirits talked through her, they didn't take over."

"They look for a host, someone who's weak, who can't resist or, sometimes, doesn't want to." Raf rested his hand on Cecily's shoulder. "Sometimes they're birds of a feather. I want you to be very careful around your husband until we get this sorted."

"You think…you think he's been taken over by Judge Whitmore!" Her voice echoed around the chamber, beating against ears that had long since ceased to hear. Her torch flickered and Cecily tapped it against her hand. The beam recovered, but only long enough to glow far brighter than it had before, then it dimmed at once and died, leaving them in darkness.

'The judge is going to get you.'

Cecily grabbed for Raf, her breathing shallow with terror. He caught his fingers around her hand and he told her, "I just want to see the judge's coffin, then we'll go back up. Keep hold of my hand, I promise I won't let you go."

Cecily held his hand tightly. She could almost see him in the darkness, a gray shape against the unremitting black. Breathing more normally now, she said, "It's near his brother's, if I remember."

He'd never be able to find it though, the plaques were indistinguishable without light, their inscriptions illegible. Yet that didn't seem to stop Raf and she could sense him bobbing his head, peering at the nearest coffins. When he gave an exclamation of triumph Cecily wondered how on earth he could have found the coffin, but nothing about Raf surprised her anymore.

Together they took a few steps then she saw the gray outline of her companion dip down and heard a long, somewhat disconcerting, sniff.

"There's nothing in this coffin," he declared. "The judge isn't here."

"How — how do you know?" Cecily dipped her head too and sniffed. All she managed to do was fill her nostrils with dust and she burst into a sneeze. "But if he's not in his coffin, where is he? He hasn't...oh, no, he's not escaped his coffin, has he?"

"I think we'd have spotted him creaking about if he had! Let's go back up top — this is no place for a cricket legend to hang about."

"The way out is over there, I think — there's a bit more light over there, that must be it!"

Together they found their way to the stairwell and Raf stood back so Cecily could go out first, the light that greeted her blinding after the pitch darkness. He emerged in her wake, holding his hand up to shield his eyes until, with a few rapid blinks, he met her gaze again.

"What can I tell you? Not only am I gorgeous, I have amazing night vision too," Raf joked. "I eat lots of carrots."

Cecily laughed. "Comes in handy if you tend to end up in pitch-black vaults with a faulty torch! Let's get the place locked up again. I'll use the key this time!"

She produced the heavy, old key from her pocket. Before closing the door, she called down the stairs, "Sorry to disturb you — sleep well, Whitmores!"

Raf took out his battered old pocket watch and clicked open the case. "I have to go and try to teach some Latin. How would you like — you don't have to but if you're not doing much later, we could share a bottle of beer?"

"I'm not doing anything at all later!" Cecily told him. "Hugh might ring of course, so I need to stay at home, but do knock when you want to pop in."

"Right after supper?" He took her hand and raised it to his lips to bestow a very chaste kiss yet somehow, even *that* seemed earthy. "And try not to worry, I've sorted worse than this!"

Chapter Ten

Not long after Cecily had headed upstairs, the telephone rang in her husband's study. She knew it was him—the black, shiny instrument lurked on his desk like a large beetle.

She trotted out the salutation and listened through the clicks and hiss on the line for Hugh's voice.

"I have arrived safely in London," he said without a greeting. "Goes the day well?"

"Yes, a very quiet day here." Cecily held her hand out and watched the gold of Isabella's ring glow in the sunlight. Hugh didn't reply and for the first time Cecily let the silence go on, listening to the sounds of the city behind him. If she had to stand here mute for an hour, she would.

"I noticed as I left that the windows of our rooms are very smeared inside," her husband said. So that was her punishment for daring to be silent, was it? To clean some windows? It was worth it. "Clean them if you would, Mrs. James."

Cecily wound her finger through the telephone's cord, for which habit he had slapped her hands before. "If I have time, Dr. James."

"Make time, Mrs. James, in between reading fanciful novels and sipping sherry with the Culpeck woman. She's old enough to know better, the painted creature."

The strong scent of perfume that had followed Hugh home from Plymouth—or wherever he'd crawled off to—returned to Cecily's mind.

And you'd know all about painted creatures.

But she didn't say anything. And Raf's words of caution came back to her. *'Be very careful around your husband.'* Goading a man who may or may not be possessed by the spirit of a long-dead, evil judge was possibly unwise.

"I only mean, if I have time with all the baking I need to do so there's biscuits and cakes on your return. But I'll clean the windows, Dr. James—I'll polish them to a shine—don't you worry about that."

"Good girl. I shall see you tomorrow. Late, I expect."

"Yes, Dr. James. See you then."

"You certainly will," he replied. Then with a click, the line went dead.

* * * *

Once evening rolled around, Cecily's arms ached from washing the windows. The glass glittered, but she knew Hugh would still find fault, so the thought of drinking beer with Raf cheered her even more. She'd baked in between washing the windows, and the kitchen had been taken over with biscuits, rock buns and fairy cakes cooling on wire racks.

By the time a knock fell on the front door, Cecily had wiped everything up and the apartment was spotless, fragrant with the scent of her baking.

Can he smell the cooking treats? Cecily wondered as she went to answer the door. *He must be able to.*

The thought warmed her almost as much as Raf's bright smile of greeting when she opened the door to the landing. He bowed low, holding up the old knapsack she had seen earlier.

"Supplies, Captain!"

"Do come in!" Cecily gestured toward the hallway. "Did your classes go well?"

"Well, we all know a few more Latin swear words." Raf looked more tousled than ever in his creased blue shirt and trousers, his feet bare again. She remembered then his bare chest, shining with sun lotion, and felt her heart beat just a little bit faster. "How was the day?"

"Dr. James demanded clean windows, so Dr. James *has* clean windows. And Dr. James will complain that they're not clean enough, but do you know what, Raf? *I don't care.*" Cecily beamed. She'd never been rude about her husband in front of anyone before, not even in front of Harriet. The occasional small remark, perhaps, but nothing too obvious. And it wasn't as if he could overhear her all the way away in London.

"Dr. James is going to carp whatever you do. He's one of those blokes," Raf decided, closing the door as he entered. "I've got beer and something a bit special — Țuică, all the way from the old country. Made by Grandpa, drunk by me. And you, if you fancy it."

"Sounds intriguing! Do you know, Raf, I'm in the sort of mood where I'll happily try *anything!*" Cecily looked away from Raf's sparkling eyes. *Anything?* "Do go through to the parlor. Would you like a glass for your beer or the *toswe—twee—* the other drink you mentioned?"

"I can carry if you like," he told her brightly. "I'm not used to having folk run about after me, I like to be useful. Besides, I'm pretty sure I can smell some amazing baking and I want to nosey at it!"

"This way!" Cecily led him to the kitchen. The smells of cooking were intense even to her, of biscuits and cakes, chocolate and lavender. Almost every surface had a wire rack weighed down with food. Raf's eyes grew wide and he greeted the sight with a low murmur of appreciation that sounded gloriously earthy, almost a growl. He dumped the bag on the floor then closed his eyes and drew in a long, appreciative breath.

Hugh would have ranted about the kitchen being untidy, but not Raf. Cecily took a plate from the dresser and began to stack it with food.

"What would you like first? I promised you a lavender biscuit dipped in chocolate, but the rock buns are rather good—they have a dab of orange in them."

"Your kitchen, you're the boss." His eyes sprang open, bright with enthusiasm. "You decide."

Cecily selected a lavender biscuit from the plate and held it up at Raf's mouth. "There you go. I did promise you one for your lock picking!"

He took a bite, his lips brushing Cecily's fingers again as he did. Then he closed his eyes again and chewed, an appreciative sound purring in his throat. She couldn't remember a time when the kitchen had seen anything so decadent, and how wonderfully forbidden it felt.

"As good as you'd hoped?" Cecily's voice caught in her throat.

"As good as I knew it'd be," Raf corrected, opening his eyes. "Because you're brilliant."

"Oh, I wouldn't say that, but I *do* know how to bake a biscuit." Flustered, she passed the plate to Raf, then grabbed some glasses for their drinks. She held up the set of plain tumblers. "Do these pass muster?"

"If they hold booze, they pass muster." He put the plates down for as long as it took to scoop up the knapsack and throw it over his shoulder. "I've been looking forward to tonight all day."

"Me too," Cecily said. She led him into the parlor and set the glasses down on the table in front of the sofa. "Drinking beer and eating biscuits, aren't we naughty!"

With a gentle laugh, Raf dropped down onto the sofa. He took four bottles of beer from the bag then a larger, unlabelled bottle that was half filled with a pale amber liquid.

"What do you fancy first?"

Cecily drummed her hands on her knees in anticipation. "I'm curious about the *tswee* — that one you said your grandpa made."

"Ţui-că," Raf said carefully, breaking the word in two. She saw the tip of his tongue touch his teeth as he did and felt herself shiver, recalling the dream of their kiss and the sweet touch of his lips on her hand earlier.

"That's the one! Let's try it — I've never heard of it before."

"First, we make a toast." Raf plucked the cork from the bottle neck and began to pour, putting a small measure in each glass. "Then, we sip."

Never being allowed anything more powerful than sherry, Cecily wondered if she should try Raf's drink. Imagine if it went straight to her head, and Hugh came home to find her rolling about drunk in a mess of crumbs? But she had tasted so little of life that she raised her glass with glee.

"Who are we toasting, Raf?"

"Us? Our friendship."

"Yes—our friendship." Cecily clinked her glass against Raf's and drank the entire contents. The glass wasn't particularly full and the drink didn't have much flavor but seconds later Cecily's stomach appeared to be on fire. "My God, what's in *that?*"

"I love how you *sip*, I'd hate to see you knock it back!" Raf took a very delicate sip from his own glass and asked, "More? It's plums, booze and a lot of optimism!"

"Go on, I'll have some more!" Cecily held her glass out to him. "But I'll drink it more slowly this time."

Raf poured another measure and raised his glass again. This time he said, "Another toast. To Sandy and Ileana, an excellent brother and a brilliant mum!"

Clink!

Cecily swung her glass against Raf's again. "To Sandy and Ileana!" She took a small, decorous sip this time. Above them a disapproving thud sounded and she and Raf looked up as one.

"Shut up, you miserable old bugger!" Raf told the judge, who bumped again in reply. "Go on, nobody cares, we're having plenty of fun without you!"

"Indeed we are. Can you imagine if that horrid old judge turned up at a party? Everyone would run off home!" *Unless you already were home,* as Cecily was. Raf settled back on the sofa, the plate resting on his knee. He picked up one of the lavender biscuits and held it to Cecily's lips.

She leaned toward Raf and slowly opened her mouth, her gaze fixed on his fathomless blue eyes. "Pop it in!"

With a smile of mischievous wonder he obeyed, something more than friendship brightening his gaze.

A tremble went through Cecily as she bit into the biscuit, which had nothing to do with her cooking. She desired Raf, and now she was sure that the feeling was returned. *I mustn't act on it, I must ignore it.* But what a thing it was, to be wanted.

"If you weren't with him," Raf said, "would you stay here at the school, or would you go off and see the world?"

"I would've gone, a long time ago." Cecily gave him a half-smile. "And if he dropped down dead tomorrow, then I'd pack my carpetbag and be out of here like a shot."

"I don't do too badly out of the gardening and the occasional supernatural house clearance keeps me in biscuits and beer," Raf explained. "But more often than not, a clearance means a *lot* of paperwork. Diaries, letters, archives, all that, and for a bloke who's word blind, that's a struggle. So if you ever find yourself in Yorkshire at a loose end and don't mind musty old documents and belligerent spooks, I could really use someone with your smarts."

"Really?" A whole new vista had opened up before Cecily, and she took another sip of her drink to steady herself. "I—I thought I'd have to be a housekeeper or a teashop waitress, or an old dear's companion. But I should much prefer that!"

"I get a lot of my work from word of mouth or Whitehall. The gardening as well as the ghosts," he explained. "And I advertise in the papers, that's how I met poor old Mr. Brennan." Raf swept up one hand in front of them, as though showing off a billboard.

"*Ghosts need laying? Rates negotiable on application.* We've been using the same ad for a century or more!"

"Certainly an unusual family business." Cecily beamed at Raf. "Are you sure you wouldn't mind me joining you, seeing as I'm not family? I can lend a hand with the gardening too, of course."

"You don't have to be family, you just have to be brave and smart. I qualify on brave but on smart?" He shrugged. "The jury's out. I make up for it with my good looks and modesty."

"You *are* smart. You're not like those people who think themselves clever but really aren't," Cecily said. "But I don't know if I'm brave. If I was, I would've left this place years ago."

"It's hard to leave the only place you've called home. I was fifteen when I lost Mum and every year we spent six months in Yorkshire, six in Romania. Everything about me was *old country*, but when the time came to choose where home was going to be, I surprised myself more than anyone." He held out the plate to her. "My head said, *you live in a castle, you'll want for nothing,* but in my soul…no contest. I love my house by the sea, with the lights at Filey twinkling way off in the dark. Home is where you make it."

Cecily pictured him peering out of the window of a fisherman's cottage, with the sound of the waves beating against the shore. "It sounds lovely! And you're right, you're quite right…" She cast a glance around the room. Evidence of Hugh was everywhere—the rigid armchair, the wedding photograph, his books, his choice of wallpaper. "This is where I live, but it's not really home. At least, it's not *homely*."

"Well, you know, there's only me rattling about back home." He shrugged. "If you don't mind a bit of mess and the odd engine part on the dinner table, you could stay with me if you like. Nothing untoward, I promise!"

Cecily patted his hand and glanced up at the ceiling. "That's so kind of you. Look…once we've sorted out all this business about ghosts and possessions, I'm going to do it, you know — I'm going to find a solicitor and I'm going to jolly well get shot of Hugh. Get a — y'know, a *divorce*." Cecily could barely say the forbidden word aloud. "But I'll need a friend and it won't be fair on Hattie, seeing as her husband has to work with Hugh. If you can help me at all — maybe you know of a super solicitor, I'm sure you must! — then I'll be grateful to you forever. I can't stay here, Raf. I don't want to be like my mother — she didn't so much pass away as fade to nothing."

"I once cleared a grumpy goblin with a chip on its shoulder for a London solicitor who buried some nasty rumors for the king himself," Raf assured her. "And I didn't charge him for landscaping his rockery, so he owes me one!"

"That would be marvelous, Raf!" Cecily squeezed his hand. "Thank you, you really are a wonderful chap."

"I've been lucky for a lot of my life. When we went into the chapel today and I saw all those names of the lads who didn't come back from the war…" He shook his head then kissed her hand. "What good is our rose garden if the gates are locked? If you want to go and live, Sissy Pincombe, then you're going to."

"You're right, you're absolutely, *devastatingly* right." Cecily rested her head on Raf's shoulder. She liked being close to him, to his scent of gardens and the outside. "Let's have another toast — you may need to top up my glass, though!"

With a laugh, he topped up both, then chose another chocolate lavender biscuit for Cecily and one for himself. "What're we toasting, Captain?"

"Freedom," Cecily told him. "In all its frightening and exciting glory!"

"Freedom!" Raf clinked their glasses together. "I can drink to that!"

Cecily took a larger swallow than she had intended to. "Whoops!" Yet Raf's reply was to down the contents of his glass in one gulp then pick up a fairy cake, as enthusiastic as a child on Christmas morning.

Cecily emptied her tumbler then picked up the bottle and refilled both her glass and Raf's. Lightheaded on both hope and țuică, she laughed, a raucous racket which set off a thud above their heads.

"Oh, do shut up, you tiresome bore!" she called. Raf let out a loud, heartfelt burst of laughter then clinked his glass with Cecily's again. How little power the spirit above seemed to have now, when all he could do was stomp and strut like an angry, chastised child.

Cecily rose to her unsteady feet. "I'm going to open a window…a bit of fresh air'll sober us up, won't it!" *Possibly not,* but it was worth a try. She crossed the room with careful deliberation, one foot in front of the other, and finally reached the curtains. "See, I didn't fall over!"

She twisted open the lock on the window and threw up the sash. It clattered and squeaked like an old guillotine as it shot up, and she grinned back at Raf as he laughed all the harder. "Ahhh, lovely fresh—oh good Lord!"

Down in the ghost garden, illuminated by the last scraps of daylight and the lights of the school that spread across the grass, Isabella had appeared once more.

Cecily heard the sound of Raf putting the plate down on the table then his bare feet on the rug. He was still chuckling but as he came to stand beside her he fell silent. Then he murmured, "So that's what our Isabella looks like."

"Yes, that's her." There was only silence from outside, no sound of sobbing accompanying Isabella now, nor the swish of her dark gown over the lawn. "See where she's walking? She's following the paths of the old garden."

"She looks like she means business," Raf said. He put his hand on Cecily's shoulder and asked, "What's the ring saying? We don't need a voice to talk, but only a few people have the gift to hear."

Cecily half-closed her eyes and turned the ring on her finger, again and again. She had grown so used to wearing it since Hugh's departure that morning that she'd worn it while baking and little bits of pastry had stuck to its stones. But somehow, it seemed apt rather than disrespectful, the ring from the soil domesticated. As she turned the ring, Cecily felt restless. Not the same emotion as earlier — not her cry for freedom. But something else.

"Discovering. Searching." The words left her lips without any thought. "She's looking for something. She wants us to look."

Down in the garden, Isabella had stopped pacing.

"Do we go down?"

"I think she wants us to. There's something in the garden. Something we can't see." Cecily turned toward Raf. In a voice that barely sounded like her own, she murmured, "Dark...so dark. Down in the soil."

"When the sun's gone, I'll go down and dig. When nobody can see." He squeezed her shoulder softly. "If anyone wants to know, there must be foxes out there somewhere."

"Shall I come with you?" Even as Cecily suggested it, she knew that wasn't such a great plan. "Although I suppose it might be...awkward if someone spots me outside with you. Because...well, you know what people are like."

"You can stay up here and watch me dig." He smiled. "Or watch the fox dig, of course!"

Cecily tapped the side of her nose. "Oh, yes, the fox! And will you be appropriately attired?"

"I'll put some boots on." He paused. "And probably take off this clean, if not pressed, shirt."

"That would be for the best. You wouldn't want to get it dirty, would you?" Cecily ran her fingertip over the collar of his shirt. Desire tightened inside her again.

But he's my friend.

"Why do you have to be so tall?" Raf murmured, turning to face her. "And so lovely?"

Cecily fanned herself with her hand. It was warm evening and she was blushing. "I'm not very tall when I sit down."

She followed Raf's gaze to the sofa as he observed, "It'll be another hour before it's dark enough to dig."

"Should we try your beer?" Cecily asked.

He nodded and took her hand, leading her back to the sofa. They sat a little closer this time, the feeling of warmth and happiness not entirely down to the alcohol. Cecily realized, as he took a bottle from the bag, that she had neglected to bring an opener from the kitchen. She was about to apologize and rush to fetch one when Raf, as though it were a perfectly normal occurrence, put the bottle between his teeth and popped the cap clean off.

Another unusual talent.

"Beer and orangey rock buns." He poured the beer into their tumblers. "And tall, lovely company."

Not wanting to look too unworldly, Cecily picked up her tumbler and took a confident swig of beer. The strong flavor took her by surprise. "How do you men drink this stuff as if it was water?"

"Practice," was his lofty reply. "I don't get through a lot of it, but the kettle's always on at home. Tea all day, a beer on the beach at night."

"Doesn't sound like a bad life." Cecily held out the plate of cakes to him. "But what about some biscuits and buns in that house of yours? They go very well with tea *and* with beer."

"I like the sound of that." He took two buns, passing one to Cecily. "I should warn you that I have a housekeeper who comes in a few days a week and thinks I'm beyond hope. She's older than the hills and twice as set in her ways. The two of you can gang up on me!"

"I'm determined to see how long it takes you to crease a perfectly ironed shirt. Ten minutes?" Cecily nibbled her bun. She'd followed the same recipe as she always used, but this evening it tasted different — decadent and luxurious in a way that no rock bun had any right to.

"Ten *seconds*." He took a bite of the bun and closed his eyes as he had before, reveling in the taste. Only when he had swallowed did he open his eyes and tell her, "I'll teach you to deal with spooks, you can teach me to bake for you?"

"That sounds fair!" The light caught Isabella's ring and Cecily felt a pang of guilt that she was so happy up here with Raf while Isabella had spent centuries in despair. But at least they had the chance now to make amends for the past. And perhaps this was what it had to take, Cecily and Raf together, the final pieces in a jigsaw that had lain unfinished for generations.

Perhaps this was her purpose.

Cecily and Raf drank beer and ate biscuits and buns, until finally the sounds of the school fell silent around them. The distant noise of water swishing through pipes and the drum of pupils' feet had stopped. Downstairs, the leaders of the future were lying under their gray blankets in the dorms. The masters were tucked up in their beds, smoking their pipes. Harriet, Cecily was sure, would be trying to get comfortable despite her helmet of pincurl clips. Just herself and Raf would still be up.

Cecily went to the window and the only light on the lawn fell from her parlor, her silhouette outlined on the lawn below. Even the little bats were nowhere to be seen and she wondered if they had stayed away because of Isabella's appearance. Somehow, it seemed as though those creatures of the night might be able to see the spiritual visitors that others couldn't.

"Time for me to get my boots on and hit the garden," Raf decided, finishing the remains of another biscuit. "If there's anything down there, I'm bringing it home."

"I've still got the torch from the caretaker's office. I'll fetch it for you."

"I can see without it." He grinned. "Some of us — *you*, for instance — can hear the echoes of those who have gone. *I* can see in the dark as well as a cat. We complement each other, you know, like chocolate and biscuits."

Cecily shivered as a sense of danger danced up her spine. "Be careful down there, won't you?"

"What do you think all those tattoos are for?" He winked. "I can see what's in front, they can watch my back."

Cecily clasped her hands. She wanted to pat his arm or take his hand or *something*, but instead she gave him a smile. "I'll see you later, then."

"You just keep an eye on that garden." He gave a polite bow. "I've a feeling Isabella won't be far away."

As soon as Raf had left, Cecily went to the window only to see that Raf was right. Isabella was standing on the same spot, her face turned up to the window. She didn't stir when Raf emerged, a spade over his strong shoulder like a rifle, nor did she seem to see him as he placed it on the grass and turned to give Cecily a thumbs-up. She could just see him in the darkness, his compact figure silvered by the moon as behind him the world fell away to night.

As Cecily watched him, she turned the ring and she saw Raf surrounded by neatly clipped hedges that had sprung back from the earth. The ghost garden as it had once been, but only a silvered memory of it that blurred as a breeze got up.

Someone had buried something there, long ago.

The ring was warm on her finger as Cecily gripped the windowsill, waiting for what Raf might find.

As Raf threw his shirt on the ground and put the spade to the grass where Isabella had indicated, it seemed as though a storm broke overhead. Cecily heard the judge thump and stamp, heard what must be his fists beat the cracking wall and heard, she was sure, a wheezing cry, as though the voice that was being raised in protest had long been silent. She breathed deeply and focused on Raf and Isabella, on those who had more than darkness in their hearts.

"My love, my secret," Cecily whispered to the night air.

Down in the garden, Raf toiled, a gray figure in the darkness. Beside him Isabella kept a silent vigil, looking up at the window still. On and on Raf went as the minutes ticked by. Then, as the bell chimed in the fearsome tower, he threw down the spade and dropped to his knees, thrusting his arms into the newly dug pit.

Cecily gripped the windowsill more tightly. The curtain billowed around her, but she barely noticed. All her attention was fixed on Raf as he reached into the ground.

Only then did Isabella seem to see him, as he lifted a dark bundle from the earth. For a terrible moment Cecily thought it was a baby, then he stood and held it above his head, triumphant.

A box.

Cecily leaned further forward, trying to get a better glimpse. Whatever was inside it, Isabella wanted them to see it. The ghost woman raised her head and Cecily at last saw her face. Not crying now, Isabella was wearing a tentative smile.

With the box on the grass, Raf began filling in the hole again. He moved fast, spurred on by the discovery and now and then, Cecily saw, he glanced up at the window where she stood.

Chapter Eleven

Cecily put the kettle on to boil. Beer and plum wine didn't seem like a good idea now, but the discovery of the box had sobered her up anyway. Tea. They needed tea.

Raf's knock on the door was light and tuneful and filled with promise, and Cecily hurried to open it. There he stood, half naked, the box under one arm and the spade under the other, his shirt thrown over one sculpted shoulder. His boots were beside the door, not neatly, she couldn't help but notice. He propped the spade beside them and said, "Delivery for the captain?"

"This is so exciting!" Cecily flung her arms around Raf's shoulders and hugged him, then quickly released him. "Sorry. But this *is* so exciting, isn't it! I hope it won't turn out to be someone's old trowel and a moldy packet of seeds."

"Don't you say sorry." He stepped over the threshold, the charms softly rattling. "I'll leave you to commune with the box while I go and have a wash. I'll even put my shirt back on since I'm in polite company."

"Please don't feel you ought to, if you're comfortable like that." Cecily was nothing if not accommodating to her guests. After all, she had so few of them. "But…people might talk. This box is locked, I suppose? I'll fetch a hair grip in readiness!"

"People," he said archly, "won't know. Where should I put it? It's pretty mucky."

"I'd dread to get mud on the carpet in the parlor — let's take a look at it in the storeroom! It's my old bedroom, actually, but it can be mucky in there without causing…difficulties." *And it's a perfect place for secrets.*

Raf followed Cecily to the room where he placed the unassuming box, still caked with earth, carefully atop newspapers she laid out for him. Then he was off again, following her directions to the bathroom with its clanking pipes and gurgling water.

She followed him and chose a towel from the cupboard. "There — use this one. It'll all go into the laundry tomorrow morning anyway. I hope you don't mind, there's only carbolic soap."

Cecily lay the towel down on the pedestal by the sink, then ran the hot tap. She caught their reflections in the mirror over the sink. It really needed a clean — how Hugh hadn't spotted it she couldn't imagine — but she struggled to see Raf's reflection and soon her own vanished behind a layer of condensation. "Sorry — it's getting a bit steamy!"

"No complaints from me," Raf teased, lowering his voice to an exotic growl before laughing. "Was she there still? Isabella? I heard him raising holy hell upstairs!"

"*He* didn't like it at all, which makes me all the keener to see what's in there. And Isabella stayed beside you all the time, and she looked at you — properly looked — when you took out the box. I saw her face! And she didn't look sad. Whatever is in there, she *wants* us to see." Cecily passed Raf the soap and a clean flannel. She would happily have scrubbed him clean herself but she wasn't quite sure she should. "She *needs* us to see it, Raf."

"I saw her properly tonight," Raf said. "He's already pretty strong, but she's getting stronger too because she's got you on her side — you're the first to hear her. The judge feeds off your husband's weakness but she needed the opposite. She needed strength. Someone who knew what she'd been through."

"We will stop Dr. James and the judge, won't we? He won't be framing *me* for murder, will he?" Cecily swirled her hand in the sink, then turned off the tap. "There we are, all ready for you to get cleaned up. Do let me know if you need...a hand?"

I really, really shouldn't. But all those years of never experiencing desire, never knowing what it was to find the man in her presence delectable had left Cecily, as she stood beside the shirtless Raf, with a deluge of emotion that she wasn't sure what to do with.

"We'll stop them." And there wasn't so much as a modicum of doubt in his voice. "I don't *need* a hand but if you're offering one, I'll happily take it. Digging's a hard business and I'm not used to being looked after!"

Cecily lathered up the flannel with the carbolic soap. The smell of tar filled the bathroom as Cecily brought the flannel toward Raf. "On your chest first?"

There's nothing wrong with lending a hand.

"Wherever you like," Raf replied. "I'm in your hands tonight."

Cecily let the flannel fall against his chest with a light slap, then she gripped the cloth and wiped it over him. Her traitorous body reacted at once, a delirious swooning sensation taking hold of her as she stroked his warm, firm body. No longer living in the shadows, Cecily hoped he would feel it in her, that need for him. That sinful need which she couldn't ignore any longer.

She could feel his heart beneath the flannel and it wasn't just beating, it was racing. Perhaps he was right and she *did* sense what others didn't, for she could feel heat in the air between them, desire like a thread connecting her body to his.

"Can I kiss you?" Raf asked, his voice low.

The flannel fell to the floor and Cecily's hand came to rest on Raf's chest, Isabella's ring tangling against the charms around his neck. "I wish you would. But ought we?"

"You're right." He nodded. "But maybe one day, if not tonight?"

Cecily let the tip of her nose brush his cheek as she continued to stroke his chest, without flannel or soap. Her lips tingled for want of him and she half-closed her eyes. "Is a kiss so very wrong?"

"Depends who's asking," Raf whispered.

Cecily touched her lips to Raf's cheek. She felt his stubble and tasted the salt of his skin. Desire shot through her and clumsily she brought her mouth to his. His arm slipped around Cecily's waist as he returned the kiss and a feeling of almost overwhelming emotion swept over her. This was how it felt to not be alone.

Trembling in every limb, Cecily sighed into their kiss as she stroked her other hand through Raf's roguishly untidy hair. He was strength and kindness all in one wonderful man.

"I'm not leaving here without you, Sissy." And she believed it. She believed it without a doubt.

"I can't stay here—not now. I don't belong here anymore." Cecily drew a shape on his chest with her fingertip, then stroked it up Raf's body to his chin. He was so lovely to touch, a playground to roam.

He kissed the tip of her finger then said, "You're lovely, you know."

Cecily blushed and glanced away from him, grinning. "You keep saying that, so it must be true, though I find it hard to believe! And you're lov—Oh God!"

A chill shot through Cecily, leaving her almost breathless. She'd only been there for a second, but the condensation on the mirror had cleared just enough to reveal Isabella standing behind them. Cecily turned round sharply and although there was now no one to be seen, Cecily knew that the time had come to stop.

"Did you see that? Did you see her? Isabella…standing right behind us."

Raf gave a good-natured sigh. "That's her way of saying *open that bloody box*, I expect. All right, boss, if you say so!"

Cecily untangled herself from Raf. She was too embarrassed to look him in the eye. "Best to put one's shirt on now," she said in an awkward sing-song voice.

"One still needs to have one's wash," he pointed out as he stooped to retrieve the flannel. "Look, I need to say this just so you know." He drew in a deep breath, holding the flannel in fingers that were still black from the garden. "Whatever you want when this is over, whether it's a mate to have a laugh with or someone to get all steamy with, I'll be waiting. I'm not going to let you down."

What a relief. At least that interlude hadn't ruined their friendship.

"Thank you. I hope you don't think I'm some sort of Jezebel after that...I've never—I got carried away." Cecily watched the bar of soap rock on the surface of the water. "I'll finish making the tea, and I'll see you in the storeroom once you've scrubbed up."

"I don't ever want to hear you say sorry again," he assured her gently. "And the next time you see me, I promise I'll be properly dressed. And properly dressed means no shoes, just so you know."

"Thank goodness you have very nice feet." Cecily gave him a grin, then went off to finish making the tea. She tried to focus on the familiar routine but how could she, when everything had shifted in a few simple seconds, when meek, boring Cecily had released the woman who had been wrapped and packed away like a piece of bone china? She could feel the firmness of his body under her hand and the softness of his lips against her own. The road that had been so mapped ahead of her had suddenly turned into a crossroads, and standing there waiting for her, a friend.

Rafael de Chastelaine, the gardener who was born in a castle, his compact body filled with energy and a spark like fire in his eyes.

And above her, the judge was silent.

The lacquered tea tray had once been her grandmother's and had never been replaced. Her mother had carried it every day of her married life, and Cecily had ever since her mother's death. Every day. And to think there might come a time now—soon— when she wouldn't see it again.

As Cecily went into what had once been her childhood bedroom, a pang claimed her. So much would change, would be lost. But it had to, because she couldn't go on. She had had a taste of what lay beyond Whitmore Hall, and she thirsted for it.

Cecily set down the tray and knelt on the bare floorboards beside the box. It had survived well in the earth, its wood still solid even though it was caked in the dirt of years.

"I hope you didn't open it without me," Raf joked as he padded along the hallway toward the storeroom that had been her childhood sanctuary. He *was* dressed now, just as he had promised he would be, but his shirt was loose rather than neatly tucked beneath his belt as Hugh's would have been and the round collar and cuffs were open. It was the sort of sight that these staid rooms were *not* used to seeing. He knelt beside her and she smelled the soap on his skin, mingling with that scent that was indefinably *his*.

Cecily pulled a hair grip from her fringe and passed it to him. "You found it — you should do the honors."

"This time, because I'm dying to see what's in there," he agreed. "But this is a skill I *will* teach you." With the grip between his finger and thumb, Raf rested his hand atop the box while with his other hand he took hold of one of the charms around his neck and mumbled a few words. Then he gave Cecily a shrug and said, "Just in case. Never know what might jump out."

Cecily gave a theatrical shiver. "I do hope whatever's in there has survived. Wouldn't it be sad if we opened it and found nothing but dust?"

"The ghost garden gives me a bit of hope that we're dealing with generous soil," he replied as he slid the bent grip into the lock. A small shower of earth tumbled down onto the newspaper and she watched in silence as Raf worked. It seemed to take forever, his eyes narrowed, his lip caught between his teeth in obvious concentration. All she could hear was the soft sound of the metal working against centuries of soil, but Cecily was sure that Raf would get the upper hand. And if he couldn't, they'd just find another way in.

It looked so plain to carry so much expected significance, though, just an old wooden box, a little bigger than one you might keep shoes in. There was nothing to mark it out as special, no elaborate decoration or mysterious runes, just the stained wood and the tarnished lock. No one would give it a second glance.

"That's it!" Raf exclaimed. He withdrew the grip and angled the box a little to face Cecily. "Do the honors, Captain."

Cecily took a deep breath. For Isabella's sake, she hoped there was something in there. Soil dropped off and skittered over the newspaper as Cecily prized open the lid. For the first time in who knew how long, the box's contents were exposed to the light and the living.

"Papers!" Cecily exclaimed. "Oh my, they've survived so well! Look, Raf, there's so many of them. Where do we start?"

She was tempted to upend the box and tip its contents across the floor, but even in her excitement, her caution stilled her. "Take one piece out at a time?"

"And they don't smell like a crypt." She could hear the relief in his voice. "You're in a select group, Sissy, you can hear the past. Is the ring giving you any clues? If not, let's try to be methodical."

"I think it might be, actually." Cecily stared down at the box's contents, all the scrolled and folded sheets of yellowed paper. "I thought it was just me being boring but actually, something's holding me back from tipping the whole lot out in one go. Something — *someone* — wants us to take our time. It's lain there a secret for so long."

"Your first investigation." Raf beamed and Cecily glanced to him. *The first of many,* she hoped. "Have at it."

"Let's start with a scroll first." Cecily pulled out a roll of paper that was tied with ancient string. "It looks like a treasure map, doesn't it!"

"X marks the spot?"

The string disintegrated as Cecily untied it and the scroll sprang open as if it could no longer bear to be hidden. Revealed for the first time in centuries was a drawing of a woman, a beautiful, well-executed portrait. She was looking up at the artist through a fringe of long eyelashes, her heart-shaped face framed by a tumble of ringlets. Even the intricacy of her lace collar had been picked out where it lay against her dark gown.

After an astonished pause, Cecily asked Raf, "You know who this probably is, don't you?"

"She's a heartbreaker." Raf smiled. "Look at those eyes."

"It's quite the flirty look, isn't it!" Cecily grinned at him. "As a man, Raf, if a woman looked at you like that, what would you think?"

"That she's the second-prettiest lass I've ever met!" He touched his fingertip lightly to the page. "And I'd think she must like me too."

Cecily beamed at Raf's compliment. "So Isabella's secret love was an artist? If he came to visit here because he was working on her portrait, and — oh my —

they fell in love! But quite a well-off sort of artist if he could afford a gold ring."

"That's a lot of gaps filled in from a drawing," Raf said gently. "Does the ring feel any different with the picture in front of you?"

"It feels...softer. As if she's happier. Wait..." Cecily looked closer at the drawing. The sitter's elegant hands were clasped on her lap. "Isn't that...isn't that the ring on her finger there?"

He nodded. "So how the hell did it end up in the rose garden? What exactly did she say in your séance?"

Cecily thought back to the evening at Harriet's séance. It seemed so long ago. "She said, '*Keep it safe, keep it from him.*' The ring, I should think. Then '*Find me,*' and...and something about wanting to '*rest as one*'."

"I don't know about you, but I don't think that '*resting as one*' is about a ring." He took Cecily's hand and lifted it, studying the ring. "'*Keep it safe*', on the other hand..."

"That definitely *is* about the ring." Cecily glanced up at the ceiling. "I do keep it safe. I only wear it when Hugh's not about. The rest of the time, it's in the hidey-hole. Hugh's never found it — and nor did my father. I keep that lotion you gave me in there too!"

"It's good stuff, isn't it? I've got funny skin, I make a lot of potions and lotions." Raf smiled. "All homegrown ingredients, planted by me and Mum."

Cecily gazed at Raf, captivated by his lively smile. She had to force herself to return her attention to the box. "There's another sheet of paper here. Let's put Isabella aside for a moment and see what's underneath."

With great care, Cecily placed the old drawing on the floor, away from the dirt of the box. There, looking back at her from the paper, was the drawing of a man. Raf was silent, studying the image. Then he took it from her and set it down next to Isabella, the torn edges lining up perfectly.

Cecily clapped. "They match! And he's certainly not the judge, is he? He's not a bad-looking chap."

"Not as good as this Romanian I can think of but..." He winked. "Is this our pauper artist? He doesn't say pauper to me!"

"No, he's not as handsome as that Rafael de Chastelaine I'm acquainted with..." Cecily returned Raf's wink. "But no, he doesn't look like a pauper at all. That lace collar probably cost a fortune, and he's wearing rings. Neat and tidy hair, and he looks quite happy with things. Especially with Isabella!"

Raf was silent as he studied the images, his finger tapping his chin thoughtfully. Cecily wondered what he was thinking, because she could almost see the cogs turning. He hunkered down, his face inches from the paper, his bottom rather prominent, though Cecily did her best not to notice.

But how can I not?

"This man, whoever he is, drew these pictures," he told her eventually, sitting up again. "Look at her. Beautiful, ideal, not a hair out of place, and look at him. Stubble, laughter lines, even a little scar here and there. He's captured himself warts and all, as they say."

"I hadn't thought of that, I just thought him rather rugged." Cecily turned pink. "But yes, I definitely see what you mean."

The ring was warmer on her finger now and Cecily turned it. "I think Isabella's happy to see these pictures again."

"We're doing our bit for chivalry," he observed softly, still studying the drawings. "Look at how their gazes line up, each looking at the other. I see two people in love. Am I just letting my romantic side run away with me?"

Cecily knelt beside him and rested her chin on his shoulder. "I don't think you are at all. They *do* look like they're in love. I've seen Hattie and Graham exchange glances like that! Is there a name anywhere? Did he sign his drawings?"

"One day, I hope someone looks at me like that. Bloody hell, I *am* an old romantic," Raf admitted, his gaze lingering on the drawings. "No signature, as far as I can see."

"Maybe someone will give you that look," Cecily said, half to herself. She turned her head and her cheek rested against Raf's shoulder. It felt so comfortable, so *right*. But she sat down again instead, breaking contact. It wasn't fair to be close to him if she couldn't offer him anything else. "Shall we see what's in the rest of the box?"

"I think Isabella would want you to do the honors," he decided. "Besides, *word blindness* and old papers aren't always a happy twosome. If I'd had my way, I wouldn't have learned to read at all but Mum wasn't having that — thank God!"

Cecily ruffled his hair. "Right…let's see what all these bits of paper are. Pour some tea, Raf, and settle in for your bedtime story."

Cross-legged, Cecily sat beside the box and took the first folded paper she came to. Unfolding it was a fraught task, and age had weathered small holes into the corners. But once she had opened it, she saw exactly what it was.

"A letter! What beautiful cursive writing. Sent from Exeter, to Isabella. *My dear Isabella…*" Cecily glanced up from the paper. "I do so wish to read it, but I feel as though I'm prying."

"You've gone all proper and queen-like again," Raf teased. "If you don't want to, we can come back to it. I don't want you to feel awkward, but she showed us where to dig for a reason."

"Yes, she did..." Cecily had the vague impression that Isabella was there in the room with them. Not just because her portrait was there, or her letters. But her presence, which was becoming stronger all the time. Cecily began to read again. *"My dear Isabella, I write to you from my inn at Exeter. I cannot express the longing in my heart for you. Oh, that we are separated from one another again. We shall be together soon, my love, my secret – "*

Cecily gasped. "Raf!"

But Raf didn't answer, because he was looking at her just as the unknown man was looking at Isabella in the drawing that somebody had torn in half. Then he blinked and said, "She couldn't even wear the ring he gave her."

"Poor woman. Oh, it really is so sad." Cecily's vision was clouded with rising tears, but she brushed them away. "We'll make it better. Won't we? We'll try, at least. *We shall be together soon, my love, my secret. Once more, I shall scatter kisses o'er your sweet face. Once more we shall... Oh, my word."*

"Come on, Captain, you've gone red." Raf took the letter from her with great care. A few moments passed as he sized up the impressive handwriting, then he cleared his throat and said, "Earthy bloke in spite of the lace! *Once more we shall shelter beneath our roses. My love – "*

This time it was Raf's turn to blush, but he went on in that decadent, exotic voice of his. *"My Isabella, my life, a thousand times I have heard your voice, a thousand times did I kiss you and by God, I long to see you ride astride me again as we did by midnight's moon."*

Cecily hid her face in her hands. "My goodness, that's the sauciest thing I've ever heard!" She dropped her hands and grinned at Raf. "That does mean what I think it means, yes?"

Raf blinked, all innocence. "I don't know, what do you think it means? I'm pretty innocent, me."

Cecily primly folded her arms. "Bedroom activities. I've heard of people doing that—and yes, I'm sure that must surprise you, but I *have*. There's a book in the school library on a very high shelf about designs on Greek and Roman pottery. Its cover looks terribly dull, but my goodness, its plate section is eyebrow-raising!"

"*Ride astride,*" he repeated. "I'm not as innocent as all that."

"It…it must have been a very passionate affair." Cecily tried not to look at Raf but her glance crept back to him and she peered at him through her eyelashes. She thought of him, lying on his back, his shirt open, his charms a tangle against his chest, and desire trembled through her. "With all that…erm…*astriding.*"

"It must," he murmured, meeting her gaze. "It sounds wild."

"Doesn't it." Cecily drew a circle on the back of his hand with her fingertip. "What else does the letter say?" She didn't want to admit it, but she hoped there was more sauciness in it. Not just because it gave her a thrill to hear Raf read it out, but because she was glad that although Isabella's life had been cut short and her end tragic, she had *lived*, even for a short while.

"*Shelter beneath our roses,*" Raf repeated. "So they made love in our rose garden, beneath the moon." He looked down at the page again and cleared his throat. *"Last night I dreamed that you came to me in this mean room and laid with me. We swore ourselves to each other and gave our bodies freely—"* Raf shifted a little, a fresh flush on his cheeks. *"How sweet you—* Should I keep going? I don't want you to feel awkward!"

"I'm a married woman, Raf," Cecily said importantly, but she was sure he'd see through her bluster. There was a great difference between lying with someone out of duty and lying with someone out of desire. And love. One day, Cecily hoped, she would experience it for herself. "Go on. Let me guess, does he say something about her bosoms?"

"Bullseye!" He laughed. *"How soft the milk white skin of your bosom, how sweet the tender bud of ecstasy, pink and pretty as a rose. How I long to kiss that bud again, my love, my secret."* Cecily saw Raf's eyes widen momentarily, then he looked at her and murmured, "That bit's not about bosoms."

Cecily frowned. The image in her mind of the female anatomy was suddenly rather askew. "So he's not talking about her...you know...*nipple*? That's very odd, Raf. I can't think what else it could be."

"You," Raf laughed, "are trying to make me blush! And they say *I'm* earthy!"

"You *are!*" Cecily giggled, elated at the freedom of discussing such things with a man. "And your nipples are very nice indeed. Very firm."

"Is that right?" He glanced down at his creased shirt. "So they're up to your high standards, Captain?"

"I'm not much of an expert, not really! But they felt nice when I was...washing you." Cecily grinned. "Sorry. Weren't we dreadfully naughty in the bathroom!"

"What's life without a bit of naughty? Isabella and her artist would agree with me!"

"I'm sure they would. But we must be careful." Cecily stroked the back of his hand again, then slid her fingers through his. "What other naughty things does the artist say?"

"*The plan is made—* Bloody hell, they were leaving!" He held the page closer. "*When I return, we fly far from the judge's lair. What dreams we will live, o'er the hills and safe, blanketed by kisses, held safe by love. And how I will kiss that bud into bloom.*"

Cecily exhaled a happy sigh and tightened her clasp on Raf's hand. "I'll pretend they did get away, and they were happy and nothing awful ever happened to them. Oh, Raf, it's so sad! But saucy all the same!" That *bud* again. The artist must've meant Isabella's lips, of course.

"I can't not put this right," Raf admitted softly. When he spoke again, Cecily heard determination in his voice. He really *was* a romantic. "Wherever they are, we need to lay them to rest. The thought of all this love, all this passion, ending like it did… They needed each other, Sissy, they still do."

Unable to look away from him, Cecily replied, "Oh, yes, you're quite right."

"We'll mend this, Isabella," Raf told the room. "No matter what, you'll be with your lover."

Cecily turned. Something—*someone*—had brushed past her. "Raf, I just felt her go by. I felt the hem of her gown, I'm certain of it."

"She's getting stronger," he said, excitement sparkling in his eyes. "We'll find her and whatever we have to do to lay her to rest with her lover, we'll do it.

And when that's done, Sis, you start whatever life you want to start, promise me?"

Cecily nodded. "Away from here. Away from...*him*. Yes, I promise. Maybe I'll give beastie hunting a go with you first."

"It's a deal." He laughed and lifted her hand to kiss it, then looked to the letter again. "Whoever this *C* was, he loved her. Bud and all. Do you think *he* was the murdered man?"

"It would make sense, wouldn't it? The judge would've been furious — I imagine he didn't find *these* letters, as a man like him would doubtless have thrown them on the fire and made Isabella watch them burn." Cecily could see the heat of the flames distorting Isabella's face. Perhaps it really had happened, somewhere in this house. "But he could easily have found something else — some other letters like this, or they were caught *in the act* and that would have been enough for him to want rid of Isabella. In the cruelest way he could engineer."

"Someone tore the picture in two. I wonder why." Raf shook his head. "So let's piece together what we know. Isabella is married to the judge, but in love with an artist. The judge somehow finds out and, what, murders the lover in a jealous rage? Then he thinks, *two birds, one stone*. He charges Isabella with the crime and executes her, then has her buried God knows where. Then he admits what he did before promptly dying."

Raf paused and Cecily saw him bite his lip, sensing his anger at the injustice. "You know what really gets on my wick? He got away with it." He looked up at the ceiling and told the clocktower, "I hope she made your life bloody miserable, you rotten old bastard, and I hope it's hot where you are right now."

"She hounded him, didn't she? All the times I've heard her weep, and I've seen her by my bed—now imagine her doing that to someone she had reason to despise." Cecily shivered. "Relentless, she must've been. Every time he glanced up, every time he heard the slightest unexpected noise—the wife he had killed would've been there, judging *him* and finding him wanting."

"And now she's earned her rest with the man who loved her." He twined his fingers with Cecily's. "We have to find Isabella, Sis."

Chapter Twelve

Letter after letter emerged from the box, each as loving and as saucy as the last. Cecily kept herself and Raf fueled on tea as the clock above chimed through the hours. She rested her head on Raf's shoulder, and as Isabella's lover spoke of kisses and caresses, she thought back again and again to her moment with Raf. No wonder Isabella and her lover had risked so much — Cecily knew now what it was to want someone.

The letters of C, filled with buds and bloom and bosom, took on a new life when spoken by Raf. She heard his breath catch, heard the heat that the writer had intended and felt the passion in the air between them.

In the box, Cecily found letters from Isabella to the mysterious C. She marveled at how a woman who had been so oppressed by her domestic life could seem so cheerful in her letters, but perhaps her writing gave her a much-needed escape. And Cecily most certainly could relate to that.

"*I walked our beloved garden this morning. The buds are growing and when you return they will bloom, I assure you. You will not be away for long, I pray you? My thoughts are always filled with you, my good, upstanding man.*" Cecily saw a grin appear on Raf's face. "So he might've been quite an important gentleman, then?"

"Good and upstanding, just like me," he agreed loftily, apparently choosing to ignore the double meaning. "No word on *his* nipples, yet, though."

"Not as such... She continues, *So often have I fallen to my knees to receive your blessing* – Raf, was he a clergyman?" But even as Cecily asked this, one of the images from the forbidden book of Greek and Roman pottery came back to her. "Oh no, could she mean she kissed him on his..." Cecily focused all her attention on the paper as her cheeks reddened. "*Down there?*"

"*Down there,*" Raf confirmed. "Just like I thought, sex. And love too. All they wanted was time and each other."

"They really were quite a couple, weren't they!" Cecily traced her fingertip down the torn divide of their portraits. "Raf, will you look after the box? I'd hate for anything to happen to these letters and drawings now that we've found them, but the hidey-hole is too small for the box. Look."

Cecily levered up the inconspicuous loose floorboard and gestured to the narrow space it revealed. Raf peered down into the gloom then nodded his understanding.

"I'll take care of it."

"Thank you." Just as Cecily was about to slot the floorboard back into place, the silver glitter of her mother's locket caught her eye. She pulled it up to the light and nudged it open with her thumbnail. "I'd like to show you this. Meet Sandy and little Cec."

She held the locket open on her palm, showing Raf the photographs it contained. Sandy in a straw boater and sailor suit, a beaming grin lighting up his round face. Cecily in the other half of the locket, unsmiling as she always was in photographs, her untidy hair escaping its ribbons. She watched Raf as he looked at the locket, seeing her and Sandy as her husband never had. What a somber child she was, what a smiling boy beside her in the locket.

"Look how alike you are, you could be twins," he said gently. "I wish I could bring Sandy back to you, Sissy. I can't imagine how alone you must've felt without him here."

"He volunteered, you know. He wanted to leave, and he knew it was dangerous. And yes, I miss him every day, but it comforts me to know that he had that life — freedom, of sorts." Cecily glanced around the room, where the utilitarian bunk beds had once stood. In the games she had played with Sandy they had become a castle or a pirate ship. "We used to sit in the orchard and read to each other. And play cricket — sometimes with the fallen apples, and we laughed like drains when they burst open as we hit them with the bat! I like to go there sometimes. I tell Hugh that I'm picking fruit, but he doesn't know I'm thinking of Sandy."

"It's a peaceful place," Raf observed. And for the first time the joyless flat felt like a peaceful place too, filled with the memory of her brother and the warmth of their friendship. "That war was…" He fell silent and shook his head, then decided, "What a bloody waste, eh?"

Cecily nodded. She laid her hand on Raf's. "Did your family… Did you lose anyone, Raf?"

"Me and my brother were lucky—we came out the other side. Mike's a vicar... Served as a chaplain. He doesn't like to talk about those years much but, yeah." He drew in a long sigh of resignation. "We lost too many on both sides of the family. *One* is too many. In Romania, it feels like every family you meet lost a boy to the Eastern front.

"For every hundred men you talked to over there, ninety-nine didn't know what the hell they were fighting for. And what *was* it? A playground spat between their *betters*, men who were too proud to shake hands and put away their sabers." Raf fell silent and she saw his Adam's apple bob when he swallowed. He pinched his fingers to the bridge of his nose then smiled, but his blue eyes clouded with sadness. "Is there any wonder those lads looked for angels in the trenches?"

"The Angel of Mons?" Cecily had read about it in the newspapers. "Did you see any, Raf?"

"What was at Mons wasn't an angel, but if it helped the blokes out there to think it was... Let them have their angel." He shrugged and squeezed her hand. "That was my war—flitting between battalions trying to separate truth from imagination."

"You must have seen... It must've been a very difficult job." Cecily kissed his cheek. "But thank you. For going out there."

"And one day, the blokes in charge will do it again." Raf shook his head. "When they do, I'm having no part of it—my days of flitting about battlefields are done. I'll be forty in a few years, so my life's gardening and ghosts nowadays."

"Hopefully a lot safer!" Cecily didn't want to lose Raf now that she'd found him. "Are the ghosts ever dangerous?"

"Not as often as the living." He let his gaze settle on the locket again. "When this is done, when you're ready to leave, bring everything that's precious. It doesn't matter how much you've got, bring it all."

"You're holding it," Cecily told him. "I had to hide the locket because Father said it was maudlin to keep mementos of Sandy—he threw the other photographs away. Or at least, he told me he did, and I've never been able to find them."

In the clocktower, the first chime of midnight sounded and Raf said, "Why don't you put your locket on and give me a nighttime tour of your favorite garden spots? He won't ring now, will he?"

"No, Hugh won't. I imagine by now he'll be happy in the arms of his floozy." Although, as Cecily closed the locket and fastened the necklace around her neck, she realized she was in no position to call another woman a *floozy*. "Right—time for a midnight stroll through the orchard."

"See, how is it that I'm single and miserable old Hugh's got a wife like you *and* a floozy?" Raf rose to his feet and gallantly helped Cecily to hers. "Is it because he's ridiculously tall? It's not his looks or personality!"

Cecily snorted with laughter. "No, indeed not! Maybe he shows a different side of himself to the *ladies*? He has a very…demanding view of how a wife should be, which I doubt extends to his mistress." It still hurt to think of it, but Cecily was glad she had found her husband out. Because Hugh, in his selfishness, had given Cecily her escape route.

"I'm a gent, so I won't say anything about the ladies concerned, but if you were waiting for me at home?" Raf offered his arm to Cecily. "If you needed proof that the bloke's not all there, that's it."

Cecily took Raf's arm, not in the least awkward as their shoulders brushed together. "You're ever so charming, Raf." Her voice caught, but she had to ask him. "Can you wait for me?"

"I told you, I'm not going anywhere," was his gentle reply. "You're not alone anymore."

Cecily kissed his cheek again, his stubble rasping lightly against her lips. Arm-in-arm, they set off for the garden through the silent school. She heard only the gentle pad of Raf's bare feet next to her own plain shoes as they went and, when he turned the heavy key and opened the door that led them outside, a cool breeze disturbed the still summer night. The stifling weeks that had brought forth the ghost garden, it seemed, were soon to be chased away by autumn.

They crossed the lawn and went across the pale outline in the grass with the freshly turned pile of earth, passing the silent walls of the rose garden. Trimmed shrubs and firs and hedges created a frame for the gardens, and Cecily led Raf through an archway of branches. On the other side, with a backdrop of stars, stood the orchard.

"Here we are," Cecily told him, only now daring herself to speak. She was sure Raf would have already found the spot, where fruit was almost ready on each branch. He closed his eyes and took a deep breath of the night air, his chest rising and falling as he did. Then those bright blue eyes opened again and settled on Cecily.

"Thank you for trusting me," Raf said.

Cecily smiled at him. "Thank you for *seeing* me."

"You're impossible to miss."

Cecily strolled through the orchard on Raf's arm. The boughs above were heavy with pears and apples. "I've felt quite invisible for a very long time. Just sort of existing. And you've made everything come alive."

Even the dead.

"There's an orchard at home too." He let his head rest on her shoulder for a moment. "I thought we could plant a tree for Sandy."

"I'd like that." Cecily ruffled his hair affectionately. "Can we take a cutting from one of these?"

"Consider it done."

Cecily grinned as she kissed his cheek. As she moved away, she paused, the tip of her nose against his. She swept her thumb over his full lips and in that brief touch felt again the memory of their forbidden embrace.

"One more kiss?" Raf asked. "Before I go back to waiting?"

"Why not?" They wouldn't go too far. Just a kiss. Even if all those letters full of longing and lust had made her feel peculiar — made her recognize an urge within her to be loving and reckless in equal parts. Raf put his hand on her face then pressed his lips to Cecily's, kissing her with a tenderness that was still filled with heat.

Cecily slipped her arms around him, holding him tight as she responded to his kiss. The affection and kindness in Raf drew her out of the shell she had built around herself. Clumsy before, she was more confident now, and mirrored Raf — the angle of his head, the gentle darting of his tongue.

She heard her breath quicken in time with Raf's and the soft sigh of pleasure in his throat. And it was for her, those little sounds of wonder were because of her touch. She wasn't invisible after all.

Cecily caressed him, exploring his strong back through his shirt, picturing the tattoos that decorated and protected him. She rested her hands on his waist to avoid traveling any farther down his body, though that firm bottom of his tempted her. One day, they might go to bed together, and the thought sent a thrill through her, which she was certain Raf couldn't have missed.

In reply, Raf's free hand settled on the base of Cecily's back and that *one* kiss deepened just a little, telling her that he shared that delicious thrill. It seemed as if the whole world was asleep, as though the long, secret hours of darkness were theirs alone to share.

Maybe Isabella and her lover had come out here at night too, when the grandparents of these trees stood in the orchard. With a giggle in her throat, Cecily thought of the rose garden—they'd certainly kissed each other there. Maybe that was when Isabella had dropped her ring, in the throes of their heated passion. And it had been left for Cecily to find, all these years later, with her own secret love in her arms.

"What're you giggling about?" Raf asked, kissing his way along her jaw. "Sounding all mischievous and saucy."

"Do I?" Cecily glanced at him. "I was thinking of…you'll think I'm a fruity sort, but I was thinking of Isabella and her *amour* in the rose garden. I suppose there can't have been many roses in there then, otherwise how did they avoid the thorns?"

"Too busy with the buds," he murmured as he nuzzled her throat.

Cecily stroked through his hair. "The impure Puritans!"

"The best kind," Raf concluded.

Cecily rested her hands on his shoulders then swept them down across his back. "You feel very nice," she told him. "You smell very nice, too. Of gardens."

And of carbolic soap, but Cecily decided not to broach that. Besides, it smelled nice on Raf, that tarry smell mingling nicely with his earthy scent.

"You smell of orange blossom," Raf replied, the scent an unexpected one. "And baking. If I could bottle that scent, I'd be a happy bloke."

"It's those rock buns," Cecily told him. "I was grating oranges all afternoon—well, it felt like it anyway. I grazed my knuckles, and I put on your lotion, and look—not a scratch!" She held her hand out for him to see. She knew he could, even though it was almost dark.

"A little bit of natural magic." He took her hand and kissed it. "My garden's a bit less ornamental than yours, it's the garden version of me. I hope you'll like it, though, it's like walking into a rainbow."

"I'd be disappointed if it wasn't!" Excitement gripped Cecily—freedom was at last within her grasp. "If only we could run away tonight, and I'd never see Hugh ever again. Wouldn't that be marvelous? Then I'd see your garden before winter sets in. I know we can't leave yet, though... Too much is unfinished."

"You'd never forgive yourself if you did. I don't think Isabella's got anybody but us just now."

"We can't let her down. And we can't let the boys down, either, nor the masters." Cecily heard steely determination edging her usually soft voice. "There's something horrible in this place—there has been for centuries—and we can put it right."

"Think of it like cleaning up an infestation." He looked round toward the clocktower and added, "Getting shot of a pest."

Cecily followed his gaze to one of the small round windows beneath the clock face, above the yawning crack. She stared in mute horror at what she saw, the sweetness of their evening vanishing in a moment. The windows had never shown anything but darkness yet now the pane was illuminated with a pale, red glow and there, splayed against it, she could make out the fingers of a withered hand, like the limbs of a monstrous spider. Someone was watching them from that empty, bleak place and one day, Cecily knew, that door would have to be opened.

"He must know she's getting stronger," Raf whispered. "I'm going to keep a sharp eye on your husband. Any trouble, you shout for me and put as much distance between the two of you as you can, as fast as you can."

"I will." Cecily nodded firmly, despite her fear. "But what if that hideous thing saw us out here?"

"Do you know what I think?" Raf said as the red glow faded. "I think it's as good as blind, it's like some ancient old creaking thing. It never speaks unless it's through somebody else and if you had one good eye and one blind, why put the blind eye to the keyhole? I need to go up into that tower, but I don't want to let anything out until I *have* to."

"But I heard him, you know, while you were digging outside." Cecily shivered. "His footsteps thudded away—he sounded furious, then I heard *him*. It was a horrible noise, a dry, wheezy croak. If Isabella is getting stronger, then is he too? Oh, if I hear him speak, if I hear words coming from him up there, I'll be too scared to scream!"

"He's pretty strong already. He hasn't had to take the time to get his hooks into someone who's weak but basically harmless." Raf slipped his arm around Cecily's waist and steered her back beneath the tree she had led him to. "He chose your husband, so it's one nasty bastard attaching to another. But he's still bound to the tower for some reason. That's why I'm in no hurry to open the door."

"Maybe it gives him a good view of the grounds. At least, maybe it did before his sight clouded over." Cecily was tempted to poke out her tongue in the direction of the clocktower, but even if the murderous judge couldn't see her, it still seemed sensible not to rile him. "Best keep him up there, horrible man!"

"What time's Hugh back tomorrow? Do we have time to go and look at our unnamed artist's grave?"

"Hugh said he'd be back late. If we nip out first thing, we should be all right. But we can't walk out of here together—we'll go separately, then meet at the churchyard." Cecily hesitated. "If—if you know the way?"

"I'll find it." Raf stroked his thumb down her cheek. "That locket's almost as pretty as you."

Cecily clasped it, the oval of silver reassuring in her hand. "It's not quite that amazing tangle you wear, though!"

He stooped to kiss her hand as it held the locket. As he stood, he told her, "One day, we'll go somewhere really special and I'll buy you something shiny to wear with that locket. Anything you want."

"Really?" Cecily almost bounced on her toes with glee. "You're the best pretend Latin master I've ever met!"

"These lads better hope Bren's back soon, or the future leaders of Britain are going to be useless when it comes to reading the classics." Raf laughed. "And twenty years from now they'll look at each other in the House of Commons and say, *I don't reckon Raf de Chastelaine was a teacher at all!*"

"When they make Home Secretary and have to hire you to sort out a demon running riot in Trafalgar Square, turning the lion statues into real ones, they'll definitely be glad you're not a teacher!" Cecily growled softly in her throat.

"With you right next to me!" He caught his arms around her waist and twirled them as though they were dancing. "And plenty more of those gorgeous growls when we get home!"

Home for Cecily at that moment, though, was the headmaster's rooms. No matter how much she dragged her feet on the way back upstairs, they would have to part. But not forever.

At the front door, Cecily whispered, "Good night, Raf. And do take care of the box — I know you will."

"Do you want me to sleep on the sofa? That's not an awkward pass, it's a genuine offer." Raf blushed just slightly and, as Cecily noticed was his habit at these bashful moments, scrubbed his hand through his tousled hair.

"I'd feel safer if you did, it's true." Cecily almost touched his chin but she lowered her hand. Just in case anyone was about. "But only if you're sure that in the morning you can get back to your room without anyone noticing."

"Saturday?" He quirked his eyebrow. "There'll be nobody around until breakfast and I'll stick a note under Graham's door saying I've had to nip into town. Nobody'll see me leave."

That decided her. "All right, then. I'll fetch you some bedding and make up a bed for you."

"You can fetch the bedding but leave the housework to me. You get off to bed."

Cecily rounded up a pillow, a sheet and a blanket. She brought them into the lounge and set them down on the sofa. "Good night, darling," Cecily said, and hugged him.

"Good night, *dragă*." He held her close. "Sweet dreams."

Chapter Thirteen

The next morning, Cecily blinked herself awake as she recalled what had happened the day before.

And Raf slept on the sofa.

She hurried into her dressing gown and slippers and bounded through the lounge door as eager as a puppy, only to discover that Raf had left.

As he'd had to do.

The bedding Cecily had given him was neatly folded on the sofa, topped with the plumped pillow. The box was gone too but he had left something in its place, a plate containing a selection of the treats she had baked for them to share.

A Raf breakfast, she surmised.

And it was the best breakfast she'd ever had.

Cecily sang to herself as she tidied the rooms, not a crumb missed. Hugh might spot something — he always did — but he wouldn't see any evidence that there had been any man there.

With her cloche hat pulled low over her face, Cecily headed to the village. Although her heart was hammering at the thought of seeing Raf again, and with the mystery of the artist to unravel, she walked with all the calm she could muster. No one seeing her by accident should be able to tell that she was doing anything other than going on a rather boring shopping trip in the village. She'd even slung her basket over her arm. Yet how free she had been last night, the silver locket around her neck and the ring on her finger as Raf spun her in his arms beneath the moonlight.

And all that talk of buds!

The locket was back in the hidey-hole under the floorboards, and although the ring was still on Cecily's finger, she hid her hand in her pocket. Her journey to the village took less time than usual — or, at least, seemed to. The ring was warm on her finger, and Cecily suspected that someone had helped her on the way.

Cecily paused by the gate into the churchyard. She looked back along the empty lane. "Don't worry, Isabella, we'll find you both," she promised.

"Mrs. James?" She'd know Raf's voice anywhere, but the one thing she wouldn't have known, had this not been planned, was that this meeting wasn't entirely accidental. He strolled out of the church in his crumpled suit, entirely missing the hat her husband would have insisted upon a master wearing on such an outing. Beneath his arm was tucked Isabella's box. "I thought it was you!"

Cecily took two hurried steps, then forced herself to go slowly, even though it was agony to see him standing so close to her but untouchable all the same. "Good morning, Mr. de Chastelaine. What a surprise to bump into you here."

"My brother's a clergyman. I thought I'd better at least pay a visit." He winked as they drew closer. "Fancy a wander with a rogue Romanian?"

"I wouldn't mind at all!" Cecily drew her hand from her pocket and the ring caught the sunlight. To anyone else, it would have seemed such an ordinary meeting, but Cecily felt an urgency that was not all her own. Lowering her voice, she told Raf, "It's the ring, Raf, it's tugging, like a piece of metal trying to reach a magnet."

"Let her lead," Raf suggested. "And if you're wondering, I've found a hiding spot for our box with my gardening gear — it fits right in. Did you get your breakfast?"

"I did, thank you — I should have more breakfasts like that. Much more exciting than bread and marg!" Cecily smiled politely for the benefit of anyone who might see them, but her arm lifted of its own accord — or perhaps the ring's — and a sharp pull forced her onward. "My word, Raf, she's so strong now!"

"I have that effect on women," he replied mischievously. "You smell even sweeter today. Like a spring morning."

The ring jerked Cecily forward again, like a keen dog pulling on a lead. "I must look ridiculous, Raf, like I'm pointing my way across the churchyard!"

"When we're working together, you'll see weirder than that!"

Cecily saw the churchyard in a flash of white stone crosses and angels. Then came nineteenth-century box tombs, and the ring dragged her farther. Gray, mossy eighteenth-century headstones showing winged hourglasses and dancing skeletons loomed toward her, but the ring was insistent — farther and farther it led her, until she and Raf rounded the corner of the church and found themselves on its north side. Cecily shivered — the sun rarely fell here and a chill always hung in the air.

"Show us, Isabella," Raf urged quietly. "Take us to your love."

Cecily stumbled in the long, unmown grass as the ring yanked her forward again. On the far side of the churchyard, by the low stone wall, Cecily spotted a woman tending a grave. "I'll have to apologize to that poor lady. This must appear terribly undigni — "

But then she realized who it was.

Isabella.

And Raf saw her too, she knew that from the gasp of surprise he gave. There she was in the hazy September sunlight, as solid as Cecily and Raf.

"This is — " Raf whispered. "They don't travel often, Sissy, this is amazing."

"Was it the ring? It was only after I found it — or it found me — that I saw her. And now we're here with the ring, and she is too." Cecily grasped for the church's stone buttress and propped herself up on it as she watched the stooping figure in black. Cecily held back tears that didn't seem to be her own — they came from something old, hidden away from the light for too long. "Isabella's mourning."

Raf nodded, watching the phantom. He reached for Cecily's hand and clasped it gently, sending a new wave of emotion washing over her.

"He's buried there, isn't he? Her secret C." Cecily leaned against Raf, drawing strength from him rather than the stone. "We need to see the grave."

"Take care on this uneven ground," Raf told her as they picked their way toward the spirit. A simple enough sentiment but one which Cecily was utterly unfamiliar with. How long had it been since anybody had shown such gentle care for her?

The long grass hid forgotten stones, broken vases and a headless angel. Each bump underfoot was either a rabbit warren or a reminder that people were buried here — the suicides, the excommunicated, the unbaptized.

And Isabella's secret love.

Cecily was glad that Raf was with her. His concern and affection for her softened Isabella's desolation, which dripped on Cecily like rain. Still the ring dragged her on, ever nearer to the wronged woman and her lover's resting place. Isabella didn't turn, only remained where she was, her shoulders heaving as though she were weeping.

Brambles and grass had climbed over the wall from the field beyond and had spread into the churchyard, and in the undergrowth something skittered away — a bird or a rabbit, Cecily had no idea. *Ashes to ashes, dust to dust.* Nature reclaims everyone in the end, but not always the spirit, Cecily realized.

They were so close to Isabella now that a broken thread on her lace collar became visible, a smudge of earth on her sleeve and a crease in her skirt. She was as real as if she still lived and breathed, until she glanced round at Cecily and Raf and disappeared. All that was left was the whistle of the wind from the hills.

And before them, a headstone.

And still Raf stood back, still he deferred to her, still, for the first time in what seemed like forever, this was Cecily's moment.

Cecily crouched down and put her basket on the ground beside her, so that she could sweep away the fringe of ivy that had grown over the stone. Its position by the wall had sheltered it from the weathering that had worn away so many of the inscriptions in the churchyard, but lichen had covered it in a green and yellow bloom. Cecily carefully flaked some of it off and the carved lettering became clearer.

"*A pauper – unknown but to God,*" Cecily read. She bowed her head, her hand resting on the top of the stone as if on the nameless man's shoulder. "I'm so sorry for what happened to you."

"Who gave you a stone, mate?" Raf asked as he knelt beside Cecily. He put the box down on the ground as though it were bone china. "*C.* I'd like to have known your name."

"Paupers don't get stones, do they?" Cecily turned to Raf, watching thoughts pass over his face. "Unless they died in a bizarre way. There's one near the gate of someone who was struck by lightning, and they only got a stone so someone could moralize on it. *In the midst of life we are in death* and all that."

"Paupers are lucky to get a marked grave at all." He reached out and placed his hand flat on the stone. Then he bowed his head and moved his lips, but the only sound was that of distant birdsong. Eventually he lifted his head and admitted, "Just being daft again. Asking Mum to look out for him."

Cecily nodded. "I'm sure she will, if she isn't already. Do you get the impression that someone's protecting him? Unnamed and unknown as he is. Because he isn't wandering like Isabella, or the judge."

"He was murdered, cut down. His name's forgotten, his killer wasn't punished." Raf placed his hand over the lettering. "I don't know is the answer, Sis, but he's not exactly the best candidate for *at peace.*"

Raf rocked back on his knees and took off his jacket, which he spread atop the uneven ground. Then he opened the box and retrieved the two drawings. Carefully, Raf laid them on the jacket, joining the torn edges, and said, "I don't know where you are, C, but we've found your girl and your letters. She loves you just as much as she ever did."

"She wants to be with you, C. She came here just now. Did you see her? She's mourned you for over three hundred years." Cecily turned the ring. She was at the grave of the man who had given the ring to Isabella, the man who had chosen the words inside it. "*My love, my secret,*" Cecily recited.

Raf glanced toward her, then took Cecily's hand in his. "You won't be forgotten again," he told Isabella and the stone as one.

Cecily glanced over her shoulder at the sound of a footstep. What on earth would the vicar make of them crouching here? But there was no one there.

A chill crept down Cecily's spine.

"Raf...did you hear that? It didn't sound like a rabbit."

"Save your strength," he told the stone. "You might need it."

Cecily closed her eyes and saw roses opening, one after another. "It could be anyone...there must be thousands of people buried here. But I think it's him — I think it's C. I can see roses, Raf. So many of them, so many colors."

"I'm going to have a day in the rose garden," he said. "Let's get it cleared and see what we can see."

"Yes, you must. Maybe there's more to find in there than the ring." Cecily chipped off some more of the lichen, but there were no other carvings on the stone. "Thank you for showing me those lovely flowers, *C.*"

"Do we have to go back now?" Raf asked with resignation. "Last night...it meant the world to me, Sissy."

"And to me too," Cecily replied. As she stroked his arm, a mixture of joy and fear washed through her. "I wish I could say to you *let's take a walk along the brook*, because it's so pretty, but if someone saw us and Hugh heard about it — even if it was only mentioned in innocence — then it wouldn't go well for either of us. Oh damn him, the tyrant!"

"One day," Raf promised, rolling the drawings up again. "We won't always be hiding from the headmaster."

"One day *soon.*"

"Should I go first or do you want to? I guess we can't knock up at the same time." He closed the box and patted the lid. Something about the gesture was so solid, so confident, so perfectly *Raf* that it seemed as though they had nothing to fear whatsoever.

"Perhaps it might be best if you go first." Cecily was glad of both a plan and a co-conspirator. "I'll go to the grocer's and buy a few things so I don't arrive back at the school with an empty basket."

"If you need me, I won't be far away." He glanced around. "I suppose we can't even chance a kiss?"

Cecily was about to shake her head, but when she realized the churchyard was empty — at least of the living — she said, "A very quick one wouldn't hurt."

She knew Raf wouldn't need telling twice and he didn't. He closed the gap between them and kissed her with the same affection and longing they had shared last night. She would hang onto these kisses when

Hugh returned, just as she had clung to the locket when Sandy was lost.

Cecily risked linking her fingers with his — only for a moment. "I'll see you back at school, then. Sometime." A wave from the upper floors as he worked in the garden. It was something to look forward to.

"I'll be in the rose garden." He winked. "Shirtless."

Cecily laughed. "I should think so too!"

She waited until Raf had disappeared around the side of the church before heading to the grocer's. In order to make her presence in the churchyard less suspicious, she tried to look as if she was tending the grave, and removed a piece of ivy that had snapped off. She tucked it into the basket — ivy was for eternity and faithfulness, and she'd bring it back to Whitmore Hall, even though she would have to hide it under the loose floorboard.

The grocer's assistant chattered away to her as usual, without expecting Cecily to contribute to their one-sided conversation. Cecily never did as she never had anything interesting to tell them. Except now. And she certainly wasn't going to mention any of that.

With her basket loaded with butter and tea leaves, Cecily made her way back along the lane to the school. As she passed through a tunnel made of trees whose boughs stretched across the road and tangled together above her head, Cecily noticed something. A bird under the branches. But as she looked closer, she realized it was a bat.

It was one of the tiny pipistrelles that she occasionally saw after dark at the school, but this one seemed perfectly happy in the daylight too. The little creature stayed with her as she emerged from the trees, flitting alongside as Cecily walked.

Alone as she could have felt, it made Cecily glad to see the bat above her. "Are you having a nice fly, little bat?"

The bat's reply was to take wing, swirling and turning above Cecily as though putting on a show just for her, though she was sure that couldn't be the case. How happy it looked, how free.

Cecily watched its acrobatics with fascination, and the bat continued to flit above her, accompanying her on her way. She'd never thought before that a bat could recognize a human, but maybe this one could, and knew where she lived. As she turned into the driveway of Whitmore Hall, her companion settled briefly on Cecily's shoulder. There it lingered for a second then lifted off again, banking low in what she fancied was a wave of farewell before it rose up into the sky.

Cecily paused to watch it go, waving herself until she could see it no more. Ahead of her loomed the school and Cecily bowed her head and made for home.

She was on the stairs that wound up to the masters' residences when she bumped into Harriet.

"Good morning, Hattie! How are you?"

"Thank heavens I've seen you before the headmaster gets home," Harriet said gravely and Cecily felt her stomach clench. *She can't know.* "We've had *letters.* Our viscount's boy has told his dear papa about the cracking wall and Papa's mobilized lots of other papas to demand action. They're worried about their little loves being squashed flat, and I don't blame them. Graham told the headmaster there'd be trouble and trouble there is!"

Cecily tried to disguise her relief, but it was replaced by a new emotion. Surely Hugh would have to act now, and Cecily couldn't imagine he would be pleased. "Thank you for warning me, Hattie."

"Just…" Harriet reached out and patted Cecily's hand. "Just keep your head down. I know how he can be."

"I appreciate it, Hattie. Thank you."

Cecily let herself through her front door and prepared for her husband's return. She could keep her head down and as she did, she would think of the box and the bat and Raf. Shirtless Raf with his breathless kisses, compact and strong as Hugh was rangy and weak. Not physically weak perhaps, but in that undefinable place that made him what he was.

A bully.

A bully in thrall to an even worse creature that had attached itself to him like a monstrous parasite.

Chapter Fourteen

Evening was drawing in by the time Hugh returned. Cecily heard his approach along the corridor, the tapping of his metal-tipped shoes. She went into the hallway, hands clasped over her apron, ready to welcome him.

"Good evening, Mrs. James," he said as he entered the apartment, a thin specter silhouetted against the landing light. He sounded almost happy, she thought, the idea a curiously ominous one. "The journey was uneventful, the conference equally so. The school is still standing, I see."

"I'm glad to see you safely home, Dr. James. I've left some supper for you." Cecily nodded stiffly. Even if he seemed happy, she wasn't about to let down her guard, because as soon as he heard from Graham... "I made a pie. Your favorite."

Hugh closed the door and turned the key with deliberate slowness. His back was still turned to Cecily when he asked in a worryingly calm voice, "And why is there a pit in the middle of the lawn?"

Cecily bit her lip. She pictured Raf digging in the ghost garden, and recalled the words of love that had lain forgotten in the ground for all that time. It was odd to think that a man like Hugh could exist in the same world as those words of passion and longing.

"Foxes, we think. Or badgers. Mrs. Culpeck thought so anyway. Rabbits, maybe. There's a lot of the little fellows about."

His head cocked to one side in a curious, jerking gesture, then corrected itself with an audible, sickening *crack*. Cecily remembered again the cloudy eye and the wheezing croak, the hellish fingers splayed against the filthy window in the clocktower.

"If I see them, I shall wring their necks with my bare hands," he said, just as the cuckolded husband had threatened to do. Finally Hugh turned, his eyes nothing more fearsome than eyes, his lips thin and bloodless as ever. "Supper, Mrs. James. I am famished from my endeavors on behalf of the school."

She thought of the terrifying hand from the clocktower window passing over a woman's décolletage. And she was glad, because now she could get away from him.

"Of course, Dr. James. Dinner in half an hour." She turned toward the kitchen, then paused. "You'll have spoken to Mr. Culpeck since your return?"

"School business is outside your concern," he told her coolly. "Mr. Culpeck has apprised me of the situation. I shall telephone the concerned parties after church tomorrow. Mr. Culpeck, Mrs. James, is an errant fool to entertain such nonsense."

Cecily decided to appeal to his vanity. "If I may, Dr. James, you have made a name for yourself at Whitmore, and will leave quite the legacy — it would be a shame if it were to be tarnished on account of troublesome masonry."

"It is more likely to be tarnished on account of my idiot wife. Supper, Mrs. James." He waved his hand to dismiss her. "Now."

If only he knew.

Cecily shut herself in the kitchen to heat through Hugh's pie and cook the vegetables she had prepared for him that afternoon. His *'idiot wife'* was indeed about to tarnish the school, but with a petition for divorce, the grounds of which were the headmaster's cruelty and adultery.

Not such an idiot after all.

As she carried Hugh's supper into the dining room, she wished she could have made the pie for Raf. *He* would enjoy it, she knew, from the filling to the edges crimped with her own hand. The thought that he was only on the other side of the wall comforted her even as it thrilled her. But the façade of the dutiful housewife had to be maintained. For now.

"Supper is served, Dr. James."

Seated at the table, his back ramrod straight and his gaze fixed on the nighttime beyond the window, Hugh said nothing. Remembering Raf's words of warning, Cecily put the plate down in front of her waxwork husband and only then did he seem to come back to life

"Beer," he told her. Then he picked up his cutlery and began to eat.

Cecily fetched a bottle from the supply she kept in the pantry. She was tempted to pop its cap off with her teeth as Raf had, but instead took the bottle back to the dining room.

"Would you like me to open it for you?"

Would you like me to tip its entire contents over your hateful head?

"Open it," Hugh instructed through a mouthful of supper. His attention was fixed only on his plate now but outside the window, Cecily glimpsed the shadow of the pipistrelles again.

The world outside.

The world she would soon be free to wander.

Since Hugh's drinking had increased, Cecily kept the bottle opener in a vase on the mantelpiece which, as long as she had lived in the house, had never seen a flower. She retrieved it and opened the bottle with a practiced *pop* and placed the bottle down beside her husband.

"There you are." Cecily waited near the table, her attention distracted from Hugh by the pipistrelles. Maybe the one who had followed her home and performed its acrobatics for her was among the flitting number outside.

One fluttered to a halt on the window ledge, landing on its furry belly with its face turned toward the glass. *That one*, Cecily decided, though she knew the idea was fanciful. Yet if there were ghosts and banshees and heaven knows what else, then why not?

She watched the bat in silence as Hugh gorged on his supper, swilling it down with beer. From above came the occasional sound of pacing feet but the judge, it seemed, was otherwise engaged tonight. Perhaps he was growing weaker, Cecily hoped, but watching her husband stuff himself with food, it seemed unlikely.

If only nameless C in his unmarked grave could grow in strength and tell them his name. It was a shame that he didn't have more power—yet—but at least his presence still lingered, because there was a chance now that he and Isabella could be reunited.

"You've got tinned peaches for pudding," Cecily told Hugh. "There's more potato if you'd like that first?"

"Hope is lost for all who were on board," he replied in a low, gloating tone. "And with it dies the last hope of my harlot wife. Will you weep, woman, and give me the pleasure of tasting your tears?"

Cecily's stomach lurched, but she set her jaw, determined not to be afraid even though the judge was speaking through her husband again. "I always weep for the dead," she replied.

"I own you now, woman, body and soul." He reached for another bottle of beer. "Look out onto your garden for you shall not see it again. I shall have it razed, your precious blooms thrown onto the flames that heat my study. Let the roses remain, though, eh, so I might always be able to watch over you?"

Cecily shuddered at the vitriol in his voice. But she was glad to think that the judge had been wrong—the garden *had* returned and Isabella still walked it. He could not take that from her, even if he had taken the one happiness she'd had. "The roses are very overgrown—I do wish they could be tidied."

"Nonsense!" Hugh laughed but it was a hollow, cold sound. "They are well-tended as ever or the gardener shall receive a flogging for his troubles! Peaches, woman, fetch!"

Cecily headed to the kitchen at a trot. Oh, to be rid of the vile man and the even more horrible man who possessed him. She shut the door behind her, desperate for space between herself and Hugh, and began to prepare his pudding. As slowly as she could risk.

At the movement of something in the corner of her eye, Cecily looked around. There on the ledge, a tiny huddle in the darkness, was a bat. Of course it must be a different bat, she knew, but if a bat *could* look familiar, this one certainly did.

Still holding the tin opener, Cecily went over to the window. It was open a crack and she peered out at the bat. "Hello. If you're the same bat I saw earlier, then I really must thank you for that fantastic aerial display."

The tiny creature fluttered up from its perch and swooped into the night sky before returning to land on the ledge again. The boys must have been feeding it, she decided, and tamed it just a little. It certainly had no fear of humans.

Cecily put aside the tin opener and held her hand out to the bat, her palm flat. "Would you like to say hello? Do bats eat tinned peaches?"

The pipistrelle boldly flew into the kitchen and, tame as a budgerigar, settled flat on Cecily's hand. It drew in its wings and snuggled down, warm and trusting. She had never seen anything quite like it, nor the bat's shining eyes as it peered up at her.

"You're the most adorable creature I've ever met. Apart from…" Cecily glanced over her shoulder. The door was shut, but she spoke quietly as she gently stroked the bat's velvety head, "A certain pretend Latin teacher. But you're definitely my favorite bat."

"Mrs. James!" Hugh bellowed. "Pudding, if you please!"

"Oh, *hell*." Cecily held up her hand to help the bat to launch. "Goodbye, little friend. I'll see you soon, maybe. I've got to go."

Off her friend flew, turning a neat loop before it darted through the open window. Somehow Cecily had an idea that when she returned to the dining room the bat would be perched on the ledge there again. She was right, for there it sat, watchful and silent.

"Your pudding, Dr. James." Cecily placed the bowl of peaches and evaporated milk down on the mat in front of him.

"Go to bed and wait for me," he told her. "And close the curtains. Those damned bats are a nuisance."

Wait for me.

Cecily flinched. "Righty-ho," she said, trying to sound brisk and assured.

She left Hugh to his lonely meal and changed into her nightie. Horrible, bland cotton thing, she wanted one of those silk ones she'd seen in Hattie's film magazines, with a marabou trim and matching slippers to swirl around the bedroom in.

Cecily got into bed and lay on her side, turned away from the door.

Now she couldn't see if the bat was still with her, for the curtains were closed as Hugh had instructed, and when he came into the room twenty minutes later, she heard him stumble and collide with the dresser. Once again came the smell of beer and smoke, once again the weight of him and the pawing hands and the dreadful, perfunctory thrusts of his body inside her. She kept her eyes closed as, above, the judge resumed that dreadful capering step and — *oh God* — the wheezing voice sounded again, letting out a strained, throaty chuckle.

It'll be over soon. All of it.

Then there would be Raf. She thought of his kiss, his tenderness and his passion. And she would never have to lie in the dark with her eyes closed again.

Chapter Fifteen

The days passed, marked by the tolling of the school's clock and the tapping of the judge's feet. Hugh still ate everything Cecily sat down before him, yet was still as thin as a whippet. And the taunts still came, for herself and for Isabella.

There was little opportunity for Cecily to see Raf, unless she slipped down to the garden. He was making good progress with the roses, as Cecily could see through the locked gate if she went down while Raf was in lessons. And when he wasn't, brief though their meetings were, the sturdy brick walls protected them from the eyes of anyone who might be watching from the school. A quick kiss and that was all.

Each evening the little bat returned and sometimes, if Hugh was occupied, she brought the creature into the apartment or watched its displays from the window. Even Isabella seemed more alert, no longer trapped in her circuits of the ghost garden but flitting across the lawns around the rose garden, her sobbing silenced.

How Cecily longed to know what else Raf had found in the box that she had entrusted to him but there was no opportunity to ask. All she could do was wait for the time when Hugh was called away again, for surely that time must be coming.

The first sign of an approaching storm came on a Friday morning, the first day in what seemed like weeks that the sun had vanished behind an iron-gray cloud. As Cecily cleaned the windows inside, she watched a black Rolls-Royce glide up the driveway and from it emerged the viscount whom her husband courted so desperately, followed by a smartly dressed man with a large, shining leather briefcase. The peer's face was not that of a happy parent, and as the two men disappeared into the school building, she readied herself for the trouble that would surely come.

Two hours later there was a cacophony on the staircase outside and Hugh wrenched open the door to their rooms, his face white with rage.

Stilling the tremble in her hands, Cecily hung her cloth over the bucket of water and suds. "Dr. James, I wasn't expecting you."

"Lord Stewart is here," he told her in an urgent hush. Behind him, Graham appeared in the doorway, waving one hand in greeting until Hugh slammed the door. "He has brought with him an architect to examine the damned clocktower. We are to go up and inspect the damage."

She remembered Raf's words immediately, his determination that the clocktower wouldn't be opened until it absolutely *had* to be, yet now here was her husband fetching the key, about to release whatever lurked behind the door.

"Can they inspect it from outside, perhaps? They could get out on the roof, I believe." Cecily wrung her hands. "That pigeon or whatever's stuck in there might be dangerous if they go straight through the door. They wouldn't want their eye pecked out, would they?"

His reply was a look of disgust as he stalked through the apartment into the study. She heard the sound of a drawer opening and closing then he emerged, the key clutched in his fist. With another warning look her way, Hugh opened the front door and disappeared, closing it behind him with a sharp *bang*.

Cecily waited, her heartbeat hammering so loudly in her ears that she couldn't hear anything else. After a few moments, calmer now, she stuck her head around the front door. Hugh had gone. She crept as quietly as she could the short distance along the corridor to Raf's room. He was likely to be in a class or in the garden, but it was worth the attempt, and she tapped on his door. If something was about to be unleashed, then he needed to know.

There was no reply, but above her she heard the footsteps of the men and their muffled voices. Their words were indistinct but something in the tone suggested surprise. Then there were knocks and bangs but not those of the pacing judge, only those of mortal men.

Cecily hurried back, and decided that the kitchen was the safest place. If the judge came at her, she had knives and a kettle of hot water to defend herself with, not that they could possibly be effective against a being made of dust and air. And Isabella's ring would be most secure in its hiding place for now.

Several sets of feet crossed above her head then she heard them descending the staircase. Hugh's voice passed the door, along with others that she didn't recognize. Cecily waited, listening to the voices fade as they continued on past the apartment and away. She had just allowed herself to breathe again when a knock sounded on the door.

Could it be Raf?

Cecily liked that thought and opened the front door only to find Graham standing there.

"Oh, Mr. Culpeck—" Cecily wondered what he'd make of being greeted with a beaming grin by the headmaster's wife. "Do come in."

"The headmaster has asked me to return his key." He shrugged meekly. "There's a heck of a to-do going on, Mrs. James! I've never seen anything like it."

"Is the masonry in a bad way?"

"Well, there's the thing!" He handed her the key. "Crack on the outside, no crack on the inside. It appears, according to our illustrious *London* architect, that our clocktower may have a false wall."

"A false wall?" Cecily wondered if she had misheard. "How on earth… How has no one ever noticed? Those engineers go up there once a year to tinker with the clock, yet they've never said anything about."

"It's what we've always taken to be the outer wall, so the engineers wouldn't have had any call to involve themselves with it." Graham shook his head. "Dreadful stench of damp up there too. Lord Stewart is demanding that restoration is undertaken or he's threatening to kick up quite the trouble."

Cecily nodded, her expression calm despite a building sensation of dread. "My husband is, I suspect, not best pleased?"

"Furious," he said, his tone the fretful whisper she knew all too well. "I have a class waiting but, Mrs.

194

James, if I were you, I would make myself as invisible as possible this evening. Harriet and I are just down the hallway should you need us."

"Thank you." Cecily pressed his hand. "I'll say you've invited me over to play rummy."

Graham gave a gentle nod before he retreated, leaving Cecily alone. Or at least, since that door had now been opened once and for all, she *hoped* she was alone.

All was eerily quiet. Cecily went on cleaning the windows, but constantly looked through them, rather than at them, in case she should spot Raf outside. He had to be told what had happened. And what would he make of the false wall?

She watched a long line of boys trek over the lawn toward the sports field and allowed herself to drift back to the afternoon of cricket, when Raf had reclined beside her and she had been named the honorary captain. The cloudy sky above made the day feel like another lifetime and as the bell chimed ominously, she fancied she heard another of those chuckles from overhead, more formed and somehow closer than the last.

"Sissy!" Raf's voice came from the other side of the door and was followed by a melodic knock. "Sis, it's me!"

Cecily hurried to open it. Breathless with fear, she asked, "Raf...oh, Raf, have you heard what's happened?"

"You can't miss it, your husband's having a stand-up row with a viscount in the middle of the assembly hall!" He caught her hand in his and wrinkled his face into a grimace. "Jesus Christ, it stinks out here. They opened the door?"

"They did. I tried to stop Hugh, but—well, I'm sure you can imagine how much he cares for my opinion." Cecily tried to swallow down her bitterness and told Raf about the false wall.

"A false wall up there and an empty coffin in the vault?" He took a deep breath, then nodded. "And that smell... I've got a feeling our rotten old judge might still be up there. I don't know why, I just— It would explain him being bound to the tower."

"How on earth did he end up *there*?" Cecily realized she'd used the same incredulous tone as she had when one of the boys had managed to get stuck on the chapel's steeple. "I mean...oh, Raf...there's been a corpse above my head all this time? And no one ever knew!"

"I suppose we're going to find out. The crack was too narrow—" He swallowed and kissed her very gently. "How've things felt since the door was opened? You've been all right in here?"

"Not to begin with, but I swear I heard a laugh. Quite close." Cecily pressed her face against his shoulder. "I'm actually rather scared."

Raf held her tight, stroking his hand tenderly down her back. "I'm always thinking about you, Sissy, never forget that."

"Thank you," she whispered. "I'm always thinking about you too. When we don't have to creep about all the time—it'll be wonderful, won't it?"

"We'll have all the time we need, just you and me."

Cecily stroked along the line of Raf's strong jaw. "I dread seeing you go, but...if Hugh finds you've been here..."

"I know." Raf caught Cecily's hand and kissed the palm. "Just remember that whatever happens, you've got me looking out for you. Isabella's been beside me in the rose garden every night. I feel like we're so close... If he's let the judge out, let's get ready to send the old sod packing."

"With a good, hard foot in the rump!" Cecily would happily have kissed Raf there and then, but held back. "Hugh might be back at any moment..."

He nodded and finally released her as, outside, the sound of a car engine starting could be heard. "I'd better go. If you need me — "

"Good day, Lord Stewart," Hugh said in a voice positively dripping with contrition. "Again, my apologies for the misunderstanding, but — "

Raf opened the door as wheels turned on gravel. He whispered, "It's going to be over." Then, as the door downstairs opened, he touched his fingertips to his lips and hurried away across the landing.

Cecily closed the front door and went back to cleaning the windows. A sense of unease crept over her like an approaching thunderstorm as Hugh's feet sounded on the staircase. When he threw the door open, the anger that came with him was like a physical force and he stalked into the office with a shout of, "Tea, now!"

"Of course, Dr. James." Cecily rushed into the kitchen, tapping her fingers with impatience as the kettle slowly boiled. She carried the tray into his study, with a homemade biscuit placed just so on the saucer. He didn't even look up at her, so intent was he on the papers before him on the desk.

Cecily went back into the kitchen and was about to start peeling carrots for supper when she heard a dull thud.

But it didn't sound as if it was the judge in the space upstairs.

She followed the noise to the bedroom. Nothing seemed awry, apart from a smell of dust. And something rotten. Then she saw, plumb in the middle of the bed, a chunk of plaster. Cecily looked up at the ceiling and saw above her an almighty crack. Some of the plaster was missing — the piece which now lay on the bed.

Fear of sleeping underneath that void battled within her against her fear of Hugh. But she couldn't not tell him. He was already furious, and would no doubt dole out a few slaps before the evening was out anyway. A couple more wouldn't make much difference.

She picked up the piece of plaster and took it to her husband, like one of the pupils taking in a trophy to show their teacher at the start of the new term.

Cecily knocked on the door and asked, "Dr. James, could you please spare a minute?"

"*What?*" he snapped.

Cecily came out from behind the door, saying nothing. She held the crumbling shard of plaster toward him. He lifted his gaze from the papers on his desk to her hand and she saw a shadow pass over his face. Then he asked, "What the devil have you there?"

"It's fallen down from the bedroom ceiling. There's" — Cecily steeled herself — "another crack."

She had expected rage but instead she got something far worse, a thin, malicious smile. When Hugh answered this time, however, his was only one of two voices that said the same thing, for he was accompanied by a reedy, mirthful voice that seemed to seep from the very ceiling itself.

"Perhaps," the two voices said, "somebody is trying to come through."

The plaster dropped from Cecily's trembling hands and shattered on the floor, throwing tiny white splinters against her legs. She looked up at the ceiling. Hugh looked up too in the moment before he rose from his chair and crossed the room, seizing her wrist in his hand.

"Do you want to see, my girl? Is that it? Would you like to meet the judge? I'm sure he'd like to meet *you*." With his keys tight in his other fist, he dragged her toward the door. "Come along, Mrs. James, let's not keep the good gentleman waiting!"

"No—no, I don't want to go up there!" In terror, Cecily tried to dig her heels into the floor but only skidded on the rug over the floorboards. She grabbed the door frame but Hugh was dragging her with such determination that her grasp slipped.

All she could picture was the hand against the window. "No, please, no!"

"I think I shall have a motor along to town tonight and find a friend or two." Hugh laughed, wrenching open the door to the apartment. "So you will have all night to get to know our friend!"

Cecily's protestations seemed only to make her husband more determined and he unlocked the door to the clocktower, the door at which Raf had seen the frightful eye peer, and thrust her into the darkness. Then he pulled it shut and turned the key, calling out, "Sleep tight, Mrs. James. Don't forget to say your prayers!"

Cecily was too hoarse to reply, too scared to speak. The unholy, suffocating stench of rot reached inside her nostrils and she hid her face in her hands as though it would make her invisible to the demonic being that had long been trapped in this space.

As Cecily now was.

She tried to calm herself, thinking of Raf and the bat and the garden, of the Culpecks' kindness, anything that would repulse the visceral terror of her prison.

Dropping her hands from her face, she could just about see the workings of the clock, those oily, metal innards that made the hands turn. And bricks – ancient bricks, and scraps of old wallpaper.

And nothing else. No judge, no looming cataract in an eye.

"I'm not scared," Cecily told the darkness.

But it was a lie.

She heard the sound of Hugh's car engine outside and the stately turn of its tires on gravel then all was silent.

Cecily listened to the emptiness until from somewhere in the shadows came the unmistakable sound that she had been dreading. The tread of a foot on the boards.

She pulled a grip from her hair and stabbed at the lock with it, but the slender metal prong dropped from her fingers. Falling to her knees, Cecily scrabbled for the grip but it had gone. And so had all hope of her getting out before Hugh came home.

The footstep sounded again, then another and another, and each nearer than the last until they seemed to be upon her, yet still the shadows were empty. Then it seemed as though the floor had opened and plunged her into a nightmare as from that same unfathomable darkness, too dark to be natural, *something* brushed lightly against her hair and a stench of decay swept over Cecily like a tide.

Cecily turned her head away and screamed, and all there seemed to be in the room at that moment was the noise of her own terror and the reeking vileness that she could not escape from.

"Your husband hates you," that ancient, dusty voice growled, and something hit Cecily from the shadows, pages or—*no, photographs*. "And your father before him. Fine, godly men both."

So her father had been possessed by the judge too? Cecily grasped for the photographs and in the dim light, she recognized them. All the images from her childhood that her father had wrested from her and thrown away.

"You miserable, horrible man!" Cecily shouted. "You deserve to be stuck up here—forever! And, God willing, you'll never hurt anyone ever again!"

"Soon enough they shall call *me* Dr. James," the voice crowed. "And you shall call me husband."

"I would rather die a thousand deaths than suffer *that*!"

Cecily pressed her back against the door, her gaze fixed on a point beyond the darkness.

Oh no, no…surely I'm seeing things?

The wall in which the crack *should* be, the false wall, was covered with the remains of a long-forgotten paper. Once deep blue as a midnight sky, now it was peeling slowly from the wall and bringing with it sheets of plaster, as though an earthquake was rocking the house to reveal the old bricks beneath. Yet beneath the torn paper and shattered plaster those stones weren't solid and immovable, standing as they had for centuries, they were—

Cecily stared at the bricks as they bulged and shifted, grinding against one another as though something were behind them, something pushing its way through. There was no light within and the sun was setting behind the clouds yet she could see some sort of illumination around the bricks. Too bright to be dusk, it was more like the flames she had seen at the window behind that hellish figure. Dust trickled down from between the bricks and a cloud of dirt filled the air as, from the door, a thunderous knock sounded.

"Sissy!"

She must have fainted — she had to be dreaming — "Raf!"

"Get back from the door!" There was no picking of the lock now, just the sound of the hinges complaining as Raf put his shoulder to them. She held tight to the photographs as the wood groaned, splintered and surrendered, flooding the darkness with light.

She staggered out of the room toward him, barely able to see against the brightness. "You must secretly be an angel, Raf — thank heavens you found me!"

He took her in his arms as the door closed with an almighty crash. From behind it, the judge's wheezing laughter mocked them in the darkness.

Chapter Sixteen

Safe in Raf's embrace, Cecily let him help her across the landing to the masters' corridor and his small room. The sound of laughter receded into silence again and from outside came the sound of boys' voices raised in cheer and laughter as they headed for the dorms and the weekend.

Cecily could barely walk, could barely make sense of anything. All she wanted was Raf. "I've torn my dress. My poor dress," was all she could say.

"I'll mend it," he promised in a whisper, pressing a kiss to her hair. The bedroom door closed softly behind them but still Raf didn't release her. Instead they clung to each other, the photographs still clutched in Cecily's hands.

Through rising tears, Cecily told him, "He said that he'd possessed my father too."

"Come and sit down." The study was far from large and scarcely equipped for two, containing a desk with an uncomfortable chair and a bookcase still filled with the absent Mr. Brennan's texts. On the dresser was a basin and jug and an assortment of jars and bottles like that Raf had given her and the one he kept in his own pocket, all made with his own hands, no doubt. Despite the presence of a narrow wardrobe, one of the two armchairs before the empty hearth was piled with Raf's clothes and she noticed only now that he was wearing a dressing gown of deep red. Raf led her to a single bed beneath the open window. It was stacked high with cushions, a cozy, chaotic nest, and it was here that he settled her, placing a gentle kiss to her forehead.

Cecily lay the precious photographs on the bed beside her then took Raf's hand. "How did you know I was up there?"

"I was sat here after my bath and I had the strangest feeling," he replied, sitting on the bed beside Cecily. She caught a fragrant smell from his skin, fresh and summery. "As soon as I stuck my head out of the door, I heard you cry out and— What happened?"

"An enormous crack appeared in the bedroom ceiling, and Hugh went spare. He dragged me up to the clocktower, saying I should meet the judge, and I begged him not to, and he *enjoyed* it—frightening me! Then he—he locked me in." Cecily couldn't hold her tears back any longer and cried.

"Shh," Raf soothed, rocking her tenderly in his arms. "You're safe now, I promise."

Cecily wept into the soft silk of his dressing gown. "The wall's falling in. I saw it. The bricks were moving."

"Don't think about it, just get your breath and take your time." He stroked her hair. "We're together now."

Cecily had stopped crying and instead let Raf's presence warm her. "I don't want to be without you."

In reply he simply held her in his arms, pressing a very tender kiss to her lips. Still she could hear the laughter of the children and the sweet birdsong and here, in Raf's messy world, the judge might as well be a monster from a childhood story.

A knock sounded on the door, not the loud rap of an adult but the tentative tap of a child. Cecily looked up from Raf's shoulder. "You have a young visitor!"

"Who's that?" Raf called, drawing a pattern on Cecily's hand with his fingertip. It was a heart, she realized, and he called again, "*Buna?*"

"*Buna!*" came the reply. "It's Blackwood, sir. I've come to borrow the book, if you please, sir!"

"Have a root in the wardrobe," Raf whispered as he hopped from the bed. "Find yourself a shirt to wear and I'll get that frock stitched in no time."

He left Cecily on the bed and crossed to the door, tightening his dressing gown belt as he went. On his way, he took a book from the shelf and held it up to Cecily so that she could read *Dracula* on the cover. Raf opened the door and addressed the unseen boy outside.

"Mister Blackwood," he exclaimed. "Are you sure you want to read this? All true, you know. It's about my grandad!"

The boy chuckled. "Very funny, Mr. de Chastelaine!"

"Do me a favor? Crack on to the kitchens and ask cook to pack up a supper and send it up with the porter, please!" Raf reached inside the door to take his wallet from the desk. He took out a few coins as Cecily opened the wardrobe quietly and began to look through the shirts, each as creased as the last. "Two coins for cook, one for you. You have a good night, don't let Grandpa give you nightmares!"

The boy gasped in appreciation, and, over the sound of his footsteps, announced, "Right away, sir!"

Cecily tried to stifle her laughter. "The boys have really taken to you! And lending them *Dracula*—you naughty fellow."

"I'm not *so* naughty—I'm not even going to look while you get changed and snuggle into that bed!" He turned his back to her, ever the gentleman.

Cecily finally chose a shirt, a sky-blue one made from brushed cotton. She unbuttoned her dress and carefully stepped out of it to avoid tearing it further, then draped it over a chair. She put Raf's shirt on over her slip. Her shoes and stockings were filthy with broken plaster and dust, so she stripped them off and bundled them on the floor. Then she unfastened the buttons and clips on her girdle and peeled it off before carefully rolling it up with her other discarded clothes. She climbed into his bed and once her bare legs were hidden from view, she told him, "It's safe to look now."

"You look *very* at home." Raf smiled at the sight of her. He made his way to the desk and the familiar bottle of liquor there. "Let's have a little taste of our Romanian booze, take the edge off the fright?"

"I wouldn't mind a mouthful of țuică if there's one going." Cecily flung her arms up above her head like a cat stretching in the sun. "I feel so decadent, lying in your bed."

"And you make the most magnificent sight I've ever seen. But a single bed?" Raf picked up the bottle and two rather battered-looking mugs. "Graham tells me that there is a *no wives* rule for the masters— headmasters and deputy only. He thinks it's a foolish idea and so do I—we're not priests! Some of us are *definitely* not priests."

He put the mugs and bottle down on the small bedside table, next to the stub of a candle. Then he reached beneath the bed and brought out a floral bag, fastened with a ribbon and covered in embroidered flowers. Cecily couldn't help but look at it and he explained, "Mum's sewing bag,"

"Did she make you clothes when you were little?" *How adorable, young Raf in short trousers.* "Most of mine were homemade. In fact…well, they still are."

"Yeah, she did." He poured a measure of țuică into each mug then settled on the bed beside Cecily and put her discarded dress in his lap. She couldn't help but notice his bare legs, though she knew she really shouldn't, and the charms that she could see so clearly now against his chest. "I'm good at patching up and mending. Your dress is safe with me, Captain. Cheers!"

"Cheers!" Cecily raised her mug and took a careful sip. Seeing the dress she had made now in Raf's hands made her happy, and she snuggled into his warm blankets. "Thank you for looking after me."

"That's what you do when you love someone," he said casually, his head bent over the dress as he began to sew.

Cecily's mouth fell open in surprise. *Love?* She took another mouthful of plum wine then, unable to stop herself, stroked Raf's arm. "Do you love me, Raf? Is that what you mean?"

He nodded, still not looking at her. Another moment passed and Raf lifted his head, then turned to look at Cecily. "I love you. You don't have to say anything, but I wanted to tell you. Because I do."

Cecily looked into his eyes and saw such kindness there and…was *that* love that she could see?

"I keep thinking about you, Raf. All the time. I'm only happy when I'm with you. And I feel so...so..." Cecily reached up to stroke his face. "I love you too. There. I've said it."

His smile grew even wider and she felt a wash of happiness and contentment that she hadn't felt in years, perhaps never had. She was loved and she loved him in return. It didn't matter what the likes of Hugh or her father or the damnable judge said, not at all.

"Then I'm the happiest and luckiest bloke in this world or the next." Raf leaned over and kissed her. As he did, the photos slid together over the blankets and he carefully set them out again, just as Cecily had. She looped her arms around his neck and kissed him back, his lips soft against her own. The silk of his dressing gown felt luxurious to her touch, and the taste of plum wine in his mouth was like coming home.

How decadent this was, how *right* and how wonderful. Their kiss went on, lingering and deep, and she heard again those soft noises of pleasure in his throat, felt her heartbeat quicken with every passing moment.

Cecily combed her fingers through his tousled hair, leaving it even more delectably untidy than it had been to start with. Her body was opening up to him, desire and love a heady, irresistible brew. She caught each of his gasps with her kiss, and drew him down closer. She wanted him as she had never wanted anyone before.

She vaguely heard the dress and bag slide from Raf's lap onto the floor and the sound of paper as he gathered up the photos and put them safely aside but it was all happening miles away. Instead there was just the two of them on this bed, their island in the middle of nowhere, a sanctuary from the madness that had descended over Whitmore Hall.

Cecily kissed her way along Raf's jaw to whisper in his ear, "Are you wearing *anything* at all under your dressing gown?"

"A light covering of skin cream. I'm sensitive to the sun otherwise," he replied in a voice rich with mischief. Then his nose twitched once and he called out, "Cheers, mate, leave the tray outside and I'll get it in a bit."

"Right-ho, Mr. de Chastelaine," the porter called back, clearly doing his best not to sound puzzled at how Raf had known he was there before he'd had a chance to knock.

Cecily giggled. "That sense of smell of yours!" She just hoped that she didn't smell of carrots or the soap she had used on the windows. He laughed softly but still his reply had sent a thrill of heat through Cecily's blood.

'A light covering of skin cream.'

"Are you not even wearing…underthings?"

"I wasn't wearing anything two minutes before I barged through that door," he told her. "So it could've been a lot worse."

"It is a very lovely dressing gown, but I wonder…would you feel more comfortable if it was a little looser?" Cecily took the end of his dressing gown tie and twirled it. She had never done anything like this before and wondered if this was what people did in bed when they loved each other.

"How about I make you a deal?" Raf touched his forehead to Cecily's. "Tonight I'm all yours to command, and if you insist on me loosening this belt, then I won't say no. All I ask in return is that you bake me those lavender biscuits again one day?"

"Command? Oh, I wouldn't know how to do that! But I'll bake you those biscuits whenever you like." Cecily tugged at his belt just enough to loosen it a couple of inches. She knew very well what was brewing within Raf's dressing gown. "Would you like me to take off this shirt?"

"I wouldn't say no," he admitted, nuzzling his lips against Cecily's throat. "All I want is for you to do what *you* want. I love you — making you happy is what matters to me."

"I desire you, Raf. Is that an awful thing to admit? It's just sort of *there*...and it's something I've never felt before." Cecily began to unbutton the shirt he had lent her. He settled back onto the pillows a little, the dressing gown *just* concealing what was beneath.

"I think you're the most beautiful woman I've ever seen," he murmured. "And it's a bloody crime if you don't know that."

"Me? I'm all gangly!" Cecily shook her head. "But thank you, handsome Raf."

"And I'm shorter than my whole family, but so what?" He caught her hand and kissed his way along her arm from elbow to wrist. "You're not gangly, you're graceful. You're like a classical statue come to life."

"Really?" Cecily felt her cheeks redden. "No one's ever said anything like that to me before. And you, Mr. de Chastelaine — you have eyes like the sea."

She tugged on his dressing gown tie again and it finally fell open. Her heart beat faster and she ran her gaze from the charms around his neck, down his toned chest and stomach to — to the firm shape still concealed by the red silk gown.

"And a permanent five o'clock shadow." He smiled. "But that's just me."

Cecily stroked the rasping stubble on his chin, then took the edge of his dressing gown. "Can I peek?"

"I'm yours. Tonight, tomorrow, as long as you want me." He shrugged, clearly trying to be casual. "You can peek all you like."

It was a novelty to be in bed before dark, and Cecily gingerly lifted the edge of his dressing gown. With a nervous giggle in her throat, she finally saw Raf's erection. "It's beautiful," she told him, which was something she'd never thought she'd say. But it was. Perky and enthusiastic, just like Raf.

"Of course," he teased. "It's mine!"

Cecily knelt up on her grazed knees and pulled the shirt off over her head without a second thought. Her slip was made from light summer fabric, and she was very aware that it didn't conceal much. So she threw that off as well, and knelt there on the bed, one arm across her breasts in a failed attempt at demureness. The horse had bolted as all she had on now were her knickers. She grinned at Raf. "We're a saucy pair, aren't we?"

"Made for each other?" With a roll of his strong shoulders Raf let the dressing gown slip down his arms and off. It pooled on the bed around him and she saw him naked for the first time, his body everything that Hugh's never would be. He reached into the tangle of charms and closed his hand around one, lifting it over his head. Cecily saw the weathered leather thong that was caught in his fist and he said, "I want to give you this, to show you what you mean to me. I made it with Mum when I was about six, so it's what you'd call *naïve*. But I want you to have it."

He opened his fist and held out his hand, watching her with wide, hopeful eyes. There on Raf's palm was a polished gray stone, a strip of leather threaded through a neatly drilled hole. On the surface of the stone was the unmistakable figure of a rooster or, at least, a child's version of one. Despite the passing years, the red and gold of its feathers blazed from the stone and he said, "At home we call him *cocosul*. He chases away the darkness and gives any evil spirits hiding in it a right pecking!"

Cecily carefully picked up the charm by its leather thong and held it up to look at it. She closed her hand around the stone and kissed Raf's cheek. It was more of a promise than a wedding ring, and Cecily slipped off her own—a thin, mean little glint of gold—and put it on the windowsill.

"This necklace is the loveliest gift I've ever had. I shall treasure it. Thank you, Raf. This means a lot."

"I thought it might go with your mum's locket." He rested his head on her shoulder. "Then you have her, Sandy and me with you all the time."

Cecily slipped the necklace on over her head and let it rest against her chest, the stone warm from Raf's skin. "I love you, darling," she told him, and kissed his cheek.

"*Te iubesc*," he whispered. "And I'm going to make you happy, Sissy, I promise."

"And I'll make you lovely biscuits forever." Cecily stroked Raf's shoulder, then moved down across his chest to gently tweak his nipples. "They feel nice."

Raf didn't answer, though the soft sigh in his throat told her what she needed to know. His eyelids fluttered and he pressed another kiss to her throat, gently nuzzling her skin.

She carried on, discovering the joy of giving pleasure to a lover. At the same time she felt Raf's hands, those unexpectedly soft hands, slide over her back, caressing and stroking her skin. He brushed kisses down over her shoulder and scattered them against the top of her breasts, soft as the silk dressing gown he had worn.

Cecily trembled, that tightening in her signaling the building of her desire. She sighed, and soft gasps of delight drifted from her lips. Raf trailed his lips lower and circled his tongue around her nipple, tender and slow. She yielded herself up to the sensation of his mouth upon her as ripples of bliss ran through her at his touch. Raf lifted his gaze to meet hers, quirking his eyebrows as though to ask if things were going as she had hoped. Then he drew her nipple between his lips, his tongue flicking and teasing.

Cecily stroked one hand down from his chest to his stomach and dipped her fingertip into his navel. He trembled under her touch, as she did in response to the tingling that ran through her. She had wondered what it would be like to be so adored that a man would willingly kiss her all over—she had never imagined that it would feel like this.

Raf's hand came to rest on Cecily's hip as his mouth roamed her breasts, trailing heated caresses over her soft skin. He lifted his shining gaze to meet hers and asked, "Can I undress you?"

Cecily tried to reply but only gasped in pleasure. She nodded instead. He was asking—not expecting or demanding. And she loved him all the more for it.

There wasn't much left to undress but as Raf slipped the last scrap of material from her body, a shiver ran through Cecily. He kissed her tummy, then her thigh, then gently pressed his lips to her knee, soothing the place where she had fallen in the darkness. She wished she could have been perfect for him, unblemished, and she turned her head away on the pillow, embarrassed. But there was something in his kiss that brought her attention back and she ruffled his hair as he kissed her knee.

"I adore you, Raf de Chastelaine," she whispered.

"The first time I saw you in that dark room at Harriet's" — Raf lifted his head to look at Cecily along the length of her body — "you knocked me sideways."

"You must've wondered what sort of a place you'd ended up at!" Cecily laughed softly. "And you enchanted me the moment I saw you."

"Must've been my irresistible messiness." He grinned. "Or my heroic shortness!"

"It was your smile," she told him. "And those lovely blue eyes."

This time the smile was bashful even as Raf joked, "I can't help being so gorgeous." Then he put his lips to Cecily's knee again and, inch by delicious inch, kissed his way up her body.

Cecily lay back, every sense alive as Raf ran his mouth over her skin. Even the sound of his kiss and the susurration of the blanket against him as he moved ever farther up the bed sent arrows of pleasure shooting through her.

As his kisses reached her throat, Raf pressed his fingers to the most sensitive part of Cecily's body, caressing with light strokes. "Can I make love to you?" he whispered.

She didn't reply at once, as she spooled his words through her mind again so that she would always remember how his question had sounded, and how she had felt when he had asked her.

'Can I make love to you?'

"Yes, Raf...please."

As he stroked between her legs, Cecily tentatively reached down for his erection and closed her hand around it. It was so strong, and it fascinated her as much as it increased her desire for him.

She had never heard a sound quite like the soft groan that slipped into their kiss and it wasn't a sound that she would have expected to tease from anyone. Low with heat and passion, it was utterly abandoned, and it was for her, because of her. One of those softly caressing fingers moved deeper in reply to her touch, seeking out the very core of her desire.

Cecily moved her hand on him, her grip light. Her hips lifted a little from the bed, a sign that she was ready for him and wanted him — Raf de Chastelaine, the pretend Latin master.

"I love you," Raf murmured as the tip of his erection pressed to Cecily's body. She knew he was taking his time, treating her with the reverence and love that the headmaster never had. For all his earthy swagger, he was more of a gentleman than that shining light of society had ever been.

"I've never felt like this before..." Cecily gazed into Raf's eyes. Their blue depths seemed as endless as the sky. "I want you so much, darling."

With the slightest movement of his hips, he brought their bodies together. They couldn't be closer than they were now, two halves of one, their hearts beating in time with each other. When Raf began to move it was with deep strokes and all the time he was kissing her, his tongue softly exploring. The pendant that rested against Cecily's skin tapped a gentle percussion on the tangle of charms around his neck, the sound mingling with their sighs.

Cecily had never felt so close to someone before, so loved. Raf's strength was filled with tenderness, and his every thrust sent pleasure shooting through her. Breathless, Cecily moaned into his kiss. How had she existed for so long without this swooning delight?

Unlike the silent, sweating minutes when Hugh claimed her body, making love with Raf was a decadent, wonderfully physical experience. They seemed to anticipate each other's needs, each touch and caress instinctive and loving. Cecily felt the slightest change in Raf's muscles, the slightest suggestion of more urgency as the minutes ticked by, but still he was devoting himself to her, every soft moan that slipped into his kisses testament to his love.

In Raf's embrace she had discovered new things about her body, even the curious fact that her neck was sensitive to Raf's kisses, making her tremble to the core each time his stubble rubbed against her skin there.

The swirling pleasure he brought her now seemed to build, and Cecily wove her legs around his, holding him close as if the lightness in her head would make her float up from the bed.

"My beautiful, *earthy*, gorgeous captain," Raf growled in a voice so rough and lusty that Cecily couldn't help but smile. He caught his hands about her waist and in one smooth movement rolled onto his back, pulling her atop him. With his tousled hair tangled on the white pillowcase, Raf blinked up at Cecily and said, "That's probably the most glorious sight I've ever seen!"

Cecily's hair flopped into her face and she scraped it aside. She felt amazing, like an all-powerful goddess, and she held Raf's hips as she moved against him. "You're not looking too bad yourself down there!"

"Well, you know..." Raf gave a cheeky shrug as though to say *of course*. When he reached up and curled his fingers around the wrought-iron bedstead, the muscles in his arms tensed and defined, she knew that it was for her benefit. He winked and told her, "When we get home to Yorkshire, we're spending at least a week in bed. Deal?"

"At *least!*" Cecily giggled, but her laughter soon changed to breathless gasps as her lightheaded thrill swept her ever higher. Raf took hold of her hips as his thrusts grew faster, his gasps of exertion louder, and together they approached the edge.

Bliss swept through Cecily, taking her by surprise. She gasped as her every nerve sprang alive and she shivered with joy. And she felt Raf there with her, their shared pleasure sending them tumbling into ecstasy.

Cecily could no longer hold herself up and she sank down onto Raf, her arms tight about him. "You're the best pretend Latin master I've ever met."

"You wouldn't say that if you had exams coming up," he said happily, wrapping his arms around her waist.

Cecily laid her head on his shoulder, her cheek against his, his dark hair mingling with hers. The sensation of being as one had not left her. Together they lay in silence, exchanging kisses and sighs, the horrors of the evening forgotten.

* * * *

The last time Cecily had eaten in bed was when she had had the flu and Harriet had brought her soup. Now she and Raf sat together under the covers eating what seemed like a banquet to Cecily, although it was simple fare. Once the cold meats and bread, the cheeses and salad, were finished, Raf took out the box they had rescued and by lamplight they went through its contents at leisure, reading letters of love and longing, reliving the affair of Isabella and C.

As Cecily read Isabella's words, she spoke with new understanding. She knew now what it was to experience such intimacy and pleasure and she was even more determined to set Isabella's troubled spirit to rest.

And not just Isabella's.

Once the box was closed, Cecily reached for the photographs. She had thought them lost and not seen them for years. She thought she had misremembered her mother's face, but as she looked through them and showed Raf each one, she realized she had never forgotten her after all. The tall, willowy lady whom Cecily so resembled, who had died while Cecily was still only small. Perhaps it was why her father had been so cruel to her, with the judge to twist him. He had looked at Cecily and seen the wife he had lost.

"She looks like you," Raf murmured as they looked at the photos. His chin was resting on her shoulder as she snuggled back against his chest, entirely safe in his embrace. "I bet she's proud of the woman you are, you know. Brave and smart and smelling like orange blossom."

"I hope so. She didn't have much of a life, poor thing. She died when she was my age." Cecily raised their joined hands to her lips and grinned. "I'm naked in bed with my lover, looking at photographs of Mummy — and I don't feel awkward in the least! I wonder if she's met your mother and they're just out of our sight drinking țuică?"

"Count on it," he laughed. "And Sandy's trying to get a word in."

"I wish you could've met him." Cecily turned over a photograph taken in the school grounds of her mother holding the hands of two chubby-legged toddlers, and beneath it found a photograph of Sandy, taken in a studio on the other side of the country. "Here he is, looking smart in his uniform."

Raf kissed Cecily's shoulder and told her, "When I said before that they don't leave us…it's true. For every bastard like the judge, there're a dozen loving spooks just keeping an eye out. You might never see them, but they're the closest we'll get to a guardian angel. Every time you think you feel a hand on your shoulder or someone sheltering you in the dark, they're there. And I'll be there with them, just not so invisible."

Cecily turned her head to catch his lips in a kiss. "Do you think they were there with me in the tower?"

"He's got the strength now to speak, to stamp about and throw stuff, but he didn't lay a hand on you in harm." Raf kissed her again. "They were there. Maybe it was them who gave me the feeling that things weren't right."

Cecily kissed him again then looked across the untidy room. "Thank you, all of you." Then she snuggled back against Raf again.

"I don't want you to go back to Hugh," he admitted, drawing the blankets higher. "Sod him, stay with me."

Cecily stroked his cheek. "I would stay with you in a heartbeat, but I have to go back. We have to finish this. We have to, for Isabella and her lover. And for my mother. We have to send Judge Whitmore back to the devil who sent him."

Realizing she was starting to sound melodramatic, Cecily returned to more practical issues. "Besides which, I want a divorce based on *his* vile behavior. If he suspects us, then you know very well what will happen — he'll find a solicitor in a snap, and it'll be me whose name is dragged through the mud. Let everyone read the newspaper and see what a bastard he is."

"At least don't go back into that tower, Sissy. Tell him *you* broke the door down if you have to!"

Cecily shook her head. "Raf, I'm the last person who wants to go back up there, but if I tell him I got out, he'll be even more furious. He needs to find me in the tower room when he gets back tomorrow — he needs to think I'm a dutiful drudge who he can push around, who hasn't the gumption to escape by herself and certainly doesn't have friends who could get her out. And as you say, the judge can't hurt me."

"He might notice the damage to the doorframe." Raf winced. "If he does, play dumb. And you won't be alone, I'll be with you until he lets you out. He won't see me in there."

"Are you sure — you'll lock yourself into that hellhole with me?" Cecily turned to Raf in surprise. No one had ever taken such a risk for her before.

"I told you," he reminded her, "that's what you do when you love someone. As soon as we hear his car pull in, we'll go."

Cecily gathered up the photographs and carefully dropped them onto the floor by the bed. Then she turned in Raf's arms and, face to face, she kissed him. A whole night together in this narrow bed in this messy room.

Heaven.

Chapter Seventeen

Determined not to be caught out by Hugh, Cecily left Raf's bed before the sun had risen. Putting on yesterday's clothes was a strange experience, as if she were a snake who had shed its skin and was trying to fit back into it. They were still covered in dust and plaster, and the knees of her lisle stockings had tiny pinpricks of blood from her grazes, but at least the tear in her dress and Raf's mending were impossible to see. Her hair had been mussed by Raf but Hugh, she hoped, would assume that more supernatural agencies had been at work.

She kissed Raf's forehead. "Good morning, my handsome man. There's some leftover bread from our supper if you want breakfast."

He stretched his arms above his head and caught Cecily, tumbling her down onto the bed for a lingering kiss.

"Good morning, sexiest woman in the world."

Cecily kissed him, and was very tempted to get back under the covers with him, but with an effort she resisted. "*There's* something I don't hear every day."

Together they breakfasted on bread and butter, then, as Cecily watched, Raf threw on a pair of trousers and the shirt she now knew would only be worn as long as it took him to reach the garden. Into his pocket went the jar of skin lotion and the little wallet of lock tools. He washed and even made an effort to comb the tousled mop of hair, but it made little difference as far as she could see. Raf wasn't made to be tidy, it seemed.

Cecily retrieved her abandoned wedding ring from the windowsill. She was resolved not to put it on until the last possible moment. Cheap, nasty little thing — it had always looked out of place on her finger. Not so the painted stone pendant around her neck, hidden beneath her dress. *That* was more precious than the Crown Jewels.

"Please keep the photographs safe, Raf, won't you?" But she knew she didn't need to ask him.

"They'll be safe in the box," he promised. "Looked after by Isabella and her mysterious C."

Cecily thanked him with a kiss, and the waiting went on, marked by the tolling of the clock. Dawn was just breaking as the sound of Hugh's car making its stately way up the drive could be heard. The moment was here and Raf rose to his feet from the bed, taking Cecily's hand in his. How different this morning was from last night as they reached the doorway with its telltale splinters showing against the frame.

"Don't forget, the door's a mystery," Raf reminded Cecily as he opened the doorway. She saw him wince at the odor she couldn't smell then he stepped inside and drew her with him. Then he stooped to pick the lock again, this time to make prisoners of them. "Not such a bully when he's got two people and daylight to face."

Cecily stood behind Raf, her hands on his shoulders. She was shaking and trying very hard not to. "When Sandy and I were children on a couple of occasions we played hide-and-seek with the boys. We weren't allowed to, of course! But I'll pretend that's what we're doing now. Just a game. Nothing to be frightened of at all."

"You stand right behind the door." With a bit of shuffling, Raf reversed their positions so Cecily faced the door, Raf's arms around her waist and his chin resting on her shoulder. Yet she was sure she heard the judge's wheezy breath in the shadows, the scuff of his foot on the dusty boards. "Nobody's coming anywhere near you — nobody can. I'll be holding you until we hear his key in the door. Be brave, Captain Sis."

"I'm trying my best. You're here, and Sandy and Mummy and your mother too — we'll ignore that huffing old beast in the corner. We'll — " Cecily froze. She had heard a floorboard creak outside, but she couldn't be sure if it was a footstep or the sound of the old house. She put her wedding ring back on.

A shadow fell across the keyhole, blocking out what little light there was, then a key scraped against the metal. Raf kissed Cecily's cheek and whispered, "I'll be in the rose garden," before he retreated back along that nightmarish corridor.

"What the devil have you been doing to the damn door?" Hugh asked as he opened it to find Cecily cowering within. "I want you out of the way today, young lady, we have *laborers* due to satisfy that blasted viscount!"

Cecily held her hands up in defense and blinked as if she'd been in the dark for hours rather than minutes.

"I was so afraid — there was so much noise — I don't know what happened to the door — I kept my eyes closed!" Her words left her in a pitiful whine which she knew very well had no chance of softening Hugh's stony heart.

"I don't want you fluttering your eyelashes at the laborers." Hugh closed the door and locked it, though she suspected that would be no obstacle to Raf. "Perhaps you might occupy yourself elsewhere today, or keep to our rooms. I shall be hosting Lord Stewart in school. Mark me, my girl, I can risk no more upset for the viscount, he shan't brook it!"

And what would the blasted viscount make of a headmaster who locked his wife in a cell while he went off to find ladies of the night in Plymouth?

"I assure you, Dr. James, that I have no interest in laborers, and I'm sure they would have none in me. I doubt they'd even notice me."

Hugh made a sound that was somewhere between mirth and disgust as he bundled her into their rooms. There they stood, her husband pale and bloodless, his eyes ringed by jet-black circles, and as Cecily looked at him she reminded herself that she felt no fear, that there was nothing in the future but freedom and happiness.

"Prepare breakfast, I'm famished," he called, stalking toward the bedroom. "The laborers shall be here within the hour and I shall be watching you, Mrs. James. Even when I am not here, I miss nothing!"

Cecily bowed her head in pretend subservience and went into the kitchen. From the window she watched Raf cross the ghost garden toward the walls, wondering what her husband would think if he knew what was happening within the roses, let alone what had happened in that tiny study last night.

'I miss nothing.'

Not much.

Cecily set a plate heaped with bacon and egg and toast on the dining table. "Breakfast, Dr. James!"

She could hear footsteps clomping along the corridor and up the stairs and for a moment panic seized her as if it was the judge at large. But the addition of someone whistling a random tune and a shout of "Careful with the hammer there, old mate!" made Cecily realize that it had to be the laborers who were going to work on the tower.

Maybe *they* wouldn't be set on by the spirit of the long-dead judge.

"Dr. James?"

For someone who was allegedly famished, Hugh was doing a very good job of letting his huge breakfast go cold. Cecily's heart sank as she approached their bedroom. She had no wish to ever enter the room again, but she would have to, until this was all over. The door was ajar when Cecily knocked.

"Husband?" She winced, regretting the edge of frustration audible in her tone, but she couldn't hear him in there. Only the sound of heavy wheezing. Staying in the doorway, Cecily pushed the door and let it creak wide open.

Her husband was sitting on the bed among the shower of fallen plaster, beneath the chasm that had opened in the ceiling just the day before. He had changed into a black suit and his gown and now sat there, jaw slack, eyes staring at Cecily. *No,* one eye was staring, for covering the other, making a marble of it, was a swirled cataract.

"Wife," he said, his slack jaw barely moving, his voice the same ancient croak she had heard in the darkness. "Once there were three brothers. Now there is but one."

"I—I've prepared breakfast for you. Just as you asked." Cecily gripped the edge of her apron, desperate to hold on to something. Was he talking about the Whitmores? But equally he could have been talking about any number of families after the war.

Hugh rose from the bed, unfurling his long limbs as though he were a marionette. He stretched his fingers, cracking the knuckles, then took a step, lurching like a man whose skin was somehow ill-fitted to his body. As Cecily took a step back from the door, he cocked his head sharply, the bones in his neck giving a sharp *crack*. Then he finally straightened and asked the space between them, "Did the rope burn, Mrs. Whitmore? Did you repent your wrongs as you swung?"

Cecily stared. There was no one else there—not Isabella, for Cecily had come to recognize her presence now, even though it was something she could not define. "She won't rest," Cecily remarked, barely daring herself to speak. "She won't lie easy in her grave."

"A woman must be punished when she sins." He circled his shoulders now, eliciting more sickening *cracks* as he did, the pearlescent eye watching her. "If you are a good wife, Mrs. Whitmore, I shall not need to punish you as I did her."

From above came a cacophony of what sounded like masonry collapsing, followed by raised voices and running footsteps. The noise seemed to shake the creature before her out of his reverie and he pushed past Cecily and headed for the door, leaving her standing in the bedroom.

Dust pattered down on her from the crack in the ceiling, and Cecily hurried out into the hallway. Hugh had left the front door open but rather than pull it shut, she went out into the corridor. The cheerful whistling of the laborers had ceased.

She headed for the bottom of the stairs to the clocktower and peered up in the darkness. Drawn back to the scene of her incarceration by a force she couldn't understand, Cecily ascended the stairs. In the distance below she could hear the builders and her husband, their voices raised, Devonshire accents filled with fear as they stammered about *'voices'* and *'knocks'* and *'something unholy'*.

'Something unholy'. The wall that had bulged now glowed red as though an inferno was raging behind the bricks. It groaned and creaked and somehow seemed to strain before her very eyes. Then, with a deafening crack of thunder, it shattered.

Cecily screamed as broken shards of brick shot through the air and scattered against her. She crouched down, her arms around her head, and peered between her fingers. Her ears buzzed and the sounds of the school were very far away.

A whole new room had appeared behind the crumbling false wall.

She rose to her feet and approached the secret chamber, her curiosity far outstripping any fear. Cecily had lived here all her life—she was not going to be afraid.

I'm the honorary captain.

The jagged hole in the wall revealed what she could only describe as a cell. A shaft of light had forced its way through the grimy window and, among the dancing brick dust, Cecily could see a figure lying on the floor. She flinched and held back, her heart thudding, until she realized it wasn't moving.

It couldn't be a mannequin, left up here as a jape by some long-gone pupil, could it?

But Cecily knew it couldn't be. Because, as the dust settled, she saw the figure's face. Papery, the desiccated skin drawn back to turn the mouth into an eternal howl — she recognized Judge Whitmore.

"Did you suffer?" Cecily asked. "I hope you did."

She climbed through the hole into the room and squinted in the powdery air at the small space. The books all said that the judge had died in prison before his trial, but was *this* his prison here?

She saw a bed, its covers a gray shroud now, and blanketed in dust and grime a chair and desk upon which papers had lain undisturbed for centuries. There on the desk was a heavy Bible beneath a thick covering of cobwebs, and scattered on the floor, the forgotten remains of food and drink. On the walls, someone — the judge, she knew — had daubed symbols that meant nothing to her, though they looked far from holy. In the center of them was something unseen, hidden by a filthy bedsheet.

Reminding herself that the spirits of those she had loved and who loved her still were around her, even in this hellish place, Cecily pulled down the bedsheet. She coughed as the dust billowed up but there behind it was a portrait.

Of Isabella and her love.

The poses and expressions were identical to those in the sketches which had lain for so long in the box under the ghost garden. And here it was, the finished portrait, in oils so perfect that Cecily could almost have been looking at a tinted photograph. Was that his punishment, then? To be bricked up with a portrait of the lovers he had so cowardly sent to their graves?

Cecily looked closer at the painting. The backgrounds had been filled in, showing Isabella and her lover sitting in front of a formal garden. Cecily recognized it at once, the garden whose shadow now haunted the dried, brittle grass.

"At least his grave was marked," a wheezing voice said, and Cecily turned to see her husband standing in the ruins of the wall, the builders wide-eyed behind him, clutching their caps as they stared at the scene. "An honor I was denied. Summon the school, Mrs. James. There is to be an assembly."

Chapter Eighteen

He thinks he's Judge Whitmore.

Cecily hurried to the school secretary's office, but before she had reached the bottom of the stairs, a thought came to her.

He is Judge Whitmore.

Her husband had disappeared, his body was only a shell inhabited by a long-dead spirit.

Hoping the secretary wouldn't ask *why* Dr. James wanted to summon a special assembly, Cecily passed on the orders she had been given. The secretary, who looked her up and down without a comment on her disheveled appearance, picked up the enormous handbell that Cecily's grandfather had brought to the school and went off through the corridors, its heavy brass clapper clanging through the building.

Cecily followed the body of the school into the assembly hall. Hugh rarely allowed her to enter, but even though it had been so long since she had been in the huge wood-paneled room, it had never changed.

The teachers took up their positions on high-backed chairs around the walls, while the sixth form sat on benches at the back. The rest of the school filed in and sat cross-legged on the floor. Cecily received the occasional bemused look, and she realized that along with all the dust and dirt that she was caked in, there was a large, dusty cobweb on her sleeve. She brushed it off and tried to comb the dirt out of her hair with her fingers.

Although the pupils and their masters were meant to be silent in the assembly hall, there was excitement in the air and whispers and laughter filled the room. The boys were not daft—they knew something odd was going on at their school.

Even Cecily and Harriet were allowed to remain, stationed on either side of the door like sentinels, but of Raf, there was no sign.

Working in the garden, Cecil knew, hoping that someone, somehow, had told him of the discovery in the clocktower.

"School," Hugh began, his one good eye looking over the bleary faces of the boys, gathered for assembly before they would usually be eating breakfast, "today has been momentous for we have discovered, just as Mr. Carter did, the hidden tomb of a great man. Our building's founder, the honored Judge Edward Whitmore."

The boys stared at him blankly, then turned to one another. The whispered sound of dozens of boys asking, "Who?" and the occasional, "What the heck's he on about?" rang through the room.

Cecily clasped her hands, willing the boys to be silent. She tried to catch Harriet's attention, but her friend could only stare at the altered headmaster in mute alarm.

"Judge Whitmore built this house," he continued. "He lived here and died here and, we now know, has lain here in unconsecrated ground for centuries. Today, he has been returned to us and the school shall be placed into formal mourning for this great man."

Someone unleashed a high-pitched giggle, which turned rapidly into a nasal snort. Before long it spread like a virus and a row of boys were shaking with mirth, chortling at the headmaster.

So much for mourning.

Cecily was powerless to do anything—Hugh would've been furious if she had intervened, and who knew what the man who possessed him would do? She could only will the boys silently to stop before they riled the headmaster and the spirit that animated him.

"You shall wear your formal dress at all times. Lights will be out half an hour earlier and we will rise an hour beforetime to pray for Judge Whitmore. Meals shall be consumed in silence." He ignored the murmur of discontentment that the unwelcome news elicited but with his next words, Cecily had to physically keep herself from wincing. "All dramatic, musical and sporting pursuits shall be postponed and all home trips shall be canceled until Judge Whitmore has been laid to rest. This school will pay its respects!"

The boys shook their heads and a grumble filled the air. The masters too looked unhappy, their arms folded as they leaned toward each other to whisper their disapproval. Finally, one of the boys stood.

Cecily recognized him. The viscount's boy.

She gritted her teeth, waiting to see what the son of a peer of the realm would do.

The viscount's son tipped up his patrician head as though practicing his maiden speech at the House of Lords and announced, "Why, sir, that's jolly unsporting of you! The Whitmore fellow was a dashed murderer, and we have a rugger match on Wednesday with that school from Truro!"

"A murderer, says Master Toby Stewart?" Hugh leaned forward, his body moving in that odd, marionette manner again. He flicked his tongue over his lips. "Well, sir, one does not rise to the rank of head boy without some pluck. Join us on stage, Master Stewart, and tell us what you know of the late judge. Come, sir, don't be shy."

The house captains who flanked Toby all patted the head boy's arm as he rose from the bench and made his way down the aisle left between the cross-legged boys. He held his snub nose in the air, his hair oiled firmly in place. Adjusting his cuffs with utmost disdain, he hopped two at a time up the steps to the stage.

"Indeed, Dr. James, I shall tell the school exactly what I know about the devilish fellow, and they shall all be just as perplexed as I am that you should bestow honor upon him."

"Please do, young sir." Hugh's smile grew. "Share your wisdom with us."

Toby nodded, then stood at the edge of the stage. "There is a pamphlet on the Whitmores in the school library, but interested boys might wish to consult Mr. Basil Angier's *Puritan Devonshire Gentry*. If one can get past the terribly dry waffle about free will and God's grace and all that, one will find a story more shocking than many a penny dreadful. Because the judge was an utter cad! Do you know, an unknown pauper was murdered in this very building?"

Gasps ran through the gathered school.

"Yes, it's true!" Toby went on, as he warmed to his theme. "And the judge's own wife stood trial for it. And *he* presided over it!"

As the sons of several judges and barristers formed Toby's audience, the understanding of such corruption was intense.

"And she was found guilty. She was hanged, and he watched—yes, he *watched* his own wife die at the end of a rope. Then he went mad. Tormented by guilt, some say—tormented by her restless ghost, say others. Until, driven to his wits' end, he confessed. *The judge himself* had murdered the pauper, and ensured the judicial murder of his wife."

"And as an act of penance had a stone carved to memorialize the luckless man!" Hugh interjected and Cecily flinched.

Toby was clearly working the room, making eye contact with all the boys, nodding in affirmation. He shrugged at Hugh before returning to his flock. "So I say to you, my fellow pupils, do *we*, the boys of Whitmore Hall, wish to honor such a man?"

Some jocular wag started up a chorus of "Boo! Hiss!"

"And what of a wife who whored herself?" Hugh spat not just at Toby, but at the assembled faces. "Who rejected him for another? Who denied his marriage rights? Should she not have been punished? Let us put it to the vote, eh? House captains, raise your hands if you support our head boy and would not see Judge Whitmore honored with a resting place in our chapel?"

With muttered remarks of "The bally rotter!" and "Bloody shameful!" the house captains all raised their hands in support of Toby. The head boy nodded to

Hugh with a conciliatory shrug, like the leader of the winning party at an election to his losing opposite.

"Sorry, Dr. James, sir, but the lads have spoken."

"Indeed. Fine boys, one and all." He nodded, his smile cold and fixed as an alligator's. "House captains, head boy, let us go to Dr. James' private study and discuss this further. School dismissed!"

Dr. James. The judge has spoken.

As the boys stood, an almighty row started up, swiftly hushed by the masters who marshaled them out of the room. As quickly as the assembly hall had filled, it now emptied, and Cecily followed them.

She was stiff with apprehension, trembling with fear. The most intelligent, most sporting, most hopeful young men in the school were being led off to the lion's den. She couldn't warn them, and the boys went unknowingly to their doom.

Cecily knew why Hugh was taking the boys to his private study, sure that the judge wished to carry out their punishment beneath his own portrait, in the rooms that had once been his. They filed through the hallways and up the stairs, past the garden where Raf worked, oblivious, past the yawning door to the clocktower and into the headmaster's apartment. Hugh stood back as the confident boys walked into his study. Cecily had no choice but to pass him and, as she did, he caught her wrist.

"Your turn soon, my dear," the judge whispered before he followed the boys into the study and closed the door.

Cecily bunched her hands into impotent fists. Nausea swept through her. Hugh was gone, and in his place was someone far worse—and who, in the eyes of mortals, was her husband. A monster.

She ran to the window in case she could see Raf there, but there was no one outside. She decided to make a pot of tea, but she spilled the leaves over the table, her hands shaking so much that couldn't even hold a spoon.

This had happened in her childhood, the boys being led into her father's study for punishment. And she knew that the head boy and the house captains would face a similar fate. But it was worse now, so much worse.

What the hell will the judge do to them?

From the study she heard raised voices, those of not only her husband but the young men too. Then she heard the snap of the cane landing on knuckles and a boy's voice raised in a cry that sounded something close to agony.

Cecily ran for the study. She couldn't bear it anymore, she couldn't sit by while a bully reigned. She wouldn't be the victim anymore, nor let anyone else be. She elbowed the door open and barely saw the pupils. All she saw was the portrait behind Hugh's head, which he was slowly morphing into.

She lunged at Hugh and tried to grab the cane from him. "Leave them alone, you bloody bully! Leave them, all of them, you hateful man!"

Toby snatched his hand back from where it had been resting atop the desk but as he did, it left a slick of bright-red blood. He clamped his hand tight under his arm and hurried for the shelter of his friends, each as white-faced as the next. Hugh relinquished the cane to Cecily and rounded on the boys, bellowing, "Every last one of you can expect further punishment before this day is done! Your headmaster had a thing or two to learn about proper discipline!"

"Run, boys! Go!" Cecily shouted. "Find Mr. de Chastelaine, find Mr. Culpeck, quick!"

The boys hesitated, as if they didn't want to leave her, but the headmaster's fury and Cecily's insistence must have worked on them, and they hurried out of the room. With all her might, Cecily tried to snap the cane in two, but it only bent round on itself.

"Your husband was as weak as your father, an empty shell to be filled," Hugh spat. He seized Cecily by the front of her dress, that glassy eye rolling in its socket. "Locked away, forgotten...but *I* didn't forget. Trapped in the darkness, waiting for the daylight."

"Let me go—please!" Cecily's voice was high and tight with fear. She almost froze then but knowing that her husband was the puppet of an ancient, furious evil, Cecily fought back and swung the cane at the judge, trying to catch his arm to free herself from his grasp. He reeled away, one bony hand clamped over his good eye as a howl of agony escaped his lips.

Fury burned through Cecily's veins like lava and she whacked him again. As she drew back her arm to switch him for a third time, she held back. Did she make herself any better than him, her tormentor for all these years, if she succumbed to her rage? "You can't make me into a monster—I won't let you! You can't bend me like you did the men you worked your evil through!"

"You will *never* be rid of me." He dropped his hand and advanced toward her. "On my life, girl, I will thrash you into line!"

Cecily renewed her grip on the cane. She stood sideways on, the cane ready as if she were in bat. "Not before I thrash *you*, you horrible old bastard! I'm a woman, not a girl!"

"A woman, she says! A wife!" He threw his head back and gave a bark of mirthless laughter. "And one day, God willing, the mother of the house of Whitmore too?"

"I'm *not* your wife and I was never willingly Hugh's. And I'm barren, so there!" Cecily swished the cane and it cracked the air like a whip. He took another step toward her and the cape billowed like monstrous wings, blocking out the morning light. She had never seen a face so contorted with fury, so utterly inhuman.

"Your husband is barren," snarled the judge. "We shall discover together over the years if the same can be said for me!"

"That's enough!" The study door flew open, slamming into the wall, and light flooded into the room again. There were some of the boys who had fled and at their head Raf, scattered bloodstains threaded across the soil-spattered white shirt he wore. He still held the hatchet she had seen him with in the rose garden, its edge keen as ever.

"Raf!" Cecily ran for him and, careful to avoid his blade, threw her arms around his neck.

"Your viscount's on his way upstairs," Raf told Hugh. "Was it worth it? Three hundred years of hate and malice for this? Bloody hell, you're a sorry specimen."

"Your employment is terminated," Hugh told Raf coldly. "Be off the premises within the hour. Mrs. James, go to your room."

Toby piped up, "That's jolly unfair, sir! We fellows rather like old Chasty!"

"Go," Hugh repeated. "Or I shall have the police remove you."

Raf accepted his fate with a nod. For a second Cecily actually thought he was going to leave the room as he had been ordered to do but instead he bolted across the study and buried the head of the hatchet in the painted face of Judge Edward Whitmore.

Hugh let out another of those animal howls and it was still ringing around the room as Graham and Lord Stewart joined the head boy in the doorway.

"Mr. Culpeck, the headmaster and I are due a long and difficult conversation," the viscount told them. "In private."

Chapter Nineteen

Cecily sat on the Culpecks' sofa, nursing a cup of tea. By her feet were two carpetbags, all she needed for her meager belongings. Around her neck, hidden under her dress, Cecily wore the *cocosul*, along with her mother's locket and Isabella's ring on the chain.

"Thank you for offering to put me up, Hattie."

"I'm sure the gents will sort it all out," Harriet told her, patting her knee, but Cecily didn't feel so sure. Nearly an hour had passed since Raf had been summoned to the study to account for the fate of the painting, and nothing had been seen or heard of him since. Whatever Lord Stewart, the headmaster and his deputy and the pretend Latin master were discussing, it seemed to be taking a worrying amount of time. She thought again of the bloodstains on his shirt, wondering where they had come from.

"I suppose Dr. James will have to go on leave?" Cecily fidgeted in her chair. "Or be put in a home, perhaps? Oh, Harriet, I can't stay married to him!"

"I don't think he shall be put away, Cecily," Harriet replied with a frown. "If we put away every master who— Well, you know what I mean. If it were up to me, Gray would be in charge, the boys would be allowed to laugh as loud as they wished and the masters could marry whenever they wanted!"

Cecily fixed her gaze onto the floor. "He's been seeing other women."

"Gray did wonder," she admitted. "There's been gossip in the village, but we didn't think— I mean, don't take this the wrong way, but *Hugh?* Now, if you had said our Mr. de Chastelaine had been entertaining ladies, I might believe it, but Hugh has always been such a cold fish."

The memory of Raf lying back on the bed, his messy hair on the pillow, warmed Cecily. "Well, indeed, it wouldn't surprise me either if Mr. de Chastelaine had been seeing someone! But Hugh…" Cecily told Hattie about the telephone call, and the strong scent of another woman's perfume on her husband. Her friend's penciled eyebrows climbed higher and higher up her forehead.

"The rotten—" Harriet shook her head as the door opened and, as one, the women looked to it. Graham entered the room alone, his face drawn with concern.

"I think we've reached an accord." He settled into an armchair and pinched the bridge of his nose between finger and thumb. "What a sorry business this is."

Cecily put aside her teacup and smoothed her dress over her knees, steeling herself for what was about to come. "So…what's going to happen?"

"Dr. James has agreed to take a short leave of absence on the coast for the benefit of his health and will pass tonight in town with Lord Stewart." Graham looked down at his hands. "He has insisted that you join him on the coast, Mrs. James, or he will initiate proceedings against you and put you out of Whitmore Hall. I did explain that you should be allowed time to consider and he has agreed to hear your decision by supper tomorrow. I'm so very sorry and I know I have no business saying it, but I wouldn't want to see you going with him for all the money in the mint!"

Cecily picked at the dirt on her dress. "*He* will launch proceedings against *me*? Of all the... Do you know how I ended up like this? He locked me in the clocktower room last night and told me he was off to enjoy the company of harlots. That's the sort of man he is. He beats me, he bullies me, he has never, ever shown me the slightest crumb of affection. But I suppose everyone will say, *Oh look, there's the headmaster, what a good man, what a pillar of the establishment, and what a harridan he married, telling all those dreadful lies about him!* I've heard the voice of the man he cuckolded — do you know that? I have, because he telephoned. So I will tell my husband my decision tomorrow night — and I will tell him that he will be receiving a letter from *my* solicitor! And I will drag his hateful name through the dirt to be free of him, because he shouldn't be allowed to pretend to the world that he's moral and good when he's foul and corrupt."

"And if you need anything, you have friends in us," Harriet told her. "I hope you know that."

Graham nodded and went on, finally coming to the person about whom Cecily cared most of all. "All of this was agreed on the condition that Mr. de Chastelaine leave Whitmore Hall and not return. I've just seen him off from the gate. I can't tell you how sorry I was to see him go."

Cecily closed her eyes and hid her face in her hands. How could she find Raf now? He wouldn't leave her, though, she was convinced of that. He'd find a way. If he knew she was in the school still, he'd surely guess she was at the Culpecks', and he'd send a message to tell her where he was.

"He was my friend," Cecily told them, and she started to cry.

"He'll send word," Harriet assured her, patting Cecily's shoulder gently. But what if he didn't? *He will.*

And what of Isabella and her lover, destined never to find rest, never to be reunited after all?

Cecily scrubbed her eyes with a handkerchief, then folded it back into her pocket. "Would you mind if I had a bath? I'm a terrible, dusty mess, and my head aches so much I fear my skull might crack."

"Help yourself to all our hot water." Harriet smiled. "You deserve it!"

* * * *

After lounging in the bath until the water had turned cold, Cecily put on a clean frock and fresh stockings, and lay down on the bed in the Culpecks' spare bedroom. She had deliberately not thought of anything while in the bath, but now, as she tried to nap, memories of all the strange events of the past little while crowded in on her and she couldn't drop off to sleep.

In one day she would lose everything she had ever known. She had nothing to her name but those two bags and the memories of Whitmore Hall but still Cecily would persevere. Better penury than another day beside Hugh or Judge Whitmore or whoever he was. The stone pendant lay against her skin, cool and smooth, and she thought again of the bloodstains and of Raf's hair against the pillow, his blue eyes blinking awake to the dawn.

The room was stuffy, so Cecily rolled off the bed and drew back the curtain to open the window. She almost didn't spot it at first, it was so small, but there it was again. The tiny bat.

"I'm very glad to see you. This might be goodbye."

It flew up from the ledge and into the room, then, with a little loop and dive, settled in Cecily's hand. Cecily stroked its head. "Maybe you can come and visit? I won't be here much longer, little friend."

The bat peered up at her and she saw that its tiny body was scratched and nicked, as though it had been in a fight of some sort. How small it was in her hand, how vulnerable.

"What happened to you? I hope you didn't get on the wrong side of a cat." Cecily nursed it against her cheek, then kissed the top of its head. To her surprise, the creature fluttered in a rather flustered manner and landed on the bed, burrowing down under the sheets as though trying to hide. It disappeared beneath the quilt and became still.

Cecily wondered how the heck she was going to explain this to Harriet and Graham. *My husband's been possessed by an insane seventeenth-century judge and I've lost a bat in your spare bed.*

"Little friend?" Cecily took the edge of the bedsheet, ready to gently peel it back to reveal its tiny occupant. "You don't need to hide from me. I'm not scary — honest! I won't kiss you again, if that's what you didn't like."

"Didn't like it? I love it!"

Cecily gasped in shock. That was Raf's voice. Coming from under the bedsheets. "Oh, God, I need to see a doctor. I'm going mad!"

"I thought—" Raf threw the covers back to his waist, revealing a very naked, very scratched chest. "—that we were going to Yorkshire! Hello, Captain!"

Cecily put her arms around him—carefully, to avoid the scratches. She was so pleased to see him that she couldn't yet work out how he'd got there. "*Please* take me to Yorkshire! I can't stay here any longer." She placed a gentle kiss on one of his many scratches. "*Was it a cat?*"

"Not quite." He kissed the top of her head. "It was a very angry vine. The judge's a pretty determined bloke, but I was the one with the ax."

"You were attacked by a plant in the rose garden?" Cecily marveled at him. "No wonder you look sore, but I've got that bottle of your lotion here with me, so let's dab it on. And will you please explain what just happened? You're my little bat friend, aren't you? Although not at the moment…"

Cecily reached for the carpetbag by the bed and took out the lotion, which she had wrapped in a cardigan. She took off the cap and inhaled the scent. Then she looked at Raf, one arm pillowed behind his head as he reclined in what had been a sorry bed indeed until a few moments ago.

"I was born in a castle on the edge of a cliff high above a treacherous mountain pass." Raf smiled, then winked one mischievous eye. "In Transylvania."

"I've read *Dracula*." Cecily tipped some of the lotion onto a cloth. If long-dead judges could possess grown men, then she wasn't about to disbelieve what Raf was saying, bizarre as it might be. "But I didn't think for a moment that — you're a vampire? But how? You're out and about in the daytime!"

"Mum was vampire, but Dad's a Yorkshireman. That makes me *dhampir*, a little bit of both." He shrugged and went on, "I'd hoped I wouldn't have to tell you. After your husband, I had an idea that you'd be glad for a normal bloke, and, most of the time, that's me. It's just on the odd occasion that — Well, sometimes I'm a bat."

Cecily pressed the cloth to one of his scratches and gently wiped the lotion on. His skin was so pale and — "Hence the lotion you put on when you go outside! Oh, Raf, I don't care if you're sometimes a bat, I love *you*. As long as you're not sometimes a maniac Puritan, I'm happy."

"I'm nowhere near Puritan." He laughed, biting back a gasp as she wiped the angry red slashes. "And before you worry, I don't drink blood. I'll eat black pudding, but that's the Yorkshire side."

Cecily paused in her ministrations to ruffle his hair, then went on applying the lotion. "I liked it when you kissed my neck, though. Do you have pointy teeth too? I can't say I noticed."

"Little ones." He grinned and she saw now that his canines *were* sharp and just a little pronounced, though hardly the terrible fangs of lore. Demi-fangs, maybe.

"Goodness!" Cecily tapped the point of one of them. She had no idea if this was correct etiquette when conversing with a dhampir, but she was curious. Suddenly a lot about Raf made sense. How else could he be so good at investigating strange goings-on that he was known to the Home Office? He had it in his blood, it appeared. "Did your mother have sharp teeth?"

"She did! Proper fangs. We called them her gnashers." He smiled. "And she taught me how to fly and do proper fancy loops and whatnot. And she taught me never to let a bastard like Judge Whitmore win."

Cecily kissed him on his mouth, but she didn't want to linger in case he was sore from the scratches. "Graham told me what Hugh—or Judge Whitmore—has decided. Did you hear about that?" Cecily rested her head on Raf's shoulder and continued to dab on the lotion.

"I heard it and I meekly packed up my stuff and drove away, because sometimes it's easier to let them think they've got you." She felt his lips against her hair again. "I nipped up to look at the judge while you lot were all in the hall. Ugly old bugger, wasn't he?"

"I suppose it'll have to be buried, won't it?" Cecily screwed up her nose with distaste at the thought of that horrible papery mummy. "But from the way Hugh or whoever he is was going on about it, it's like he thinks there should be a ceremony at Exeter Cathedral!"

"You saw the writing on the wall up there?" His tone was light but she sensed the daubings were anything but.

Cecily shook her head. "I saw a lot of symbols scrawled onto the wall, but I couldn't make head nor tail of them."

"It's black magic. Some sort of binding spell," Raf explained. "I think our judge was worried about his day of reckoning so he bound himself to the house, ready for death. Somewhere in here there'll be a physical *something*, an anchor that he's latched onto. I thought it might be the painting of him but it isn't. I shredded that thing and he's still here."

"What on earth did you say to them when they asked you about the painting? Which, I have to say, I'm very pleased you shredded!"

"I told them it was the painting or the headmaster, so I chose the painting." Raf smiled. "And I *know* there's something out there in the garden. The vines were alive, like whips. Look at the state of me! I'm coming back in the morning once I know he's gone and the coast's clear and I'm going to hack the whole bloody lot down. If he's anchored to something in there, I'll find it."

Cecily shivered. "This is all too horrible! And to think I've lived my whole life in this house, and all along there's been an unburied corpse in the attic—it's vile!"

"I've got a confession," Raf admitted, his voice filled with that characteristic naughtiness. "When I was up there earlier, I pinched the portrait. I know I shouldn't have, but Isabel and that poor nameless bloke don't deserve to be left up there. It's in my car with the rest of my gear."

Cecily took his hand. "I'm glad you rescued the portrait. If only we knew who the poor man was, then at the very least he could have his name on his headstone."

"I just wish we knew how the judge ended up walled into the clocktower." Raf snuggled Cecily into his arms and held her to his chest, his lips resting on her hair. "Just so I know, you sure you're going to be happy with a gorgeous, sexy, admittedly not too tall dhampir like me? I don't make a habit of the bat thing, I just had to make sure you were safe and since I'm not exactly a threatening, scary bat, it seemed like the best way!"

"I love you, Raf." Cecily kissed him. "The fact that you don't like the sun and you have the power to turn into a bat sometimes doesn't change a thing."

"I used to be able to turn into a bat whenever the mood took me," Raf told her. "But maybe I flew over a few too many battlefields because for a few years after the war, I could hardly do it at all. Since I met you, I seem to have a pretty good batting average, though! I tried to squeeze into the crack when it opened but it was a bit too snug—I didn't want to get stuck!"

"I suppose you'll have to turn back into a bat in order to leave." Not that Cecily wanted to think of him leaving but, unless as a bat he wore tiny underpants that could increase in size on his return to human form, Raf had to be completely naked under the bedclothes. And if a naked Raf was found in the room with her, it might make life rather awkward. "You could take a leaf from Bonnie Prince Charlie's book and put on one of my dresses!"

"I'm not in a hurry to fly away just yet," he assured her. Nor was Cecily in any hurry to see him go. He was the only thing that had been constant, even if he *did* have a rather unexpected ability to turn into a pipistrelle.

"If Hattie wants me, she'll knock—she's not the sort to come barging in." Cecily hugged Raf, trying to avoid his scratches. He held her close and she reveled in it, in his secrets and his love. Even the creak she heard sent no shiver through her for it couldn't be the judge now, could it? After all, the judge was to spend the evening in town with Lord Stewart, no doubt to discuss how all this might be brushed under the carpet without causing embarrassment to any member of the sainted *establishment*, Hugh included.

"I need to find the anchor," Raf murmured as another creak sounded. "Otherwise he could be hopping between bodies for another three centuries, getting stronger with every passing year."

Cecily noticed a movement from the corner of her eye. Had she left the window open? But it wasn't the window. As she looked up from Raf's shoulder, she saw the wardrobe door had come ajar, and inside it—

"There's someone in the wardrobe!"

She could see a dark shape among the hanging clothes, and the light reflected from something—not a mother-of-pearl button, but a cataract.

"It's the judge!"

"He can't leave." Raf dragged one of the sheets from the bed and wrapped it around his waist. He sprang to his feet and wrenched the wardrobe door open, revealing nothing within but winter coats. "He bound himself so tight to the house that he can't leave it—he's not strong enough yet. He might be out of his cell, but old Whitmore can't get any farther than his precious estate—for now." Raf closed the door and turned back to Cecily. "Fancy a night out? That rotten old sod can't, but you can."

Cecily forced herself to look away from the wardrobe. *He can't hurt me. The judge can't hurt me.*

"Leave? Just for a night—" She clasped her hands. "Oh, even just for a night would be splendid!"

"We can go now if you like, if Harriet lets you!" He caught her hands and squeezed them, letting the bedsheet fall. "I drove a couple of minutes down the road and parked in a little lane just over the bridge. It goes off into the woods, do you know it?"

"Yes, I do—it's the bluebell woods!" Cecily closed her eyes. She couldn't get nostalgic for the school—her future lay elsewhere. She opened her eyes again. "I'll tell Harriet that I'm going down to the Royal Oak in the village to find out about their rooms. And that I might stay there for dinner—to put some distance between myself and this place. She'll understand."

He raised her hands to his lips and kissed them. "Is this what you want? You've been ordered around all your life. I'm not going to do that."

"I *want* to go. I wanted to ten years ago, but I didn't get the chance. And if I don't leave now, I never will." Cecily stroked Raf's jaw and ran her hand up into his hair. "I do have happy memories here—but they're so often crowded out by the bad. As you said, Mummy and Sandy will be with me wherever I go. And if they're at my side, then I'll carry those happy memories with me."

"And every step you take along the drive, you'll have the world's least-threatening bat flying alongside." Raf smiled and Cecily could suddenly see the similarities in this compact man with his shock of dark hair and that determined little pipistrelle. It was the perfect bat for a man like Raf.

"One kiss before we leave?"

"One kiss from a naked dhampir," he agreed, taking her face in his hands. "Never forget that I love you."

"Nor I you." Cecily brought her lips to his and as they kissed, she put her arms around him, holding her *naked dhampir*. As the kiss finally ended to allow them to draw breath, Cecily found her arms empty but the air was anything but, filled as it was with the beating wings of the bat. He settled on her shoulder, the warmth of his body proof that this was as real as it seemed. As real as the fearsome creature in the clocktower.

"I'll see you outside soon." Cecily stroked the bat's velvet fur. Raf lifted from her shoulder and fluttered out through the window, leaving Cecily alone once more.

Chapter Twenty

With a carpetbag in each hand, Cecily walked out of the school. Down the stairs from the masters' residences, through the door, across the lawn and onto the driveway. The poplars framed her route as she strode along, each step taking her farther away from the place that had for so long been her prison.

She was leaving, at last, and as she'd told her white lie to Harriet, she had smiled. It wasn't easy fibbing to one of her very few friends, and she felt no pride in it, but she was so happy to go that she couldn't hide it.

Cecily only paused to glance up at the sky overhead for a glimpse of Raf. Just as he had promised, he was there above her, banking and swooping as he accompanied her along the driveway to freedom. Cecily put down one of the bags for long enough to wave at him, then picked it back up again and continued on her way, walking faster now that she could see the school perimeter ahead.

The imposing iron gates were open and Cecily inwardly cheered as she crossed the threshold and was at last out on the road. She could already picture the lane and the bridge, and tried to picture Raf's car. How well it suited him, that little red Austin 7, and how Sandy would have loved it. It couldn't be more different from Hugh's stately vehicle, yet it was that car that now purred to a halt alongside and it was the thin figure of her husband who climbed from within, leaving the unimpressed viscount in the passenger seat.

"Mrs. James," he called, his eyes now nothing more horrible than their usual rheumy selves. "Do I take it you have made your decision?"

Cecily stopped. She gripped the handles of her carpetbags more firmly. "I made my decision ten years ago." Raising her chin imperiously, she strode on.

"The judge is a great man. *I* am likewise," he informed her. "He and I together shall make another Eton here, Mrs. James, would you not like to sit beside us as we do? To be the mother of our children?"

Cecily halted again. Revulsion crept through her as she looked at the man who had crushed her dreams a decade ago. The man who had never loved her and who now played host to a monster. That demon was not in him now, she realized—Judge Whitmore was bound to the grounds of the school. But even without his puppetmaster, there was nothing pleasing in her husband at all.

"Never! I would rather beg for scraps on my hands and knees than be wife to you and that beast!"

"Then I *will* destroy you," Hugh whispered, any further threats silenced when Raf swooped down to flutter in the headmaster's face, his wings batting and jabbing until Hugh finally returned to the car. At the door he called, "Be sure of it, madam!"

Cecily glanced at the viscount. Could he hear all this? Did he really want the man to be in charge of his son's school?

I am the honorary captain.

She returned her attention to Hugh. "You've already spent ten years trying to destroy me, Hugh—and you couldn't bloody well manage it!"

As Hugh started the engine and drove past Cecily, she could see the anger in his companion's face, see the viscount's finger jabbing as he remonstrated with her husband. What the two men could possibly hope to achieve in their summit she hardly knew, for it didn't look as though Lord Stewart was going to be sympathetic to the headmaster after all.

Hugh. She hadn't called him that since their wedding breakfast, when he had twisted her hand back on itself and demanded that she only ever call him *Dr. James.* She had tried to be affectionate with him, to start with, but he had rejected her attempts and had never been affectionate in return, so she had soon stopped. And that had been the pattern of the last ten years.

Not anymore. Cecily continued along the road until she saw the lane. She ran part of the way, ignoring the carpetbags thudding against her legs, the jewelry around her neck jangling.

Up ahead was Raf's car.

"Raf?" Cecily glanced about, wondering if she would see a man or a bat.

"I'm here, Captain!" She saw his arm wave from behind the car. "Fancy helping me get dressed, you gorgeous thing?"

Cecily approached. "It won't be as fun as *un*dressing you, I suppose?"

He shrugged as he placed the tangle of charms around his neck. "And I'm not wearing a bloody tie!"

"You wouldn't be Raf if you were wearing a tie." Cecily rounded the car and dropped the carpetbags. Her hands were sore, and she flexed them as she looked Raf up and down. He really had a marvelous figure, even with those scratches, so firm and strong. A tingle ran through her as she remembered their night together. "Right, what would you like me to do?"

"If you do *that* here, we'll get arrested." Raf winked. "Why don't you just enjoy this amazing Carpathian view and tell me what you want to do with this afternoon?"

Cecily leaned back against the car and breathed in the scent of the nearby woodland as she ran her gaze over Raf's muscled body. "Why don't we go for a drive, up on Exmoor?"

"We could find a little pub." He nodded, glancing down at the cuts and scratches she had cleaned. "Somewhere with pretty rooms for the prettiest woman in Devon?"

Cecily unpinned her cloche hat and ran her hand through her hair. "Are you suggesting we spend a naughty afternoon together, Mr. de Chastelaine?"

"Hmm." He buttoned his trousers and paused as though considering the question. "I'm suggesting that you take me to bed and ravish me, Captain Sissy. Or, even better, let's ravish each other?"

"That sounds like an admirable plan. We could instead go for tea somewhere, I suppose. Somewhere nice for scones with lots of cream." Cecily ran her tongue over her lower lip. "But the ravishing sounds more fun. And we can always have the scones and cream for supper."

He scooped up his shirt. How strange to think that just minutes ago this man had flown overhead as a bat, yet her world seemed full of such strangeness now. Now she could wear the ring and the locket as often as she wished, for Cecily was about to embark on a life of her own. She lifted the locket and Raf's *cocosul* from where she had hidden them inside her dress. Cecily unfastened the locket to remove Isabella's ring from the chain and put it on her finger again.

"Such a pretty ring..." Cecily nodded toward at Raf. "Exmoor will be lovely this time of year — we might just be in time to catch the end of the heather. It'll all be purple, as far as the eye can see."

Raf buttoned his shirt and stooped to fasten his shoes, offering her a rather eye-catching view of his bottom. Even as he did, he said, "Stop looking at my bum — I know you English girls."

"You have a fine rump, sir!" Cecily giggled as she put her hat back on. "Raf, I have a confession to make. I'm ever so sorry, but could I borrow some money from you? Or come to some sort of arrangement? I'll pay you back, I don't know how, but I will. I wouldn't want you to pay for the whole of our day out."

"Yeah, we need to talk about that." He nodded. "But I'd like to pay for the day out, either way."

How embarrassing for us both, Cecily thought, bracing herself for his polite rebuttal. Raf picked up her bags effortlessly and put them into the car, then opened the passenger door for her. Cecily nodded her thanks as she climbed in, brushing toffee wrappers from the seat.

"I know you said I could help you out with your…your work, Raf, but I really wouldn't want to be a burden."

"The thing is, I don't need *helping out*. You'll be a partner," Raf replied as he climbed in beside her. "And being a partner means getting a proper day's pay for a day's work. So I won't give you a loan but I'll give you an advance on your first earnings as a *spiritual operative*, how's that sound? Once Whitmore Hall's settled, I'll stick an invoice in and your name'll be on it next to mine. You won't be in debt to me, and I've got no plans to keep you under the thumb, that's not how I do things."

"A *spiritual operative*?" Cecily raised an eyebrow. "I've never had earnings before, or appeared on an invoice either, for that matter—oh, this is so exciting!"

She leaned across and kissed Raf's cheek. "That's so lovely of you, I really appreciate it." Another thought occurred to her and she blushed. But it would have to be broached, though she wasn't sure how. "So it's a family business, then?"

"It has been up till now." He smiled, showing off those sharp canines again. "Did you just propose?"

"Erm…perhaps a little!" Cecily took his hand. "What I wanted to say was, I'd thought…*assumed*…that I couldn't…and—well, Hugh—the judge—maybe you overheard?" Cecily tightened her grasp. "Oh, Raf, put it this way—I thought I couldn't have children, but it may well be the case that actually…I might be able to. I wanted you to know, what with all the ravishing, in case we end up with little bats flying about."

"I'd like that," he laughed. "Me and you, Mr. and Mrs. D.C.? The answer's yes, but until we make it official, how much convincing would you take to live in glorious sin with a good-looking lad from Transylvania?"

"Very little convincing at all!" Cecily rested her cheek on his shoulder. "We're going to have a wonderful time, aren't we, you and I?"

"We're going to laugh a lot and eat way too much chocolate," he replied. "And we're going to leave this place happier than we found it. I love you, Captain Sissy."

"I love you too, Raf!" Cecily kissed his cheek again, then settled back in her seat. "And off we go to Exmoor—I'm so excited, Raf, I haven't been on a day out in ages!"

Raf beamed as the car pulled out onto the narrow road and together, they left Whitmore Hall behind. The air was filled with the scent of flowers and the song of birds and Cecily could hardly bring herself to believe that this was truly happening. What would Sandy say if he knew?

Probably 'it's about time'.

The world seemed somehow different now, as though someone had taken a paintbrush and made the colors more vibrant, the air clearer. Yet somewhere in the wide blue sky Isabella still waited, and Cecily knew that the solving of that long-buried mystery would herald the end of one story and the beginning of another. She wouldn't let Isabella Whitmore down.

How long had it been since she had traveled so far from the school? So long that she could hardly remember, for her horizons had long since shrunk down to the school grounds and, more often than not of late, the apartments where little trace of Cecily could be found. It was as if she were a ghost herself, passing silently through the shadows, occasionally glimpsed at the windows of Whitmore Hall.

"What's on your mind, gorgeous?" Raf asked after a while of contented silence. "Not worrying about my fangs, are you? I'm not the sort to carry a wench off to my castle, don't worry."

"I rather like your fangs, actually! Gosh, it's been so long...can you smell the heather? It's like honey!" Leaning forward in her seat, Cecily peered out at the road ahead as it wound between the hedges. She knew this road, she was certain of it. "There's a turning just up ahead, a crossroads—you need to turn right."

Raf was happy to obey, following her directions without question. This would take some getting used to, Cecily realized, but she'd manage it.

The road *felt* familiar, but Cecily knew she hadn't seen it before. Unless it had been so long ago, in her childhood perhaps, that its route was there in her mind even if she wasn't sure how. It headed over high land and the view, when they could see between the gaps in the hedges, was of rough moorland spreading far away in all directions, striped with sunlight falling between the passing clouds. Human habitation looked tiny from up where Raf now drove, as if the broad hills and sudden valleys, the bare rocks and stubby trees, were a world apart.

Which they were. Something ancient, as if the passing of a decade in Cecily's world had passed here in only a second.

"How does this compare with Carpathia?" Cecily asked.

"It's a lot more purple." He smiled, bringing the car to a standstill at the top of the hill, the heather here far more abundant than Cecily had been expecting. "But you'll be able to make your own mind up once you've seen both!"

"Go abroad?" Cecily stared open-mouthed. "I've only left Devon a handful of times, and that was to go to Somerset! Truly? Oh, I should love to—and see you family castle?"

"And the family that live in it!"

Cecily shuffled over to sit closer to Raf. "Are they all vampires, or...dhampirs too?" She asked the question as simply as if she was asking him the color of their hair.

He slipped his arm around her shoulders and admitted, "They're vampires, but there are humans and dhampirs in the family too. And every one of them's housetrained."

"Good to hear." Cecily thought once more about Raf lunging, in bat form, at Hugh. "Only flying in the faces of particularly obnoxious people!"

"God, I enjoyed that!" Raf laughed. "I'm the littlest bat in the family, but I do all right."

"You were fearsome!" Cecily chuckled. "Doesn't matter if you're tall or short, does it?"

"Not a bit! I still gave him something to think about." He winked. "He won't forget me in a hurry."

"He certainly wasn't expecting it."

Cecily watched the light change over the hills as the clouds drifted on overhead. She twisted Isabella's ring and felt restless. Was this freedom, a yearning to be off and moving? "There's a house..."

Cecily could picture it, though she wasn't sure why. Sturdy and made from stone, its windows set deep into its thick walls to survive the winter on the moors. She knew she had never been there—had she dreamed of it? But why did it appear to her now?

"Let's get back to it." Raf kissed her cheek, as easy and natural as lovers should be. "Where am I headed?"

"Keep along this road, then there's" — Cecily closed her eyes — "a tree at a fork in the road, and you need to turn left. There's a stream running alongside, and the road is very narrow and steep. You'll think you can't go along it, but you can."

She opened her eyes. "Raf, I'm remembering this from somewhere, but I don't know where. Is it — could it be Isabella? Is she showing me the way?"

"Like I said, some people can hear them, and not always as voices." He reached across to squeeze her hand. "In my business, we call people like that *sensitives*. I think that might be what you are. If it is, it's nothing to fear, it's just one more talent."

Having been told throughout her life that she was good for very little, Cecily struggled to conceal her surprise. "So along with not being too bad at cricket and baking, ghosts can show me things, and make me feel what they did? How very odd — I'd never heard of that before."

"Turn left at a tree at a fork," Raf repeated as they arrived at a towering oak where the road divided in two. He took the left-hand turn as instructed. "It's not something people tend to realize. They just think they've got a vivid imagination or, worse, they're told it's *nerves*."

Cecily held on to the strap above the door as the car turned. "Nerves? Oh, yes, I've been told that often enough! *Cecily, you're a weak woman*. I'm bombarded by emotions sometimes — I'm glad to know it has a name."

"It's a big deal in my game," he assured her merrily. "I wish I could do it!"

"I never thought of it as a strength, as something that might be useful. At least, I *hope* it's useful." Cecily jumped as branches squeaked against the window. "Wherever is Isabella taking us?"

"Which way now?" He peered through the windscreen at the narrowing road. "So this is the bit I think I can't fit the car down?"

"Yes," Cecily said, her voice soft and faraway. "It spooks the horses." She looked at Raf with bemusement. "Sorry about that—*what* horses?"

"You started it," he laughed. "Breathe in, this *is* narrow!"

The road was penned in between a steep rise on one side and the stream on the other. Trees overhead arched across the road and turned it into a tunnel of green and gold light, their branches scraping along the paintwork of Raf's car.

"Gosh, I wish we had a map!" Cecily gripped the strap more tightly. "I hope you don't get a scratch. No wonder the horses were spooked!"

"I'm scratched enough," he grinned. "Perils of gardening for a miserable old judge."

"Whenever you need more lotion on, you just let me—oh, God!" A flash of brown and red shot across the road, vanishing through the trees. "That *was* a pheasant, wasn't it? Not a ghost."

"I have to put a *lot* of lotion on." He pouted, nodding. "Before sun, after sun, battling with possessed vines. It's a full-time job."

"I'm a willing spare pair of hands, Raf...so you know."

The light suddenly changed and they were out of the tunnel of trees, the lane widening before them.

Dizziness crept up on Cecily, and she clutched the edge of her seat. "We're nearly there, I'm certain of it!"

"Keep following Isabella, but keep talking to me," Raf instructed, stroking his hand against hers. "Remember she's only visiting."

"All right, let me just…" Cecily closed her eyes and the impressions came to her quickly. "We're so close now…the house is by the stream. At least…is it a house? No — it's an old inn. A coaching inn. There's a high archway. I can see the sign swinging, and it's got a red frame, but I can't read it."

Raf said nothing but kept the car inching forward toward their mysterious destination. Cecily, her eyes still closed, felt the car take a tight corner, as if pulling out of the lane, and once the road straightened out, she said, "We're here."

She opened her eyes and after miles of uninhabited moorland lanes, they were on a wider road outside a large stone-built inn. Smoke rose up from its chimneys and its door and window frames were painted a cheerful red. A sign creaked back and forth, announcing it to be *The Captain's Rest.*

"What a wonderful place to come and hide away in! Shall we have a cup of tea?" Cecily asked.

"At least a cup of tea. I'm in the mood for scones!"

Cecily kissed his cheek. "Do you think they might — perhaps — have a room for us?"

"For Captain and Mr. Pincombe?" He turned off the engine and opened the car door. "I'll ask for the best they have."

"Captain and Mr. Pincombe!" Cecily held out her left hand toward Raf to show him her wedding ring. "It's as well I've still got this! Though I should rather throw it away. But people will assume *you're* my husband, and I don't mind that at all."

He kissed her hand then climbed from the car. Before Cecily had the chance to open her own door, Raf was there to do it for her, something that Hugh had certainly never done. She wasn't even allowed to carry her bags to the inn, as Raf took Cecily's luggage and his own tatty old knapsack, hefting them as though they weighed next to nothing. The box was safely tucked beneath one arm while the painting, covered by a sheet, remained safe in the car.

Cecily spotted someone at the window, and the door of the inn was flung wide for them by a rosy-cheeked woman in a polka dot dress.

"Welcome, welcome! Come in, do!" she said, in a warm Devonshire accent. "You've traveled a long way, by the look of it! And you'll be wanting a room, I shouldn't wonder?"

"We're eloping," Raf whispered in his most exotically lustful Romanian tones. "Captain and *Mr.* Pincombe. We're desperate for a big bed and a warm welcome."

Cecily blushed hotly. *Eloping* — if only.

"I've got the perfect room — right at the other end of the inn. We're quiet this time of year, see, not as many charabancs passing by. You'll more or less have that whole side of the place to yourselves!" The woman giggled like a girl half her age, and beckoned them to follow up the stairs. "You want a hand with those bags, sir? And did you say, your lady here is a captain? Well I never!"

"I'm a strapping lad, you leave these bags to me." He winked, as though sharing a secret. "If you've got scones and clotted cream in the house, I might just have to kiss you!"

She hooted with laughter and tucked escaping tendrils of gray hair behind her ears. "You naughty fellow—as it happens, I do have scones and finest Devon clotted cream too, and whortleberry jam as well. That's our local speciality, that is. I can bring it to your room and leave it by your door, if you'd rather not come to the dining room."

They had reached the top of the old, carved wooden stairs now, and a carpeted corridor led off, left and right.

"This'll be the way, then," she said, and headed off past the closed doors of apparently uninhabited rooms.

"And what do we call you, other than an angel?"

"That'd be Mrs. Holberton, sir," she told them. "Me and the husband run the place."

At the end of a corridor decorated with velvet wallpaper and a motley collection of portraits and landscapes, Mrs. Holberton pulled a bunch of keys from her pocket and opened the door in front of them. "If you like dancing, by the way, we've got a gramophone downstairs—we like to have music here of an evening, and Mr. Holberton and I take a turn around the floor."

Raf looked to Cecily with a delighted grin. "I love to dance. Can you believe, I've never danced with my girl?"

Cecily slid her arm through Raf's. Mrs. Holberton, this jolly stranger, was the first person to see them together as a couple. "It's true, we've never had the chance."

"Well, you shall have the chance tonight! Anyway…is the room all right for you? It's got its own bathroom, by the way."

"What do you think, gorgeous?" Raf looked to Cecily. "Special enough for my lady?"

The room was dominated by a large, curtained bed, and was full of heavy, dark wooden furniture and velvet upholstery. It was a place to be cozy, and a place to be free. Cecily was aware that she was seeing it from a double perspective—Isabella was there somewhere with her, appraising the room and believing it to be in the highest fashion.

Perhaps she even stayed here.

"Yes, it's lovely, thank you, Mrs. Holberton."

"Our rates, Mr. Pincombe..." Mrs. Holberton nodded, as she passed Raf a discreet card. "Very reasonable, I assure you."

"You're underselling yourself," he assured her. "And that's before I've tasted your scones."

"Oooh, now!" Mrs. Holberton exclaimed. "You two get yourselves settled in and I'll bring you your scones. I'll leave them outside your door."

Mrs. Holberton placed the room key on the bedside table and closed the door behind her as she left.

Raf put the bags down. He placed the box carefully on the bed and turned to take Cecily in his arms. "*Our* castle," he told her.

Cecily sighed happily and wrapped Raf in an answering embrace. "What a wonderful place to run away to—Isabella has excellent taste, doesn't she!"

"Is she here with us?"

"I have a sense that she might be." Cecily scanned the part of the room she could see over Raf's shoulder. "But I can't see her or hear her. She brought us here, I know that, though."

"So, what would you like to do now?"

Cecily drew her thumb over Raf's lips and stroked her other hand across his shoulders, passing lower until it settled at the small of his back. "Kiss you, rub lotion on you, ravish you…how does that sound?"

"It sounds like a perfect way to spend an afternoon." He kissed the pad of her thumb. "Ravish me, Captain. Go wild."

With one hand, Cecily unpinned her hat and threw it to land wherever it would. Then she rushed her mouth to Raf's and caught his lips in a kiss. There was no tentativeness now, but passion, and Cecily let herself be carried along by it, their kiss deepening.

'Go wild,' he had said. She had never gone wild in her life. But she had never met a dhampir or heard a ghost either, so perhaps now was the time for firsts.

She ran her hand lower, over his bottom, and held it there, feeling the firmness of his buttocks. Giving free reign to her desire to touch and enjoy a man, especially the man she loved, was new to Cecily. Beneath her hand his bottom tensed, then he dotted kisses down her jaw and over her throat, trailing heat over her skin.

Not wanting to waste a moment, Cecily began to unbutton Raf's shirt, her fingers clumsy with haste. As soon as she reached the hem of his shirt, she unbuttoned his trousers and stroked her way inside. She was surprised at her own boldness but Raf's answering gasp and the press of his erection against Cecily's hand told her that she had no need to be shy. He grazed his teeth lightly against her skin and whispered, "You caught yourself a dhampir, Sissy."

Cecily trembled at the sensation of his teeth, but went on stroking him. "I'm very glad I did!"

"You know I don't expect anything from you, don't you?" This time his voice was softer. "I'm not him —

your life's your own now. If you want to share it with me, that's *my* good fortune, not yours."

Cecily ran her other hand up Raf's back as she went on stroking him. New sensations ran through her body just to touch her lover. "Oh, Raf, you have no idea, to have a choice—to decide what *I* want to do…and right now, I want *you*. If you don't mind." His body's reaction suggested he didn't mind one bit.

"One thing you'll learn about me once we get back to the garden." He danced another flurry of kisses against her neck. "I don't like shoes and I don't like shirts. Which can be a problem for a bloke who's sensitive to sun."

Cecily chuckled. "So I've found myself a half-naked dhampir who needs lots of lotion rubbed on? I don't see a problem there at all." She mimed stroking lotion on his tattooed back, circling her hand against his skin. She felt the heat of Raf's laughter against her throat and heard the soft sound of fabric as he let the shirt slide down his arms onto the floor.

"I think we're going to get on fine," he teased. "So what about this ravishing?"

"I can't ravish you with your trousers on." Cecily allowed his trousers to fall, but nothing fell with them. Raf de Chastelaine, it appeared, had no truck with underpants. "Raf!"

He gave a carefree shrug and kicked off his shoes. Now Rafael de Chastelaine, gardener, dhampir, occasional bat and pretend Latin teacher, was naked before her but for the charms around his neck and *that* smile. That wonderful, disarming smile.

"Lie down on the bed, darling." Something stirred in Cecily as she gave her order. *More a polite request.* "If you would."

"You'd better not be about to produce that cane." Raf bounced onto the bed and settled there, his hands pillowed behind his head. How decadent he looked and how utterly wanton with that perky erection the proof of his desire.

Cecily snaked her arm around the bedpost and peered at him from behind it. "I want to look," she admitted. "And admire."

"Do you want to watch me looking earthy," Raf asked, as though this situation happened all the time. He lazily lifted one arm from the pillow and drew his finger down the length of his erection. "Or do you want to watch me *being* earthy?"

Cecily gasped and tried to hide behind the bedpost. *Should* a man do that, in front of a woman? Though she couldn't see why not. She grinned around the post at him. "Are you going to commit the sin of Onan?"

"I don't see any stony ground," he told her, stroking with his fingertip again.

Toying with one of the tassels from the bed curtain, Cecily made her decision. "Go on, then…"

As though he had all the time in the world, Raf wrapped his fingers around his erection and, with his blue gaze still fixed on Cecily, began to work his hand back and forth. She had never seen anything quite like it, even in those forbidden books that resided on the high shelf of the library. It was decadent and primal and forbidden, from the quickening of his breath and the rise and fall of his chest to the look in his eyes, so filled with desire and heat.

Cecily's dress began to feel tight, and she untied its sash to loosen it. Her body was heating all over, inside and out, and as she watched Raf, she finally managed to take her dress off completely. Her underwear followed, yet she still peered at him, concealed behind the velvet curtain.

And all the while he watched her, raking that heated gaze over her as she revealed herself to him. And all the time was touching himself, enjoying his own body in a way that Cecily had barely dared to imagine in her miserable years.

Life with Raf was, she knew, going to be very different indeed.

Cecily crept from behind the curtain and sat on the edge of the bed, turned toward Raf. She ran her fingertips up and down his leg. "I said I'd lend a hand when you put on your lotion, but I'll help you with *anything* else, if you'd like."

"I wouldn't say no…" He ran his tongue over his lower lip. "I'm all yours."

Cecily laid down beside him and kissed him, before joining her hand to his, moving it up and down his length. "You're a very naughty dhampir!"

"Isn't that the best kind?"

Cecily's answer was a kiss, deep and loving. Then she broke away from Raf's lips and, a little embarrassed at what she was about to ask, peered at him through her eyelashes. "You know in the letters, when Isabella said about kneeling for her lover's blessing — and she meant something *other* than blessing — can we try it? Only, you see, I have the strangest urge to kiss you *down there.*"

"Will you let me return the favor?" He trailed his fingers down her side. "All that talk of buds, I reckon."

Cecily propped herself upon her arm. A thrill trembled through her at the thought. "*Would* you? I can't begin to imagine what it's like."

He pressed a kiss to her lips, their hands still moving together. Then he whispered, "Anything you want, it's yours."

"I want *you*," Cecily told him, words she had never spoken before last night with Raf. She placed a soft kiss on his lips, then kissed his chest, trying to avoid his scratches as she worked her way down his torso. She heard him sigh, felt his body arch up to meet her lips in an unspoken gesture of need.

"I love you," Raf gasped. "I'm proud to be your *Mr.*"

"And I'm proud to be your captain." Cecily reached his erection and wondered then what she was supposed to do. So she kissed their joined hands and somewhere between them was the warmth and hardness of Raf's erection. A quiver ran through her as she realized what she'd just done — something so forbidden but at that moment quite perfect.

In reply he gave a low, breathless moan of encouragement and a shiver seemed to run through his whole body. She had never imagined anything quite like this, let alone that she could elicit a sound of such ecstasy from someone.

So Cecily decided to go on, kneeling beside Raf as she took her hand away from his erection and replaced it with her lips. She placed one slow, gentle kiss after another between his fingers onto his hardness. Each touch drew another of those delighted and delightful sounds from her lover, his body responding to her touch. *My lover. Not husband, not headmaster. Lover.*

She kissed the very tip of his erection and parted her lips, only a little, as if she was tasting a rare fruit. She glanced up at him and saw that he was already gazing back.

Raf's full lips were parted, his dark hair black against the white pillow, and she saw such love in his eyes that it almost felt like a kiss. He smiled softly and murmured, "No fangs, I hope?"

She shook her head, her lips still around him, then ventured a short lick, wondering if it was what she was meant to do. The low, heated groan that was his reply seemed to suggest that this was a good start and Cecily felt Raf's hips lift toward her, sensed his efforts to keep them still.

Cecily gave him a longer lick now, and another—and another, each a little longer than the last, until she licked his entire length and finished with a kiss on his erection's tip. Every touch of her tongue met with another of those impossibly lustful moans and he peered at her from beneath his eyelashes as he reached down and stroked her hair, caressing tenderly.

Cecily lifted her head. "Was that nice?"

"Smart, gorgeous...and talented too."

Cecily lay down next to Raf and ruffled the modest patch of hair on his chest, then began to look at each of his charms. They were a cluster of pottery, glass and even—

"Is this a bone?"

"If I say yes, is that all right?" He slipped his arms around her. "It's not human, at least."

"Yes, as long as it's not human!"

"I'm not sure what it is," Raf admitted. "I got it in... I want to say Egypt. Maybe? Pretty sure Egypt."

"You've been to Egypt?" Cecily stared at him wide-eyed. "I should *love* to go there! Did you see the pyramids? You weren't dealing with a mummy, were you?" Though she hoped he would say yes.

"A mummy? Try the most grumpy mummy you've ever crossed paths with!" He widened his eyes to match hers. "Shall we go? You and me?"

"Oh, *can* we? And ride a camel, too!" Cecily held the bone between finger and thumb, trying to discern the tiniest trace of sand trapped in its contours.

"We can go anywhere you want." Raf kissed the tip of her nose. "Name it, any adventure you want. The world's yours to enjoy now!"

"I really want to see your house in Yorkshire." Cecily let the bone hang once again with Raf's other charms. "Is that silly, when we could go anywhere?"

"What're you picturing, when you think of my house?" He twined a few strands of her hair around his fingertip.

Cecily snuggled against him. "A cozy fisherman's cottage with a wonderful view of the sea. Ever so homely and warm."

"It's homely and warm," he admitted, cuddling her close. "And it's got its own bit of beach and a lovely big garden."

"Its own section of *beach?*" Cecily stared at him, amazed. "I can't wait to visit!"

"Are you planning to visit, then?" Raf blinked. "I sort of hoped you were moving in. I'll even clear the engine bits off the kitchen table!"

"Visit and *stay!*" Cecily grinned. Raf kissed her in reply, letting the locket and charm Cecily wore tangle with those around his neck, memories of adventures already past and promises of shared adventures yet to come.

"I've been all over the place in my business but when I walked into that room in Whitmore Hall…" He sighed happily. "It was like a wallop between the eyes."

Cecily looped her long legs around his, bringing him close. "I wondered who on earth was at the door when you came in. For a moment, I thought we'd summoned a spirit! But a dhampir is just as good."

"Did you look at me and think, *one day I'll ravish that gorgeous bloke*?"

"No! But you seemed to me the most extraordinary person I'd ever met." Cecily kissed him. "And with the loveliest blue eyes."

"And if we *can* reach your brother, we will," he told her softly. "I know some people, people with your gift. We won't ever stop trying."

"I hope so." Cecily cupped Raf's face in her hand and gazed into those lovely blue eyes again. "And maybe these people you know...would they help me, Raf, to understand what I have?"

"They will." He danced his fingertips against her hip. "And so will I. We don't just go wading in after banshees without a bit of prep!"

"Does this count as prep too?" Cecily rolled onto her back and brought Raf on top of her.

"Valuable field work for you," Raf decided. "Getting to grips with a dhampir."

"Am I doing a good job of seducing him?" Cecily raised an eyebrow. "He's been particularly troublesome, luring unsuspecting women with his beautiful blue eyes, making love to them until they're breathless with desire for him."

He nuzzled her throat and she heard him whisper, "It's the fangs that do it."

"Oh my word, yes it is!" Cecily gasped as she felt the light scuff of his teeth against her skin. Raf let them graze a little harder, still no harder than the rasp of his stubble.

He soothed the spot with his tongue then whispered, "So can I return that favor for you?"

"Gosh, *that* favor..." Cecily's cheeks heated at the memory of what she had done, and her hips stirred against Raf's. "I would love you to."

"*Gosh*," he teased. Then he embarked on the most wonderful exploration of Cecily's body that she might've imagined in her wildest dreams, kissing what felt like every inch of her as he moved over her breasts. Raf spent long, loving minutes devoting himself to her pleasure as her husband never had.

The cool charms around Raf's neck marked his path, resting against her skin before his lips followed. He dotted kisses over her stomach and lower until Cecily knew, for the first time, exactly what Isabella and her lover meant by their breathless talk of *buds.*

Bed had never been a place of pleasure for Cecily, only a place of duty. Until last night, she hadn't known what bliss she could feel, nor could she have known how each intimate kiss could bring her and her lover closer. Her body tingled with pleasure as one wave after another of joy washed through her.

On and on it went until Raf lifted his head and peered at her with a dreamy look. "I reckon freedom suits you."

"It most certainly does." She sat up and ruffled Raf's hair. He pushed himself up to kneel on the bed, a picture of decadent, puckish mischief.

"So, what's this talk of ravishing?"

Cecily slid her arm around his shoulder. "I think it's high time we ravished each other."

Raf's reply was to kiss her with that heat that was by now so familiar and so wonderfully welcome. What a world waited out there for them to discover, a world of adventure and things unseen.

As Cecily kissed him back, something she kept locked deep inside her opened and she was passion and fire. She craved Raf's closeness, wanting to forget where each other began, and she climbed onto his lap, taking him inside her in one movement. For a moment she didn't move, apart from to kiss him, absorbed by the sensation of their linked bodies. She heard his answering gasp of pleasure as he thrust his hips against her and they gave themselves to each other, abandoned and primal.

Lightheaded with passion, Cecily grabbed for something to keep her steady. She heard something clatter to the floor, but paid no notice as all her attention was focused on Raf and their carnal coupling. His teeth grazed her skin, sending darts of erotic pleasure into the core of her. They were nothing but sensation and desire, scaling the heights and reaching the pinnacle together. Intense pleasure swept through Cecily again and she tipped back her head and moaned, totally unrestrained now that they were alone in their own corner of the inn, their own corner of the world.

As his muscles relaxed, Raf sank against Cecily's body. He laid his head on her shoulder and kissed her collarbone, murmuring, "I love you... Did we break the bed?"

Cecily kissed his messy hair. "I have no idea! I hope not. Oh, hang on...there's something on the floor."

She turned her head as best she could to see the folded papers on the floor that had spilled out from the box.

The lovers' letters.

"Oh, Raf—we've knocked the letters all over the floor…" Cecily stroked his back as if following a trail through his tattoos, her brain too addled to process what had happened. Was the box's lid meant to be at an awkward angle? "We can tidy them up in a mo', can't we?"

"Mm," Raf murmured, completely occupied with the soft kisses he was placing on her shoulder. "In a bit."

"No rush," Cecily whispered, her skin tingling where his kisses fell. "Shall we wriggle down under the covers?"

Together they snuggled beneath the covers, against the cool sheets, as afternoon sunlight warmed the room. Safe in each other's embrace, they whiled away the time with soft kisses and words, ghosts and mystery forgotten.

Cecily had no idea how much time had passed. She was too happy to care. But at the sound of a distant door slamming, she was reminded of the world beyond their room. "Shall I stick my head round the door and see if the scones have arrived?"

"Go on, and I'll admire the view," Raf teased drowsily. Cecily kissed him, then climbed out of bed. She pulled on Raf's discarded shirt, which rendered her almost decent, then she opened the door a crack.

Mrs. Holberton had excelled herself, having set out for them the biggest scones Cecily had ever seen, with a large bowl of clotted cream and a pot of dark purple jam. The simple earthenware teapot was covered in a brightly colored cozy promising a hot cup of tea no matter how long the tray had sat outside.

Cecily brought the tray in and closed the door behind her with her foot. "What a feast! I swear I could live on cream teas."

"Back to bed, Captain, get it served up!" Raf sat up against the plumped pillows and clapped his hands. "This is life now, I hope you're up to it!"

She got back under the covers and chuckled as she stuck her finger in the cream. "I'm truly in heaven."

Raf caught Cecily's hand in his and brought her finger to his lips. He licked it clean in the most decadent display of teasing that she could possibly imagine, then told her, "Tastes even better like that!"

"How about this?" Cecily put her finger in the cream again, then stuck out her tongue and placed it on the end. She brought her mouth to Raf's in a ridiculous creamy mess of a kiss.

"Best of all," was his verdict. "I bet you make a mean scone."

"Not too bad... I don't make them as big as this, though. Maybe I'll have to try!" Cecily imagined herself in the small kitchen of Raf's cozy fisherman's cottage, a mixing bowl in the crook of her arm. She could picture the oven, and a view out of the window across to the sea, but the more she thought about it, the larger the kitchen grew. Her mind had decided it wasn't so small as she had assumed. She laughed to herself as she poured the tea.

"What're you chuckling about?" Raf began loading sugar into his cup. "Not my hair, I hope!"

"Your house. Sorry...I know how silly that sounds, but I was thinking of myself making scones in your kitchen, and in my head, the kitchen was huge!" Cecily grinned at him over her cup. "Which it can't be in a cottage, can it?"

"Keep talking," he said, adding milk. "Describe chez Raf?"

Cecily set her cup back on its saucer. She closed her eyes and took Raf's hands. "I can hear the sea, and then...there's a hotel, it's huge. Made from stone. But I can't see your cottage. I can see a door now, and behind it...my word, there's so much *stuff*. What a glorious mess."

Cecily laughed. "But even with the mess, there's lots of space. What is it, a barn? Is that it? But there's stairs..." Cecily opened her eyes. "Are you sure I'm a sensitive? None of that makes any sense."

"Are there portraits on the walls as you go upstairs?" Raf squeezed her hands. "Remind you of anyone?"

"There are...in a barn! Is it a barn? Someone went to a lot of trouble carving the bannister." Cecily saw a row of portraits along the wall. "And the paintings—they all look like you, but in different ways. That one's got your eyes...this other one has your grin... Wait—I'm walking on carpet. Why is there carpet in a barn? No...it's not a barn. It's a house. Is it—am I seeing the inside of your family castle in Carpathia?"

He shook his head slowly, a rather cheeky grin brightening his face as he said, "You're seeing home! I'll pretend you didn't call it a barn."

Cecily blinked open her eyes. "Raf, it's—it's enormous!"

"It's biggish, but it's not as big as the Romanian place." Raf laughed. "Do you like it? Dad's family have lived there since the year dot."

"If what I see is right, then yes—I love it!" Cecily hugged him. "And to think I assumed you lived in a little cottage."

"It's homely, but it really needs a gorgeous woman to complete it," he commented. "You, basically. Making scones if you're willing?"

"Oh, yes — and slathering you in cream!" Cecily kissed the tip of Raf's nose. "I hope we can go soon. I want a home, Raf. I want to make cushions and choose wallpaper and have the place smelling of fresh biscuits. And I want to curl up on the sofa with you when it's cold outside and be all nice and warm."

"Once we find Isabella and lay her to rest with her lover," he said, "*and* sort out the one or two lingering issues with the judge, we'll be gone." He slipped from the bed and picked up the scattered papers, placing them atop the covers. Next he retrieved the box, with a murmur of, "What's this?"

"I think we might have broken the lid, or — it's the lining, it's come loose." Cecily gasped. She felt as if she'd smashed a priceless museum exhibit. "One of the letters has got stuck down the side, look."

Making sure she had wiped the cream off her fingers first, Cecily took the corner of the folded paper and tugged it free of the box. But it wasn't like the other letters — this one was long and rectangular with a wax seal. "I don't think we've read this one yet."

She turned it over, looking for an addressee, even though whoever the letter had been intended for was long dead, though perhaps not long gone. Taking the teaspoon, Cecily carefully levered off the seal and laid it on the tray. The old paper creaked as she opened it.

"It's not the same handwriting as the other letters." Cecily looked up from the paper. "I'll read it to you."

Raf picked up his cup and settled back against the pillows, crossing his legs at the ankle. He took a sip and inclined his head politely, as though awaiting an oration.

"The shadows lengthen as the year dies. This is the last confession of the house of Whitmore, and I pray that it shall hereafter be steeped not in blood, but in fortune. Into this chest I place the worldly evidence of the love between those whom should not have loved. In the earth I lay it, as my brother will not be laid." Cecily glanced at Raf. *'Should not have loved.'* But they did. And Isabella and her mysterious *C had.* She read on.

"Edward Whitmore shall know no grave. He who committed the most grievous sin lives on in limbo, imprisoned not by the law and lash, but by his own guilt. For the sake of the good name of Whitmore, let him be placed into the clocktower with the Good Book and the image of those whose blood stains his hands. Let him be fed the meanest scraps from the table. When the scraps grow rotten and the air grows silent and fetid with death, let the last brick be placed and let Edward Whitmore be forgotten, eternity counted by the chimes of the bell. For his crimes we, the house of Whitmore, pass our own sentence."

Cecily's voice had begun to crack with emotion. So this was how the screaming mummy in that narrow room had died, and why his footsteps echoed back and forth as he paced his tiny prison. She turned the sheet of paper and continued.

"Let the stone that marks that nameless grave bring peace to the man that I now know rests beneath it. Let the chimes number the days of my brother's punishment and let his unquiet bride torment him in the darkness as he tormented her in the light."

What had that been like, for however long — however many years Judge Whitmore had been walled up, dead as far as the rest of the world knew — while his wife's weeping filled his ears? Cecily shuddered.

"God forgive me. God preserve me and let this confession see me safely through the gates of paradise. God show mercy to my brother and may the devil take Edward when the darkness claims him. Lord have mercy on the brothers of the house of Whitmore, in this life and the next.

"Benjamin Whitmore."

Cecily folded the confession back up. "His own brother—he walled his own brother up, kept him prisoner. Have you ever heard of anything so awful? But what else could he do? The judge was drunk on power and revenge, and if Benjamin had murdered him, run him through with a sword or blown his brains out with a musket, then he would only have been as bad as Judge Whitmore! What a choice, though...how it must've weighed on the poor man. And he lived such a long time, too! And all along, there above his head — oh, Raf, it's frightful!"

"It's...*different*," Raf decided. "Prayers for heaven for the *brothers*, so that's Matthew and Benjamin, hell for Edward. You know what, though? Ben *knew* who was in that grave, he says so right there, so why couldn't he bloody tell us?"

Cecily groaned in exasperation. "So close—we're *so* close to finding out who he was!"

At the sound of a swish of fabric, Cecily turned to look across the room. There was nothing and no one there. "Sorry—I thought we had a visitor."

Raf took the letter from her. Silently, he ran his eyes over the page before carefully folding it. His next target was the box itself and Cecily watched as Raf went over every inch of it, from hinge to lining and back, but there were no more secrets to reveal. Instead, he placed the contents safely inside and returned to the pillows and his cup of tea, his expression thoughtful.

"I think they used to come here, you know. Isabella and her secret love." Cecily coiled herself around Raf, stroking his leg with her long toes. "That's why she guided us here. Maybe she's never been back here in all that time—I don't know. But I hope it has only happy memories for her."

"I think best when I'm trying not to think," Raf said. "We need to find where she's buried and who's in that pauper's grave and put them together, like she told you. And I want to know what old Judge W.'s anchored to. Something personal, significant to him, maybe something in that rotten little cell. He's already latched onto Hugh, so he can hitch a ride with him for as long as he likes. All he needs to do is jump into the next host before the first one dies and he can go on forever. Life'd be a lot easier if—" Raf fell silent, his gaze skittering away.

"If...?" Cecily stroked the back of her hand against his stubble. "How horrible, all that business of hopping from one host to another like a hermit crab."

"I've seen this before," Raf admitted. "If the host dies before they latch onto another, it ends. But I'm not in the business of playing executioner—I couldn't do it."

Cecily would happily have sat and listened to Raf tell her about his previous adventures, although she realized it could take an extremely long time to hear everything. The very idea that he'd seen possession like this before fascinated her, at the same time as it spooked her. The world was a stranger place than she had ever imagined.

But the import of his words finally sank in and she drew up the covers, shivering at what he'd said.

"So Hugh would have to die suddenly, so that the judge would have no time to find another host? Because if Hugh were to die of old age, the judge'd be at his leisure, then, to find someone else?" Cecily wiped her hand across her eyes. "A car crash. Or a fall down the stairs. We can't—we can't kill, you're quite right, it's like Benjamin Whitmore—you can't sink to the judge's level. It's wrong."

"They move on long before old age," Raf told her. "And leave behind a husk of a person, every ounce wrung out. There are ways to separate the two but I need to find the anchor, and believe me, Sis, I will."

"He made the jump from my father to Hugh. When?" Cecily chewed the edge of her thumb as she tried to make sense of what Raf was telling her. "My father wasn't old when he died, but he was ill with shock after Sandy was killed. Do you think he did it *then*, decided to possess Hugh?"

He shook his head. "I don't know, but they're like leeches. If the judge had the fortune to leech off someone as rotten as him, he'd be stronger all the faster. The lazy metaphor is a vampire but *I'm* not going to use it."

"I'm not surprised you won't." Cecily ruffled Raf's hair. "I bet Hugh was the answer to his prayers! He's horrible even without a mad old judge possessing him. It's funny that Mrs. Holberton should mention dancing, because, do you know, I don't think I've been dancing since…since… I really couldn't say. Because Hugh wouldn't let me, and he wouldn't take me. Harriet wanted to organize a joint dance with a nearby girls' school, and he hit the roof!"

"So let's go dancing," Raf decided brightly. "I'm Transylvania's favorite barefoot-dancing dhampir!"

Cecily clapped her hands. *Dancing, at last!*
"I'll put on my best frock and I'll comb my hair."
"So will I—just not the frock bit."

Chapter Twenty-One

They followed the sound of the gramophone into the wooden-floored room. It was possibly the dining room but the furniture had been stacked up around the sides of the room to create a dancefloor, and Mrs. Holberton stood by the door, ready to welcome them.

"Good evening! I'm so glad you've decided to join us. Mr. Holberton, these are our other guests."

"A pleasure," the small, neat man at her side said as he gave a polite nod. His bald head was red from the sun but his suit was immaculate, as was the angle of his pince-nez. "A continental gentleman, I understand?"

"Transylvania," Raf growled, flashing a beaming smile. "But I only turn into a bat on special occasions!"

Mrs. Holberton laughed. "How very droll! There's a complimentary sherry for you each, and do take the floor whenever you wish. We've got waltzes and jazz and goodness knows what else—just tell us what you'd like to dance to. If you're lucky, we'll have your favorite tunes!"

Cecily nodded politely even as her stomach lurched. *Favorite tunes.* There were so many that she had listened to on the radio, the volume low to avoid detection, but she wasn't sure what they were called.

She felt so unworldly, especially when Mrs. Holberton was wearing a silk dress and heels with rouge on her cheeks and the best Cecily could manage was a dress made from rayon with practical pockets and flat, buckle-up shoes. But one day—and soon, Cecily hoped—she could go dancing in a silk dress and shiny heels.

"Hostess's choice." Raf beamed. He took a glass of sherry from Mr. Holberton before accepting one for himself and bringing them together. The glasses made a cheery *clink* as they touched. "To love and dancing!"

Mrs. Holberton flicked through the records and, having made her selection, set a lively jazz number blaring from the gramophone. Cecily sipped her sherry and held Raf's hand, swinging their arms back and forth in time to the music. Their hostess took her husband's arm and they executed an energetic routine across the dining room, with the vim of a couple half their age.

"They're really good, aren't they!" Cecily laughed.

"Fancy joining them?"

Cecily watched the Holbertons' quick feet skim across the polished floor. She put down her glass and took Raf's other hand. "I don't think I'll be very good— but I'm willing to try!"

"I don't care how good you are, just have fun!" He led her to the floor and whispered, "You're taller than ever."

Taking him at his word, Cecily whirled Raf round in a circle, then put her arm around his shoulder and tried to dance. She let the music surround her and guide her, and even if she wasn't dancing the exact steps, it was fun nonetheless—to have her arms around Raf and not be worried who might see.

They danced the day away to dusk, sometimes fast, sometimes wonderfully slow, always together. In a world of spirits and banshees, of vampires in castles and dhampirs on the beach, they had found each other.

"One last dance!" Mrs. Holberton announced, as she put another record on the gramophone. "A nice slow one," she told them with a wink.

Cecily draped her arms around Raf's shoulders and touched the tip of her nose to his. "I love you, my handsome dhampir."

"I love you." He smiled. "And I think you've healed my rose scratches. But a nice hot bath might put the cherry on top."

"I think it might. Let's go." Cecily glanced over at the other couple. They were barely moving from foot to foot, taking the chance instead to embrace. "Good night, Mr. and Mrs. Holberton! Thank you for a lovely evening."

After a moment, as if she had forgotten the other couple were there, Mrs. Holberton waved. "Good night, Captain and Mr. Pincombe!"

"Good night, Mr. and Mrs. H!" Raf called as he twirled Cecily toward the door. "Sleep tight!"

Raf danced Cecily along the hallway to the staircase and only then did he stop and kiss her again. They danced and kissed upstairs and along the landing to the room, barely pausing to set the bath running. They undressed each other, their clothes lying in a muddled heap on the floor, steam obscuring the bathroom mirror.

Cecily could barely comprehend how much change the day had brought.

And all of those kisses…

"With all of this not thinking," Raf murmured, "I reckon I know where our old judge's anchored himself."

Cecily was halfway into the bath and paused, one leg still on the bathmat. "You *do*? Where?"

"The rose garden." He settled back into the water and gestured her to join him with the slightest crook of his finger. "Not the whole garden, maybe one of those flailing roses. Before dawn tomorrow, I'm going back in there, ax swinging."

Cecily sank in the bath at the opposite end from Raf and lifted one of his feet into her lap to stroke it. "It would make sense if it was the rose garden. But do be careful — I can't bear the thought of you being scratched again. *You know who* won't be back until later in the morning, I suppose, but you never know who might tattle on you, then you'll be accused of trespassing."

"It's not the scratches that worried me, it was keeping my eyes," he admitted with a casual shrug. "If we get that again tomorrow, I'll set the whole bloody thing alight. Don't you worry about your Raf, I'm fearless, me!"

Cecily was glad of his confident swagger. "I know you can shift for yourself well enough, but should I come with you?"

"I'd rather you were safe and miles away," he said. "But you and Isabella are connected… What do you reckon?"

Cecily looked down at the ring. "I can't leave her, not yet. And after tomorrow evening, I can't see me being allowed back onto school grounds. It's the only chance I have to help her."

He nodded, but she saw the reluctance in his face, born not of annoyance, but of love for her. "One thing, though. If it starts to get dangerous, I want you to run for it—don't wait for me, just go."

Cecily blinked at him. "And leave you behind?"

"You're not starting a new life just to throw it away for a short, gorgeous Transylvanian if things go wrong," he said lightly. "Promise me?"

Cecily reached for his hand. "I—I can't promise you that. I *love* you."

"I love you too." Raf twined his fingers with hers. "And I've made it out the other side so far, so let's not worry?"

"All right, let's not worry." Cecily leaned toward Raf to kiss him, but her anxiety remained. "Can we have a hug?"

"I promise you, this time next week, we'll be home." He moved through the water to embrace her, holding her tight against him.

"*Home.* I like the sound of that." Cecily twined her arms around him, never wanting to let go. Raf might do this sort of thing all the time and she might not be the most experienced at understanding the sensations that assailed her, but even if she had barely considered what it meant to be *a sensitive*, Cecily could guess the gravity of what was to come. Raf wasn't telling her of the danger but it didn't keep her from knowing that it existed. Like the prickle of a distant storm, she sensed the vile threat of the judge even from here.

"I reckon I'm on to something with the roses," he whispered, nodding across the room. "Look."

Cecily followed his gaze and a shiver went down her spine. There, in the steam on the mirror, a drawing of a rose had appeared, traced by an invisible finger.

"What in the world — Isabella?" The ring clicked against the bath as Cecily gripped its side. "What a mean thing, for the judge to anchor himself in a place that was special to Isabella — he did it to spite her, I'm sure of it."

"And she's lost," Raf said thoughtfully. "Buried beneath her husband's gaze until the day of — " His blue eyes grew suddenly wide. "The clocktower. It's the only place in the hall where you can see into the rose garden!"

"He's buried her there? Of course!" Cecily gave Raf a loud kiss on his cheek. "He was powerful enough to get his own way and if he wanted to bury her there, then he would."

"Bloody hell," Raf murmured. "But they gave her lover a stone. What do you feel, Sis, right now? Isabella, you asked us to find you. We think you're in the rose garden, could that be right? Can you give a sign?"

Cecily heard a rumbling sound, then the clanking of pipes. She jumped as a gurgle came from the sink and suddenly water spurted from both taps.

"Unless this inn has plumbing problems, I think that might be the sign." Cecily closed her eyes, turning and turning the ring, as water still gushed from the taps. "Isabella, are you buried in the rose garden?"

In reply, the bathroom door swung wide open then slammed shut hard and the ring grew warm on Cecily's finger. Cecily's eyes sprang open. The image of the rose grew more vivid than ever on the mirror, untouched by the moisture around it. Raf nodded as though in conversation, his gaze moving between the door and the mirror.

Cecily stepped out of the bath, barely noticing the cold air of the bathroom or the dripping pools of water at her feet. Her hand rose toward the mirror, the ring dictating. Her fingertip hovered over the rose then met the mirror.

"Isabella...?" Cecily asked.

Her finger moved across the glass, forming a half circle. As it left the glass, Cecily realized she had written the letter C.

She glanced over her shoulder at Raf as her finger touched the mirror again, drawing by itself. The uncanniness was almost frightening. "Raf, should I stop this? Is this the right thing to do?"

"Set the boundary." Raf climbed from the bath as he spoke. He reached for the towels and wrapped one around his waist before he gently put the other around Cecily, securing it at her breastbone. "Tell Isabella what she can do and how much control you're willing to give. If you're happy to help her write, tell her, but only if you're happy."

"Thank you, darling." Cecily took a deep, calming breath, then addressed the unseen spirit. "Isabella, I don't want to be possessed. Not like my father or Hugh. I know you're not a bad person, Isabella, but please don't possess me. Write through me, but don't take me over, gentle lady."

The next letter began to form, a shaky circle. *Co?* But a tail appeared on the letter and it turned into an *a*. Then a long line, terminating in another circle. Cecily looked at Raf. An idea was beginning to form in her mind but it was as blurred as their reflections in the misted mirror. "*Cap?*"

"Captain?" Raf asked, furrowing his brow.

"The Captain's Rest!" Cecily glanced around the bathroom for Isabella, but still couldn't see her. Her finger was moving again, a new letter. A lowercase *t*. "Why the name of the inn? She came here with *C* – Raf, what if her lover was a *captain*?"

"But which one?" He frowned, still gazing at the mirror. "You lived there all your life, Sissy, does it mean *anything* to you? Did Hugh say anything that might give us a clue?"

"Depends what sort of captain..." The ring seemed to glow with heat then and Cecily bit her lip. "Isabella, please don't hurt me." She watched as her finger formed another letter *a* on the mirror.

"Hugh went on about shipwrecks," Cecily recalled. "A sea captain, perhaps? Oh, wait – one of the brothers was a sea captain, wasn't he? Brought all those exotic plants back from his travels." Cecily closed her eyes and the name appeared before her as if it was written in glowing coals. "That's his name – Matthew!"

Cecily's finger slipped on the mirror and a letter *M* appeared as a breeze blew through the room even though the door and the window were both closed. The taps turned themselves off and Cecily slumped against the sink, laughing. The tension in the room had snapped.

"I'm so happy! So, so happy!" Cecily embraced Raf. It wasn't Cecily's happiness, but Isabella's, and, with effort, Cecily controlled her laughter. "Isabella, it's all right, please be calm, please... You fell in love with your husband's brother, didn't you? We're coming back to Whitmore Hall, I promise! We'll lay you to rest with your captain."

"God bless two brothers, the devil take the third!" Raf clung to her. "*The most grievous sin* — Edward murdered his brother and framed his wife for it. It's Matthew Whitmore in the churchyard!"

"Buried as a pauper, with only the ghost of his lover to weep over him." It all made sense now. "We need to go back there, together. We know now, and with knowledge, as Hugh likes to say, comes power."

"Can you wait until dawn?" Raf asked, blinking at her in the dim light.

Can I?

Can Isabella?

Cecily saw the outside of Whitmore Hall in darkness, as though standing in the ghost garden where Isabella had so often walked. The pink of the advancing day tinted the school's windows and birds swooped over the grounds.

"Yes," Cecily replied. "Yes, she can."

"Let's go to bed," Raf suggested softly. "By the time dawn breaks, we'll be back at the school to get this sorted once and for all. If Isabella's in there and I'm going to bring her out, I'll need something to wrap — You leave all that to me."

He was trying to be delicate, Cecily knew, but this was his life, his work. He was going to dig up a skeleton after centuries in the ground and somehow reunite it with the body of Matthew. It was rather more complicated than planting a clipping.

They climbed into the bed together and curled up around each other. Cecily tried not to think about the danger they would face. She didn't want to think about the fact that this could be the last time they ever shared a bed.

As the minutes ticked by, she listened to the night and the steady sound of Raf's breathing. So gentle was it that she assumed he must be asleep until he whispered, "I'm not planning on dying anytime soon, Sissy, don't you worry."

Cecily laid her head on his chest and felt his breath, gentle against her hair. "I'm very glad to hear it."

"Try to sleep," he murmured. "And tomorrow night, we'll stay here again and celebrate a job well done."

* * * *

Cecily must have fallen asleep, because now she was waking. For a moment, she thought she was back in her old bedroom lying beside her husband. But Hugh had never held her as she slept.

She was with Raf.

The darkness was almost total but Cecily knew there was a third person in the room with them. She heard the rustle of fabric as they drew nearer to the bed, and Cecily gripped the bedclothes. Perhaps it was someone who had stayed here years before and had left an imprint on the room.

But at the low sound of weeping, Cecily realized exactly who it was.

Isabella.

"Please don't cry, Isabella — please. We'll go back to Whitmore Hall in the morning."

But the weeping grew louder, with an urgency and fear in it that Cecily hadn't heard before. She nudged Raf. He murmured and snuggled closer, kissing her shoulder. "What's up, gorgeous?"

"Isabella's crying. Can you hear her?"

Raf shifted again then bolted suddenly upright against the pillows and peered into the darkness. He couldn't only hear her, Cecily realized, he could see her too. Only then did she see Isabella emerge from the shadows into the moonlight, her hands worrying against each other, her pale cheeks wet with tears.

She stopped at the side of the bed, mere inches from Cecily, then said in a voice that sounded as delicate as a breeze through petals, "The judge has come home."

Acting on impulse, Cecily held out her hand in friendship to the ghost. Isabella must mean Hugh, sneaking back under cover of darkness to his demon. "What's he doing there, Isabella?"

"Summoning the roses." She reached out and placed her hand on Cecily's palm. It felt like silk, cool and soft and smooth. *A ghost's hand.*

Cecily glanced at Raf. "That's not good — that's more crazed, thorny branches, surely?"

"That's not good at all," he confirmed. "I might need to nip out and save the world. Will you stay here?"

Cecily shook her head. Her gaze on Isabella, she replied, "You're not going to that place alone, Raf."

"I'd rather you stayed here." He dotted a kiss to her cheek. "But if you're set on coming, a couple of ground rules. I'm going to use some spells, protection, unbinding, general possession stuff that'll sound like something out of the Hellfire Club. It'll sound creepy but I'm one of the good guys so don't worry. Second, take no risks, and I mean that. This is just first day on the job, Sis, agreed?"

"Yes, I'll do exactly as you say." Cecily tried to look into Isabella's eyes. "We're on our way, kind lady."

She kissed Isabella's hand and the ghost faded away.

"I don't suppose you've got any trousers?" Raf asked as he threw back the covers. "Those thorns're no joke — we need to cover as much skin as we can."

"Trousers?" Certainly not something Hugh would have ever allowed Cecily to wear. "No, I don't have any, but I've got very thick stockings."

"I'd lend you a pair but you insist on being tall." He grinned, showing the sharp points of his teeth. "Stockings on, Captain, and let's get this done. We'll leave Mrs. H. a note to let her know that we'll be back in time for a fry-up!"

Chapter Twenty-Two

Cecily pulled her coat around her. There was an icy nip in the early morning air, and no sign of sunrise. Three o'clock wasn't a time Cecily ever saw. As Raf drove back through the lanes, his headlights picked out the road ahead. There was no other traffic — the rest of the world was asleep.

Although Cecily couldn't ignore her fear, she was excited to think that the possession of Whitmore Hall by the devil of a man might all be over in mere hours. Yet the hazards were almost too great to countenance and she could scarcely allow herself to imagine those vines, studded with keen thorns that had already lashed Raf once. She could lose him tonight, but she wouldn't let herself think it.

Every so often, Cecily stole a glance at Raf, at his set, determined expression and the serious light in his eyes. How often he must have faced such terrors before, but he was utterly unwavering.

All too soon, they were at the padlocked school gates.

Raf climbed from the car and she watched as he made short work of the lock and pushed the gates wide. In silence he returned to the car and extinguished the headlamps, but Cecily knew that he didn't need them anyway. As the vehicle advanced along the driveway toward the glowering building, Raf reached out and squeezed Cecily's knee.

"Whatever happens, you look after you."

Nodding, Cecily turned her head away. She saw Sandy again, leaning out of the train window, waving goodbye. The last time she had ever seen him.

"You know what you're doing—I shan't be scared." Cecily kissed her palm and pressed it to Raf's cheek. In the distance she saw the gray walls of the rose garden and, from within, a pale glow that illuminated the night sky with an uncanny light.

Her stomach gripped with apprehension. "What on earth is that man doing in there?"

"Gloves, ax and a kiss from my lady?" Raf turned off the car engine. "Let's get this miserable bugger sorted, once and for all."

Cecily slipped her arms around Raf's neck and brushed her lips against his. "Whatever happens, I love you."

"I love you. And I'm coming back."

With that, Raf climbed from the car. He retrieved the ax, a spade and his thick gloves, finally throwing a folded blanket over his shoulder. Then he began the trek over the lawn toward the ghost garden and that unearthly light. As Cecily watched, the light went out and the world was plunged once more into darkness, with only the moon left to illuminate the grounds. Raf didn't look nervous, nor timid or hesitant, and she knew that he had faced such danger before, yet something in the sight of him disappearing into the gloom filled Cecily with dismay. If he passed through those gates and left her here, she had the feeling that he would be lost to her forever.

Cecily twisted Isabella's ring on her finger.

My love, my secret.

As carefully and as quietly as she could, Cecily opened the car door and got out. She crept over the lawn, the sense of menace building the closer she got. She had no idea what she would do once she reached the rose garden, only that she needed to be there.

"I know you're here, Whitmore, I can smell you," she heard Raf call from within the garden. "I'm going to start cutting, and when you're ready to come out of hiding, you and I can settle this! We know what you did and we know that Isabella's here. You're finished!" Then came the sound of the ax falling and splintering wood.

Cecily pressed her back against the wall and inched her way toward the rose garden's entrance. It wasn't just a garden, she knew now, but a tomb.

Evil seemed to drip from the air, as heavy as mercury. She clutched her locket and the *cocosul*, and whispered one line of the Lord's Prayer, over and over again, and finally she could peer around the entrance and into the garden.

"*Deliver us from evil, deliver us from evil, deliver us...*"

Raf swung the ax again and again, hacking his way through the thicket of thorns and vines that seemed blacker than night itself. With each falling branch he was closer to the center of the garden, yet something in that seething air was more than nature and, as Cecily watched, the thick rose boughs seemed to weave and twine, advancing just a touch for every length of foliage that Raf hacked away. From deep within the tangle of roses came a low, steady voice, speaking in a tongue that Cecily didn't recognize. Yet she did recognize the voice, and as Hugh spoke his hellish incantation, what seemed like a pulse at the heart of the garden began to glow.

Raf didn't stop in his toil for so much as a moment but, instead, his voice broken by exertion, he began to recite his own words. It sounded almost like a song, melodic and exotic and warm on the chill air.

Cecily wondered if she would ever know those words herself — whether they were for protection or unbinding, she had no idea. But there was something beautiful in Raf's words that was utterly lacking in Whitmore's. He continued to intone as the vines whipped at his legs and chest and lashed for his eyes, meeting them with the keen blade of the ax and sending them splintering.

"I know you're holding on to this place," Raf shouted, plunging headfirst into the deep thicket and snapping vines this way and that with his gloved hands. There was something in there, Cecily saw, a statue illuminated by the ghost light that, with each discarded branch, revealed itself to them a little more. Yet the enchanted boughs were fighting back, whipping across Raf's face and torso, leaving beaded trails of bright-red blood.

Isabella Whitmore, whose earthly remains lye interr'd elsewhere, under her husband's connstant gaze untill the Daye of Judgement.

The statue's gaze.

"Is this it?" Raf shouted. He looked round at Cecily and told her, "This is the anchor, it has to be!"

Cecily stared at the weathered marble statue, transfixed. Thirty years she had lived here yet the house had kept its secrets.

Until now.

"It must be!" Cecily replied.

Still Raf pulled the thick rose branches from the towering statue as his incantation did battle with that of the unseen judge. It was then that Cecily saw her husband as he stepped from the shadows, his black robes and white face making him a ghoul in the moonlight. At first she thought he was wearing his academic gown, but something about it seemed ancient and Cecily realized that Hugh was clad in the robes that had swaddled the judge's corpse, that death shroud billowing around him like a monstrous bat in silhouette.

Nausea rose in her throat at the realization of how debased her husband had become. She turned away, her mind overpowered by death. Crouching down, she rested her head against her knees. "Deliver us from evil, deliver—"

There by her foot she saw a plant, dark green with needle-shaped leaves. *Rosemary.* One of the herbs Raf had hidden around the garden. She snapped off a sprig and brought it to her nose, breathing in the scent.

'Remembrance.'

Hugh raised his arms above his head and his voice grew in volume and force as those hellish vines surged forth with whip-crack precision, smearing freshly spilled blood across Raf's shirt and skin. Even that didn't stop him and he stepped into the tangle and began smashing at the statue with the ax, chipping away at the effigy of Judge Edward Whitmore.

The statue stared with a blank frown, the judge's pose stiff as he held a rolled piece of paper in one hand, gripping the edge of his coat with the other. In the uncanny light, it was if the statue were breathing, though the judge had come alive again in her husband.

Something drew Cecily into the garden. Raf's wounds, her own fascinated terror, the shock of seeing her husband so changed. She crept in, keeping against the wall, trying to avoid the sharp, thorny rose bushes. She needed to be there, she decided, out of respect for the woman who lay buried beneath the untended soil.

Hugh moved with the speed of a striking snake. He darted past Cecily, long limbs spindly as a spider, the glassy blind eye rolling in its socket, and as he went he snatched up one of those thorn-throttled vines, swishing it once like a cane. At the moment Hugh sprang, the boughs lashed again, rearing back before lunging forward.

Raf, meeting them with the blade of the ax, turned his back on Hugh for one second, no more. It was all the time the headmaster needed to swing his arms over Raf's head and catch the vine around his throat like a garrote, drawing a cry of agony from him. He dropped the ax to the ground and reached up to do battle with the strangling vine as blood began to seep from his thorn-ravaged skin.

And Hugh smiled with a warmth that Cecily had never before seen in her husband's face.

He's enjoying this.

"Fear not, Mrs. James," Hugh crowed, tightening the vine around Raf's throat. "We shall forgive you your trespasses. You may come home and be a good girl once more."

"Let him go." Cecily's voice was firm despite the horror of witnessing Raf's struggle against the thorns in the hands of the possessed man. "I won't do *anything* unless you let him go."

"You overestimate our fondness for you. We shall find another wife when you are dead." Hugh laughed. His mirth was cut short when Raf propelled them forward toward the statue and, as the struggling men collided with it, it gave the slightest suggestion of movement, shifting just a touch on the uneven ground. Now the vines rose again, dragging at Raf's legs, holding him beneath the judge's empty marble gaze.

"You were never in the least fond of me – nor I of you!"

Cecily swallowed her repugnance and grabbed at the judge's shroud, trying to pull Hugh away from Raf. The fabric crumbled into dust in her hands, but still she went on, clutching at air as she tried to save her lover. Was this how it had happened all those years before, the judge strangling Matthew as Isabella had tried to fight him off?

She stepped away. There was nothing more she could do, she couldn't even pick up Raf's ax as the vines had consumed it.

But in her pocket she had the sprig of rosemary.

"Deliver us from evil," she recited once more, and threw the sprig into the tangle of vines.

"Willful, deceitful, whore!" Hugh thundered as the vines that had clung to Raf's limbs fell away, withering before Cecily's eyes like dead branches in winter. All around the garden the thick branches began to snap and crumble until only one remained, the one that was slowly strangling the man she loved. Hugh wrenched his arms back then propelled himself forward, shoving

Raf ahead of him so his forehead glanced off the statue's stone plinth and once again, Cecily saw the effigy seem to shift, a sound of marble grinding on marble shuddering from the monument.

"The statue—" Raf gasped as he fell to his knees, bringing Hugh down with him. As though the headmaster sensed what he was trying to say, he clamped his hand over Raf's mouth, but this time the howl of pain that followed was his own. He tried to drag his hand away as quickly as it had landed and Cecily saw that Raf had bitten into it with the fangs that had seemed so insignificant, tearing a chunk from Hugh's hand as though her husband were nothing more than the papery mummy in the clocktower.

"Destroy the statue," Raf told her, locking his hands around the vine, forcing his fingers between the thorns and his throat as the two men battled.

Destroy it.

But if it fell, it would crush both her husband and the man she adored.

Hot tears began to slide down Cecily's cheeks as she contemplated what she must do. The world needed to be free of Judge Whitmore, the demon who had blighted nearly every moment of her life until she had met Raf.

"But I love you, Raf!" Cecily clenched her hands, a terrible pain in her chest as she realized her heart must be breaking. She would never be rid of the judge unless Hugh died, but she could not save Raf from the vines.

"Do it," Raf gasped, his hands still holding the vine around his neck as Hugh tightened and twisted it with maniacal glee. "*Te iubesc.*"

Cecily gazed once more into Raf's blue eyes, then looked away, not wanting to see the moment the statue fell. She ran at the marble figure and, with all her force, pushed it over onto the struggling men. All at once the light went out and it seemed as though the whole world had stopped. She saw Hugh's unmoving leg protruding from beneath the statue then from the clocktower came an almighty crash. Cecily stared open-mouthed as the clock that had stood atop Whitmore Hall for centuries seemed to split in half. For a moment it teetered, then it tumbled down into the quad in a deafening sound of splintering wood and smashing glass.

Wiping away her tears, Cecily fell exhausted to her knees. What could she do? Go to Hattie and Graham? Call the police? All the school would have been woken by the clock collapsing — someone would find her here, beside the fallen statue and the bodies. Then she'd be hanged liked Isabella for the murder of not just one but two men. A burial in the prison grounds, vilified then forgotten.

"Oh, Raf...darling...I'm so sorry. I will love you forever, I swear it!"

She hardly heard the sound of raised voices as the masters and boys flocked from the school, nor the soft beat of wings. When the pipistrelle bat alighted on her shoulder and began to fuss at her hair, however, there was no ignoring it.

Cecily cupped the bat in her hands. "I thought I'd lost you. My sweet Raf!"

The battered creature nuzzled Cecily's nose for a few seconds then fluttered up into the air and, with what seemed like a supreme effort, flitted down to land beside the fallen statue. In the time it took Cecily to blink, she found herself looking at Raf once more, his naked body a map of bloodied cuts.

"I'd better get dressed," he told her with a rather disbelieving smile. "Then let's get digging. I've got a funny idea that the school's going to be a bit distracted just now."

"Raf, what on earth do we say to them? I've just killed my husband..." Cecily glanced at the leg that stuck out from under the statue then looked away. She felt numb and cold inside—free of him and his cruelty, but she had his blood on her hands now. "Surely I should be in handcuffs? Unless he's still alive. Is he? I can't bear to look."

"The last thing I remember is him going loopy and slamming my head into that plinth." Raf paused in gathering his clothes and touched his hand to the vivid purple bruise that already colored his forehead. "I'm guessing he did it so hard that he managed to dislodge the statue and..." He stooped to peer more closely at Hugh then laid his jacket over what Cecily now knew must be her late husband. Only then did Raf begin to dress as he asked, "Would you rather wait in the car? I'm sorry about Hugh, it's— I'm sorry."

"Don't be. It's over, isn't it? The judge has gone." Cecily tipped her face up to the sky. It was beginning to lighten as a new day approached. "The air feels different, doesn't it? The sky looks bigger."

"Yeah, it does." He smiled, but as Raf continued dressing, Cecily wondered what reserves of strength were even keeping him standing. His throat was a mess of wounds, like someone had wrapped him in barbed wire, and his clothes were stained with blood and dirt yet still he didn't falter, still he told her, "You let Isabella know that she's cried her last tear. She'll have a proper place to rest now."

Cecily nodded. She held her hands out in front of her, palms upward. "Isabella, are you there? He's gone. He won't torment anyone else, ever again. We're both widows, you and I. And we can move on now to love whoever we choose, without fear."

As Cecily waited for Isabella, Raf crossed to the wall to retrieve the spade from where it rested against the wall. He paced the length of the statue and began to dig at the point where its empty gaze would've been focused, softly singing more of those gentle, mysterious words as he worked.

Cecily heard footsteps crunch over the fallen parched garden, but saw no one enter. The soil moved, as if someone else were there with Raf, helping him. Cecily moved nearer and as Raf's spade fell, she saw the distinct shape of a hand in the soil, as if someone were scooping the earth away. A large, powerful, invisible hand.

"We have a visitor, Raf. Captain Whitmore, is that you?"

"Isabella." Raf broke from his song. "There's a gentleman here looking for you."

Cecily felt a surge of joy as Isabella began to materialize in the garden. The dark ringlets and the pale face, the black gown and the bright, white lace collar came into view once more. Perhaps, Cecily realized with a pang, for the last time.

"She's here." Cecily dashed away a tear of happiness. Raf glanced up and greeted the ghost with a polite nod, then he went back to the business of digging. The noise around the school building seemed to be happening in another world and the deeper Raf and his unseen helper dug, the stronger the fragrance of roses became. A sound like whispering silk filled the air around them as the garden, once a place of terror and threat, began to bloom into life once more. Those nightmarish thorns were gone, replaced by blossoming roses in every conceivable color and, among them, sprigs of heady rosemary.

Eventually Raf paused, standing in a hole no more than a few feet deep. He set the spade down beside it and asked Cecily in a voice that was filled with respect, "Can you pass me the blanket, Sissy? I've found the lady."

As Cecily went to fetch the blanket, she glanced at Isabella, not at whatever might be in the earth, but at the spirit that had taken form before her. *That*, Cecily knew, was Isabella, not the bones that had been left behind for Judgment Day.

She came to the graveside with the blanket and passed it to Raf, leaning to kiss his blood-smeared cheek. He took the blanket from her, then returned to his work. Cecily felt Isabella at her side once more and, as Raf carefully set a wrapped bundle down on the emerald grass at the side of her no-longer-forgotten grave, another shape shimmered into life.

The specter of Matthew Whitmore, as handsome now as he was in the painting, stepped forward and held out one ethereal hand to Raf. There in the moonlight, as Cecily and Isabella watched, Raf put his hand in that of the phantom and allowed Matthew to help him from the grave. Raf's knees buckled as soon as his feet hit the earth and he caught his arm around Cecily's waist, staggering against her.

"Darling..." Cecily kissed the top of his head. "Sit for a moment."

"Don't mind me," Raf told the ghosts, sinking to his knees. They didn't seem to mind anything, though, gazing as they were at each other. Matthew held out his hand to Isabella, a gentle smile of love illuminating his features.

"Isabella and Matthew," Raf sighed in a happy whisper, running his hand around his wounded throat. "Captain Sissy, you're a hell of a woman."

"And you're a hell of a man! I've never seen bravery like it—I wish I'd remembered to bring your lotion out of the car." Cecily watched as Isabella gave Matthew her hand and he gently kissed it. "But it's worth it—for that. To see a wrong righted after so long."

"This goes a bit beyond lotion," he admitted, and for just a moment, Cecily's stomach lurched. "This calls for scones, țuică and lots of kisses."

"Let's stay at our lovely inn for a couple of days, make sure you're recuperated before we drive north." Cecily kissed him, then rose to her feet. "There's something I need to do."

She twisted Isabella's ring from her finger and walked toward the ghost couple, who were so busy gazing at each other after so long apart that Cecily felt rather rude for interrupting. But it had to be done.

"Isabella...thank you for lending me your beautiful ring. Here—will you have it once again?" Cecily held her hand out toward Isabella, the ring resting on her palm. Isabella looked down at it, then lifted her gaze to meet Cecily's.

"Thank you," Isabella said as she placed her hand around Cecily's fingers, gently closing her fist around the ring. "My friend."

"From one captain—" Raf began.

"To another," concluded Matthew with a tender smile, slipping his arm around Isabella's waist.

"I'll look after it, I promise." Cecily knew then that Isabella had wanted her to find the ring — she had meant for her to have it. She knew too that the time had come to bid farewell to the reunited couple. They had centuries to make up for and she had a new life to live, in a world where forgotten rose gardens blossomed anew and she wasn't *Mrs. Headmaster*, but *Cecily*.

Isabella and Matthew held hands then leaned toward each other. As their lips met in a kiss, even more roses came into bloom, and the ghostly lovers faded away.

Chapter Twenty-Three

Rafael de Chastelaine, it seemed, was made of stronger stuff than anyone Cecily had met in her life. *'Little but fierce'* was right. Over the next two weeks they barely left the cozy bed in Mrs. Holberton's house as Raf's wounds healed, and though his body was battered, his spirit was as buoyant as ever. With the cheap wedding ring long since forsaken, Cecily nursed her lover and shared his beloved cream teas, dancing the evenings away and loving into the dawn. It was decadent and indulgent and utterly, perfectly wonderful.

Two weeks without mysterious footsteps, midnight weeping or cracks in the masonry. Two weeks of making plans for their future life together.

Cecily didn't consider herself widowed but engaged. Unable to mourn the tormentor she had never loved, she didn't attend Hugh's funeral. Harriet rang the inn to tell Cecily the verdict of the inquest. The coroner had returned a verdict of death by misadventure, commenting on the dead man's parlous mental state at the time of his death. Perhaps, he had noted, the collapse of the clocktower on that same night had contributed to Hugh's strange behavior in the rose garden. After all, it was a miracle that no one in the school had been injured.

I'm not a murderer, Cecily told herself as she ended her call with Harriet. Only she and Raf would ever know the truth.

But other truths *were* known. Matthew and Isabella now slumbered together in the chapel of Whitmore Hall and their joint portrait looked out over the school from pride of place in the assembly hall where no more fearsome sermons were to be read. For the desiccated mummy of Judge Edward Whitmore, however, the collapsing clocktower had provided a final resting place of a different sort. What was left of him had been swept away with the rubble, that hideous cadaver becoming nothing more than dust and an unwelcome, unmourned memory.

The school looked so different. *Felt* so different. Cecily stood arm in arm with Raf on the lawn as they said their farewells to the new headmaster and his wife.

"What a happy school this is now," Cecily observed. "It's in capable hands."

"Whitmore Hall's been allowed to fossilize," Graham told her with a beaming smile. "I like to fancy that the clocktower's collapse was but the cracking of one of Harriet's baking eggs and, between us, we'll bake a fresh Whitmore Hall. A Whitmore Hall with wives, should the masters wish to plunge into the waters of wedded bliss. One or two of them have admitted already that they *do!*"

"So I'll have plenty of ladies to share a sherry with when you're off having adventures." Harriet beamed, clutching her hands together in delight. Then she took Cecily's hand and said excitedly, "I have something to show you. Come and see our ghost garden!"

"I hope it won't disappear back into the ground," Cecily said, but as she walked along with Harriet, she realized there was no risk of that. The garden that had been etched on the parched grass was a ghost no more, but a thing of breathtaking, glorious beauty, bursting forth from the ground just as the rose garden had been reborn. Those silhouettes on the flat, yellow earth were walkways and hedges again, the walls of the rose garden now surrounded by bright blooms and vivid blossoms.

"We noticed on the morning after the headmaster was— Well, that is to say, after the late Dr. James and that frightful statue were taken from the premises," Harriet told them, nodding up toward the scaffolding and industry that was taking place in the jagged hole where the clocktower had once stood. "It's been good as a beanstalk, growing an inch or more every day. The boys call it a miracle, with our little secret rose garden at its heart!"

"It truly *is* a miracle. I could never have imagined something like this growing here." As Cecily patted Harriet's arm, the autumn sun glinted from the gold of Isabella's ring. "But it's such a different place now. It'll be a wonderful school with you and Graham to lead it—I'd love to come back and see how you're getting on. I can't stay, though, Hattie, you do understand?"

"I shall miss you dreadfully, Cecily," Harriet replied, though her expression became a little saucier when she winked and whispered, "but I can see that Yorkshire has some raffish charms of its own!"

Busily chatting to Graham as they took in the miracle of the newly regrown ghost garden, Raf gave no indication that he had heard other than the slightest quirk of a smile. There in the autumn sunlight, surrounded by bright flowers, his clothes rumpled and his hair tousled, he made a glorious sight indeed. As the thought entered Cecily's head, Raf met her gaze and mouthed *Love you*.

Cecily gave him a wave. She wasn't sure the school was quite ready for the late headmaster's widow to blow a kiss across the grounds, but she did so anyway. "My world has changed so much, I barely recognize who I used to be."

"We'll always be chums, you and I," Harriet assured her, watching as Raf and Graham made their way over the lawn toward them. From the school building came a happy clamor of fists at the windows and Raf greeted the boys he had taught with a wave and a bow as innumerable hands waved back from behind the glass. "And Mr. Brennan is good as new, even if he isn't *quite* as legendary in school as our temporary Latin master!"

"Ready, Sissy?" Raf asked. He slipped his arm around Cecily's waist, earning another round of clamor from the watching pupils. "Ask those lads to look after this garden, Gray, and it'll look after them in turn."

"They're very proud of it." Graham beamed. "And of being able to honor the captain and Mrs. Whitmore. We all are. Our honorary Captain Cecily has certainly earned her place in Whitmore Hall history too!"

"Let's take a cutting before we go," Cecily suggested. "Something to remember the *good* of Whitmore Hall by."

Among hugs and handkerchiefs, they said their goodbyes and best wishes, and made their promises to write and visit when time allowed. Graham slipped a protective arm around Harriet's shoulder and together they departed for the building, ready to rebuild the school in a new image. As they disappeared inside, Raf pressed a kiss to Cecily's cheek.

"There's no rush," he whispered. "Take your time."

Cecily scanned along the plants in the ghost garden, wondering what to take. She crouched down and snipped off some lavender, which she folded into her handkerchief. As she stood once more, Isabella's ring grew warmer against her skin. Someone was there, she realized. An old friend.

She looked up and there, on one of the ghost garden's paths, was Sandy. Solid, real and apparently alive. He smiled as he lifted his straw boater and waved to Cecily. Beside her, Raf responded with a polite bow, the gentle smile on his lips as warm as the sun that fell across Sandy's face.

"Look after the place for us?" Raf asked him. "I promise I'll look after Sissy for you."

Sandy turned toward Raf and nodded.

"Goodbye, Sandy." Cecily wanted to give her brother one last hug, but didn't want to approach in case she put her hands around nothing but air. "I miss you."

"I won't ever be far away." Sandy opened his arms to her and said, "I never have been."

I'll always regret it if I don't at least try.

Cecily headed toward Sandy and hugged him. He didn't melt in her embrace—the woolen weave of his striped blazer was soft against her cheek as she laid her head on his shoulder. She felt his arms embrace her in turn and there they stood, the simple hug between brother and sister just one more miracle in the blossoming ghost garden.

What would they see from the windows of the school? Cecily alone with her arms around nothing? But it didn't matter, because she had discovered that there were worlds within worlds filled with wonder.

"Goodbye, dear brother!" Cecily kissed his cheek and took a step back from him, her arms dropping to her side.

"Cheerio, Cecily." Sandy inclined his head. "Now on you go."

Cecily looked back over her shoulder at him as she walked away. She took Raf's hand. "I'm glad you've been introduced."

"If you love someone, they're never really gone." Raf kissed Cecily's cheek and, together, they walked across the lawn toward the car. "Now let's go home and get the kettle on."

Want to see more from these authors?
Here's a taster for you to enjoy!

Captivating Captains:
The Captain &
The Cavalry Trooper
Catherine Curzon
& Eleanor Harkstead

Excerpt

Northern France
1917

The wagon carrying Jack Woodvine bumped and jerked along the poplar-lined lanes, a fine spray of mud rising up each time the huge wooden wheels splashed through a puddle.

He had given up checking the time and, even though the journey was far from comfortable, tried to doze as he passed along under the iron-gray sky. A chateau, they'd said. Different from the barracks he'd been in when he was first deployed. Doubtless it would be a dismal old fortress, but was it silly of him to hope for bright pennants fluttering from a turret?

Finally, the wagon drew up at a gatehouse of pale stone. As Jack climbed out, dragging his kitbag behind him, sunlight nudged back the clouds and turned the gray slate of the roofs to blue.

"You the new groom?" A soldier appeared from the gatehouse. His cap was so low over his eyes that Jack couldn't make out his expression.

"Yes — Trooper Woodvine. Jack Woodvine." He took a letter from his pocket and held it out to the man. "I've been transferred from another battalion. This is the Chateau de Desgravier?"

"Yes, Trooper! Turn left at the bottom of the drive for the stables. Quick march!"

The last thing Jack wanted to do was march, quickly or otherwise, but he shouldered his kitbag, jammed his cap onto his head and marched down the tree-lined avenue.

It was thickly leaved, but through the branches he could see the white stone of the chateau ahead. He rounded a bend in the driveway and he saw it — Chateau de Desgravier.

An enormous tower rose up in front of him, its roof reaching into a delicate point. Jack sighed, the spots of mud on his face cracking as he smiled. It might not have had pennants floating from it, but it was exactly like something from a fairytale. Beside the tower were the stone and brick and filigreed windows of what looked to Jack like a palace. Who would ever think that the front was only a few miles to the east?

Quick march!

Jack continued on his way, turning to his left just as he'd been ordered. The path here bore evidence of horses — straw, manure, the marks of horseshoes. Ahead, an archway, figures at work. A lad of Jack's age maneuvering a wheelbarrow, another leading a horse out to the paddock.

This wouldn't be so bad. It seemed to be a peaceful place, and easy work for a lad like Jack. He raised his hand and grinned at the grooms as he headed under the archway and into the vast stable yard.

Then he heard singing. In French.

Jack dropped his kitbag and looked round. The voice was that of a man, yet heightened slightly, giving it a teasing, effeminate edge, and Jack couldn't help but follow it like a sailor lured by a siren, pulled along the row of open stables toward that lilting chanson. Inside those stables young men labored and sweated, brooms swept and spades shoveled, yet one of the boxes at the far corner of the yard seemed to have been transformed into an impromptu theater.

Jack hardly dared glance through that open door, yet he couldn't help himself, blinking at the hazy darkness of the interior where half a dozen grooms lounged in the straw, watching the *chanteur* in rapt silence.

Right in front of Jack, his back to the door, was the figure of a young man, clad in jodhpurs, polished riding boots and nothing else. No, that wasn't quite true, because he *was* wearing something, the sort of something Jack didn't really see much of in Shropshire. It was some sort of silken scarf, a shawl, perhaps, that was looped around his neck twice, the wide, dazzling red fabric decorated with intricate yellow flowers. They were bright against the pale skin of his naked back, as bright as the tip of the cigarette that glowed in the end of a long ebony cigarette holder that the singer held in his elegant right hand. He gestured with it like a painter with his brush, making intricate movements with his wrist as he sang, his voice a low purr, then a high, tuneful trill, then a comically deep bass that drew laughter from his audience.

He moved with the confidence of a dancer, hips swinging seductively, head cocked to one side, free hand resting on his narrow hip and here, in this strange fairytale place, he was bewitching.

The singer executed a near-perfect pirouette yet quite suddenly, when he was facing Jack, stopped. He put the cigarette holder to his pink lips, drew in a long, deep breath and blew out a smoke ring, his full lips forming a perfect O.

"Well, now." He sucked in his pale cheeks and asked, "Who on earth have we here?"

Jack blinked as the smoke ring drifted into his face.

"Tr-trooper Woodvine, reporting for Captain Thorne. I've been transferred — I'm his new groom. I don't suppose — "

The words dried in Jack's throat. As enthralling as this otherworldly figure was, with his slim face and high cheekbones, there was an unsettling glint of mockery in his narrow blue eyes.

"Sorry." Jack took a half-step backward. "I interrupted your song. I should…"

The singer moved a little, just enough that he could dart his head forward on its slender neck and draw his nose from Jack's shoulder to his ear, breathing deeply all the way. They didn't touch but the invasion, the *authority*, was clear. However lowly their station, Jack had wandered innocently into someone else's domain.

When the young man's nose reached Jack's ear he threw his head back and let out a loud sigh through his parted lips, arms extended to either side. Then he finally spoke again, declaring to the heavens, "I smell new blood!"

Behind him, his small audience tittered nervously and his head dropped once more, those glittering blue eyes focused on Jack.

"Trooper Charles, *sir*!" He executed a courtly bow, the hand that held the cigarette twirling elaborately. "But you're so darling and green that *you* may address me as Queenie. Aren't you the lucky one?"

Jack reached for the doorframe to casually prop himself against it and essay the appearance of calm. *Queenie?*

"You may call me Jack."

He extended his free hand to shake. A handshake showed the mettle of a man, his father was always telling him so. A good, firm hand at the market and a fellow would never have his prices beaten down.

Queenie's narrow gaze slid down Jack like a snake and settled on his hand. He didn't take it, didn't move at all for a few seconds as the silence between them grew thicker. Then, in one quick movement, he placed his cigarette holder between Jack's fingers and said, "Have a treat on me. Welcome to Cinderella's doss house!"

Jack brought it hesitantly to his lips, smiling gamely at the grooms who made up Queenie's audience. He pouted his lips against the carved ebony and inhaled.

The cough was so violent that Jack nearly dropped the holder, but an instinct in him born of a lifetime on a farm of tinder-dry hay meant he clamped it between his fingers. As he heaved for breath, he stamped on the nearby straw, suffocating any sparks that might have fallen.

The other grooms laughed and Queenie's head tipped back to emit a bray of hilarity as a strong hand walloped Jack's back.

A friendly Cockney burr chirruped, "Cough up, chicken—there's a good lad!"

"We have a new little chicky in our nest," Queenie told his audience, turning to address them. "I want you all to make him terribly welcome, or he might burn down our stables and then where would your Queenie sing?"

The stocky lad who had rescued Jack from his coughing fit was a head shorter than him. He pulled a face that could have been a smile or a sneer and took the cigarette holder from his fingers. He passed it to Queenie, all the while fixing his stare on the new arrival.

"Trooper Cole. Wilfred, that's me. You're Captain Thorne's new boy, aren't you?"

He laughed, then turned his head to spit on the floor, pulling a skinny roll-up from behind his ear.

"I'm Jack Woodvine. I mean…Trooper Woodvine."

"I s'pose me and Queenie better take you to your quarters?"

"That would — But…oughtn't I to introduce myself to Captain Thorne?"

"I'd say that's a bit difficult, seeing as he's not here at the moment." Wilfred picked up Jack's kitbag as easily as if it were spun from a feather. "Come on, soldier. Your palace awaits!"

"Captain T is an *angel.*" Queenie draped one arm sinuously around Jack's shoulders and walked him back across the stable yard, his naked torso pressed to Jack's rough tunic. "You're going to have a bloody easy war, he's soft as my mother's newborn kitten."

He glanced back at Wilfred and asked, "Wouldn't you say so, Wilf?"

"Not half!" Wilfred laughed, striking a match to light his cigarette. "You couldn't find a nicer bloke in the entire regiment."

Jack grinned as they headed up the creaking wooden stairs above the stables. New quarters and new friends, and he wouldn't have to rough it in a tent. Maybe there'd even be warm water for a bath.

"Well, that's good to know. The officers were a bit…brusque at my last place."

"Brusque?" Wilfred raised an amused eyebrow. "That's a fancy word for a groom!"

"Ignore our lovely Wilf. Strong as an ox, bright as a coal shed." At the top of the stairs Queenie turned to address Wilfred and Jack, his pale hand resting on the crooked handrail. "Thorny is adorable, not *brusque* at all. Welcome to our little slice of heaven!"

With that he lifted the latch and threw the door open, directing Jack to enter with another low bow.

The loft's low, sloping ceiling made it difficult to stand anywhere other than in the middle of the floor. Dormer windows with murky, cracked glazing made no attempt to lift the gloom. The beds were lined up with military precision, as was to be expected, but they were a mixture of sturdy metal bedsteads and low camp beds. Above each, the soldier-grooms had left their imprint of personality, albeit their personalities were almost all the same. Images culled from the pages of gung-ho magazines, of tanks and explosions and enormous guns and heroic men leaping through barbed wire. Shapely stars of music hall and burlesque in enormous hats, elaborate costumes cut to show the boys a lot of leg. The occasional postcard from home had been tucked beside a poster of a woman wearing rather little.

At the far end of that simple loft, someone appeared to have opened a door to an exotic land, a place far removed from the simple rustic pleasures of the grooms. From floor to ceiling hung richly embroidered tapestries depicting scenes of battle from another time, long since lost. Knights jousted on a field of emerald green, a sapphire sky above, dotted with pristine white clouds. Innumerable jabs of the needle had gone to create the sun that blazed down on the curiously bloodless battle, each thread of tapestry teasing out a story from another century.

Between the two tapestries stood a tall screen of black lacquer that served as a door to the mysterious realm beyond, the sort of screen behind which a gentleman's mistress might tantalizingly undress. A rainbow of butterflies fluttered over its polished surface but only one of its panels was folded back, affording no glimpse of the treasures within.

Was it Queenie's place behind those tapestries? Was that the peacock's nest? The only thing Jack knew was that this wasn't *his* chamber.

"Now, little Jack, where shall we plant your magic bean?" Queenie strolled along and pointed to one of the metal beds, addressing his followers in a drawl. "Our lovely young Trooper Miles pissed all over this mattress on the night before he got shipped out. He was terrified, poor thing."

He took a draw on his cigarette and gestured with it toward the bed, its single scratchy blanket concealing that same soiled mattress.

"Mardy Miles was gassed last weekend, so I'm sure it must be dry by now. Your home from home, little Jack!"

The smile was fading from Jack's face. *Sleeping in the piss of a dead man – they never mentioned that in* Boy's Own Paper.

"Thank you." Jack forced a grin. "You've made me feel very…welcome."

Wilfred threw Jack's kitbag onto the bed.

"The crapper's through that door at the other end. You want to get on it early in the morning — it's been known to flood."

"Smashing. Thanks for the tip, Trooper Cole."

All three of them turned at the sound of feet hammering across the floorboards. A breathless groom ran into the attic.

"Just heard — the officers are nearly back! They rang in from the village."

"Don't forget, Jacky," Queenie twirled the end of his scarf, whirling it before Jack's eyes, "Thorny is sweet as cherries, and Apollo is a donkey at heart!"

Jack followed Wilfred back down the stairs and into the yard. Hoofbeats were approaching, drumming down the avenue like a distant storm drawing nearer. Jack fidgeted with his buttons, his cuffs, straightening his collar to look smart for his captain.

A voice could be heard in the distance, raised in a furious bark. It was the voice of an officer, a voice that could never belong to a trooper.

"Get out of the bloody way!" Those plummy vowels sang of Sandhurst and swagger sticks, of punting down the river on a balmy afternoon while other men toiled in the fields. It was the voice of rank.

"Next time, Trooper, next time!" The owner of the voice clattered into the yard at a canter, mounted on a perfect gray stallion, its snow-white mane flying with each movement of its muscular neck. The captain sat tall in his saddle, still looking back over one shoulder at whoever had come close to falling beneath those pounding, powerful hooves. His whip was raised in a warning to the unfortunate soldier, brandished high in the air, dark against a clear blue sky.

The horse pulled itself back with the barest twitch of the rider's gloved hand on its reins. It was something that Jack had rarely seen, a suggestion of a man and animal in perfect harmony.

"You're a damned fool!" The officer gave one last bellow then, with a creak of the leather saddle on which he sat, he turned to survey the yard.

None of the grooms approached. Jack was still listening for other hooves on the avenue, because this couldn't be Captain Thorne. The officer's dark eyes blazed their way around the grooms in the yard and finally alighted on Jack.

"Oh, Lord." The captain heaved a theatrical sigh at the sight of him. He leaned forward to tuck his whip down the side of one highly polished boot. "Are you the chap they've sent Apollo for supper? Woodvine, is it?"

Could this really be Captain Thorne, after what Queenie and Wilfred had just told him? Jack felt the eyes of the other grooms on him as he tentatively crossed toward the officer and his horse. He saluted and dropped his arm to his side.

"Yes, sir, Trooper Woodvine, sir… Captain…? You have a very fine horse, sir."

"Thorne!" Captain Thorne snapped his gloved hand to his brow in a sharp salute. "I hope you've a firm hand, Trooper, you're going to need it."

Brusque. That described his new captain after all.

Jack approached the horse. Its round black eye twitched at him as he came nearer. Jack made a soft clicking sound in his throat as he lightly stroked the back of his hand to the side of Apollo's face.

"Handsome fellow, aren't you?" he whispered. The horse flinched back a step, eyes growing wide then it bowed its head to accept the touch. From his place in the saddle Thorne murmured, the words indistinguishable, his fingers working softly at the nape of Apollo's neck.

"A firm hand, Captain? But a gentle touch will do as well, sir."

Jack looked up at the man in the saddle. He struggled to see his face with the sky so bright behind him, his face thrown into shadow. Jack had an impression of those blazing dark eyes, a strong jaw and a mouth set into a straight line. Which, as Jack continued to smile up at him, showed the slightest sign of an amused quirk at its corners.

"Forgive me, Trooper, because I *may* have misheard." The captain shifted in his saddle and asked, "Did you just presume to tell me how best to handle my mount?"

"Gosh, sir…no, I would never… I only… It's my way, sir. See? I think Apollo likes me."

Jack looked away from the captain, conscious of his *faux pas*, and continued to stroke the horse, running his hand along its nose but careful to avoid Apollo's impressive teeth.

"Fear not, soldier!" Thorne dropped his feet from the stirrups and, in one fluid movement, swung his leg round and hopped down to stand beside Jack. "I'd sooner thrash you than thrash Apollo, he's *far* less trouble!"

Jack's glance fell to the whip that poked over the top of the captain's boot. He bit his lip and met the captain's eye, then returned his attention to the horse.

"I'll…I'll gladly take him off you now, sir."

"Apollo has his routine, Trooper, you're on *his* watch now." Thorne drew the whip from his boot and gestured as he spoke. "Saddle off first—he *won't* like you fumbling his girth, so I hope you're sure-fingered. Then brush, water, down to the paddock, bridle off and let my boy have his pasture."

He swept the whip down, cracking it against his boot, and commanded, "Jump to it!"

Jack shuddered at the snap of the whip then took the reins. As his eyes met the captain's glittering gaze, his heart began to beat just a little faster.

"You must excuse me, sir, I have only just arrived. Would you show me where Apollo's stable is?"

Thorne, however, was preoccupied with lifting the horse's hooves. He held out one hand and clicked his fingers without looking to Jack. He commanded, "Pick!"

"Sir, I haven't one to hand."

The fingers clicked again.

"Captain Thorne, sir… I'm—I'm new."

Something in those words or perhaps what Jack knew was a gently imploring tone appeared to reach through the officer's concentration and Thorne set Apollo's hoof on the ground once more. He returned the whip to his boot and straightened, cocking his head to one side as he peered at Jack through brown eyes so dark that they were almost black.

"Of course you are, yet you've survived two minutes with Apollo, so the signs are good." He nodded once and moved to roll up one stirrup, calling to Jack, "Deal with the other stirrup, Trooper, and Apollo and I will show you the lie of the land!"

Jack went around to the other side of the horse, nimbly working the leather straps. He secured it and patted Apollo's flank.

"Good boy."

There was so much power in the creature. It was in perfect condition, its muscles firm. The captain seemed to have ridden it hard — or at least, the last couple of hundred yards as he knocked grooms flying — and yet Apollo didn't seem tired at all. Thorne was watching him all the time and when Jack's hand touched the horse's flank, the captain visibly tensed, as though he thought he might need to leap forward and intervene. Apollo, however, gave a snort of approval and lowered his head a little farther, glowering from beneath long eyelashes at the grooms who moved this way and that across the yard.

With a soft murmur to comfort his steed's dark expression, Thorne swept his cap off and tucked it beneath his arm. He smoothed his hand over his already immaculate black hair and told Jack, "Come along then, soldier!"

They walked on either side of Apollo as Thorne led the horse across the yard to the stable which had earlier played host to Trooper Charles' command performance. It really wouldn't do for Jack to say anything to the captain about Queenie smoking in Apollo's stable. But there was a pang in Jack's belly. What if a spark had fallen from the cigarette? What if there had been a fire and Apollo —

Jack dismissed the thoughts, because he knew his face would betray him. In fact, he was worried that it already had.

Jack's breath hitched as he looked over at the captain and remembered his words.

'I'd sooner thrash you than thrash Apollo.'

It had been in jest, of course.

Thorne twitched his nostrils and grimaced, setting his cap firmly back on his head. "You've been smoking again, Apollo." Then he snatched up a bucket crammed with brushes and combs abandoned by one of the grooms who had been enjoying Queenie's show and told Jack, "Your fellow grooms are a slovenly bunch, soldier. I hope you'll prove to be stronger meat!"

He pulled a currycomb from the bucket and tossed it across to Jack. "Saddle off, give him a good rub-down and I'll see to the hooves!"

"Yes, sir."

If Thorne heard, he didn't acknowledge, already occupied with scraping at the bottom of Apollo's hooves. All the time Jack could hear him murmuring to the horse in a soft coo, a world away from the furious character who had ridden into the yard as though charging up from hell itself.

Jack reached under Apollo to unfasten the girth then lifted the supple, well-cared-for saddle. He strode past the captain, almost brushing his knee against his bowed head as he passed in the cramped space, and hung the saddle over the stable door.

He unbuttoned his jacket, threw it onto a hook on the wall and rolled up his sleeves to comb the horse. He was aware of the amused quirk of the captain's mouth again but went on with his work, picking loose hair and bits of mud out of the comb as he went.

"That's it, Apollo, aren't you a good boy... You're enjoying this, aren't you? Yes, you are!"

"You're our third chap in the last twelve months," Thorne told Jack, his voice growing more stern with every word. "First one got his foot smashed by this cheeky lad. Second couldn't get anywhere near him to begin with. I don't know what magic you're working, Trooper, but do it with your jacket on, or ask an officer's permission to remove it."

Jack's cheeks flamed and he tugged awkwardly at his shirt.

"Sorry, Captain. May I ask your permission now, please?"

"You may, soldier." Thorne fell silent at a soft whinny from Apollo. He furrowed his brow as though listening and said, "Apollo has his doubts, Trooper. He's finding the baby-talk disconcerting."

Jack met the captain's eye. There was a flash of humor there, he was sure. But he wasn't going to laugh, even if he started to grin.

"*What a big, brave, handsome chap you are, Apollo!* There, is that better, Captain?"

"Are you patronizing my horse, Woodvine?" Thorne returned to his task, his head bowed. "He'll have your guts if you don't watch out."

After a pause, Jack said, "He's a very fine horse, sir. Have you had him long?"

"From his first months." The captain straightened and threw the hoof pick into the bucket with a clatter. "Gather up the reins, Trooper. I'll show you the tack and feed, we can pick up some water and get him into the grass."

Jack shrugged himself back into his jacket but didn't button it up. He had to draw near to the captain in order to take the reins, but he found himself distracted by an extraordinary smell — the spicy scent of expensive pomade, blended with warm leather and saddle soap. He tightened his grip on the reins, aware of a slight tremble in his hands. What a contrast that masculine scent was to Jack, who used only carbolic soap and cheap peppermint shaving cream.

"Right you are, Captain."

Jack smiled at his officer, but when the captain's gaze swept over him, Jack avoided his eyes and closely examined the reins instead. He was relieved when they stepped back into the sunlight, then there was no time to think of anything as Thorne toured him around the yard, pointing out tack rooms and feed stores, and listing the names of horses and their riders that Jack couldn't hope to remember. All the time he was issuing those barked orders and criticisms to the grooms who were laden with saddles and sacks and they jumped at the officer's say-so. This was clearly not a man to be trifled with.

A bark of the word *bucket* to one slight red-haired lad resulted in the sudden appearance of the requested item and Thorne drew the whip. He flourished it and Jack interpreted the gesture as a command to take the bucket from his fellow groom. Then they were off again, Captain Thorne striding out ahead like a king surveying his court.

Jack followed obediently behind. He couldn't help but be impressed by the captain. He knew he really shouldn't, but he stole glances at him, at the breadth of his shoulders in his tailored tunic, at the suggestion of his firm thighs inside his spotless breeches, at his thick sweep of dark hair tapering down to the nape of his neck.

He had to stop. He couldn't afford to moon after officers. Last time it had been one touch, a stray hand on a knee as he passed a captain a whip. Just a brush of his fingertips, but it had been enough, because the look in his eyes had given him away.

And now he had been sent here, to work for this man. The universe was taunting him for his unnatural desires.

As they moved through the yard and its bustle Apollo grew more fractious, a little less willing to go along with his new groom and a little more agitated with each passing second. Eventually they passed through a narrow avenue between two stable blocks and there, in the shade of the structures, was a water pump. The ground around it was saturated and Thorne reached to take the reins from Jack. He placed the tip of his right ring finger between his teeth and plucked off his brown leather glove before placing his bare palm against the horse's muzzle in a gesture of calm.

"Fill the bucket, soldier, then put it down for Apollo." Thorne tucked the glove into his pocket and removed the other, slipping that into his pocket too. "You and I need a quick parley."

Jack swallowed and stepped into the mud to reach the pump. Water spilled out as Jack worked the handle. He kept his back to the captain, drawing out the moment until the captain told him what he had to say. *I saw how you looked at me, you ought to be court martialed.* That would be it. He'd barely been at Chateau de Desgravier an hour and his card would already be marked.

"The bucket, sir." Jack paused, running his wet hand through his too-long chestnut locks.

"I'm not going to drink out of it, Trooper." He sighed deeply. "Put it down for Apollo, he's parched!"

"Yes, sir."

Apollo tried to push his muzzle into the bucket before it was on the ground, and Jack stroked the horse. Feeling the captain's gaze on him again, he came forward and stood to attention.

"Sir?"

"Your hair is—" The captain seemed to reconsider whatever he was going to say, instead withdrawing the whip once more. He held it out, touching the tip to Jack's face. "You're muddy, Trooper Woodvine."

Jack brought his fingertip to his cheek, the whip whispering against the slender digit.

"Golly, sir... I am sorry. The roads were very muddy. Unless you mean my freckles, sir? I-I hadn't... I'd only just got here when you arrived, sir, or I'd have scrubbed properly before I ever... You must think me a terrible slob, Captain Thorne. I'm sorry." Jack braved himself to meet the officer's eye. "I didn't want to disappoint you."

Thorne didn't speak, but reached into his pocket and produced a white handkerchief. It was pristine, and he unfolded it with a flick of his wrist then held it beneath the pump to catch a few of the drips of water that fell from it. Then, like a father with an insolent boy, Captain Thorne pressed the wet handkerchief to Jack's cheekbone and began to gently scrub at the mud.

Jack, still standing to attention, tried to distract himself by watching Apollo with the bucket, but the captain was so close to him that he was overwhelmed once more by the scent of the man. He felt the captain's warm breath on his neck and, as if in answer, a blush broke over his face again.

"At ease, soldier." It seemed like a low purr, the captain's hand on his cheek more of a caress than— Jack pushed the thought aside as soon as it occurred to him.

"Thank you, sir."

It was a whisper, and Jack glanced at the captain. He saw something, then, in the captain's eyes. Something that he —

"Thorne!"

The voice was a parade-ground bark. Jack flinched away from his captain. Whatever connection he had thought — imagined — for a moment, snapped.

Thorne pressed the handkerchief into Jack's hand and winked, whispering, "Our secret, Woodvine. One can't put a wet hanky back in one's uniform."

Then he stepped back and snatched up Apollo's reins a moment before the horse began to pull against him, its nostrils flaring and dark eyes rolling to reveal white at the edges.

The officer was fastening his flies as he approached, with a glare for Captain Thorne and an interested stare for Jack.

"This the new boy, eh? Is it?"

He leaned in toward Jack, his lips slightly parted, his breath smelling of stale tobacco and booze.

Jack wasn't sure if he was supposed to speak, and waited for his captain to say something. Still Apollo pulled, shying back from the new arrival, and Thorne's arm visibly tensed inside his uniform, one strong shoulder setting firm with the effort of holding the reins that he now wrapped around his knuckles.

"This is Trooper Woodvine. Woodvine, Captain Marsh." Thorne made a gesture with his eyebrows that was clearly intended to suggest the younger man should salute. Yet Marsh was peering ever closer at Jack, freezing him with that rheumy, pale stare, and Thorne thrust the reins toward his new groom, filling Jack's hands with the leather and saving him the awkwardness of that missed salute.

"Excuse the lack of ceremony, Marsh, you know what a two-hander Apollo can be." Thorne patted the horse's snow-white shoulder. "You'll have to excuse us, Captain, I'm just showing our new arrival the ropes."

"The ropes, eh? Yes...the ropes." Marsh cleared his throat and stood to his full height, aided, Jack noticed, by strategically stacked heels to his boots.

"Sure this isn't a girl, Thorne? Eh?" Marsh's gloved hand slid toward Jack's chin but stopped an inch away. "Ought to be a milkmaid with a face like that, what? You smell of the country, boy..."

Jack saluted at last, hammering out the words in basic training staccato.

"Captain Marsh, sir. Pleasure to meet you, sir."

"Ha! Very good. Got manners after all, boy, haven't you?"

Thorne's hand pressed into the small of Jack's back, urging him to move even as he told Marsh in those same withering public school tones, "We can but hope, Marsh. Excuse us, old man?"

Jack moved forward, guided by the captain's touch.

Marsh leaned against the pump, mud seeping around his boots, his oppressive stare not leaving Jack even after they had rounded the corner and were out of his sight. Thorne's hand, however, pulled away and he walked ahead once more as Apollo relaxed, the tugging at the end of the rein ebbing to a gentle amble.

"Captain, sir...may I tell you something?"

They were out of earshot now of the stables, following a path to the paddock.

"You're not a bloody woman, are you?" Thorne's voice was deadly serious but he glanced back and winked. "One hears such things nowadays. Tell away."

Jack allowed himself a chuckle, then looked Thorne carefully in the eye.

"One mustn't tattle on a fellow, sir, especially not when one shares quarters with them. But…I felt I really ought to say…about…that smell in Apollo's stable, sir. The cigarettes."

Jack waited for a reaction on the captain's face. Did he realize what would happen if he betrayed the other grooms? But Jack Woodvine always did the right thing. Jack Woodvine, who had broken his shoulder falling off a horse just before conscription began. Jack Woodvine, who had healed, and who had answered the call to do his bit for King, Country and Empire. Jack Woodvine, who had left his father and the farm behind him because ten boys in his year at the grammar had already been killed and he couldn't chase their faces from his dreams at night.

"Sir…I know who it was. Who was smoking. I cannot tell you who, sir, but I want you to know that, as Apollo's groom—as *your* groom, sir, I won't allow it anymore. Apollo is my concern, sir, and I…I won't have it. That shilly-shallying about—I simply won't!"

The captain looked back at him, his face set in a stern expression, those full lips a hard, tight line. When he spoke again, his voice was that of a commander once more.

"The grooms here are a shower of layabouts, rascals and hooligans. Don't let them draw you into their ways, Woodvine, I won't tolerate it."

"Don't worry, sir. I won't."

But even so, Jack didn't like the idea of lying on that mattress with its ammonia stink of fear, alone, without some fellows to talk to. Even if he had to make up some ludicrous story, as he had before—of losing his virginity to a farmhand's buxom daughter in a hayloft. When he hadn't even held a girl's hand.

And hadn't wanted to.

At the end of the narrow path was a bright green paddock where half a dozen other horses grazed contentedly, with no idea of what was happening just a few miles away. It was fenced all around and bordered with trees that provided cool shade for those that might wish it. Threaded along the fence and off through the trees was a stream, deep and wide, the sunlight glittering and dancing on the surface like stars in a night sky, and they walked alongside it to reach the gate, which was held in place by a heavy iron bolt.

As soon as Thorne pulled back the bolt and opened the gate Apollo began to surge toward the paddock, the mighty creature pulling at Jack with enough force to have him trotting to keep up. The captain darted out one hand and seized the reins, admonishing the horse with a swift, "Fall back, Apollo!"

The horse responded immediately, though not without a certain insolence as he pulled just a touch, just to make the point that the choice was his to make, not that of the captain or the trooper. When the trio stepped into the paddock, Thorne unbuckled the bridle in a few swift movements and pulled it gently over the horse's head. He patted his elegant hand against Apollo's firm shoulder and told him, "Go on then, lad."

And the horse was gone, cantering as happily as a pony across the paddock and into the shade. There he dropped his head and began to drink from the stream, leaving the captain to watch him with a soft gaze.

As he watched the gentle glee of the great stallion, Jack beamed. He looked back at the captain and tried to push aside the wavy hair that had fallen into his face.

But a breeze was stirring up from somewhere, and Jack's unruly forelock flopped back again.

"What a…a lovely paddock."

Jack shoved his hands into his pockets. He must've broken some protocol somewhere—*should one be so casual when faced with one's captain?* What did he remember from training? Being shouted at a lot, shimmying on his hips face down through mud with a lump of wood that was supposed to resemble a gun and finally, when he had been given a real gun, and had been hopeless at firing it. He'd had more luck with the bayonet, but in reality he didn't fancy his chances if he had to look a fellow in the eye and twist a sharp bit of metal into his guts.

"Loveliest paddock I think I've ever seen."

"And not even twenty miles from here…" Thorne knitted his hands behind his back, his shoulders squaring, his feet set apart in their shining leather boots. He drew in a deep breath and surveyed the horses as they grazed in peace, all except one gathered at the far end of the field. "You'll soon learn, trooper, Apollo likes his own company as a rule. Perhaps he might make an exception for you, we shall have to see."

"I…I hope so, Captain." Jack peered at him from the corner of his eye. The captain's face was set in a firm expression, as if it were hewn from stone. "I should like, sir, to please you."

He stared ahead, tugging at a loose button on his jacket.

"Work hard and show proper respect and you and I will get on." Thorne took a long, deep breath before speaking again. "And if you see anyone raise a hand to Apollo, I want his name, groom's code or no. Understand?"

Jack nodded.

"Yes, sir. And…I'm sorry, Captain Thorne, if I didn't show you respect earlier. With my muddy face and taking off my jacket without your permission. It won't happen again, sir. I promise."

"You'll find me a fair master, but I brook no nonsense." Thorne took the gloves from his pocket and slipped his hands into them, flexing his fingers a couple of times as if to test the supple leather. "Now back up to the yard and get yourself settled. Tomorrow we'll go through your duties. Really put you through your paces, eh?"

"Yes, sir."

Jack began to walk away, realizing that the captain was standing still, as if his feet had grown roots and those fine, sturdy legs had become tree trunks. He gave a salute.

"Good evening, sir."

With a strange feeling of loss that he couldn't quite account for, Jack went back to the stables.

Home of Erotic Romance

Sign up for our newsletter and find out about all our
romance book releases, eBook sales and promotions,
sneak peeks and FREE romance books!

About the Author

Catherine Curzon is a royal historian who writes on all matters of 18th century. Her work has been featured on many platforms and Catherine has also spoken at various venues including the Royal Pavilion, Brighton, and Dr Johnson's House.

Catherine holds a Master's degree in Film and when not dodging the furies of the guillotine, writes fiction set deep in the underbelly of Georgian London.

She lives in Yorkshire atop a ludicrously steep hill.

Eleanor Harkstead often dashes about in nineteenth-century costume, in bonnet or cravat as the mood takes her. She can occasionally be found wandering old graveyards, and is especially fond of the ones in Edinburgh. Eleanor is very fond of chocolate, wine, tweed waistcoats and nice pens. She has a large collection of vintage hats, and once played guitar in a band. Originally from the south-east, Eleanor now lives somewhere in the Midlands with a large ginger cat who resembles a Viking.

Catherine & Eleanor love to hear from readers. You can find their contact information, website details and author profile page at https://www.totallybound.com

9 781786 863980